The dead mother's hand lay still ⌐ waited but sensed nothing. She ⌐ face, a face with one pale green eye open and the other crushed into the back of the skull. The cheekbones were flattened nearly to the floor, and her teeth lay in the glistening mass of blood and pulp that once was her jaw. There was no nose to speak of, and pink brain tissue oozed out through the top of her head into the hat that clung precariously to the tangled, crusted hair like a frightened animal.

"Anything?" asked Lieutenant Granger.

Suzanne shook her head. She hoped there would be nothing. But nothing for Granger would be nothing for the butchered family. Nothing for justice. No movement toward forgiveness. And so she focused. She drew down hard in her mind. Waited. Then, "I have nothing for you. Nothing other than her family way condition."

"Did you try?"

"Would I waste my time coming here just to have a look at dead bodies?"

She tried again. Tucked her head. And there. Faint but certain. The prickling at the corner of her eyes, the tightening, the sense of lightheadedness. She drew air through her teeth.

A sudden flash of white. A blast of fierce cold that takes her breath away. It slammed into her consciousness, as if the spirit of the dead mother was demanding vengeance, demanding to be heard.

Or perhaps the evil deed was an entity unto itself, and wanted to play with Suzanne's soul and heart, to torment and haunt her.

"You're shivering," said Granger.

The white whirls round and round, erasing everything beyond it. Suzanne feels herself spinning, too, round and round with it, slow at first then faster faster.

"Miss Heath, are you ill?"

Faster faster faster faster. Dizzying. Horrific.

"Miss Heath!"

Round round round faster faster faster faster. She begins to sweat in the cold white, sweat from nausea and the thick dread that wells in her stomach like rancid bile. Round round round round round round...

HELL GATE

by ELIZABETH MASSIE

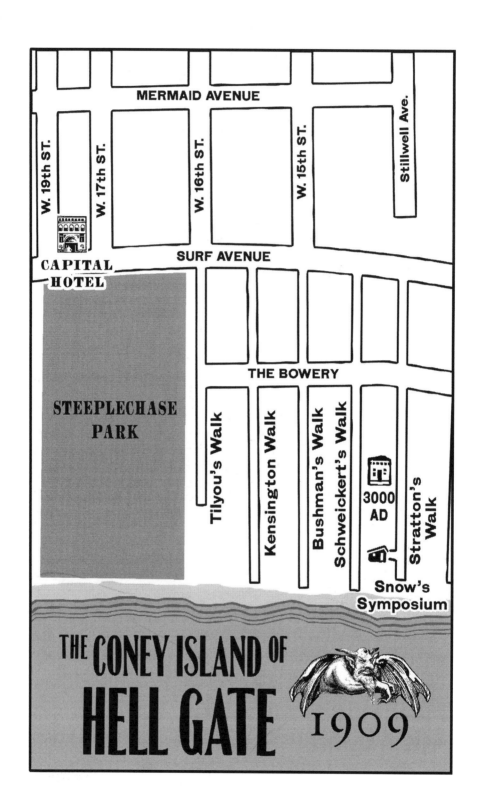

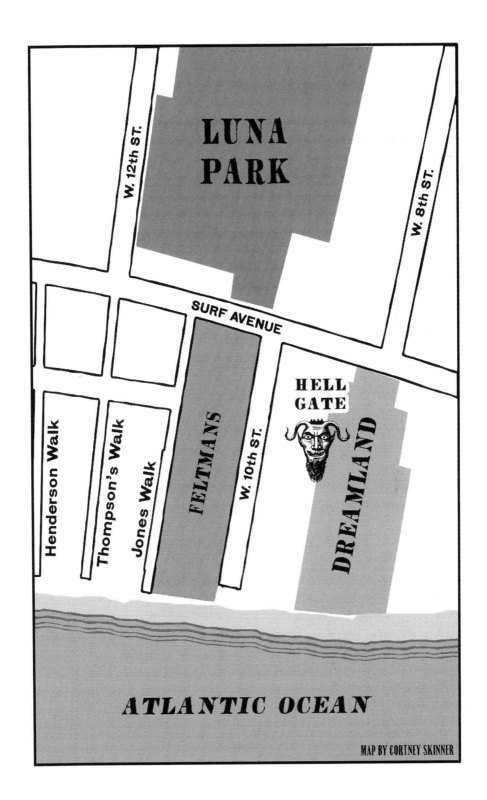

"(Coney represents) a different world, a dream world, perhaps a nightmare world, where all is bizarre and fantastic…."

- Frederic A. Thompson, "The Summer Show," *Independent*, 62, June 20th, 1907

"The long elaborate dream of mine hadn't lasted a second. It wuz staged in the real Dream Land, for the awful drayma so soon to be enacted there, by the terrible actor, Fire! The most fearful and tragic actor on the hull stage of life."

- from *Samantha At Coney Island and a Thousand Other Islands* by Josiah Allen's Wife, 1911, *The Christian Herald*

ONE

June, 1901

The woods were vicious, uneven, with a ground-level tapestry of jagged stones, briars, and saplings that caught her legs, causing her to stumble. Her face was bruised and bleeding, her scalp raw where hanks of hair had been ripped out. Beneath the skin her knee shifted painfully as if the cap were dislocated, and a raw strip of blood-spotted flesh dangled from her elbow. A molar had been knocked from her jaw and coughed out into the weeds somewhere behind her. Trails of pinked saliva clung to her chin and neck.

The intensity of pain squeezed her mind until there were no thoughts, only the instinct to get out, get away, to run from the agony, to escape the torment.

She ran, away from what she not did not know, toward what she could not fathom. She could no longer feel her feet in her shoes, could no longer focus on what lay ahead.

But on she ran.

At some point in time she came upon a hard-packed road that stretched in both directions, shaded by arms of tall and endless trees. Time was meaningless, as was the road. She only knew to take it, though not which direction to go. She turned and moved on, through the dust and insects and filtering sunlight, her feet dragging the road, her throat dry as old leaves.

Then came a wagon.

It moved up behind her, the wheels creaking, the leather harness squeaking, the mule's hoof beats slow and determined.

A voice called out, "Ah, look'a there! It's a girl! She's hurt bad!"

It was a young voice, a boy's. A colored boy's.

"Johnny, slow up. We gotta help her."

A man's voice answered, the words deep, slow, measured. "We stop to help that young woman, and you know we be accused of doin' whatever been done to her. Best say a prayer on her behalf and let her be."

"But she's bleedin'! She's cut up, banged up!"

"I got eyes, Cittie. I see she's bleedin' and banged up."

The wagon moved up and around the young woman, so now she could see it out of the corner of her eye. There was an old, white-haired black man leaning over the reins. In the back were six or seven boys sitting on straw bales, all dark-skinned, all gazing with fascination and sadness.

"Johnny! Stop!" It was one of the boys, one a head shorter than the others. He had close-cropped hair and his jacket was dark blue.

The old man turned his head back. "Cittie, we got to be back home shortly. What you suggest we do with her?"

"What would the Lord want us to do?"

"Ah, now, don't be throwin' that at me! Lord know I mean well, best I can!" The old man drew the mule up. The animal snorted and stomped a front hoof on the road. Flies buzzed about its head. The young woman felt herself stop, too, as if someone had reined her in as well.

"We got a doctor at the home," said the boy. "He can fix her then send her off. Ain't nobody gonna think nothin' if they don' know nothin'.'"

"Cittie..."

Several other boys now spoke up.

"Yeah, Johnny, that's the Christian thing to do. Don' leave her here."

"We keep it quiet and nobody'll know. Doc Fitzgerald won't say nothin'."

The old man rubbed his mouth, sighed heavily, and then looked at the young woman with troubled eyes and furrowed brow. "Miss, you need a ride?"

"'Course she needs a ride!" said the boy called Cittie.

"Hush, now! Miss?"

The young woman turned fully toward the wagon, with its dark driver and its dark, wide-eyed passengers and the white lettering on the wagon's side that read, "Hudson Colored Waifs' Asylum."

She tried to nod, but the weight of the movement pitched her forward onto the road, and just before she passed out, she saw sympathetic faces swarming around her and felt small but steady arms cradle her and lift her up and off the cold, callous earth.

TWO

July, 1909

The wooden chair was built to spin round and round, worked by a foot pedal in the closet and a hydraulic hose that ran through a hole in the wall and across the floor. There were four leather straps on the chair — one to secure each arm, one across the chest, and on down tight over the thighs — so that the man or woman on the ride would stay in place and could watch the scenes that would soon be flashed on the wall.

So the rider couldn't escape when he or she began to feel sick. Or justifiably terrified.

At this particular moment, there was a dapper, pudgy gentleman in the spinning chair, though his dapperness was long gone. His eyes rolled and his mouth hung slack from the spinning. He tried to speak but the motion drove the words back into his throat, and only a pathetic whine escaped his lips. His skin was damp and pale, as if the color had been spun away against the walls. He smelled of sour sweat.

The proprietor pumped the pedal in the closet and watched the spinning chair through a tiny window in the door. The proprietor's grin was wide and quite pleased.

The chair ride was located in the backroom of a tar-black, two-room shack. The shack was situated among countless other independent exhibits, trinket shops, shows, and snack booths within an area called the Bowery, a maze of stuffy, smoke-scented, alleyways between Coney Island's Surf Avenue to the north, the shoreline to the south, Steeplechase Park to the west and Dreamland's park to the east. Located at the back of a very narrow dead-end corridor off one of the main walkways, the tar-black shack was not the most popular amusement in the Bowery by any means. Most folks never saw it back in the shadows and passed on by, opting for the dance halls, snack shops, and stereograph booths where, for a penny or two, they could gaze into a wooden viewer at three-dimensional photographs of wild elephants or naked women. However, as long as enough holidayers found the shack with its intriguing red lettering — "Snow's Symposium of Secrets and Surprises!" — and their curiosity was enough to cause them to part with their nickel to see the magic within, the goal was accomplished. All were welcomed to sit on a bench in the front room to view the sleight of hand and parlor tricks performed by Rex, the proprietor's bald and towering assistant. Children and old folks alike were enthralled when cards disappeared and re-appeared, torn paper was made whole again, and coins were pulled from behind a customer's ear.

However, the backroom was reserved for those few special thrill-seekers. Adults only, lone souls. Those who inquired, asking, "What, may I ask, is in the room behind those curious velvet curtains?"

Only those who would not be missed were invited to see.

The proprietor pushed the pedal harder and the chair went round-round-round- round. The man's arms spasmed on the rests. His chest heaved against the straps. His face contorted, his lips drawn back. Then the light went out and the projectors clicked on. Sharp-toothed rabbits and horned devils appeared instantly on the walls, dancing, dancing, up and down amid flashing reds and oranges.

The man cried as round and round he went. Round and round as the devils and rabbits danced. Round and round, until the light in his eyes winked out.

THREE

August, 1909

1

Late summer had found a fat, fanciful plaything in Coney Island. Breezes, laced with grit and salt, pelted the bathhouses, pavilions, eateries, theaters, and rides in steady blows, tossed as a child would toss baseballs with giddy humor and anxious furor. Humidity lay on the land like an enormous dog, licking the skin of the revelers to taste and savor their sweaty delusions. The sun itself longed for the grand amusement parks as much as New York natives and foreign-speaking immigrants did, and spent its lazy hours gazing down through dazzling white turrets, spiraling spires, and grimy yet elegant Oriental towers to the streets and walkways, alleys and niches, jealous, as if wishing it could leave its lofty confines and join the gay merrymaking below. It busied itself as it could, burning the noses of children as they splashed in the briny waves along the shore, baking the paving blocks on the roads until they burst, and chasing shadows from alleys and doorways like a copper chasing pickpockets from the Culver Depot train platform.

The four-storied Capital Hotel at the corner of West 19th and Surf Avenue was not exempt from summer's sweltering taunts. The glass in the front door reflected a glare as harsh as a July firecracker, and the new pink paint on the exterior wall, dabbed on prior to opening for the season in May, was already splitting its seams. The hotel's first-floor lobby window was pushed up and the counter clerk and hotel manager, momentarily disengaged from customers, took turns gulping air from the opening like fresh catch on a fishing boat. The faded blue and white awning above the entrance sagged mightily, as though Dreamland's own Jolly Trixie had sat herself down on top of it to have a rest.

There was a woman standing on the sidewalk outside the hotel, and she was screaming.

An assembly of Coney visitors were gathered on Surf Avenue near the screamer, just off the trolley's track so as not to be struck as it hummed its way east and west. The curious waggled fingers and walking sticks at the woman as if poking at her would help them understand what had her in such a state. She was not the only thing making a racket by any means; the air was littered with the loud rumblings of the nearby coasters on their steel tracks, the shrieks of the riders on Steeplechase's wooden horses as they came around the bend across the street, festive men barking at passersby, offering etched ruby glass trinkets and postcards from pushcarts, brass bands bleating out one tune to the west and another to the east, and haughty new green Model T Fords honking at stray pedestrians along the avenue.

But the screams of the woman outside the Capital were not of joy nor excitement nor surprise; they were of terror.

Children with candy-stickied hands watched the woman from beneath droopy lids as if this were just another amusement put on for their entertainment — another Johnstown Flood or Fighting the Flames show. Mothers tugged at the children, pretending to pull them back and away, but not hard enough so that they, themselves, could stay and have a look at the shrieking lunatic. A few single girls in plume-covered hats and white shirtwaists were clustered by a telephone pole, holding on to each others' arms, giggling and grimacing, while young single men in boaters and pastel vests feigned concern for the wailing woman but in truth kept an eye on the giggling girls.

"Ohh, m' God!" the woman bellowed in a heavy brogue, her fingernails digging tracks down her face. "M' God help me help me, ohhh!"

"Look at her," said a teenaged boy in the crowd. "She's ready to be bundled up and locked away in Bellevue, you ask me!"

The boy's friend, another teen with pimples the size of dimes, grinned broadly.

"Oh God, what am I to do?" the woman cried. She shook like a dog in the cold.

Suzanne Heath stood behind the group of gawkers, her arms wrapped about her waist, her fingers plucking a loose thread in the side seam of her yellow cotton blouse. A loose curl of auburn hair tickled her cheek. She tried to shake it back, but it stuck tightly to her damp skin. Her broad, unadorned straw hat protected her face from the sun's harsh eye, yet it did nothing to keep her from perspiring profusely. She had changed as quickly as possible from her red bolero jacket and black Mexican skirt before coming to the Capital Hotel, figuring she already had one strike against her and that was being female. A woman and a lowly, costumed Luna Park ticket seller to boot, she knew she wouldn't be taken seriously by many, especially not the officers of the Coney Island police force.

Suzanne could see several tall, rounded police helmets above the crowd in front of the hotel. According to the lieutenant, the dead couple had been discovered just before six that morning, long before Coney's parks and attractions were open for the day, before the first excursion boat and train brought a shipment of vacationers to the Coney Island piers and depots. It was now ten-thirty. Those who had spent the night in any of the local guest houses and hotels were up and about, breakfasting on fried egg sandwiches, boiled sausages, and glasses of milk or beer, waiting for the parks and independent attractions to open at ten. The Capital Hotel maid had begun her daily duties as the guests got up and went out, and had discovered the murdered couple in a fourth-floor room. The hotel manager alerted the police who blocked off the hotel for their investigation. Police presence usually didn't cause a stir on Coney. Officers were kept visible by order of Captain Williamson so visitors would assume the place safe and swindlers and whores might think twice about plying their trade in plain sight.

The hysterical woman had caused this stir on her own.

"God help me, oh Lord m' God, what am I ta do?" the woman wailed again. "Ohhh! She was with me jes yestiddy! Not ten hours 'go she was, with me in all of one piece! Ohhh sweet Jaysus!"

Suzanne moved around the side of the crowd to have a better look, watching not to step in a fresh pile of horse manure, trying to avoid the pinwheeling arms of a young boy with fists full of melting, unwrapped chocolate.

The screamer was middle-aged, with a face more masculine than feminine. Her light brown hair was knotted at the back of her neck, though she'd pulled quite a few strands loose in her terror; her hat was a flat pie pan of gray felt. There was a large mole on her cheek and her blue eyes were nearly invisible in the flush of her face. Vicious red streaks coursed her cheeks where she repeatedly slashed them with her nails.

"Madam," said one of the police officers in a stern voice. He was young, obviously a new recruit in his crisp double-breasted frock coat, and his frustration was clear. "Madam! There's no need for the ruckus. We'll be taking care of this. You'll just make matters worse. Calm yourself."

"How can they be worse than they is?" the woman continued, her knees knocking beneath her skirt, making it flutter as if she was standing over a grate. "Yestiddy afternoon she tol' me she was goin' to get us tickets to Steeplechase, twenty-five rides for twenty-five cents, you know. She was goin' to bring them tickets back to our room at the Seaside, and then we was goin' to go there after havin' a bite at the Clam Shack. 'Tween you 'n' me, I thought she was tryin' to get away to see that bloody devil she'd met on the Bowery, and might be she was. But I've not seen 'er since she left and now there's that dead couple in the Capital, mashed up! And no one will let me 'ave a look to see if it's her!"

"Get hold of yourself, madam," said the policeman, "or I'll have to haul you in for disturbing the peace and disrupting an investigation." His compatriot, who had been stationed at the door to keep anyone from leaving or entering, nodded in agreement.

"Ohh!"

"I mean it. I'll throw you in a cell until you are quiet! You been in a cell, all wet and full of maniacs and criminals? And spiders?"

The woman just covered her face and continued to wail.

Suzanne shouldered past the gawkers, removed one white cotton glove, and put her hand on the woman's elbow. The woman turned instantly to Suzanne, flinching as if something painful had passed through her. She gave Suzanne a look which to others would have seemed quite odd, but a look which had become intimately familiar to Suzanne in her twenty-four years of life — a combination of shock, caution, and hope. The woman had sensed something peculiar and charged in that touch, something that caused her mouth to snap shut and her wail to dry up in her throat.

"Who is she?" Suzanne asked gently. "Is she your sister?"

"M' sister, yes," said the woman. Her voice was now raspy, almost a whisper. "My silly, careless, dearest sister! I'm brutal worried."

The young police officer stepped forward, shaking his head at Suzanne. "Go on now. We don't need no others involved with this. We got enough to deal with, young lady."

Suzanne ignored the cop, and spoke again to the woman. "Why do you think something has happened to your sister? She's gone off on her own before, hasn't she? Gone off until morning without telling anyone?"

"She…well, s'times she's done that," the woman said. Her brows drew together then. "How d'you know she's done that before?"

Suzanne knew, but didn't say why she knew. "She's a pretty woman, isn't she?" she offered. "Brown hair like yours? Blue eyes?"

The woman nodded, brows drawn.

"Single women are likely to go off nowadays, don't you think, with so many of them having their own spending money. Your sister makes her own money, doesn't she?"

The woman nodded. Her pie pan hat bobbed.

"She sews garments during the week, the same as you?"

The woman nodded again. "Yes, but how do you…?" she began.

"Miss," said the police officer, stepping between Suzanne and the woman and shaking his finger in Suzanne's face. His breath smelled of coffee and there were some tiny, stray biscuit crumbs in his mustache. "I got this lady taken care of. Get on, now, out of here you go! This is police business." He took her arm and tried to steer her away.

"Yes, it is police business," said Suzanne, pulling her arm free, "and that is why I've been called in. A boy brought me a note just a half hour ago."

The officer barked laughter. He turned to his partner barring the door. "Do you see this, Osier? Did you hear her? She says she's been called in!"

"What for?" asked Osier, a short, pale-haired officer who seemed to swim in the bulk of his uniform. "For moppin' up the blood? The hotel's got a maid for that, Miss, unless you got a special way with a bucket of water!"

"What's your sister's name?" Suzanne asked the woman.

"Her name's Maude O'Connor."

"And yours?"

"Mary O'Connor. We got them free tickets in the mail for the parks here. Never been, and so we was lookin' forward to the trip. Now, oh! What am I t'do?"

"Why don't you give your report to the patrolman," said Suzanne. She nodded toward the mustached officer. "That's his job, to take notes. I'll bet he even has a little pad of paper and a pencil in his fine new jacket there. He'll need the details if your sister is truly missing. Try to calm down if you can. Right now, there is nothing else you can do. Do you understand? The best you can do for your sister is to cooperate with these men."

"I…" the woman began.

"Do you understand? Tell him everything you can think of about your sister and her disappearance."

The woman nodded then glanced up at the officer, who scowled.

"Just who the Hell do you think you are?" he demanded of Suzanne.

A loud voice came from the crowd. "She's here at my request."

The officers stared. Their lieutenant stood among the people at street side, his eyes shaded by the black brim of his flat cap, his single-breasted jacket set with the badge and the bar of his rank. He was a tall, heavyset man in his late fifties with a tanned, leathery face, silvered hair and a ragged scar on his chin.

"Sir," scoffed the mustached officer. "We appreciate a good laugh like the next fellow, but…"

"Martin," the lieutenant said, "take Miss O'Connor aside, transcribe her statement and do it carefully, as has been suggested. And the rest of you!" He gestured to the crowd with a wide sweep of his arm. "Be off, now, or I will authorize my men to thwack you on your ears with their clubs. Do you want to spend your holiday in the parks or in the hospital?"

"You can't do that," challenged one of the young dandies, who had moved closer to the girls by the telephone pole. He winked at one and she winked back. "We ain't done nothing wrong."

"Thwack him," the lieutenant said to Officer Osier by the door.

Osier snatched his club from his belt and went after the young man. The young man backed up, stepping into the manure Suzanne had avoided, his hands raised apologetically.

"Joking, my man! Just joking!" the young fellow said.

The crowd dispersed, the spectacle all but gone now that Mary O'Connor was no longer scratching her face and tearing her hair.

The lieutenant waved Suzanne inside the hotel.

The hotel manager and the clerk were still at the window, but they glanced around as Suzanne entered. Clearly they were as curious about the enlistment of this plain young woman as had been the officers outside. Around the lobby on threadbare upholstered chairs and settees were clumps of men and women, last night's Capital's guests who had not gone out for early breakfast, less-affluent Coney visitors dressed in their best yet well-worn skirts and blouses, jackets, trousers, and cracking leather shoes. They grumbled amongst each other, the ladies wilting into their handkerchiefs, the men scuffing their shoes back and forth on the floor and waving their faces with their hats. Two little boys were stretched out on the faux Turkish carpeting, grabbing for the hotel's cat that had hid itself away beneath a small writing desk. An elderly officer, short and gruff and near-bald, was interviewing a man near the steps. Another officer was making sure the seated guests did not discuss the crime that had befouled the hotel.

"Lieutenant Granger," called the copper by the steps, pausing with his pencil raised, "they need you and," he nodded at Suzanne, "and *her* upstairs. We're staying with the guests down here until they can all be interviewed."

"Good, Wescott, thank you," said Granger.

"Room forty-six. Fourth floor. It's a mess, sir, but you might already have guessed that." The old officer watched Suzanne as he said this, as if certain no woman, regardless of the supposed value she might have to an investigation, would want to see what was up the flights of stairs.

"I suspected it would be nothing short of a mess," said Granger.

The lieutenant headed for the stairs, Suzanne not far behind, wishing she was alone so she could wipe the tickling sweat from between her breasts. She was glad this hotel did not have an elevator. She had traveled on elevators several times, and several times was enough. She'd heard rumors that cables could snap and send one flying to the basement in a moment's time, crushing thighs or breaking backs or worse. She didn't doubt it for a moment.

Granger bounced up the first flight of steps to show what a lively cop he was, then slowed down beneath his substantial weight on the last flight. Suzanne caught up with him on the third-floor landing, and, clutching her skirts to avoid tripping on the splintery boards, moved ahead of him.

The fourth-floor hallway was long and narrow, with a blue-and-orange runner traveling its length. Faded bird-of-paradise wallpaper clung to the walls. Brass sconces with electric light illuminated the corridor poorly. An abandoned maid's cart sat laden with linens and towels. The maid was near the far end of the hall, sitting on a stool with her face in her hands and her maid's cap hanging precariously by a hairpin. She looked up at Suzanne and Granger, and Granger held up a finger for her to wait longer. She dipped her head back into her hands.

Standing in the doorway of room46 was a police sergeant, black hair, crooked nose, his arms crossed and his eyes narrowed, not at the carnage inside the room but at Suzanne. It was clear he was disgusted by the idea that a woman had been called in to help on a case. A woman, no less, who didn't even work in the precinct house as a clerk or telephone operator, but who sold tickets at the entrance to one of Coney Island's amusement parks.

"So this is your wonder lady?" he asked with a snort. "I don't see much to her, you ask me."

"Let me introduce Miss Suzanne Heath, Sergeant Whitman," said Granger, ignoring Whitman's tart quip. "The young lady I spoke to you about at the station. She's a friend of my girl, Coralie."

No, not a friend, really, thought Suzanne. *She's a co-worker. We both sell tickets at Luna Park, that's all. I have no true friends but Cittie.*

"Miss Heath has come here to give us a hand."

"A hand of what?" asked Whitman. "Spooks and spells and tea leaves? I can't believe you've fallen for whatever shit she's fed you."

"Mind your words, Whitman."

"Dung, then, or excrement. We get a call this morning that there's been a murder, two murders, one of them a big shot. You tell me your daughter knows some Luna loony who claims to be able to see and feel things we can't, and that perhaps she'll be able to aid us on this case. Josiah, you want captain so badly you'd risk it on queer talk of reading minds or whatever magic Coralie claims your young lady can do?"

"It is not magic, Whitman. I would call it a psychic connection, and I'm not risking a thing," said Granger. Suzanne could hear it in his voice — he really wasn't certain but hoped to heaven Coralie was right. "When a good police officer finds a useful tool, he uses it. Miss Heath can help or she can't, we'll see."

Suzanne didn't give a donkey's ass how Whitman felt about her. She knew men like him, knew their narrow minds and haughty attitudes. She had work to do, a duty to society, as much as she didn't want to do it. She lifted her head high and turned sideways and made to go around him. He blocked her with his arm. She stopped short to keep from touching him.

"So," he said with a thin smile, rocking on the heels of his boots and pushing her back slightly with his arm. "Who do you think did the bloody deed? Perhaps the silly little maid out in the corridor, a jealous lover of the dead man here? Oh, no, that would have no drama, would it? How about President Taft? Your visions could throw our president into jail for murder, perhaps. I don't have much of a liking for the fat old boy, anyway. Or maybe the owner of this rat's nest of a hotel is the killer? Maybe the woman looked like his bad old auntie who used to beat him senseless, so he returned the favor. What'd you think?"

"Too early to say," Suzanne said. And then she leaned forward, narrowed her eyes, and whispered, "But one thing I can say for certain is that you best watch the way you treat your wife. Women are known to rise up when you least expect it, and bring you down quickly."

The sergeant drew back, stunned. Suzanne nodded at the thin, scabbed scratches on his face and the bruised knuckles on his left hand. Whitman's teeth barred, but he said nothing. Suzanne and Granger entered the room.

The bedchamber was a poor imitation of the upscale hotels east on Manhattan Beaches, with thin, moth-eaten curtains, a wobbly chair over which a green cotton skirt and gingham blouse had been draped, and a highboy with a door that hung at a tilt. A badly-silvered mirror was mounted on the wall over the washstand. On a bedside table was an electric lamp with a dragon base and red, tasseled shade. The place employed a maid, but clearly her only responsibilities were replacing linens on occasion. There were cobwebs in the corners of the ceiling and sandy grit and cigar ash on the floor.

Suzanne removed her second glove and put the two into her skirt pocket. She glanced quickly past the tarnished, warped mirror then looked at the bed. She closed her eyes, caught her breath, and looked again.

She had seen violent death before. During the cold months of her first off-season five years earlier, Suzanne had lived in a Brooklyn apartment several blocks from the East River's Hell Gate. She'd worked as a clerk in a mattress and pillow shop, sharing a cramped flat with two other girls, hotheaded and determined greenies from Scotland. One worked as a chicken decapitator in a poultry factory and the other a sanitary assistant in the local hospital. In this city, far removed from the elegance of Tarrytown on the Hudson where Suzanne had been born and had spent her earliest years, death was harder, faster, and angrier. In Brooklyn there was a world of possibilities when it came to illness, injury, and demise. She'd seen bodies in all stages of disrepair and dismemberment: children dead from consumption and starvation, women dead in the midst of childbirth with the babies' wet heads staring lifelessly from between their mothers' legs; bodies of bargemen pulled from the East River, mottled and fish-gnawed; corpses in sweltering tenements, undiscovered for days, bloated and whistling with escaping gasses.

And there was never a time that her heart did not leap and twist, not a time she did not offer a brief prayer for the soul of the one who had died...if there was a God listening or caring. If there was such thing as a soul.

Usher this poor spirit into Your presence for ever and ever, and into something better than that which grim life has offered. If You are real. If You care.

The face of the woman on the bed had been smashed beyond recognition. Her features were gone, ripped away, leaving little but bone fragments, bloody tissue, and some glistening brain matter on the pillow sham. Dark blood had soaked into the pillow, the bedspread around her shoulders, and into her partially unfastened corset. At the foot of the bed were her gingham blouse and green cotton skirt, tangled up, spattered. The man was dead on the floor beside the bed, on his knees and leaning against the mattress, his head likewise crushed, with rivulets of blood and strands of bone and flesh dangling down his back and chest. He was dressed still, wearing an expensive starched shirt and vest, black tie, tan trousers and well-polished shoes. His stiffened fingers were raised and linked with the fingers of his dead lover, much the same as they might have been linked hours earlier while laughing and tripping on Steeplechase's Funny Staircase.

"Mary O'Connor was right," said Suzanne. "This is her sister Maude."

"You know that for certain?" asked Granger, while at the door Whitman blew air noisily through his lips.

Suzanne nodded. "Outside, I touched Mary. I felt myself then as her, sometime yesterday afternoon. She was talking to her sister, talking to Maude." For the barest moment, Suzanne had been the woman, standing on a wooden plank walkway in the fading sunlight, shaking her head and saying in a particularly amused and shrill voice, "Oh, Maude, 'ave you heard of the Blowhole Theater? Ladies' skirts fly up and everybody laughs whilst their chumps has their bums stuck with a cattle prod by a little clown! We'll go there and we'll have ourselves quite the lark!" Suzanne had felt the uncomfortable tightness of the woman's sweaty corset and the pinch of her too-small shoes. She could taste remnants of the corn and cabbage Mary'd had for lunch. She felt a rush of the woman's excitement and sheer joy, passing through her heart like a flock of butterflies, and then it was gone, there was nothing more. But there was no doubt that the woman to whom Mary had been talking was Maude O'Connor, dressed in her green cotton skirt and gingham blouse.

Whitman sneered. "Mary O'Conner could've told us that herself, should we'd let her up here to have a peek at the dead woman. Surely you can do better than this, Miss Heath. See if you can determine what weapon was used to cause all that blood there. See if you can describe the face of the killer for us."

Suzanne moved to the foot of the bed, keeping her eyes averted from the carnage. She touched the blanket roll and took slow breaths, waiting for something, anything…

Then there was a tug at the corner of her eyes and a sense of lightheadedness. Across her field of vision a sudden snap of something white, something like an egret's wing or a sheet flapping on a line.

Bright, swirling white.

Then it was gone.

"Where you get this talent, Miss Heath?" said Whitman. "Who whispers in your ear and tells you things we can't hear?"

This killing had something to do with the color white, she was certain.

"Must be old Satan himself talking to you, little lady," snorted Whitman. "You and the devil bosom buddies?"

Suzanne turned to glare at Whitman, who flinched though just barely, clearly surprised by the venom in her eyes.

Satan himself has got you in his clutches, Suzanne's mother had said when Suzanne was a child. *Right there in the palm of his red, fiery hand, whispering secrets into your very ear. What a curse I have with a daughter such as you! It would have been better if you had died in my womb.*

Suzanne shook her head to hush her mother's voice, and then focused on the crime scene.

Maude O'Connor's petticoat was twisted beneath her but not torn, her stockings were snagged in several places but not ripped. There appeared to be no scratches or bruising on her arms or legs. Likewise, her one-time lover seemed to have been caught unawares, kneeling by her bedside, drunk and sappy and perhaps proposing marriage to the girl with whom he had spent the afternoon, who might have let him fondle her breasts inside the dark, warm recesses of Luna's Dragons Gorge ride. A marriage proposal after such a day, regardless of how insincere, might give him access to the girl's own dark, warm recesses for the night.

Then someone had come into the room and killed them. Unheard, unseen by the lovers. Maude had wet herself as she died. The scent of urine on the bedspread was strong.

Suzanne waited, her stomach roiling, her jaw tight, bearing down into her mind, waiting for something, anything more than just a vision of white, to help her know who had done this hideous act.

"Tell us what you found before we got here," Granger ordered Whitman. "You had a full half hour in this room before we arrived."

"I've made my sketches," said Whitman, tapping his pocket where the outline of a notebook could be detected. "And I, myself, found the weapon. It's right there, under the edge of the rug by the window." He walked to the rug and pushed back the corner with the toe of his boot, revealing a claw hammer covered in rust.

"What were you waiting for, in not telling me?"

"Oh, you'd have found it," said Whitman. "But I wanted that woman to prophesy where it was, what it was."

Suzanne said, "I'm quite certain that isn't the weapon. I believe you brought it here, rubbed it in the blood, then hid it beneath the rug so you could claim a bit of credit for the find."

Whitman stalked forward into the room, his hand lifted, as if he would slap Suzanne. Suzanne drew up her shoulders but stood still. Were he to strike her, she would strike him back with her fist, and for her size she could pack a fairly powerful punch.

But Granger said, "Whitman! Halt right there!"

Whitman stopped but did not look at his superior. Rather, he continued to stare at Suzanne. "Bitch! How dare you accuse me of tampering?"

Suzanne stared at him coolly. "I don't make casual accusations." She wouldn't be surprised if he'd planted the weapon, the way he had glanced at the rug's corner with a certain dark glee. And why would the murderer have hidden it in the room rather than take it along with him? Any sensible person would question that. So no, Suzanne wasn't sure Whitman had planted the weapon, but either way it didn't hurt to knock him down a couple pegs.

Granger looked between the two, his face hard, his breaths coming through his teeth. Then he jabbed a finger at Whitman. "Get out of here! Get back to the precinct house! On my return we'll both see the captain, and he'll hear tell how you tried to interfere with these investigations."

"But you can't believe this witch!" declared Whitman. "She's lying! I'm honest as the day is long!"

"You'll have your chance to state your case when I get back. Now go!"

"Damn this whole thing! Damn it to Hell, and this bitch with it all!" Whitman left the room, casting an enraged glance over his shoulder at Suzanne. Weapon-planter or not, with such a temper she hoped his career would be done for in short order.

"So," said Granger, pushing the door shut. His face was flushed with anger or embarrassment or both. He mopped his forehead with his handkerchief. "Can you help on this, Miss Heath? You proved yourself to Coralie regarding her...incident. But can you help us find the killer?"

"We'll see." She stepped over the body of the man and stood flush against the bed. Slowly, reluctantly, she walked her fingers across the coverlet to the dead woman's hand and cupped it. She held and waited, looking up at the cheap painting of a flower garden over the headboard so as not to see the head of Maude O'Connor, so as not to look at the smashed and bloody bits on the pillow sham. Life here one moment and gone the next, and often in tragic, hideous turns of fate.

The hand was cold and stiff, the skin tight and dry like that of the crippled crocodile "Bullrushes" in the poorly-attended Pharaoh's Daughter show in Luna Park. Cold, knotted, and offering nothing.

Come now, she thought. *If I have to do this, let me do it and have it over.*

She let out a breath, bore down, waited. But there was nothing.

She let go of the hand. Bracing herself, she placed her hand gently on the mangled forehead. It was pulpy, sticky, chilled. She pressed down slightly and felt a very slight warming beneath her fingers, waited. Her visions came in two fashions — some came without coaxing, unexpected and unbidden, others came through careful focus that more often than not left her with a headache that lasted for days. Never were the visions truly wanted. Most often they were dreaded.

Dreaded and dreadful.

Such was the case of Faith Gansy, many years in the past. Suzanne didn't want to know but it was her chore to know, and when she experienced the dreadful truth and told what she knew, she had made to suffer for knowing, for telling. Faith, sweet little Faith. Such tragedy, such a cruel act of...

"Miss Heath?"

Suzanne shook her head and stepped away from the bed, over

the dead man on the floor. She knelt, touched him for a moment, and again, sensed nothing. Standing, she wiped her bloody hand on her skirt, causing Granger to cringe. "I'm sorry," she said. "The woman is Maude O'Connor, but that's all I know. I saw something white a few minutes ago, but I have no idea what that could mean."

"White. Do you mean a name, White?"

"I don't know. I don't think so, but I'm not sure."

"Oh."

"I'm sorry."

"All right."

"Perhaps something will come to me later."

"Perhaps."

"When you sent for me your message said you already knew who this man is." Suzanne nodded at the body on the floor.

"Yes," said Granger. He hesitated. "It's Alexander Harper, assistant Alderman. In spite of the...damage...I recognized him the moment I got here this morning, those shoes, that ring. And there is a leather pouch in his pocket with his calling cards. I'd always knew he liked a shoddy trifle every now and then. Oh." He shook his head. "His wife will blame everyone but him, even though she never cared much for her husband. Feel sorry for his young children, though. Four of them, you know."

Suzanne didn't know.

"What kind of man would kill, and in this manner, I wonder? What kind of hideous animal is he? And to kill such a prominent figure."

"I read in the news of a killing in Coney just two weeks ago," said Suzanne, one hand going to her hip. "A young man. No one knew where he was from or who he was. He got drunk and in a fight. He was robbed, stabbed, and left under Steeplechase Pier."

"Without meaning to sound incapable or inefficient, Miss Heath, yes, we do have our occasional murders on Coney. That in and of itself is not unusual. And between the two of us, some of the dead are those who, well, are just as well off dead."

"Better off dead?"

Granger nodded, obvious to Suzanne's expression of disgust. "But now it seems we have a murderer that not only killed two persons, and in a more hideous fashion I cannot imagine, but he killed a very important man. I think our killer might have political retributions to make, a bloody statement he may want known. It does not seem careless, this killing. It was planned by a devious and diseased mind. Will he kill again? That is what I'm asking myself now." He hesitated, looked the floor, his eyes spinning for a moment as if he were watching an insect. Then his voice steeled and he said, "You must swear to keep Harper's name to yourself."

"I don't swear."

"Apologies, Miss Heath, but hear me. I know, Whitman knows, you know, and our captain knows. The rest of the officers will catch wind before the day is up and they'll be sworn to secrecy. But no one else can find out, do you understand? It is as important to keep this under wraps for as long as possible as we hunt Harper's killer and bring him to justice."

"And for justice for Maude O'Connor, as well."

"What? Oh, yes."

Suzanne tilted her head. "And what about the man found under Steeplechase Pier? Have you spent a great deal of time and effort searching for his murderer?"

Granger opened the door and the two went into the hallway. The maid was still there, and she glanced up, her eyes weary and wrung out from crying. "Go on down," said Granger. "Wait for me in the lobby." She nodded, pulled herself up, and moved off toward the stairs. "Damn Whitman," Granger grumbled. "His job was to talk to that woman."

"What of the stabbed man's justice?" Suzanne pressed.

Granger shrugged. "Chippies and drifters are just that, no surprise, no real matter to anyone but their family and friends, if they have any. I don't mean to sound harsh, but that's the truth. I only have time to deal in the truth. Alexander Harper is…was… young, rich, and popular. Alderman George Mansfield's favorite nephew. Harper's fellows liked him quite a bit. He was primed to move up." Granger tugged at his cuffs then headed down the hallway. "I'm lucky to be a police lieutenant, Miss Heath. A bad turn of luck can pull that out from under me. Mind you, I wouldn't tell you who he is…was…if I didn't have high hopes you could help. I am not into magic. Magic is for children and ignorant immigrants and savages. We've in an age now of science and sensible thinking.

But I thought that, I hoped maybe…" He trailed for a moment. Then, "We must find the killer in this case." He stopped at the top of the steps, holding his head up high as if feeling that the more he spoke, the more authority he lost.

"Again, I'm sorry I was no help."

"All right, then."

As Granger started down the stairs, Suzanne paused to gaze out the hall window overlooking Surf Avenue. Across the street was Steeplechase Park, its enormous glass-enclosed Pavilion of Fun dominating the scene, along with George Tilyou's self-proclaimed "World's Largest Ferris Wheel," the now-defunct steel Giant Seesaw, holding its two empty wheels at arm's length and boldly advertising "Steeplechase Park" with letters made of twisting wire and tightly-strung electric bulbs, the undulating steel tracks of the Steeplechase Ride, and the colorful flags atop poles and towers, batting madly at the wind off the Atlantic. Beyond the park, the blue slice of ocean and an excursion boat pulling up to the pier to deposit visitors from Manhattan. The ship's horn sounded long, faint, and balefully on the air. The window had no screen, and flies buzzed in and out on their own particular whims.

Halfway down the stairs, the precinct photographer, a short man with dark eyes and square shoulders, passed them on his way up, all huffs and puffs, a cigarette in his teeth and pince-nez gripping the tip of his bulbous nose, a leather case slung over his shoulder, lugging a tripod and a bellowed, mahogany camera. Granger stopped on the second floor landing. "Can you see yourself out, Miss Heath? I need to supervise the photographing."

"Yes, Lieutenant," said Suzanne.

Granger's opened his mouth and Suzanne expected him to say, "Thank you for your time," but it was clear he was disappointed and didn't want to make more of it in front of the photographer. His mouth snapped shut and he merely nodded.

The rest of the way down, Suzanne let her fingers brush the wall, thinking perhaps there was something in the paper-covered plaster, something in the grime of a handprint to help her know what had happened.

Not that she really wanted to see. Not that she really wanted to know. If she could never again be asked to detect something with her visions she could live a life of relative normalcy.

But she had debts to pay, sins from long ago to make right. She didn't know if they would ever be paid in full, but as best she could she would continue to offer bribes to Heaven, to grease God's palm a bit to keep from going to the Hell her mother so often swore her into. If there were a Heaven that heard appeals. If there were a Hell beyond the gore and heartbreak of everyday life.

She left the hotel, past the few remaining guests who were now being interviewed, out from the sweltering shade into the sweltering sun. The crowd was gone from the walk, as was Mary O'Conner, though patrolmen Martin and Osier remained by the door, arms crossed. Surf Avenue hummed with horses, carriages, trolleys, a few scattered automobiles, and pedestrians. The air was thick with the smell of fried lunches from the small street-side vendors and the sweat of beast and man alike.

Suzanne let out a long, deep breath then moved to the streetlight to watch for a break in the bustle to make her way to the other side. She watched as a young girl pulled her mother down the walk past the hotel. The mother laughed and skipped along, trying to keep up. There was love there. There was a bond, the bond that should be between mother and child.

Tell me, Mother, Suzanne thought, *now that you're dead. Now you know for certain. Is there a Hell? Are there flames to consume those like me, those who see things we aren't supposed to see? Who know things we aren't supposed to know? Who do things they aren't supposed to do?*

A mule-drawn wagon filled with rags passed by. Suzanne put her hand on the light pole, ready to cross…

And the vision struck her full force. She felt herself crashing backward, falling away from the moment and into another place, another time…

The woman Maude is smiling into a mirror. Suzanne is Maude, and she looks at herself as she unpins her thick, rather coarse hair. She is trembling with anticipation, and her neck and cheeks are slick and pinked. There is movement behind her. It is a smiling man. Handsome, well-groomed. His eyes are shaded by thick brows. This man is rich, clearly. He is the dead man in the room. The politician.

Blink.

She is on the hotel bed now, lying across the pillows, dressed only in a corset and damp petticoats. Her hair falls across her shoulders like tangled, copper-colored batting. She is breathing heavily, and her heart is pounding. She knows this man only wants one night with her. He is only after her woman's goods. Yet that is all right with her. He's promised to make her feel good. He promised to bring her as close to Heaven as any woman on Earth could possibly be. She needs to feel him on her, in her. She's been untouched too long. Most men think she is plain, but this man said she is pretty. She knows what her sister Mary will think of all this but she doesn't care. Mary, who is also considered plain, has a beau named Bill.

Maude's mouth moves, and she says, "I'm ready" but the words are silent on the air. The well-dressed man is beside her now, his hand reaching out for hers, clutching her fingers and wiggling playfully. She laughs, her laugh inaudible. There is no sound at all. Nothing but...

Nothing but a distant man's voice saying, "Miss, are you all right?" and the muffled thump as Suzanne's head strikes the ground.

...the smell of talc and the feel of the man's fingers as he touches her face teasingly, putting one finger in her mouth like a child's lollipop. The finger tastes like warm butter and has a ring on it. Maude laughs again, silently, and shuts her eyes to savor the sensations of taste and touch. The man's finger pulls out, and then the mattress shudders and then it bounces. There is a heavy vibration as if he has gone down on his knees beside the bed.

Blink.

She is no longer in the hotel room. She is no longer Maude. There is darkness, and in the center of the darkness, a fire. At first it looks like the fire inside a cook stove—small, red, flickering. But this fire suddenly leaps upward, forming a raging, blistering column that lights none of the darkness but only itself. The heat is so intense that the black air crackles and hums.

Blink.

She is Maude O'Connor again, gurgling without a sound as her head crushes in like a tin can and her eyes are blown to the back of her skull.

"Miss? Miss!"

Blink.

The fire column again and a faint sound of laughter. There are shadows now, as if on the walls of a narrow alley or cave, shadows that bow and bend and contort, dancing like dark and skeletal savages.

Wings rise from the flame, flapping, whirring, but not burning, lifting from the conflagration, as cheerful as a child on the last day of school. The bird is pure white.

"Miss, please!"

She was being shaken, quite roughly, and she tried to scramble back and away because it hurt her neck. "I'm…" she begins.

"Miss!"

"I'm all right," Suzanne managed. "Let go of me."

Surf Avenue re-appeared in a nauseating swirl of gold and blue. Osier was in the center of the swirl, his face distorted and wobbly. Suzanne planted her palms against the steaming road and waited for it to stop moving. She swallowed once, twice. "Damn this," she muttered.

"What did you say?"

"Nothing." Suzanne pulled her knees beneath her and pushed herself upward. Her head throbbed. There was a tear in the hem of her skirt. She must have kicked up quite a fuss while on the ground, catching the heel of her shoe in the fabric.

"Do you need a doctor?" The question was more irritated than concerned.

"No," Suzanne managed. *Damn, my head hurts!* She gave Osier her best look of stoic resolve. "I'll be fine."

Suzanne adjusted her straw hat, pulled on the little white cotton gloves from her pocket, and started east up Surf Avenue, through the milling hoards of holidayers going about on foot, in carriages, wagons, fancy black Ford automobiles, and trolleys; past hawkers with their souvenir teacups and ashtrays, candies and teacakes, fried clams and boiled sausages, ice cream sodas and hot dogs; past the façades of countless restaurants and hotels with their colorful signs and awnings; past cigar shops and beer stands; past the rattling coasters run by independent investors and the painted fronts of shows and rides with talkers that called to all who passed, "The best you've ever seen!", "The most fun to be had for a nickel!", "Your sweetheart will hold on tight to you in here, just see if she won't!"; past clots of families of all shapes, sizes, and backgrounds, dammed up on the side of the avenue to discuss what they should see next, what they should ride next, how much money they had to last them until midnight. Up five blocks to Luna Park's enormous entrance arch where her fellow cash girls sat in their little carts dressed in Mexican red and black, mindlessly trading paper slips for coins over and over and over again, smiling hard as if the smiles had been nailed on by some cruel, divine carpenter.

2

The hot dog smelled like an old tramp who hadn't taken a bath in a year, but Coralie Granger took a bite, anyway, chewed it up and swallowed it down. It didn't taste as bad as it smelled, and Coralie's stomach had managed foods much worse. She watched as Suzanne Heath, seated in the brightly-painted cart a good six feet from her own, sniffed the meat in one of her sandwiches then put it down beside the other on the narrow counter next to the roll of paper tickets. Coralie had gotten dogs all 'round for the cash girls; she'd slipped a couple nickels into the hand of a wide-grinning young man who'd bought a Luna Park entrance ticket from her and asked if he might find the time to come back to the front of the park with a couple dachshund sausages. Coralie never had trouble getting men to do what she asked, and within twenty-five minutes the pleasant young dandy had returned with enough dogs for each of the cash girls to have two.

There were five cash girls, side by side in their Mexican carts in the shadow of Luna Park's tall entrance arch. At one end sat the new girl Adelaide Groche, buxom and shrill and twenty-two, then came Suzanne Heath, nineteen-year-old Coralie Granger, stout little seventeen-year-old Jennie Baker, who weighed as much as two of the smaller cash girls together, and lastly, eighteen-year-old Eliza Jameson, thin as a pole and charmingly coy, with pale skin and straw-colored hair. All the girls except Suzanne chewed on their hot dogs between brisk ticket sales. Coralie could see that Jennie was well ahead of the other girls, having downed one and a half in a matter of minutes, and was having a hard time keeping the dripping grease off the bodice of her Mexican blouse.

"Don't you like the hot dogs?" Coralie called over to Suzanne, no longer able to hold her tongue. With just a sideways glance, Coralie snatched two dimes from an elderly man on whose arm was draped an elderly woman, dropped the coins into the steel box on her cart shelf, and handed the man two tickets. Immediately behind the elderly man was a young woman in gloves and a bright blue gown and flowered white hat, apparently alone, and then a father herding three eager adolescent children and a timid wife. Customers were steady this time of day — early evening — when the hot air was beginning to ease ever so slightly within lengthening shadows. Folks paid their entrance fees then entered Luna Park, a world filled with coasters and cafes, marching bands and giant slides, diving horses and elephant parades, ice cream stands and Oriental promenades, and tall white electric towers that would, in a few hours, cut the sky and hold back the night like glimmering, sparkling tent poles.

"Well?" Coralie demanded as she gave the woman in the blue gown a ticket. "Suzanne, are you listening to me?"

Suzanne glanced at Coralie, her eyes barely visible beneath the brim of her silk rose-covered Mexican hat. There was a drip of sweat on the tip of her nose, and the cotton gloves she always wore were dark on the palms where she had handled countless nickels and dimes. "I appreciate it," said Suzanne, "but I don't feel comfortable having people spend money on me. You may have them back."

Coralie blew air through her lips. "Can't you just lie and say you aren't hungry?"

Suzanne said, "But I *am* hungry."

"Then why don't you eat? You didn't take your lunch break at one-thirty and we don't get off until seven. That's a full hour away."

Suzanne took money from a gruff-looking, bristly man and handed him a ticket. He licked his lips at her and she scowled, which sent him off into the park without comment. Suzanne looked back over at Coralie. "First," she said, "the sandwiches reek. I know you noticed that but chose to ignore it. Second, I don't want you spending money on me. You need to keep your money. We all do. We work too hard and too long to waste it."

"You sound like an old woman." Coralie pruned up her lips and her voice picked up a raspy, quivery tone. "Don't do anything for me, sweetie. I don't need any help. I'm just fine as long as I can have my cane and my ear trumpet." Then she shook her head. "You want to be old before your time? You prefer to be a matron instead of a miss?"

"I'm fine. You don't need to worry about me." Suzanne looked back at the row of people lined up before her cart. Took money, handed a ticked. Took money, handed a ticket. Coralie turned her attention back to her own antsy, noisy customers, laughing, bumping into one another, stamping their feet on the dusty ground and watching her as anxiously and hopefully as children waiting for birthday ice cream.

Take the money, hand the ticket, take the money, hand the ticket. One face so much like the next, regardless of age or height or weight or sex or breeding. Faces that blurred one into the other as the day and weeks went by.

Coralie wrinkled her nose. It cracked with burned skin where she'd gone to the beach Sunday without a hat. She glanced at Suzanne again, and at the uneaten hot dogs beside her. So she didn't like the food. She didn't like having money spent on her. Hadn't her mother taught her the etiquette of the white lie? Suzanne was so infuriatingly honest. So dreadfully blunt. Coralie couldn't remember anyone as completely, painfully truthful since her last beau had ridiculed her club foot, saying it looked like she was the product of a human and duck coupling. She'd been shocked, and had struck him, hard. But, yes, he'd been honest. That was exactly what her foot looked like. Such things didn't bother her for long. Very little got under her skin, very little irritated her. She'd lived with her father long enough to form a fairly heavy crust for bad truths. Truth about her mom leaving them. The truth about her brother's suicide. The truth that rich boys usually preferred to dally with poor girls but rarely married them. The truth that if you didn't mind being dallied with, you could get yourself a fine meal and perhaps even a nice gift before having to give in to the rich boys' animal lusts. No, few things got under Coralie's skin.

But Suzanne Heath certainly did.

Earlier that day, when Suzanne returned from the Capital Hotel, Coralie had tried to learn something, anything, about the murdered couple, about any vision Suzanne might have seen, about the room, the blood, the smell, the condition of the bodies, and the reaction of her father, Lieutenant Granger, to it all. But Suzanne remained infuriatingly tight-lipped and silent.

Coralie had demanded, "Gracious sakes, I'm involved here, too, so you best tell me what you know. Papa was so upset this morning when he got the news. He said there'd been a murder on Coney, an important murder though he wouldn't expound. And it was *I* who said to him, 'Get Suzanne Heath, she'll help you.' I said to him, 'Suzanne can see things. We both know that, Papa. Call her in. It can't cost you a penny for the time!' And he did, right like I said. He sent a note for you and there you went, missing out the first hour of work to do a civic duty. I know you helped him. I knew you would."

"And I was docked pay for that hour of work I missed," Suzanne had replied. "You heard Timothy. He was very happy to tell me." Timothy O'Rourke was the man who supervised the cash girls. He was a whistley-nosed bastard who never could look another person in the eye — not out of modesty but out the purest sense of superiority Coralie had ever run up upon.

"But what did you see there, at the Capital Hotel?"

Suzanne had only waved her hand to chase away a clot of gnats. Coralie wanted to slap her. The next few hours drove Coralie to distraction, wanting to know what had gone on at the hotel. Suzanne merely did her job, speaking only to answer direct questions, being careful not to touch those to whom she handed tickets.

"Are you going to just waste the dogs?" Coralie hitched her thumb in the direction of the two unloved frankfurters on Suzanne's cart. Her curly blonde hair caught up with a breeze and several strands caught on her lip. She spit them out. More customers paused at her cart and the carts of the other cash girls, trading money for tickets. "Pass them over if you won't eat them. I'll give them to a deserving child. Food shouldn't go to waste, you realize that."

"That's why I ask you to please not spend money on me."

"Fine, then. Puh!"

Suzanne leaned from her cart, holding the dogs out as far as she could. Coralie snatched them up then nearly dropped them as three juvenile boys ran between the carts without paying. Eliza waved her arms and shouted, "Wait!" but the boys ignored her and the cash girls let them go. O'Rourke's big bully boy, Griffin Gold, would catch them and send them back. And if O'Rourke were watching, he'd give the boys a cuff on the ear, to boot.

Coralie tucked the hot dogs into her deep skirt pocket. It was already filthy from the week's work, so a bit of stain wouldn't show. She didn't really know what else might be available for dinner tonight — her father often worked very late and she hated cooking — so these would serve nicely, even though they did have that stink.

Coralie was used to Coney food, hot or cold, fresh or stale, steaming with delicious aromas or prickling on the edge of rancidity. Oh, she had been ill before from something she had consumed, had been laid up for days with cramps and sweats, but she was always able to rise again, no worse for the wear, no more worried about getting sick again than she was about flying to the moon. She loved Coney like she had loved her brother William. She trusted it, in all its uncertainties and dangers. It pumped hot and alive in her veins as much as did her red, American blood.

Coralie had been called many things by those who knew her — "wild as a leopard in Bostock's Animal Arena" and "as unsettling as a spin on the 'Roosevelt's Rough Riders' coaster." She knew the comments were more insult than compliment, but she took them as the latter. She was a dyed-in-the-wool Coney kid, born in Brooklyn but relocated south to West Brighton in 1897 when her family took jobs at Sea Lion Park. The huge, wall-enclosed playground, along with its competition, George C. Tilyou's Steeplechase Park which sat across Surf Avenue along the beach to the west several blocks, offered what had not been offered to the American public in the past — fun and recreation in its purest form, with no responsibilities, no repercussions, no strictly-enforced moral codes to keep one's enjoyment within socially-acceptable limits.

Everyone in the Granger family worked at Sea Lion — six-year-old Coralie, the ten-year-old twins Della and Maude, fifteen-year-old William, and Mr. and Mrs. Josiah Granger. Josiah assumed the role of an operator on the Shoot-the-Chutes ride, an enormous sliding board down which flat-bottom boats filled with passengers would plummet from a lofty height into a man-made lagoon then bounce along the water's surface and slowly glide to a stop. Mrs. Granger was a cook at the Sea Lion Lunch Bar, offering up batches of buttery clams, green corn, and potato chowder for starving guests. William took tickets for the "Flip Flap," though there were few takers on this circular-looping ride. Too many people got off complaining of wrenched necks, and so in a short time the "Flip Flap" became more of a spectator's amusement than a rider's pleasure. The twins Della and Maude were featured swimmers in the Aquatic Show and Water Circus held at the south end of the lagoon. Little Coralie danced for pennies at the park's entrance, dressed in a frilly costume that made her look like a poodle. She loved the attention; women gave her hugs, children patted her head, and men presented her with pennies for "being so precious." Once, she earned a whole quarter for sneaking away behind the sea lion pen with a man who pulled down her poodle panties and spanked her bare bottom.

At nine, Coralie got a job singing as "Little Lily, Angel Child" in Kramer's Music Hall in Sea Lion's competition, Steeplechase Park. This was a fine occupation until she was eleven, no longer little and no longer in possession of a sweet, child's voice. By then her father was shut of the park business, having paid his three hundred dollars to join up with the Coney Island police force and her brother William, who had struggled with long bouts of melancholia, had hanged himself. Also gone were Maude and Della, who had moved to Manhattan to get jobs as typewriters, and Coralie's mother who had just up and left. Coralie, however, was part of the lights and the noise and the garish, constantly changing world that was Coney.

In 1902, Sea Lion Park closed due to too much rain and Boyton's refusal to bring in new amusements to appease the crowds. When Luna Park opened May 16th, 1903, on the same plot of land where Sea Lion Park had died, Coralie was hired to play a young moon maiden in its "Trip to the Moon" cyclorama. She spent the next five seasons dressed in a silver blouse, skirt, and leggings, dancing amid incandescent lights and spraying fountains, tripping over children and midgets dressed as tiny, jabbering "Selenites," and offering rocket passengers bits of green cheese from a dimly lit stage plastered and painted to look like the moon's surface.

"Trip to the Moon" closed at the end of the 1907 season, and the next year Coralie took on the part of a young, beautiful maiden, along with over a hundred other young, beautiful maidens, in the "Man Hunt" show, in which horses plunged down inclines into man-made rivers and a Mexican-Indian was burned at the stake during the climax. She didn't much like being one of over a hundred, and so kept her eyes and her options open for another move.

Opening day in May 1909, at age nineteen, Coralie found herself dressed as a Mexican lady and selling tickets at Luna's entrance with four other girls — Emma Zedeck, Eliza Jane Spilman, Jennie Baker, and Suzanne Heath. This position suited Coralie's seething curiosity, for while she was on duty she saw each and every person who passed through Luna's gateway. She could wink at the young men, tease the children, poke fun at the girls she found silly or prudish, and roll her eyes behind the backs of the grumbling dowagers who had come to the park only to suit their husbands' demands.

Yet within the first few days, Coralie noticed that there was something not quite ordinary about the quiet, copper-haired Heath girl. She rarely laughed, but when she did it was one of the most genuine, startling sounds Coralie had ever heard. Suzanne did not make mockery of park-goers as Coralie, Eliza, Emma, and Jennie did throughout the long, hot hours. Suzanne was a solemn, pretty enigma.

And so Coralie relentlessly prodded and chided her co-worker. She tried her best to make Suzanne angry or defensive or gay, to get her to chat about boys or money or boys with money, to get her to laugh at the fat man who ripped the seam of his trousers when he bent to pick up a penny or to make a guess as to what the giggling young couple might do while in each other's arms once they climbed into the car to ride through Dragon's Gorge. Coralie picked at Suzanne like a scab, digging and scratching for something, hoping for a glimpse into the mind of her stoic, oft-silent coworker. Yet Suzanne was the hardest nut Coralie ever had to crack, and what Coralie knew of Suzanne could fit into a teaspoon.

But sometimes a teaspoon could be just enough to sweeten the cup.

It had been a Wednesday in mid-June, a strangely angry night full of salt, sweat, and brawls in the dust along Surf Avenue. The five Luna cash girls were working their usual, six-day-a-week shift from 11 a.m. until 7 p.m. Another crew of girls came on at seven, and took the shift until the park closed at 2 a.m. The girls preferred the longer daytime shift because with more hours came more coins in the pocket. But on that Wednesday afternoon, Timothy O'Rourke told the cash girls that one of the late-shift girls would not be coming in that night. She had turned up "sick in a most unfortunate way," he said with a sniff of his superior nose. Coralie knew that could only mean one thing; the girl would be off to visit a maiden aunt in the Connecticut or Massachusetts countryside at least until Christmastime.

Coralie quickly offered to work the late shift. She would be happy to have the extra dollar.

The night had grown windy, misty, and unseasonably chilly by the time Coralie left Luna at 2:15 the next morning, her shawl about her shoulders, her hair coming loose from its pins, her hat bobbing atop her head in the wind. She walked quickly, turning off Surf Avenue, heading north and home.

A sudden gust caught her hat and tore it free from her hair, then sent it rolling up the road like a child's hoop. Coralie stumbled after it, exhausted from the long day but refusing to let one of her two favorite hats get lost. The felt roses and satin ribbons trailed dust and dirt, and the hat scooted up and out of reach each time Coralie reached down for it. She passed the depot and the wearied merry-makers buying their tickets for the Culver Depot train. Several laughed as she ran by, but none came after to help.

The hat snagged itself against a light pole and Coralie grabbed it up — battered and torn — and held it to her chest as she caught her breath. A rattling automobile, full of young men not ready to give up the ghost and go home, rumbled by and one drunkard shouted out, "I can smell you from here! Ah, ripe and ready! I have what you need right here in my trousers!" The other boys hooted with the wit of their friend, while one lone voice said, "Ah, leave 'er alone, Paulie."

Coralie shouted back, "Get lost, little boys!" Her voice was strained with panting, and made her feel vulnerable. "Curse it all," she whispered as the automobile drove around the corner and out of sight.

She walked on. Home was a mere fourteen blocks from Surf Avenue but tonight it felt like miles. She leaned into the wind, holding her damaged hat to her chest.

A stray dog, matted and likely mad, lumbered from behind a rain barrel and snarled at her. Its teeth glistened and white drool dripped down its muzzle. Coralie froze, hoping the animal would move on. "Go away dog, get!" she whispered. But it didn't get.

With a sudden lunge, it flew at her, chasing her several blocks east and into a dark residential area where sloppy flats leaned this way and that. She prayed as she ran, and God took a bit of her appeal to heart, causing the dog to trip and stumble against the strong wind. Coralie found an empty wagon and clambered up and over its tall sides into the bed, the heel of her right shoe broken, her lip bit through and bleeding, her heart beating wildly, her hat gone once more. Deep in the damp straw, she waited for the dog to leave.

It began to rain.

Yet it was neither the dog nor the rain that caused Coralie the most trouble that night.

The creature growled, leapt, and slobbered about the wheels of the wagon for many long minutes, then stumbled off in search of something within easier reach. Coralie held still, holding her hand to her heart. When it had slowed, she climbed from the wagon. She cursed through clenched teeth, rain dripping from her nose, staring down at her broken shoe. And for one of the rare moments in her life, she was truly afraid.

The street was lined with houses, shops, and electric street lamps offering up auras of yellowed, hazy light into the rain. It was quiet except for a few drunks a block away on the sagging steps of a bar, wobbling in the yellowed light of an electric lamp, batting away the bugs and singing to each other and swearing allegiance to their mothers, sweethearts, and Ireland.

Coralie wondered if she should walk back to Luna and see if perhaps one of the men who worked the security shift might let her into the park, let her find a dry booth or shop in which she could spend the night. It was a shorter walk back than it was on to home.

"That would be the thing to do," she told herself as the Irishmen singing down the road rose and fell. "I could offer the man the extra dollar I earned tonight for his trouble, for letting me in. What choice have I?"

She turned around, facing south into the wind.

And there in front of her was a huge bear of a man, his face scrunched in anger and jabbing his finger at her face. He barked, "I seen you get out of my wagon, girl!"

Coralie flinched, drew herself up. "A mad dog chased me."

"You playing games with me? Truth now, girlie! Why you really hide in my wagon?" He was a drunk. An angry, strong drunk. His body steamed and his breath was thick as spoiled fish.

Coralie tightened like a spring. If she were bigger and he smaller, she would have punched him in the face. Her hands balled into fists but she kept them to her side. "It's the truth. A dog...."

The man shoved Coralie's shoulder and she stumbled backward. "I know what it is. You's playin' saucy with your beau, make him come look for you in the straw. You cheeky little puss!"

Coralie gasped, lifted her head, narrowed her eyes. "I did no damage to your filthy wagon. Now if you'll excuse me…"

But he did not excuse her. He dove for her then, grabbing her arm and then spinning her about to clamp his hand over her mouth. She tried to scream but all that came out was a grunt. He chuckled foully and struck her on the side of her face.

The world disappeared in a shattering of rain, pain, and yellowed light.

A jostle brought Coralie back around. She opened one eye to the black, cloth-covered ceiling of a rattling, horse-drawn ambulance. A young orderly with a scrubby beard and kind brown eyes peered down throw the black haze and stuttered, "We'll be th…there in a m..m…moment. Don't be frightened, m…ma'am." A fire exploded on the side of her head then, forcing her eye shut and throwing her, mercifully, back into oblivion.

There was an insistent and irritating patting on her cheek. Coralie tried to ignore it but it grew more persistent, harder, and so she opened her eyes and prepared to shout, "Leave me alone!" but her throat was too raw to make a sound.

Above her was a nurse in a white uniform. Behind the nurse, on the white and night-shadowed wall, a gas jet was turned low. Coralie's nose pricked with the sharp scents of disinfectants and heady medicines.

"Miss, are you awake?"

Coralie licked her lower lip but could not answer.

"You're in a hospital," said the nurse. "The best hospital to be had, so you're lucky there." She paused. "Though, ah, you're not so lucky otherwise. You've been hurt, I'm afraid. Ho there, are you awake? Miss?"

Coralie tried to nod, to slide her head up and down against the pillow, but she could not.

A doctor came later, how much later Coralie couldn't fathom. He told her that she had been taken advantage of and that, unfortunately, a portion of her left ear had been chewed away.

"Can you tell me your name, Miss?"

Coralie rolled her tongue around in her mouth and tasted blood. There was a ragged spot on her tongue and it felt swollen. She mouthed, "My name is Coralie...Coralie Heath."

"Heath, yes? Where do you live?"

"I...forget."

"You forget?"

Coralie nodded slowly. God, but her head hurt. Her ear, her swollen tongue...

"I need to contact your family. What is your father's name? Or your mother's?"

Coralie swallowed air and grit. She twisted herself upward until she was sitting and looking at the doctor. He bobbed up and down in her wavering vision.

"Lie down, Miss Heath." The doctor took Coralie's arm and tried to steer her back. She wrenched free.

"No, I'm all right." Her voice was audible now, and the sound stung her ears. Her ear. "I've got to go. What time is it?"

"Now think. Where do you live? Who is your father?"

"I live...over on Tierney. No father."

"What's the number?"

"I can't think," said Coralie. She closed her eyes. "I want to sleep."

"Nurse," she heard the doctor say. "Find out about any Heath family living on Tierney."

"Yes, Doctor Green."

Footsteps, then the doctor saying, "Get some sleep, Miss Heath. We'll get hold of your family as soon as we can."

Then he, too, was gone.

Coralie opened her eyes and sat up slowly. Her head spun and her ear throbbed. She could feel bruises up and down her body.

The room was long and narrow, and filled with white-sheeted beds and moaning or sleeping patients. A nurse down near the door, talking to someone with a casted leg.

Then, another voice, soft but insistent. Familiar.

"Coralie."

It was Suzanne.

"Coralie, look at me."

Coralie looked. Suzanne was leaning over her, the expression on her face as much quizzical as sympathetic, as if she had a puzzle to piece together. It was most peculiar, that expression.

"They came for me at my flat, telling me my sister was injured. I had no idea what they meant, until they said, 'Coralie, the young lady with the blonde hair and the little Spanish outfit.' I still have no idea why they came for me, but knew there was trouble."

"I didn't want my father to know what happened."

"And what did? Was this an accident or an attack?"

A surge of agony swept through Coralie's skull and she moaned.

"Coralie!"

"I can't say," she managed. "I won't say. Should word get to my father, he'll lock me up for good. Or he'll send me away. He detests I'm so free."

"Coralie. We cannot let cruel people get away with their crimes. We must make right what is wrong when we can. If I've learned anything in life, that is it."

"Go away. I'll be all right. I'm out of here as soon as the guards aren't looking."

"I care for nothing but the truth, Coralie. I won't tolerate lies. You've brought me into this as you tried to get away from it. Now, tell me what happened?"

"Go away!"

"No."

Suzanne pulled the wicker visitor's chair close and sat as carefully as if she were posing for a photograph, her blue jacket buttoned neatly, her linen skirt smoothed tidily, her plain, broad hat straight on her head. She said nothing for a moment, breathing slowly, her eyes dark and mouth set. Then she removed her white gloves and took Coralie's hand, so firmly that Coralie didn't have the strength to pull it away. Suzanne's jaw tightened, her face tilted back and she gazed at the ceiling. Her hat trembled. Coralie watched with fascination. Was the young woman praying to God to make this right? For what could God do, as the deed was done?

Down the aisle of cots, an old woman down the ward began to grunt and call out, "I got a itchin' under this bandage! I can hardly stand it. I have to take this bandage off!" Someone else said, "Don't take it off, Mary." Another said, "Take it off, Mary, and have at it. I'm sick of your complaining."

A nurse went to Mary's aid, and Mary went quiet.

Suzanne held motionless, her body in an odd, arched position for what seemed like minutes, her head tilted upward, her hand clutching Coralie's. Coralie didn't like the feel of the grasp. The hand was dry, the touch intrusive.

Then Suzanne shuddered, and a strange sense of sudden warmth shot up Coralie's arm. "What was that?" Coralie exclaimed as she jerked away and held her arm protectively to her chest.

Suzanne lowered her head. She rubbed her eyes and stared at the gas jet over Coralie's bed, then at the floor, and then hard at Coralie.

"What's wrong with you? What happened just now?" Coralie asked. "Are you sick?"

"In many ways, I suppose I am," Suzanne said, more to herself than to Coralie. Then, to Coralie, "I need you to talk to your father and tell him what happened. Such men as the one you encountered should not be loose on the street. Do your duty."

"What man? Wait, what duty?"

"You know exactly what I mean."

"I…"

Suzanne's expression and words were not to be challenged. Coralie's jaw clenched. How did Suzanne know a man was involved? Oh, probably because of the injuries. They surely looked like she'd been beaten. And it was a rare woman to punch that hard.

But then Suzanne said, in a low, guttural voice, "You's playin' saucy with your beau, make him come look for you in the straw. You cheeky little puss."

"How did you know what he said to me?"

"He beat you," said Suzanne, "and tried to have his way with you, though he was too drunk to do it."

Coralie slid back on the cot, trying to get away from Suzanne. What devil had whispered in her ear what had happened?

"His name is Charles O'Reilly. Has friends named Biggy and Lou, though I don't know more than that about them. They drink over at the Slate and Shamrock, a little den beside Concourse Park. They were talking about going there. Might be there still, as drunk as they were."

"Shut your mouth, Suzanne. Don't say any more." Coralie was

nearly whining now. Her heart thundered.

Suzanne sighed. "It's as troubling to me as to you," she said. "I don't care to see what I see, hear what I hear, but I must use it for good, if it is to be used at all. Call your father. Tell him about Charles O'Reilly. Have the man arrested. And you. You must be careful. The world is treacherous. You are young and beautiful. I know you want to have fun. But you're too careless, Coralie. Be smart. Be wise."

And so it was that Charles O'Reilly was arrested and confessed to the assault after a bit of a go in a back station room. And so it was that Coralie recovered over a period of five days, went back to work, and had pestered Suzanne about the experience at the hospital.

"I am your friend, am I not?" Coralie had asked the day she returned as she and the other ticket girls got into place at their booths. "If so, tell me what happened."

"I can't explain it to you. Please leave it at that."

"So, am I a mouse who cannot understand, or a child? I'm not so much younger than you."

"No."

A trolley slowed in front of the hospital with a grinding of steel wheels, and stopped. Cheerful people bumbled and fumbled from the grit-covered vehicle, catching up skirts and holding the hands of wild-eyed children, then rushed off in different directions to take the fun at the parks and other amusements up and down Surf Avenue. A goodly clot of them headed toward the Luna entrance.

"You don't care for me in the least, you never have or you would tell me," Coralie said as the trolley lurched into motion and the first customers reached the booths. She could barely hear her own words above the rattling, groaning vehicle and the loud voices of the customers. Dust drifted front the street into her nose and she sneezed. "Is it my background you don't care for? I suppose that's it, yes! You were born into wealth, anyone can see that. The way you speak, behave. You come from money, not from West Brighton."

Suzanne silently began collecting coins and handing out tickets.

"Do I offend you?" called Coralie over the tumult.

"Let it be, Coralie."

"Am I so careless, so careless and *crazy*, that you won't confide in me?"

Suzanne turned sharply and lifted both her hands, flat out, as if she meant to slap both of Coralie's cheeks at once. Instead, she stepped over, bringing them close to Coralie's face without actually touching her, and gazed at her with an expression both patient and pained. Coralie had the sudden strange sensation that even though she was not being touched, she was being caressed, ever so firmly yet ever so gently. In that brief moment Coralie thought of her mother, Millie Granger, always present with a caress, a cup of tea, an encouraging word to her daughter, yet tough as steel when it came to work and to life, who was kicked by an angry mule when Coralie was eleven and died two days later.

"I've lived only a few years longer than you," Suzanne said quietly, though the voice cut through the din in a low, rumbling way much as soft thunder could be heard amid shouts, "but those years seem a lifetime, more than a lifetime. I am worn out by what I am and what I've been through."

"Are you a fate teller, a gypsy witch, like Madame Mysterio, who sees things with her crystal ball? How did you know about the man who hurt me?"

"Hey, there!" shouted a grumpy old man who stood beside his grumpy old wife. "We're here to buy tickets!"

Suzanne had lowered her hands, stepped back behind her booth, and sold the old grumpy couple some tickets.

"You have to tell me," Coralie had insisted.

Suzanne had not replied.

So it was that early this very morning, as Josiah Granger buttoned the jacket of his uniform and told Coralie a couple had been brutally murdered in the Capital Hotel — that it was bad, it was serious, and would be a difficult solve — Coralie had reminded him of Suzanne. He had sent for her. And Suzanne had reluctantly left her post and gone to the hotel.

"Coralie!" shouted Jennie Baker from behind her cart. "You got plans for those hot dogs Suzanne gave back to you?"

Coralie looked at the pudgy girl in her Mexican skirt and hat. Her face was taut and hopeful, and at that moment she looked for all purposes like a hot dog herself, red and shiny, squeezed into a bun and ready to pop with the heat. Coralie took two dimes from a middle-aged man and his date and gave them two tickets. She pulled a paper-wrapped sandwich from her pocket and hurled it at

Jennie. Jennie squawked and threw up her hands. Jennie's customers dodged the flying meat, and burst out laughing.

Jennie whined, "You should be glad Mr. O'Rourke didn't see that! He'd have you dismissed for unladylike behavior!"

Coralie ignored the girl, and the sandwich was soon squashed by ticket buyers' feet. Not long afterwards, the white-uniformed street sweeper came by and scraped it up along with other bits of rubbish with his big brush. The evening passed along until seven when the cash girls traded their posts with the evening girls.

Jennie and Adelaide went off together, arm in arm, chatting about new shipment of hats they had seen at one of Manhattan Beach's more elegant milliner shops. Eliza's beau escorted her away to dinner at Feltman's. Coralie, having learned nothing of the dead couple at the Capital Hotel from the girl who could have shared such delicious and secret details, put her parasol over her arm and scowled as Suzanne Heath strolled away down Surf Avenue.

"I didn't get a single tidbit from her," Coralie said to a stray mutt that had stopped to sniff the spot where the squashed sandwich had lain. "Not a hint, not even a suggestion, as to what she saw in the hotel and what she saw in her mind. Well." She stomped her foot lightly. "I didn't get what I wanted, and she won't get paid for the time she was gone. Ha. And I'm going to find me a nice fellow to take me up the Iron Tower for a view, then over to Henderson's Music Hall in the Bowery for a concert. After that, maybe a moonlight stroll on the beach and a little sparking if the fellow was handsome and dapper enough.

The dog licked the spot on the ground then snarled at Coralie and trotted after a child with an ice cream cone.

"Ha!" barked Coralie at the dog. It didn't look back.

3

Suzanne and Cittie Parker sat on the damp and lumpy sand, staring out over the dark ocean at the quarter moon and the hazy clouds that ran like thin, threadbare ribbons across the horizon. The sky was never fully dark along the Coney shore, but at the most a deep blue-violet, the purest black held back by the lights of the parks and the myriad independent amusements that crowded the seaside land. The parks were closed for the night, but nearly half of the millions of lights still burned. Night crews were busy, sweeping the trash from the day's customers, mopping spilled ice cream and vomit from the wooden walkways, replacing bad bulbs, hammering back boards that were popping up on the walkways. It would be three-thirty before the crews left and the switch was thrown in the main power buildings. And by five-thirty, the summer sun would be stretching its blood-red fingers from the east, tickling the crests of the coasters, the towers, and the flags that held eternal vigil from the highest vantage points.

But while the parks behind them still seethed with light, they were fairly silent. The last of the patrons had been ushered out at 2 a.m. and the gates locked. It was now nearly two-thirty. A couple Bowery bars and dance halls were still open and music piped from their windows and floated on the damp air down to the shoreline. On the beach, not far from where Cittie and Suzanne sat, lovers giggled beneath a blanket. Down shore fifty yards and out in the water, several tipsy sailors and tipsy young girls, laughed and clung to the tow ropes as the inky waves rose and fell around them.

Cittie took an apple from his cloth sack and handed it Suzanne. She took it with her gloved hands, smelled the summer-tart skin, and then sunk her teeth into the flesh. It was a bit bruised, but the flavor was sweet. She chewed and watched the sailors and girls in the waves. Cittie ate his own apple then hurled the core into the water.

"That's quite a throw," said Suzanne. "You could join the Cuban X Giants and play some of that tricky baseball."

Cittie smiled broadly, his even teeth very white in contrast to the uneven brown of his skin. "I'd be a terrible bad baseball player. I throw bad much as I throw good. Only thing my arms and fingers is good for is playing my music. I think I should jest stick with Dreamland where know I got a check every Saturday."

"Hmm," said Suzanne. She stretched back her head and worked her neck. There was a burning between her shoulders, a pounding weariness in her eyes. Yet she wasn't ready to go back to her flat. At least twice a week, in the wee morning hours, Mandy and his wife Ruth, who owned Moon's Confections and Cigarette Shop above which Suzanne had her one-room flat, would get into a row that rattled the walls, and then into intimate relations which shook the windows. They'd been quiet four nights straight, and she knew tonight they were due. She picked a piece of apple peeling from her tooth. "How are you getting along with the new rattle man?"

Cittie scowled, and stretched his long legs out in front of him. "Lightnin'. Huh. He ain't makin' no friends in the band, I can say that for sure. Got hired 'cause he looks more savage than the rest of us what with that long face and big ole bugged eyes, and he can keep up a pretty good rhythm. But he's got me an' Alfred spooked, though we ain't sayin' nothin' to the boss man. We want our jobs and we ain't rockin' no boats. I'm hopin' he gets tired real quick of shaking that *ganza* and hires hisself out to play Satan over at the Creation Show. That'd suit him better, suit me an' Alfred better, too."

Suzanne nodded. Cittie was part of a band that wandered the walkways and bridges of the Dreamland amusement park, pounding out their savage music and occasionally gathering tips from startled yet pleased listeners. The band was called "Dreamland's Band of Bloodthirsty Zulus," and was made up of the tallest and darkest Negroes to be found. They wore colorful wrapped skirts or animal skin loincloths and jewelry made of bone and twigs. Sharpened ivory skewers ran through their noses, and they wove birds' claws into their hair. They were not allowed to speak to customers, only go about, banging the *djembe*, blowing tunes from carved flutes, and shaking woven rattles and brass bells. A stern-faced white man, dressed in safari clothing, a helmet, and carrying a rifle, walked with the wandering musicians, swinging his weapon slowly back and forth as if to keep the savages in line, as if to protect innocent onlookers from wild men who might just fly off into a rampage and break their necks with their long and savage fingers.

Of course, none of the Bloodthirsty Zulus were from Africa. How expensive that would have been, finding and rounding up musicians on that far continent. Cittie Parker was a twenty-year-old drummer who had run off from the Colored Waifs' Asylum of Ulster County, New York. Alfred Johnson was a thirty-year-old ex-cotton chopper from South Carolina. Cletus Robinson was in his twenties, and had come to Dreamland from Chicago when he got in trouble with some white men over a black woman and they'd swore to cut his balls off with rusty razors. Moses, who could have been thirty and could have been fifty and who swore he had no surname, had worked meat packing in Atlanta. Others came from various east coast states, various occupations. The new man, Lightnin' Veney, was an antsy, twitchy dock boy from Battery Park.

"Dreamland put up a new sign just outside the park this morning, advertisin' Lightnin' as 'Kolo, the most savage beast-man to ever stepped onto Coney Island soil.' Thought that'd get more interest in the Zulu band, more ticket sales, more tips for our manager."

"Yes?"

"Sign spelled it 'salvage.' Most salvage beast-man. Had to laugh. They took it down. Made another one to put up."

Suzanne smiled and shook her head.

They sat without speaking for several long minutes. Suzanne slipped her feet from her shoes and dug her stockinged feet into the cool, wet sand. She took another large bite from her apple then handed the core to Cittie, who threw it toward the dark, foamy water. Suzanne watched the white bristle up on the tops of the ebony waves, dissipate, and then churn up again. The sea's struggle with itself never ended — boiling, spitting, hissing at the world, part of Earth yet eternally separate. Suzanne's understood the sea.

"Was that policeman mad at you 'cause you couldn't help him?" asked Cittie.

"Just disappointed."

"You wanna go back up to the hotel now everythin's calmed down? Pat around, see if you can get a vision there?"

"No."

"But you wan' help the police find that killer."

"I know I'm supposed to. I don't really want to. I never wanted to be compelled to use my…talent. I just wanted to live with it as best I could."

Cittie nodded encouragingly. "You got chores to do in this life, and it's somethin' more than sellin' tickets to Dundy and Thompson's amusement park."

"I know, Cittie."

"Don' mean to be bossy. But you hear what I's sayin'. God's sayin' it, too."

"I hear you, Cittie. Not so sure about God."

Cittie took a cigar stump from his pocket and lit it with a

match. It was damp, and took a moment to catch. He stared at the flame then shook out the match. He drew on the stogie and let the smoke out through his teeth, slowly, like an old man who'd been smoking his whole life. Suzanne watched his eyes as he smoked. She remembered his eyes when she first saw him, peering down at her from the back of a wagon, surrounded by the lush green of a forest. She'd thought he'd been an angel from heaven.

There was a squeal out in the water, and a girl came splashing back toward shore. Her pale swim dress clung to her legs; her dark stockings made it look, for a moment, that she had no legs at all. One of the sailors stomped through the water after her, grabbed her around the waist, lifted her up and carried her back into the deeper waves. She screamed and laughed.

Faith Gansy screamed and laughed as she was carried off, Suzanne thought. *She thought it all a game, just like that girl and the sailor. He had said to her, "I've something oh, so funny to show you, Faith! Come with me, quickly!" Faith had hesitated, for she had meticulously set out a tea party for her dollies under the mulberry bush and didn't want to be disturbed. But he had scooped her up and told her that there was the silliest cat in the stable, doing something he'd never seen a cat do before. She giggled, and she did not resist.*

Suzanne had felt his arms, his clammy hands. She did not want to be there, was not really there at all, but had felt herself carried into the cool shadows to the stable where lingered the smell of newly cut hay and leather but where there was no silly cat at all. In that moment she was Faith.

And then the man had killed the girl.

Faith — Suzanne — had looked at him openly, trustingly, and minutes later she was dead.

Cittie took several more puffs on the stogie then said, "You wanna puff?"

"No. You know don't want to, you know I might...." Her words trailed.

"Yeah, okay." Cittie stubbed the cigar out in the sand. He stood and brushed his legs, his ass, stretched his arms and neck. "I'm headin' out, Suzanne. Gotta get some shut-eye, even if Cletus does kick hard and take up mos' the mattress. You gon' stay here alone? That might not be a good idea, what with a killer runnin' round."

"I'll sit a few more minutes."

"Want I should wait with you?"

"No thanks, Cittie."

He reached out his hand toward her and she nodded. She would not take the hand, even though she wore her gloves. The fabric was enough barrier to keep her from having visions from objects she touched, but she feared they wouldn't be enough for human contact. Cittie knew this, and his reaching out was merely a gesture.

Cittie was gone a full half hour before Suzanne slipped into her shoes, dusted off the grit, and walked home through the blue and breezy night to her one-room flat above Marty and Ruth Moon's dingy shop. It was a long hike, nearly a mile from Coney, but such a familiar stretch that it seemed a blink of an eye that she was home. She climbed the shaky wooden steps from street side to her private door, holding her skirt with one hand, the railing with the other. The door opened with a jostling of the key, and she entered and locked the door behind her.

She shook off her shoes, rolled off her stockings, and sat on the divan in the dark, her legs tucked under her, staring ahead at the wall. There was little to see, but she wasn't looking. The room was sparsely decorated, for Suzanne had long ago lost her taste for anything fancy. The divan, which was on loan from Marty Moon's wife Ruth, served as Suzanne's only seat and her bed as well. It was not long enough to accommodate her five feet four inches; she had to draw her legs up a bit to sleep. She didn't mind. She felt safer that way. A soft blanket was folded across the back of the divan, though during the summer months it was much too hot and humid to use it. The rest of the pieces in the room — a nightstand with washbasin and pitcher, a battered wardrobe, a once-white basin with a spigot that sputtered water, a galvanized bathing tub, and a table with drawers — also belonged to Mrs. Moon. The little cast-iron stove was rarely used for cooking, but was used to boil and cleanse the white cotton gloves she wore most of the time to keep from picking up too much relentless and worthless psychic information throughout the day. There had been a mirror once, but she had covered it without gazing into it, and had requested that Mrs. Moon remove it from the room. Ever since her arrival at the Waifs' Asylum, she had preferred not to look at herself. There was nothing there she cared to see, and certainly nothing there to admire.

A small leather-covered steamer trunk by the wardrobe, however, did belong to Suzanne. It was a gift from the boys at the Colored Waifs' Asylum, and was adorned with hand-painted, colorful flowers and a scrolling "R," for at that time she only knew herself as Rachel. The gift had touched Suzanne more than anything she could remember in her whole life. Nothing her mother had ever done for her had made her feel as warm and cared for as receiving the trunk; nothing her father had said ever made her heart rise up with such joy.

Joy was a rare thing, a fleeting emotion.

Suzanne peeled off the gloves and dropped them to the floor. Too tired to boil them, and there were several other clean pairs folded on the table. She eased over up on her side on the divan, her arm under her head, the other folded at her chest. She knew she should change into her nightgown, but she was so very tired. Four hours until she had to get up again to get ready for work. She shifted slightly to get more comfortable and closed her eyes. It was a long time before she slept. And as she prayed to the troubling, mysterious darkness for oblivion, visions of her mother drifted down to chide her, recollections of her childhood rose up like a monster of the deep to slash her.

Memories that washed upon her like dark, briny ocean waves.

Waves that chilled her to the core.

The Heath homestead, Riverton, sat on the Hudson River just north of Tarrytown on a boxwood-rimmed hill high enough to see up river a good mile and down the river clear to the sharp bend. Built in 1852 by Suzanne's grandfather, a wealthy importer of Asian and European art and owner of a fleet of merchant ships, the estate house held court upon its fifty-two acres proudly, not the largest of the area manors but by far not the smallest. Suzanne's father, Geoffrey, had joined his father in business and inherited the home when the old man died. Geoffrey was an even-tempered yet distant parent who preferred to leave the raising of his only daughter to his wife, Olga. Geoffrey was gone much more than he was home, and Suzanne's only true memories of him were that he wore a mustache, drank rum, smelled of cleaned leather, and that he loved to expound on the virtues of hard work and the sins of frivolity. He wanted his daughter dressed properly, to be silent in his presence and trained in manners, music, and social etiquette so as to be a shining member of the society into which she was born. Suzanne's mother did as best she could to follow her husband's wishes regarding their child, but Suzanne was not, for whatever reason deemed fit by God or Satan, cut of the same cloth as the delicate and proper girls and boys of the neighboring manors.

Suzanne, as her mother came to believe, was cursed.

Suzanne was five the first time her mother sent her to her room without dinner and punished her for "dabbling in devil's work." There had been an Easter gathering at Riverton, an afternoon of elegantly gowned ladies, top-hatted men, girls in new frilly dresses and boys squirming in their velvet Little Lord Fauntleroy outfits and brutally stiff sailor suits. The estate lawns, already heavy with oaks and maples and elephantine boxwood hedges, were freshly trimmed and adorned with new plantings of dogwoods and fire-red azaleas. Cloud-white canopies were erected on the south and western yards, under which silver and crystal serving platters were kept constantly filled with roasted game hens, pheasant, glazed hams, lamb, breads, and dressings by the Heath serving staff. Wine bottles from the Heath cellar were emptied nearly as quickly as they had appeared. A string quartet played in the gazebo. Every neighboring family of importance was there — the Tesses, the Argenbreits, the Jensons, the Newtons, kind Doctor Brenton and his wife, and scads of others Suzanne knew only by sight. The children sat on their chairs in the grass, ate their meals and drank their milk obediently and silently, until they were excused to be off to play.

Seven-year-old Cynthia Tess taught Suzanne how to do a cartwheel that day, telling her she must do them only when boys weren't about as they would see her undergarments. She also let Suzanne hold her new pet rabbit, Benjamin, whom she had brought to the party in a little wooden cage. Suzanne got a grass stain on the front of her yellow gown when she kneeled down to look at an earthworm, but Cynthia pinned a daffodil over the stain so Suzanne would not get in trouble with her mother. Suzanne was merry that day.

When finished with her own meal and conversation, Olga Heath called the children together and explained that they would have an Egg Roll, "just like they do at the White House." Four dozen hardboiled eggs had been dyed by the Heath cook, Deirdre, and put into two wicker baskets. Suzanne had not been allowed to help dye the eggs ("You'll get colors on your hands and it won't come off for weeks," her mother had explained. "Hands reveal so much about a lady.") but got to help carry the baskets out to the party when it was time. Each child selected a long stick from the grounds, chose an egg, and then stood side by side at the top of the knoll on the west lawn facing the river. Suzanne's mother clapped her hands and the race began. Children urged their eggs down the hill with their sticks, laughing and screaming as the eggs refused to roll straight but rather zigzagged back and forth, thumping into other eggs, some of them suffering small cracks in the process. Suzanne looked back up the hill at her mother's face, and was thrilled to see it alight with fun and expectation.

It was the last time she could remember seeing her mother truly happy.

A boy whose name she had since forgotten won the Egg Roll and was presented with a prize of chocolate and licorice. The other children were allowed to eat their hardboiled eggs, and all were served ice cream and cake.

Then, from beneath a flowering dogwood tree, Cynthia shrieked, "Dear no! My Benjamin is gone!"

Suzanne, sitting on a bench nearby, jumped to her feet and rushed over. Benjamin couldn't be gone! Such a sweet, brown bunny, out in the wild where any fox could grab him and gobble him down!

"Where did you leave him?" Suzanne asked her friend, but Cynthia could only weep and hold up the little empty cage, its hatch hanging open.

The children went on a mad hunt, in spite of the warnings from parents to stay out of the trees along the property for there was poison ivy and snakes there. Several fathers joined the search, giving winks to their wives as they departed, certain they were not to find the rabbit but willing to pay lip service to the children's concern. Suzanne's mother beckoned her daughter to stand with her. "You'll not go getting your new dress spoiled, rooting around like a dog," she whispered in Suzanne's ear.

And so, helpless, Suzanne watched as the west and south lawns were scoured and bushes were shaken, then as the children and men vanished around the other side of the mansion. Even out of sight, she could hear them calling "Benjamin!" as if the rabbit knew its name and would come on command.

Cynthia was too distraught to join the others, and sat beneath one of the white canopies, holding the cage in her lap. Cynthia's mother and father sat with her, consoling her, telling her rabbits knew how to live in the wild and that Benjamin, if not found, would still be safe with his big ears and spry legs.

Suzanne went to Cynthia and sat beside her. Then, she reached her arms about her friend and hugged her.

She'd never felt such a sensation before. It started slowly and then grew, a mild buzzing in her head and then a warm sensation behind her eyes. At first she wanted to let go of Cynthia, to stop the strange feeling, but she held on because...

...because she was seeing something, then. She saw the little brown rabbit, not far from the dogwood tree under which Cynthia had stood, beneath an azalea, his hind leg caught in a tangle of wire that had held the root ball together. He kicked and twisted, sniffed his foot, then twisted some more.

Suzanne felt the cool ground beneath her hands; she could smell the sharp acidic leaves of the bush. She leaned in close to the rabbit, her face gazing at his, looking into his little black eyes and feeling his fear.

"Suzanne!"

Suzanne yanked her arms from around Cynthia and blinked. Her mother was standing over her, frowning.

"You're mussing Cynthia's curls!"

"I..."

"Cynthia," said Olga Heath, reaching out tentatively to put the coils of brown hair back into place. "I'm sorry, dear, Suzanne has a lot to learn about good manners."

"I saw Benjamin," said Suzanne.

"What!" exclaimed Cynthia.

"I know where your bunny is!" Suzanne stood, feeling a bit wobbly from the experience then clambered down to the dogwood and the rows of blooming bushes, her arms out for balance, her vision still swimming. Cynthia followed, as did her parents and

Olga Heath. Suzanne went to the azalea bush and parted the scratchy branches with her hands. There, trapped by a knot of wire, was Benjamin.

"Daddy! Help him out of there!" said Cynthia. "Poor, poor baby! He's got his little foot trapped!"

Mr. Tess eased the rabbit from its snare then handed it to his daughter. Cynthia buried her face in the thick, soft fur. "Benjamin," she cooed. "My baby bunny, you are safe with me again."

Suzanne smiled, waiting to be thanked.

But Olga spun Suzanne around on her heels and snapped, "How did you know the rabbit was there?"

"I saw him there, Mother. When I hugged Cynthia, it came into my mind where he was."

"And it tickled!" said Cynthia.

"Did you take the rabbit and put him under the bush to play a trick on Cynthia?" asked Mrs. Tess.

Suzanne was stunned. "What? Oh, no, ma'am! I don't do bad things like that!"

"Don't you?"

"Oh, no, ma'am!" Tears welled in Suzanne's eyes. She could not believe she was being accused of doing such a dreadful act.

"I saw him in my mind, when I put my arms around Cynthia. It was like a dream. I saw the bunny, all tangled. I saw the bush and knew he was there."

"Suzanne couldn't have taken Benjamin from his cage, Daddy," said Cynthia, her tears near gone, her cheek still pressed to the rabbit. "He was in there when I went to eat my cake under the tree. I talked to him. Then I gave him a crumb but he wouldn't eat it. I put the cage down and finished my ice cream. When I looked back, the hatch had come open and he was gone. Suzanne was on the bench the whole time, Daddy."

"Very well, then, Suzanne, I apologize," said Mrs. Tess, though her voice didn't sound very nice.

But the worse came next. Her mother ordered her into the house without bidding farewell to any of the other children, and told her to put on her nightclothes and go to her room. She was to wait there until her mother came for her. Suzanne knew better than to argue. Even though the evening was still young, and from her window she could see the sun hanging on the tops of the trees across the Hudson, she dressed for bed, put her dress in the wardrobe, and sat on her stool. And waited. Her heart pounded and her chest hurt. What had she done wrong?

All the guests were gone, the sky had turned dark, and the sliver moon was up over the water before her mother joined her in her chamber. Her face was tight and her breath smelled of wine. She stood in front of Suzanne and rubbed her hands together as if they were cold.

She said, "Tell me again how you found that rabbit."

Carefully, slowly, Suzanne told the story again, knowing it was wrong to lie and so leaving out no detail, recalling the tingling sensation, the buzzing in her mind, the darkening of what was around her and then a light coming up again to reveal the bunny deep in the shadows, caught in the wire. She said she could feel how afraid he was. She could feel his little heart beating and his quick, painful breaths. She felt so sorry for the rabbit, and was getting ready to tell him everything would be all right when her mother called her name and then she was back under the canopy with Cynthia.

"You saw a vision, did you?"

"I don't know what you mean, Mama."

"You saw something in your mind, did you? Something that wasn't near you at all."

"Yes, ma'am."

"You touched Cynthia and then knew where her rabbit was."

Suzanne smiled a little. Maybe her mother understood after all. "Yes, Mama."

"How do you think that happened?"

"I don't know."

"How do you think something came into your mind like that?"

"I don't know."

"People don't have visions like that, Suzanne. Not good, God-fearing people."

"Ma'am?"

"Something is playing with your mind, girl."

"What do you mean, Mama?"

"Something has made a deal with you, with your soul."

"Ma'am?"

"The devil has got a foothold with you. What you've done is magic. Magic is devil's work, daughter. What you've done is let Satan come into your heart and mind. He's giving you little treats, little favors, for welcoming him."

"Ma'am?"

"Devil's child, you are."

"Mama?"

"Devil's child!" Olga stepped up and slapped Suzanne so hard across the face that she was knocked from her stool and landed on the floor on her knees. Suzanne was too stunned to cry, though she felt a trickle of blood at the corner of her mouth. She looked up at her mother, who had brought a thin, long switch from behind her back.

"Pull up your nightdress, girl," said Olga.

"Mama, no!"

"Stand up! Pull up your nightdress!"

Suzanne pushed herself slowly to her feet. She stared at her mother, at the switch in her hand. She could not pull up her nightdress. She backed toward the wall.

"Don't make this any worse than it already is!" said Olga. "I'll beat the devil out of you and maybe God will forgive you for your selfishness and me for my blindness!"

"I'm not a devil's child!" said Suzanne.

Olga dove for her daughter, and wrangled her up into her arms. Suzanne twisted, kicked at the air, and slashed with her fingers, wanting her mother to let her go but afraid she might hurt her mother in the struggle. "Stop it!" screamed Olga, and outside in the hall, beyond the closed door, Suzanne could hear one of the maids, old Jennie Sue, call hesitantly but clearly, "Is everything all right, Mrs. Heath?"

"Yes! No!" said Olga. "Leave us be, Jennie, Suzanne's got a tantrum, that's all."

Olga dragged Suzanne across the room and threw her down onto the bed. Before Suzanne could slip away, her mother rolled her in the bedspread, leaving only her lower legs exposed. Suzanne coughed and spit, trying to catch air through the heavy blanket.

And then Olga whipped her daughter's legs until the skin split, singing, "Jesus Loves Me," all the while.

Suzanne steered as clear from her mother as was humanly possible after that. She skittered around far sides of rooms as casually as possible when he mother was present, she hung close to Jennie in the kitchen and the yard staff while outside. She sat beside her mother during the evening Bible readings and never in her lap anymore. She spoke when spoken to, but tried her best not to be in situations where he mother would want to talk.

The months went on, and the visions continued sporadically, always unexpected and unwanted. Most were brief, incidental, and inconsequential, touching a wall or railing or door and smelling pine, hearing violins or a barking dog, or seeing indecipherable flashes of light or darkness. Others were more troubling. A touch of her mother's napkin revealed a dreadful fight her mother had had with her father the night before. A game of hoops with the maid, Della, which gave Suzanne a brief glimpse of Della weeping at night, crying for something she didn't have, or something she'd lost. Suzanne made a point to limit her physical contact with others, the experience with Cynthia and her subsequent beating seared into her mind. She tried her best to act as she was expected to act, sitting primly for her reading lessons with Madame Ingles, silently and obediently following the instructions from Mister Kaine during her piano lessons, bearing the corrective, wooden ruler hand-smacks without complaint.

Years passed then, and she was eight, nine, ten, living carefully, playing with visiting children cautiously, though her mother never invited Cynthia or her family to Riverton again.

And then Faith Gansy came to visit.

Faith was a tiny young thing, seven years old and the daughter of Olga's second cousin, Emily Emerson Gansy. Pretty, black-haired and pink-cheeked, from the outset it was clear Faith was the child Suzanne's mother wished she'd had. Emily had become ill and her father too engrossed in his business as a lawyer to mind his daughter, and so they had shipped Faith to Riverton for the summer.

Suzanne immediately liked Faith. The little girl was cheerful though frail, thoughtful and considerate. She seemed to sense Suzanne's need to be alone and to stand apart. That didn't diminish her smiles, her willingness to share, her kind words. She demanded nothing of the Heath family and even offered to help Della straighten Faith's bedroom and to help Edward, the yardman, rake clipped grass.

Then, like the bunny Benjamin, Faith disappeared.

She had been on the side lawn in the shade of the mulberry bush having a tea party with her dollies. Suzanne's father was in New York City and Olga was in the parlor composing a letter to Faith's ailing mother and Della was washing dishes and Suzanne was in her bedroom reading *A Dog of Flanders*. When it was time for the mid-day meal, Della went out to the lawn and found the tiny teacups and pot on the blanket, and Faith gone.

Panic ensued. Edward, Della, Olga, the gardener Ralph and the stable master Sean searched the grounds while Suzanne stood on the porch, too terrified to help, for if she did and if she discovered Faith's whereabouts, she would certainly be beaten again for it, even if she had seen nothing in her mind at all.

"The river!" cried Ogla when the lawn and hedges had been thoroughly covered, and the adults raced to the high ground and peered down the sharply sloping bank to the rushing Hudson below.

"Faith!" Olga screamed.

They stared, shouted, and cried, then turned and hurried back to the house, Olga and Della wringing their hands, Ralph, Sean, and Edward talking together, likely planning a wider search. If Faith had gone into the river she was surely washed away. If only she'd run off after a stray kitten or puppy, there was still hope.

Suzanne clutched one of the bright white porch posts, her face pressed to the cool wood, as Ogla and Della climbed the steps, panting, sweating in a most unladylike manner. Della held Ogla's arm comfortingly. Ogla cast a quick, agonized look at Suzanne then disappeared through the door. Perhaps her mother thought it was her fault Faith was gone? Perhaps she resented Faith's vanishing when it would have been better to have been Suzanne?

Out on the front lawn, Ralph gestured toward the stables and Edward nodded and pointed in the other direction. The three men hurried off — Edward and Ralph along the hard-packed road that circled the south side of the house, through the trees, and down a quarter mile to the edge of the property where the horses, wagon, and carriage were kept, Sean across the lawn, over the fence, and through the black-eyed Susan-filled field to the home of the nearest neighbors, the VanDorns. Suzanne watched as the men vanished. Then her fingers loosened from the post and she walked down the steps and over to the abandoned tea party by the mulberry bush.

Kneeling by the tea set, she glanced back up at the house. If her mother were watching there would be Hell to pay. She would suspect only the worst. But Suzanne couldn't resist the dreadful urge. She put out her hand. She picked up a teacup.

There was nothing.

Overhead, a mockingbird chided her with a raucous string of calls.

Suzanne stroked the cup handle with her thumb. She closed her eyes. She thought of Faith, little Faith, sweet Faith…

Faith giggles as she is lifted and carried off the lawn and down the winding path toward the stable.

Suzanne's eyes flew open; she dropped the cup to the grass.

Faith thinks they are playing a game. She bounces along in the man's arms. He smells good, like pipe tobacco and verbena.

Suzanne stifled a cry and shook her head, trying to rid herself of the vision. Yet it remained, a film over the real and current world where grass tickled the palms of her hands and a chipmunk gazed at her from beneath the mulberry bush, and in the vision, she was Faith. Faith, laughing, asking where they are going, jostling in the man's strong arms.

She isn't looking at his face but down the road where tall oaks and maples spread their substance-less, inky shadows across the ground. He says into her hair, "I've something oh, so funny to show you, Faith! It will make you laugh! There is the silliest cat in the stable, doing something I've never seen a cat do before!"

Suzanne felt the man shift her in his arms, his hand moving up to cup her bottom in a most uncomfortable, unseemly way, but still she did not look to see who he was. Down the road, giggling, to the stable. They reached the large sliding door and the man puts her down. He slid it open, releasing scents of newly cut hay, clean leather, and horse sweat.

Faith peers into the stable and says, "Where is the cat?" She turns to look at him, her face tipping up, her eyes squinting against a spear of sunlight.

It is Doctor VanDorn who lives in the house to the north of Riverton. Olga Heath has invited this man and his wife to Riverton numerous times. Doctor VanDorn has seen Olga for headaches and lethargy, prescribing medicines and giving advice.

"Where is the cat?" she asks, stepping inside the stable. "I don't want to startle the poor puss, but I want to see her!"

"It's a tom," says Doctor VanDorn. "Come, I'll show you. You'll laugh and laugh!"

He takes her hand, and his is cold and clammy and Suzanne wants to pull away but Faith doesn't. She follows trustingly into an empty stall. Doctor VanDorn smiles down at her then puts his large, damp hands around her neck.

"What are you doing?"

A hand whistled through the air and Suzanne was slapped hard against her head. She was knocked to her side in the grass. The vision shattered and was gone. Olga stood over her, eyes huge and reddened with rage. "Are you such a twisted child that you would play with the teacups of a little girl gone missing?"

Suzanne's ears rung and painful stars pounded her brain. She started to cry.

"Stop that, you're only wanting my sympathies but it won't work!"

"Mama, Faith..." began Suzanne.

"She's missing, and you dare play with her toys! Are you so morbid, Suzanne? Get up now, and go to your room! I will deal with you later!"

Suzanne stumbled to the house and up to her room where she stood at the window to watch over the front lawn and the river. And wait.

Long minutes, Suzanne wiping angry tears from her cheeks. An hour. The sun reached its pinnacle and then began to lower over the rushing water of the Hudson.

And then she heard the shout and saw Olga and Della rush out onto the lawn. She leaned out of the window, craning to see, and then her knees buckled. Ralph was carrying Faith's limp and lifeless body to the house, with Edward close beside him. Olga wailed and fainted. Della fell onto Faith's body in Ralph's arms and wept.

Sean was determined to be the murderer. He was the stable

master, and he had volunteered to go seek out help of the neighbors rather than offering to search the road and the stable. Faith's body had been hidden in the corner of the tack room beneath a thick pile of straw where Sean could later take additional advantage of it or hauled it away to bury. Sean denied it vehemently with furious tears, but the authorities arrested him nonetheless, and in the days that followed the whispered conversation in and about the house focused on Sean and how he would be executed in the electric chair up in Auburn once he was convicted.

It was a full week before Suzanne told Della what she'd seen. She could not sleep, but faced relentless nightmares that drove her so deep into her mattress she could barely breathe.

Della, having heard the story, sat down onto a kitchen chair and stared at Suzanne with horror and wonder. Then she tipped her head up and said, "You must tell your mother. We must see if what you say is true. Sean was…is…my friend. For him to die for a crime he did not commit is as much a sin as for a guilty man to go free."

"But…" began Suzanne, and Della nodded.

"I know, dear. I know your Mother wants to hear nothing of what you see. But I know you found that rabbit so long ago, and I know you've seen other things, too. I've studied your face, and know that sometimes there is something dreadful and true playing in your thoughts, things you don't what to know but which God wants you to know."

"God?" said Suzanne. "Mother said the devil, rather."

Della opened her mouth then hesitated, clearly unwilling to contradict Olga Heath. She planted her hands on her thighs and said, "I will stand with you when you tell her. I will do all I can to make sure she does not do anything terrible to you, and that what you saw is investigated."

Suzanne knew Della was right. She had to confess her vision. She hoped Della would stand true to her promise.

Doctor VanDoren was arrested, with Faith's panties and hair bow discovered in a box in his study. Sean was set free. Della did not need to intervene and prevent another beating, for Olga Heath had other plans.

Three days later, Suzanne's trunk was packed, and she was shipped off to Madame Harlow's School for Young Ladies ninety-three miles away in the wilds at the foot of the Catskills.

Suzanne drew her legs up even closer to her chest, shifted her weight on the divan, and stared through the darkness of her room toward the single window. Faint moonlight drifted through like swirling gnats, landed, and flickered on the bare wood of the floor. Downstairs, Marty Moon was snoring, the sound like a distant and struggling freight train....

...the train that used to travel past Madame Harlow's School, crying and reaching out as it rushed forward into the dark unknown.

Suzanne closed her eyes against cold tears that welled then slid down to her pillow.

4

The proprietor of Snow's Symposium of Secrets and Surprises stood against the wall in the low-ceilinged, windowless back room as Rex, the towering brute, unfolded the cot, unstrapped the dazed man from the spinning chair, and laid him flat out. Leaning over with a surgeon's precision and a shiny straight-edged razor, Rex cut the man's clothing away in tidy strips then proceeded to shave every hair from his body. The man stared up at Rex, not really seeing him, not really knowing why he was being shaved and well beyond caring, the scrape of the cold straight razor making his flesh quiver instinctively as if it, alone, realized the terrible circumstance into which he had stumbled. The chest, arms, face were first cleared of all hair. Then the ample, pumpkin-shaped stomach, the legs, the trembling, startled groin. Rex then flipped the man over so his back, shoulders, and buttocks could be shaved. The razor nipped several large blackheads on the man's ass, causing them to bleed. The proprietor glared at Rex and so he leaned over and licked the blood away.

When the man was hairless as a fat and knobby-kneed baby, Rex helped the man to his feet. He wobbled but remained upright. Rex turned him around slowly for the proprietor's inspection. His bare feet slapped and dragged against the wooden floor.

"Very well, then," said the proprietor with a rub of the chin. "Ugly, ugly chap, this, but another mindless one, another obedient soul for my army."

"Yeah," said Rex. He nodded and grinned, revealing the few teeth that were determined enough to remain in his rotted mouth.

"Get him dressed. Take him over to the theater and lock him up with the others."

"Yeah."

"And wipe that damned blood off your lips. You look like a mongrel who just ate a rabbit."

Rex dragged the back of his hand over his mouth, removing the blood and the grin. He yanked open the door to the closet and tugged a folded piece of fabric from a shelf piled with other, likewise-folded pieces of fabric. He shook it open to reveal a thin, sleeveless cotton shift. Rex dressed the hairless man in the shift, tied a little towel around the man's face, and then opened the rear door and led him out into the humid, pre-dawn blue. Down the short dead-end alley then onto the slightly larger corridor called Stratton's Walk they went, on to a small, locked theater entitled "3000 AD." The large broadside by the front door declared that within these very walls was "A Warning to All Humanity to Be Ware and Be Aware, or Our Race Shall Perish and Our Very Souls Shall Be Consumed!" And so it was that from 7 p.m. six days a week, after the proprietor had shut down the Symposium, hairless, mindless people shuffled about on the 3000 A.D. theater's stage as a phonograph recording explained to the audience that they were witnessing a horror beyond horrors, the offspring of humans and aliens from other planets, aliens who had come to earth over the last fifty years and raped the earthlings so as to infiltrate the planet.

The man's bare feet were scratched and scraped on the alley's gravels and bits of litter by the time they reached the theater, but he didn't complain. He no longer knew how to complain. He was taken into the darkened theater and locked into the room behind the stage with mindless, hairless, gaping beings. Seventeen now. When the number reached twenty-five, the proprietor would open a second theater farther east, near Brighton Beach perhaps, and choose a second, suitable Rex-type to help manage that. When another twenty-five were collected and the needed seed money was secured, they would make the big move south. Georgia, perhaps, or Mississippi. Somewhere a vast chunk of farmland could be had at a good price and where the nosiest neighbors were miles away and busy with their own dark and secret activities. Set up the starter plantation. The drones would work, build, plant, tend, serve. The foundation of the new nation would be constructed and the plans carefully laid out. And then the true work would begin.

Power, the proprietor thought with a hardened, almost painful smile. There is no other reason to exist. Increasing power, my power over all. It is why I am as I am. It is why I am who I am.

The proprietor stretched out on the cot, which was covered in shaved hairs both soft and wiry, and smelled of sweat and resignation. The light bulb overhead flickered and hummed, drawing toward it several suicidal moths that had come in through the open door. The spinning chair sat motionlessly in the center of the room, straps dangling, ready for a new victim in a week or so. Perhaps only a few days from now.

Focusing on the light bulb, the proprietor concentrated, stared, and then the bulb shattered with a loud pop. Glass bits rained down onto the floor. Rex could clean it up on his return.

Yes, power was the goal. There was nothing to stop its progress now. Everything was rolling smoothly as planned, and the proprietor would enjoy every moment of it, savor it, taste it, and claim it. And like the shambling idiots in the "3000 AD" show, eventually the world would be conquered.

Though by one of its own.

One of its most talented and formidable own. Aliens be damned.

FOUR

May 1902

Madame Harlow's School for Young Ladies was an enormous red brick, ivy-covered compound situated on 143 acres of field and forest, the main compound surrounded by a massive wrought-iron fence and backed up against the sloping mountainside. The grounds were dotted with hedges and benches, arbors, flower gardens, and walkways, where students could wander and read poetry, or visit with family members on "visitor weekends." The school had been built in 1831 and, with its less-than-modest motto of, "Educating Young Women of Breeding to be the Stewards of Home, Family, Church, and Society," boasted that it was the most prestigious school for young ladies in the Northeast. Most of the girls who attended the school were fluffy, silly, giggling creatures from wealthy homes in New York, Connecticut, and Rhode Island, homes where money flowed like water. They ranged from age ten to eighteen. All of them were expected to become the pillars of the societies from whence they came once they were graduated, pillars of grace and dignity and poise and wisdom, able to play at least two instruments, paint a decent landscape, quote poetry and great passages from the Bible by heart, discuss classic literature, plant a flower garden, manage finances, sew an outfit, and sing a variety of hymns as on-key as possible, depending on the girl. Of course, Suzanne was of the same secure financial background as the gigglers, but none other than Suzanne had been sent away because her mother deemed her demonic. And of course, Olga had not mentioned a word of that when filling out Suzanne's application and when she and Suzanne's father deposited her at the school, she had even feigned affection on their parting, with a brief kiss and embrace.

The school had become home over the years that followed, nevertheless, and at seventeen Suzanne was third eldest girl at the school, wise in the ways of keeping out of trouble, her grades admirable, and her poise perfect. No one in charge suspected a thing. Suzanne was punctual to classes, ladylike at meals, obedient to the rules, attentive to the care of her school uniform and silent when silence was required. She was considered the second best flute player and third best at piano. She never received letters or visits from her mother and only an occasional note from her father. She never went home over breaks or vacations, but rather stayed on to study and celebrate Christmas and Easter with the staff. They did not mind. The girls' tuitions were based on the number of days on campus.

And Suzanne hid her secret life very well, from the adults.

From most of the other students.

They called themselves the Order of Morgans after the mythical sorceress from the ancient classic Le Morte d'Arthur, Morgan le Fay, who, according to legends, was able to transform herself into various shapes, fly, and cast spells. There were seven Morgans at Madame Harlow's School, a strong and magical number for such a group — Mary Alice Broome, Caroline Rittenhouse, Darlene Mannetti, Rosemary Reynolds, Tirzah Simmons, Polly Harrington, and Suzanne, all between the ages of fifteen and eighteen, all of whom had discovered in themselves varying talents with the supernatural and a desire to fine tune it. It was no surprise to any of the Morgans that the seven had found each other; they sensed one another's sensitivities like a handful of dogs could detect each other in a room of a million cats.

The girls' little society was well hidden from the school administration. The Morgans gathered on the broad lawns three afternoons a week, wandering about in their proper school-issued black skirts and cream-colored jackets, holding books by Dickens and Alcott, sitting primly on benches with ankles crossed, talking so calmly that anyone at a distance would imagine they were discussing music theory or the Bible. But their conversations were not of symphonies nor of God, but rather of spells and potions, curses, visions, and other unearthly skills. Their code forbade any talk of the Order of Morgans beyond themselves, and each had taken a blood oath of secrecy with a prick of the thumb.

The newest member of the Order of Morgans was sixteen-year-old, who had arrived from New Milford, Connecticut, at the beginning of the second term in January. The faculty deemed Rosemary Suzanne's twin, for the girls were very similar in height and coloring, with dark, thick brows, small, straight noses, and high cheekbones. Even Rosemary's auburn hair was similarly wavy. Suzanne and Rosemary began affectionately calling each other "Twinnie," and very soon Suzanne realized she had fallen in love with the younger girl. In spite of or perhaps because of her ability to detect and experience the physical pain of others, Rosemary was more gentle and thoughtful than any other girl Suzanne had ever met, except for poor little Faith Gansy, rest her soul. With Rosemary, Suzanne felt safe, at ease, and, she hoped, loved. The two talked quietly and late into the night in the dorm room when lights were out, chatting about favorite classes and least favorite teachers, about the food and the cat they smuggled into the dorm and kept hidden from the prying eyes of the Dean of Ladies, about home and family and friends, though Suzanne spoke little of this and encouraged Rosemary to talk on all she wanted to, for the pictures she painted of their estate on Cape Cod were pleasant and dreamy.

When, at last, Rosemary fell asleep in her bed next to Suzanne's, Suzanne would wrap her arm around the lazy, contented cat, stare into the gloom and dared imagine a life where the two of them could live together, away from prying eyes and condemning sermons. Suzanne kept her feelings to herself, however, and never allowed herself to touch Rosemary or Rosemary's belongings. She feared having a vision in which she witnessed Rosemary confiding in another schoolgirl that she found Suzanne to be sullen or irritating. Suzanne had had her heart broken by her mother. She knew she couldn't stand having it broken by Rosemary.

Of the seven Morgans, Suzanne and Tirzah developed their abilities more quickly and to a finer point than the others. Tirzah, eighteen, was a tall brunette with piercing green eyes who embraced her power with a vicious and haughty pride. She had dabbled in black arts before attending Madame Harlow's School, and came to the school already able to make classmate or teacher to become nauseous or dizzy by sheer focus and will of her mind. Tirzah adored her abilities from the beginning, and was most happy when spending time with the Morgans out on the lawn, talking about mind power, studying the precepts of mind power, and practicing to grow more adept. Suzanne, on the other hand, had only reluctantly accepted the fact that her clairvoyance was part of her, realizing as the years passed that she could not stop the visions, could not prevent herself from seeing details of other people's lives, and so should try to control and make the most of them. And while controlling them continued to be a struggle, making the most of them did not. When bumping against Miss Ardou, the eternally-arrogant French teacher one morning at breakfast, Suzanne had had a vision of the teacher talking privately in the teachers' parlor about how much she hated Tirzah. "Irritating little miscreant," she'd said. "There is something in her eyes I don't trust. Should the whole school burn down someday, I'd place my penny on Tirzah as the arsonist." Suzanne shared this vision and Tirzah, at once outraged and thrilled, was able to cause Miss Ardou to double over during class one afternoon, and scuttle from the room with wide eyes, muttering over her shoulder, "You girls read your chapter, I will be back momentarily!" The momentarily ended up being the entire class period, which allowed the girls fifty minutes to sit and relax and tell jokes. When touching a doorknob that the headmistress had touched, Suzanne learned that the headmistress was going deaf, even though to witness one of her stern strolls through the dining hall, her head whipping back and forth like an eagle listening for mice, no one would ever suspect. Following this revelation, Suzanne slipped an anonymous note to the cook, Judith, to let her know that she could prevent future unwarranted tongue-lashings by making sure she faced Madame Harlow and spoke to her directly rather than trying to hold conversations over the clattering of pans with her face turned away. Another vision revealed to Suzanne that her favorite teacher during second term, Miss Garrison, had left the school not because she needed to go home and tend her sick aunt, but because she had become pregnant by one of the Irish boys who did repairs around the school. Suzanne mailed Miss Garrison a letter of encouragement and support, hinting that the baby boy, for it was to be a boy, would become her pride and joy in spite of his beginnings. She still was uneasy with the visions, still resented the intrusions they forced upon her life, but if nothing else it gave her membership into the Morgans and the first true sense of belonging she'd ever experienced. She was not alone, for if she was a freak then she was a freak among freaks. And surely, with someone as sweet as Rosemary among their number, then it could not be a bad thing to have supernatural talents.

With books on the black arts smuggled in to them by the school's custodian in return for a few spare dollars, the Morgans studied telekinesis, pyro-kinesis, clairvoyance, psycho-kinesis, astral projection, and time travel. While all the girls were psychically sensitive, their actual, applicable skills were "unfortunately and pathetically limited," as Tirzah put it. She said it was their duty to learn all they could, to absorb everything they could possibly absorb, master everything they could possibly master, and then find ways to use these talents. "We are the goddesses of this school," she said time and again, "but infant goddesses, each of us. We must become all we are to become, for if we don't, we have pissed in the face of our destinies." And so they studied. And they practiced. More often than not, Suzanne returned to her dorm room with an excruciating headache from trying so hard to project out of her body, set some leaves afire, or move herself back in time even a minute. Most of which were futile attempts.

Tirzah and Suzanne were the first to find success with telekinesis. On their "Morgan afternoons" they would sit side by side on one of the tree-shaded benches and stare at the geese by the pond and see if they could cause one of them to trip over their own feet. Sometimes it worked, other times the geese, sensing something strange in the air, would turn and glare at the girls with tiny, angry goosey eyes. Or Tirzah and Suzanne would gaze intently at two stones Rosemary held in her hands and try to make them roll or flip up and away. Sometimes the stones would fly off, other times they would vibrate, while other times they would lay still and unmoved. The younger girls watched in awe, applauding quietly if the stones moved but remaining mute if they did not, for they held the two elder girls in high esteem and knew if they angered Tirzah they might find themselves with several stomach aches.

The girls studied. They practiced. Slowly, steadily, each strengthened her innate skill and attempted new ones. Mary Alice, who sensed luminous auras around people but had never understood them, learned to interpret the auras to determine someone's mood, intentions, and sometimes even fears by carefully considering the colors, and at times was even able to absorb energies from other people's auras. Caroline, who could on occasion read fleeting thoughts in the minds of others, was now better able to focus and pick up more of the mental vibrations. More than half the time she could read at least a portion of a thought projected at her from one of the other Morgans. Darlene's precognition was slow to improve, and for the longest time Tirzah criticized the younger girl for nothing more than good guesses as to what a teacher might wear at a particular time, what might be served the next day for lunch, or what student might be the last to climb into bed at lights-out. Yet Tirzah eased up on her scoffing when Darlene correctly predicted several comments by the music teacher during class and reported two hours ahead of time that during elocution class, a squirrel would get in through the open window and wreak temporary and gleeful havoc. Polly was a sensitive who claimed she could speak to the dead, but as of yet neither Suzanne nor Tirzah was convinced. They let Polly remain, though, because several times she went into a trance and said things that startled Darlene and Mary Alice and made them swear that Polly had connected, if only briefly, with Darlene's great-aunt and Mary Alice's departed infant brother. Rosemary soon picked up a bit of telekinesis and was able to stir papers in dead air. And with the power of her mind she was also capable of easing some of the sicknesses brought on by Tirzah's spells. She confessed of her healings only to Suzanne for fear of having Tirzah's spell cast on her in revenge.

Yet in spite of the gradual increase of powers among the members of the Order of Morgan, Tirzah became increasingly unhappy. On their afternoon outings, she became more likely to pitch a fit as she was to sit and study and practice.

On one particularly chilly May afternoon she gathered the Morgans beside the tall boxwood hedge at the lawn's east edge and said, "Look at us! Just look at us! Seven of the most preternaturally-inclined women in the country, perhaps even the world, and yet we sit or stand around, watching stones fly and finding hidden spoons, predicting squirrel attacks and who might wear what hat to dinner.

We should be in control of this place by now. We should have taken over everyone and turned their energies into serving us!"

Caroline, Darlene, Polly, and Mary Alice nodded solemnly. Rosemary stood apart slightly, staring out at the trees, clearly uncomfortable with Tirzah's selfish goals. Suzanne crossed her arms and gazed steadily at Tirzah. She understood the older girl's frustration but not her lack of patience. Anyone who knew about such things, anyone who had studied and practiced as much as they had, must know that these talents were lifelong skills, developed with often-painful slowness. And it especially angered her that Tirzah was upsetting Rosemary.

"I shall burst, I shall come apart from my very bones should we not make more progress than this!" Tirzah continued, pacing back and forth. "Yes, I shall explode and take you all with me, should we remain as petty and pathetic as we are in this moment!"

Rosemary sighed and closed her eyes. Caroline, Darlene, Polly, and Mary Alice continued to nod.

Tirzah let out a loud breath and shook her head, causing the pinned mass of brown hair on her head to wobble like a mountain in an earthquake. Her upper lip drew back and her eyes narrowed darkly. She had never looked so old, or so mad. The other girls shivered. "I promise you this!" she said, pointing at each Morgan in turn. "I am due to graduate from this ghastly institution in but five months. Should we have accomplished nothing of note in that time, then I will indeed leave here a mark among the six of you, a mark so deep no one will ever forget me!"

"We'll make you proud, Tirzah," said Caroline. Polly, Darlene, and Mary Alice nodded. Rosemary glanced at Suzanne, and Suzanne shook her head.

"Tirzah," she said, "think rationally. What will passion do, but cloud your head and fog your thinking, like the air this morning?"

Tirzah sneered. "Suzanne, you have such a little mind. Your talent is wasted on you. Wasted! You're like a dog that's been given run of an estate but are too afraid to leave the yard. Barking, barking, as if your voice commands anything more than your own silly daydreams."

"We've sworn to careful exploration and growth," said Suzanne. "What now are you suggesting? What, exactly, are you saying we should do?"

"If you have such little imagination," said Tirzah, "then I pity you all the more. You'll wallow and whine in your own filth without the slightest understanding that you could climb out, could be free!"

At that moment, the bell in the chapel tower rang, clanging a heavy, monotonic command, calling the girls and staff together for some announcement or other. And so the Morgans went, their skirts trailing the grass, each in silent contemplation with Tirzah in silent furor, joining the other school girls whose bright and unknowing faces registered little more than gossip about boys they wish they knew and dresses they wish they owned.

The chapel was a stone room, apart from the main school building, complete with white towering steeple and elegant stained glass windows with images of Jesus in the manger, Jesus being baptized, Jesus on the cross, Jesus rising from the earth in His resurrection. During the spring and summer, fresh flowers from the school's gardens were placed on the altar in brass vases, with holly and brightly-colored oak leaves adorning that same spot in winter and autumn. Today, the vases were filled with sweet-scented purple lilacs and pink roses. Suzanne wanted to love the chapel, and the peace it seemed to want to offer her, but she could not feel it. She could only sit and watch the other girls who were able to embrace the comfort of the place.

Once the students were settled in the chapel, with the older girls in the front and the younger ones to the rear, Madame Harlow came before them, stood at the pulpit where Reverend Alfred Sours preached each morning as well as Sunday and Wednesday nights, and announced that they would all be attending a camp meeting in the mountains. The girls listened silently, obediently, hands folded in their laps, ankles crossed. The teachers stood along the walls as they always did during important meetings, dressed in their matching blue skirts and pale blouses, their gazes flicking back and forth between the students and Madame Harlow, watching for any talking, any disturbances, which were quite rare at the Harlow School.

"We have learned that evangelist Snavely Leeman, former associate of the most godly Billy Sunday, will hold a revival beginning Thursday a mere three miles from our school, up in the Brake's Knoll Clearing," the headmistress said, one palm pressed to the black lace on the bodice of her black gown. She was nearly breathless with excitement, and there were spots of unladylike perspiration on the creases of her forehead. A humorless, pious matron, there was nothing she loved more than a chance to become more pious and to see that her charges had that chance, as well. "What a joy, to have such a holy and godly man come to the Catskills and share his wisdom and inspiration. And we shall be attending. Every one of us. We shall hear God's word from the lips of an anointed one!"

Madame Harlow won't hear much at all, Suzanne thought with a sour and silent chuckle. *Though I understand that some evangelists get louder and louder as a day goes on, shouting and banging and stamping around like proud roosters, so perhaps she will hear a bit, after all.*

"I, for one, am greatly anticipating this event and the changes in our lives it may well herald. I hope you, likewise, find joy in this announcement."

Madame Harlow lifted her face to the ceiling as if praying or looking for cobwebs. Her iron-colored hair, twisted and coiled against the back of her head like a snake, shimmered with hair tonic and the overhead chapel lights. Then she looked back at the girls. "We have never taken a trip as an entire school before, and we haven't enough wagons to carry us all to and from. We shall be borrowing two additional wagons from the Brenner farm, but that will make only four wagons, and four cannot accommodate all sixty-eight girls. However, Miss Williamson has suggested that some of you might care to walk to the clearing. She even suggests it could be a healthy and thus godly activity. After a bit of consideration, I concur."

"Oh, puh," muttered Tirzah, who was seated next to Suzanne. "Too cheap to hire out enough wagons or carriages and expects some of us to walk under pretense of our health. Had we accomplished flight, we'd be there ahead of them all, and should have spit in their faces when they arrived."

"Had we accomplished flight," whispered Suzanne, "we should have flown from here long ago and made our fortunes performing for kings and queens. Now hush."

Madame Harlow scanned the room with her pale gray eyes. "Tomorrow, during your physical culture class with Miss Woods, she will take the names of those who volunteer to hike to the meeting. We shall need about twenty volunteers."

Rosemary, behind Suzanne, leaned forward and said, "I'll volunteer to walk. I love the forests and mountains. My mother used to take my sister and me hiking when I was younger. Before my sister died."

"Well, doesn't that make you quite the little pioneer woman," said Tirzah.

Rosemary's brows drew together and she sat back.

"Now," said Madame Harlow, "let us pray for Reverend Leeman's safe travels, and that we shall all benefit from his holy wisdom. That what we learn from him shall increase our own faith, faith to hold us 'til our death or 'til the blessed Rapture."

Tirzah let out a noisy breath. "Rapture, my lily-white behind. Nonsense is what it is. We're to suffer chapel every day, Sunday services each weekend, and Bible study Wednesday nights, and now we'll be forced into tramping up into the mountains to listen to some wretched self-proclaimed John the Baptist who claims to have the answers to all life's questions, to sit there and shout, 'Amen,' and 'Hallelujah,' and 'Praise the Lord.' Well, I tell you right now, I'll shout none of the kind."

"Shh," warned Suzanne.

Tirzah's voice lowered but she continued. "You hold and wait. Some day it will be 'Praise Tirzah!' Someday there will be camp meetings, not to worship some imaginary deity but to worship and praise me."

"Shut your mouth. I don't want trouble and you don't need it, either. You know Madame Harlow hates you and is looking for any reason to throw you out of the school."

"Oh, how I would praise the god Madame Harlow praises should she kick me out," said Tirzah. "But she knows better. She knows my grandfather has promised to leave a considerable sum of money to the school should I be graduated from here with honors."

"And bless us, each one," prayed Madame Harlow at the front of the room, her old voice wavering up and down, emotion nearly getting the best of her. "Grant us courage to face the Evil One when he tempts us and the humility to give all the glory to You. Give us courage to live as godly women should, chaste, charitable, hopeful."

Suzanne let out an exasperated breath. "So run off, Tirzah. Escape. I will vouch to your grandfather that Madame Harlow had nothing to do with it. That, say, you were snatched away by goblins or thieves."

Tirzah's eyes narrowed. "That's what you would like, isn't it, Suzanne?"

"What does it matter what I would like? Run off, Tirzah."

"Why not? You think the Morgans need you as what, our leader? We don't."

"Hush!" hissed Rosemary behind them.

"I'm as powerful as you," said Suzanne. "We'll be fine, we'll carry on. Run off into the wilderness. Practice your skills on the raccoons and skunks."

"I won't," said Tirzah.

"And why not? Are you afraid?"

Tirzah glared at Suzanne. Suzanne braced for a brutal stomachache, willed her body to resist what was coming. "I'm afraid of nothing."

"Nothing but..." began Suzanne, but the words clicked off in her throat when she saw Madame Harlow looking directly at her. The old woman had paused in her praying and was waiting for Suzanne to notice. All the girls' eyes were likewise trained on her, as were those of the faculty. Suzanne's heart clenched but not by any curse from Tirzah.

"Miss Heath!"

"Ma'am?"

"You surprise me with your disrespect."

"I'm sorry, ma'am."

"As well you should be. You shall come up here and finish the prayer for me."

Suzanne's jaw tightened but she stood, lifted her chin, and walked to the front of the room. Madame Harlow said, "You obviously had no need to listen to our appeal to our Heavenly Father, for perhaps you knew well ahead what I was going to pray."

Yes, I did, though in this case it doesn't require any special skills. I can imagine every student in the school knew what you were going to pray, for you rarely vary from one prayer to the other.

"Finish the prayer," said Madame Harlow down her nose, "and

then you and I shall have a little chat in my office."

Suzanne closed her eyes, folded her hands, and finished the prayer, filling it with "glories" and "praises" and "earnestly beseechings" and several requests for wisdom, humility, and an unquestioning desire to be obedient to the Word as written in the Holy Scriptures. Followed, of course, by a reverent "Amen" that was echoed by all in the room.

The visit to Madame Harlow's office was brief, with the headmistress sitting behind her huge oak desk as Suzanne stood on the oval braided rug, the old woman expressing her dismay over Suzanne's behavior ("My dear, you have always been one our most superior students in both academics and deportment. Your behavior startled me, to say the least. Please remember yourself in the future and act like the young lady you are. Also I suggest you stay away from Miss Simmons, for she is a bad influence.") and making little tsking sounds and shakes of the head. Suzanne had promised to remember herself and act like the young lady she was. She didn't promise to stay clear of Tirzah Simmons.

Thursday morning came, cloudy and warm. The girls gathered outside on the lawn beside the drive, most dressed in their freshly pressed school uniforms, shading their eyes against the haze and awaiting the wagons that would carry them to the camp meeting. The others, who had nicknamed themselves the "Mountain Climbers," stood in small clusters, dressed in sturdy walking shoes, casual skirts or exercise bloomers, and small straw hats adorned with white ribbons. Madame Harlow worried that the Reverend would find the girls' clothing to be unworthy of a sacred gathering, but Miss Williamson reassured her, saying that the girls' behaviors and attendance would speak much louder than their clothing.

The wagon-girls clambered into the beds of the wagons, sat down atop prickly bales covered in blankets, adjusted their hems, and picked bits of straw from the lower portions of their stockings. Several of the teachers joined the girls in the wagon backs while the others, along with Madame Harlow, claimed more choice spots on the wooden seats up front. With a jerk, the four wagons, driven by the farmer, his brother, and two of the school's custodians, took off down the lane, through the open gate, and into the distant darkness of the forest's shadows.

"Well, now, ladies," said Miss Williamson with a clap of her hands. She was a pleasant enough woman, no more than five years older than her eldest student, with small, bird-like eyes and thin mud-colored hair that could not hold a bun for long. She was dressed in her gray instructor's bloomers and walking shoes, and wore a broad-brimmed hat with silk cherries pinned to the brim. "Let us be off! A brisk pace to begin with, breathing deeply, drawing in that healthy air. Heads up, arms swinging, and we can sing as we hike!"

Miss Williamson led the pack along the lane, through the gate to the road and up the western fork at the divide, into the fading dust of the wagons that had gone before them. Very soon the road steepened, rising and rising into the mountains, curving around shady bends, shadowed by overhanging branches heavy with late spring foliage. It was pitted in many places with foot-deep ruts, and covered with rocks washed out of the ground by hard rains. Most of the girls sang together in harmony the songs they had learned in music class — "When You Were Sweet Sixteen," "My Wild Irish Rose," "I Can't Tell You Why I Love You But I Do" — along with numerous Protestant hymns while the remaining girls remained silent, saving their breath for the strenuous hike. Crows called from treetops. Squirrels darted across the road, tails puffed and indignant. Grit from their footfalls tumbled in the air as if unwilling to come back to earth. Half an hour into the hike, the singing petered out.

The Morgans brought up the rear, pretending to be listening to Miss Williamson's lectures on the flora and fauna as they climbed steadily upward. Tirzah was surprisingly quiet, obviously deep in thought. Suzanne left the older girl alone, when Tirzah was pondering it was never good to interrupt. Rosemary kept pace with Suzanne, while the other four girls trudged along a good ten feet behind, complaining within minutes that they wished they'd gone on the wagons.

"My feet hurt," said Polly. "This was a mistake. I can't hike the whole way."

"I think I just swallowed a fly," said Mary Alice, grasping her neck and coughing. "Nasty! I think I shall vomit."

"Wish yourself back in time and change your mind," said Suzanne. "Will some other girls to take your places here on foot."

Darlene and Caroline chuckled while Polly and Mary Alice made little disgruntled sounds.

Upward they hiked, chatter growing spottier among all the girls as the slope of the roadway increased even more. Miss Williamson encouraged them with claps and shrill commands, "Pick it up, ladies! No scuffling! No lollygagging!"

After a while, Rosemary began to fall behind, and when Suzanne looked back at her, the younger girl held out her hand. Suzanne paused, blinked, and looked at the hand. She wanted to take it, to hold it, to help her friend along. It was an awkward moment before Suzanne pretended to slip on a rock herself and look down and away. Then she picked up her stride to catch up with Tirzah, saying with a chuckle, "We should be exempt from physical education classes for a week after this."

Riders on horseback passed them, and several wagons, rocking and creaking, on their way to the camp meeting in the clearing. Families, lone men, groups that appeared to be Sunday School classes from the area's Baptist and Methodist churches. They nodded or spoke pleasantly to the hiking schoolgirls and continued on, disappearing around bends and over tree-shadowed rises.

At last the girls reached Brake's Knoll Clearing, and collapsed into the daisy-speckled grass where gnats and butterflies chased one another. Men in shirtsleeves had put bricks down to level the poles for the huge, canvas preaching tent and were hoisting the tent into place. Families who had already arrived were busy spreading blankets and baskets on the ground. Dogs chased each other and toddlers stumbled about, picking up sticks and chewing on them. Young boys played catch and tag, babies wailed, and gray-haired old men stood chatting with one another and rubbing their chins as old women sat in the shade of their parasols, looking starched and impatient.

The four wagons from the school had arrived well before the girls on foot, and Madame Harlow was directing the men to remove the straw bales from the wagons and place them side by side to serve as prickly pews for the preaching. The horses were already bored, and pawed the soft earth with front hooves in hopes they could be moving again soon.

Miss Williamson hurried across the uneven ground to Madame

Harlow to check in. The student hikers bee-lined, sweating and panting, to the back of one of the wagons where a barrel of water had been tapped. They eagerly accepted tin cupsful then joined the other girls on the straw bales. All but the Morgans, who hung back near the edge of the pasture, watching the hubbub.

"I wonder where the oh-so-holy Reverend Mr. Leeman is keeping himself?" mused Tirzah. "I suppose he waits until everything is set and ready, not willing to pitch in a hand himself. All pomp and pomade, pince-nez and pride. Perhaps sipping from his flask in a private carriage that has yet to arrive."

Polly batted gnats from her eyes. "I wonder if he's handsome. Handsome men seem to draw bigger followings than homely ones. I could sit and listen to a handsome man much more so than a man who is unappealing, no matter what they chose to talk about."

"Polly, you're pathetic," said Darlene.

"Oh, Darlene, you feel the same way. You adore listening to Madame Harlow's fetching nephew Richard when he comes to visit with his wife. You watch his face, his hands, his body. You flush and smile, even if he is only discussing the weather or the price of pigs."

Darlene scoffed.

"But should Reverend Leeman be a fine-looking man, it will make the afternoon all the more tolerable. Not that his preaching would sink in, but I do hope he is attractive. Attractive attracts, does it not? And why shouldn't it? That is the way of nature."

Tirzah scoffed. "Handsome means nothing. It's power that attracts. That, Polly, is the way of nature. The preacher could be the most beautiful man on this green earth or could be the most ugly creature ever to walk on two feet, but his power is what draws people to him. That's the way it always has been and always will be."

The girls were silent, considering Tirzah's proclamation.

Then Mary Alice asked, "Do you suspect he has special...talents, like we do? That he gained his initial following through some sort of mental trickery? I bet he is quite wealthy as well as popular."

"I don't know," said Tirzah. "Perhaps he does and most certainly he is rich beyond belief, though he may feign being poor to relate to the masses. I suggest we pay close attention and see if we can determine that. I would love to throw a fly into his ointment. No, a million flies. Give him a true challenge."

Suzanne chuckled. She, too, suspected it would be wonderfully humorous to startle the man a bit as he expounded on the virtues of biblical obedience and humility. Even Rosemary covered her mouth and grinned.

Snavely Leeman wasn't handsome nor was he unhandsome, but rather an ordinary-looking man whom someone would pass on the street and not remember having seen. He was in his forties, perhaps, with graying hair and pointed chin and a bit of a bulge at his waistline. But that didn't stop most of the women in attendance from swooning and writhing as he spoke, nor keep the men from shouting "Glory!" It was Leeman's voice and body movements that commanded, the shouts, the pauses and the inflections, the folded hands, the trembling appeals, the pointed accusations. He marched back and forth on the stage beneath the tent where as many people as possible had crowded, leaving the rest to press in close on the outside, mopping his brow with the white handkerchief he kept tucked in his rear trouser pocket. No doubt Madame Harlow could hear the man, for his voice was as piercing as a rusty gate swinging in a storm. He held his Bible aloft like a black bird he'd brought down during a hunt, shaking his free fist and promising Heaven's most bounteous rewards for those and only those who claimed God's son Jesus as their personal Savior. He called out names of the sinners in the crowd — Joseph! Mary! Martha! Helen! Elizabeth! James! Florence! Edward! William! John! Ruth! Louis! Theodore! — to which every Joseph, Mary, Martha, Helen, Elizabeth, James, Florence, Edward, William, John, Ruth, Louis, and Theodore in the crowd cried and fell to their knees if they had the room to do so. Suzanne watched, mesmerized not so much by Leeman but by the audience. None of them seemed to consider the fact that in any given gathering of people there would always be those named Joseph, Mary, Martha, Helen, Elizabeth, James, Florence, Edward, William, John, Ruth, Louis, and Theodore. But to the ones bearing those names, the reverend was most certainly calling them because God had whispered in his ear, declaring that these folks were the ones most in need of saving.

Suzanne was as fascinated by Tirzah as she was Snavely Leeman. Tirzah, along with the other girls from Madame Harlow's school, sat on the straw bales to the rear of the crowd, just outside the tent in the sun. But Tirzah was the only one with the obvious disdain for the man and his proclamations. With her arms crossed tightly over her chest, Tirzah glared at the man as he paraded about, grimacing every so often as she wished upon him a particularly sharp stomach pain. This, in turn, caused the man to flinch. However, he kept on preaching. It was likewise funny to see Rosemary staring at the preacher long and hard until the page of the open Bible flipped over, leaving him staring at a passage he wasn't planning on reading.

Yet it wasn't long before Suzanne began to feel uncomfortable. Reverend Leeman started to sound like her mother, warning his listeners about those in league with the devil, with those who embrace Satan's destructive and godless ways. Adulterers. Fornicators. Lusters after unnatural affections. Tellers of lies and those who dabbled in witchcraft and who led astray the innocents.

"For it is better for the sinner to have a millstone tied around his neck and to be thrown into the sea than for us to allow one of the innocents to be deceived!" thundered Reverend Leeman. Men, women, and teens in the crowd wailed, "Amen, Lord!" as the babies whimpered or slept. "It would be better for the sinner to be engulfed in flames and roasted alive than to allow them to bring one of God's children into the abyss!"

"You look ill," said Polly from Suzanne's right.

Suzanne closed her eyes, grit her teeth against the nausea that swam at the base of her throat. She ran her fingers over the scratchy straw, feeling it carefully, hoping for some benign vision of the farmer who raised and chopped and tied it to take her mind off what Leeman was saying. But no vision came.

In the darkness behind her lids she saw Snavely Leeman and her mother, standing together, faces ablaze with holy intent, screaming, "Child of the devil! Child of the damned!"

"Suzanne?" This was Rosemary on the left, close in to Suzanne's ear. "What's the matter?"

I'll be all right, Suzanne tried to say, but only her lips moved with no sound uttered, and Reverend Leeman's voice and her mother's voice grew all the louder and more condemning, tangible now like a hot wind buffeting her ears, her body. Her stomach clenched, threatening to vomit.

"Suzanne?" Rosemary's hand touched Suzanne's shoulder, and Suzanne flinched and pulled away. "I'll be all right," she managed. She slipped from the straw bale and hurried across the downward slop of the clearing and into the trees. There, she clutched the low branches of a sapling and heaved into the weeds, spattering the leaves, the tips of her shoes, the hem of her skirt. The world bobbed, swayed, and Suzanne rode with it, praying for not the first time in her life that she would just go on and die.

"Suzanne!"

Suzanne looked up into Tirzah's stern face.

"Suzanne, enough of that nonsense. Wipe your mouth. Stand up straight!"

Suzanne ran the back of her hand across her lips, spit, and then licked the crust away.

"That best be a bad egg from this morning," said Tirzah, "and not some reaction to the blubbering Snavely Leeman!"

"No..."

"No, what?" Suzanne saw the other Morgans now, behind Tirzah, peering over her shoulders, their faces mottled with leaf-shadows.

"No, it must have been a bad egg." She spit again, hard, onto the ground. "That must be it."

"Good, then," said Tirzah. "Now, listen to me, all of you. Madame Harlow and the teachers are enraptured, and they haven't any idea what's going on around them. Raising their hands and praising the Lord! No surprise there, eh? Hypnotized, the lot of them. The other students are likewise feeling the spirit or are at least pretending very well. You see Maggie Doyle? Crying and waving her hands and pleading for salvation. They all make me sick! But here me. Now's our time. Come on!" She slapped Suzanne's shoulder, and then trotted off down a briar-shrouded knoll. The other girls followed, holding their skirts up and out of the grasp of the tangled undergrowth. Suzanne brought up the rear. She had no idea what Tirzah had in mind but was too wrung out to argue. It didn't really matter, as long as they were out of earshot of the roaring Reverend Leeman.

They gathered in a small, fern-covered grotto beside a stream. Several sat on a fungus-covered log, others sat directly on the ground. Suzanne leaned against a scabby oak tree. Then Tirzah stood before them, her chin lifted definitely. The preacher's voice was no longer in the air; it was replaced with the call of crows and gurgling of the creek.

"Do you realize," Tirzah said, "this is the first time we have gathered beyond the walls of the school? The first time we have been totally free from the gazing eyes and curious ears of the staff? Do you feel it, this freedom? Out here in the wilds of the world is where we belong, not barricaded behind brick walls and iron gates."

Caroline, Polly, and Darlene nodded. Mary Alice chewed her lip. Rosemary stared at the creek, and it looked as if she were counting the ripples. Suzanne watched Rosemary out of the corner of her eye. Such a beautiful girl, always so calm, so thoughtful, so pleasant, no matter what the circumstances. I love you….

"Now that we are free from scrutiny and free from the physical constraints of that dreadful institution, it's time we determined our next move," said Tirzah.

"Our next move regarding what?" asked Suzanne. Her tongue still tasted foul, and she scraped it with her teeth.

"That you ask that only emphasizes the need," said Tirzah. "Our next move as Morgans, our next move toward increasing and perfecting our power. I'll be leaving the school soon, and I want you all to join me."

"Join you?" Polly frowned. "You are asking us to leave, too?"

"To run off and away?" asked Caroline.

"Run off and away? No, run off and toward. Toward our new life. To rise up like fine birds, to rise to our destinies. Together, the seven of us, growing steadily stronger, finding our place, finally taking what we deserve without others marching us here and there at the clang of a bell or bark of an order!"

Suzanne held up her hand. "Just wait a minute. You're not being reasonable, Tirzah. I have another eight months before I'm done with my schooling. The other girls, a year or even more. You aren't willing to quit before you've graduated, yet are asking that of the rest of us?"

Tirzah sat on the log beside Darlene and unbuckled her shoes. She slipped them off and tossed them aside. She ran her toes through a patch of dark green moss, smiling briefly. "One of us must lead, and that is me. There is no question in my mind and shouldn't be in yours."

"You can't lead unless you have a diploma from Madame Harlow? Really, Tirzah? Would you explain that to us, to those you clearly see as your inferiors?"

Tirzah's lip curled slightly. She continued to run her feet across the moss. "It's more than the diploma, Suzanne, but I'm not required to explain myself to you. As the Morgan with the most power, it's high time I took total charge of things. Otherwise, we'll only continue to flounder and play with no true progress toward our destinies."

Darlene tried to scoot a bit away from Tirzah, and Tirzah noticed immediately. "What, do you hate me?"

Darlene said nothing.

"What, do none of you care to join me when I leave the school? Do you all hate me, then?"

No one answered.

"Ah, but I hate you all even more! Oh, you'll be sorry you ever knew me!"

"I've figured the reason you want to wait until you have been graduated," said Suzanne. "It has nothing to do with our talents but all to do with your purse. It has nothing to do with power but with pennies. If you were to leave without graduating, your parents would disown you and give your inheritance away to, what, some charity or other? Or perhaps some distant cousin you've never met?"

Tirzah looked up sharply. It was clear Suzanne had struck upon the truth. "How dare you speak to me and about me in such a way!"

"I'm smart enough to know what's going on," said Suzanne. "All this time you've railed against Madame Harlow, the teachers, the school. And yet you've never made a move to leave. You've said Madame Harlow won't expel you, but how would that stop you from expelling yourself? The only thing I think you love more than your dark talents is money. Or perhaps you love them equally, which is a mighty love, indeed. You can't imagine having to start your life without a hefty bank account. Now, tell me that I'm wrong and I'll be silent on the matter. But you've a gathering of psychically skilled young ladies here around you, and you can bet some of us are able to see your fears as surely as if you were wearing them as a brand on your forehead!"

Tirzah jumped to her feet and slapped Suzanne soundly across the cheek. Suzanne's head snapped back, sending stars through her field of vision. Her face flamed hot. The other Morgans gasped. Polly grabbed Caroline's hand.

"How dare you speak to me in such a way!" Tirzah shrieked. "You stinking little witch, you! And yes, little, for you'll always be little and timid and lazy!" She spun about, jabbing her finger in the faces of each Morgan in turn. "Why have I wasted my time on you? Reading, practicing, planning, talking! For what? For nothing! For disrespect and doubt! A bad egg makes you vomit, Suzanne? Well, you, little girl, make me vomit! You've lost everything of value, for you've lost your determination and the sense of who you are!"

"And you, Tirzah, have lost your mind," said Rosemary simply. She glanced up from the creek. Blue light flickered across her face, reflected from the water.

Tirzah's hands drew into claws. She spoke through clenched jaws. "What did you say?"

"This was never your group," said Rosemary. "You are part of it but no more than the rest of us. Do you listen to yourself, Tirzah? Your anger serves no one, not me, not the other Morgans, and certainly not you. It only tangles you up inside. Knots and tangles, which lessen your skills, not increase them. It makes you lose control of your emotions. Yes, take off your shoes and become one with nature, or whatever it is you're trying to do now. Become a powerful earth crone, a magical Druid, whatever you imagine. But don't try to convince us that you are our leader. We are equals in every way."

Tirzah's hands flew to her head, and she tore her hair down, where it caught a breeze and fluttered around her face like a living spider's web. Her eyes flashed a strange, almost unearthly red, like every dreadful sorceress Suzanne had ever read about in the smuggled books. It was a terrible Halloween transformation, a girl into a banshee. Collectively, the Morgans gasped.

"Listen to this, this pathetic, mealy-mouthed child!" Tirzah cried, shaking her finger in Rosemary's face. "Do you see, now? Do you understand? Mewling, worthless! A weakling! How I tolerated you all for as long as I did is beyond me!" She turned and shouted to the other girls. "We have to purge ourselves of our weaknesses! We have to prove our strength to ourselves and to the powers that await us! That nothing will stop us, no school, no pathetic emotions!" She snatched up a large stone beside the creek and slammed it against the side of Rosemary's face. Rosemary's eyes flew open wide, and then froze in a blink-less stare as she fell over onto her side. Suzanne dropped beside her, stared at the blood welling up beneath Rosemary's soft hair.

"My God, Tirzah! Oh, no, no! What have you done?"

"Only what needed to be done." Tirzah stood, swaying, glaring. Insanity rolled off her in waves. "We cannot tolerate deadweight! We cannot allow such girls to slow us down, to water us down! Clear away the brush, shake ourselves loose and free!"

Rosemary groaned and trembled on the ground. Blood oozed out from between her lips and dripped to the downed leaves beneath her head. Suzanne touched her for the first time — let her hand brush against her friend's cheek. There was no vision revealed, no secrets sprung to her mind, but Suzanne felt the fevered agony and fading consciousness of her dear one. She leapt up and shoved Tirzah with both hands. Tirzah stumbled backward but retained her footing. "What is wrong with you? How dare you! I could kill you!"

"Oh, please try," said Tirzah. She snarled, snapped her teeth, and glanced at the other Morgans, who sat in stunned, horrified silence. "You have played at power, but you, in your pathetic love for Rosemary, have become soft. Yes, I know of your affection for her, and it disgusts me in more ways than one!"

Rosemary! Oh, God, please don't die!

Tirzah took a threatening step forward. "Your power is little more than a puff of air, a stinking scent that blows away in a breeze. Now, let's see just what you have left!" Tirzah angled her face and stared at Suzanne. Immediately, a surge of pain coursed through Suzanne's gut and she doubled over, clutching her stomach, gritting her teeth.

"You are the demon," said Suzanne. "You are the devil my mother told me about!"

"How is your stomach, little girl?" chided Tirzah. "Let me twist it for you even more!" She angled her head and more pain, red-hot and hard, sawed Suzanne's insides. Suzanne bore down so as not to cry out. "You couldn't stop me if you wanted! See? What have you gained all this time but some more worthless visions and a bit of telekinesis? While I've perfected my talents without hesitation or apology! Call me what you will, you're no more than a flea, an irritating mosquito!"

Suzanne tasted blood, acidic, bitter blood, though had not bitten her tongue or lips. Red-hot pressure billowed behind her eyes, and she lunged forward again, this time bringing her fist into Tirzah's face. Tirzah screeched with glee and pain, grabbed a thick, thorny branch, and held it before her like a sword. "So it's us, is it? So be it! I knew it would come to this."

"Polly," cried Suzanne, "go get Madame Harlow! Rosemary's in a bad way!"

Polly looked between Tirzah and Suzanne. Her eyes were wide as quarters.

"My God, Polly, go!"

"You do, Polly, and you'll face my wrath! You are mine! Obey my words!" screamed Tirzah.

"Caroline, Darlene, anybody! Get help!"

The girls sat in stunned silence.

Tirzah slashed the thorny branch, bringing it against Suzanne's neck, tearing a strip of flesh away. Suzanne wailed and fell forward into Tirzah, fingers flexing, grabbing for Tirzah's throat. The pain in her stomach grew, twisting, tearing up her insides, causing her knees to buckle. But she held on to Tirzah's throat, squeezed.

"Please, somebody! Go!" cried Suzanne.

The other Morgans did not move. They looked for all the world to be a garden of statues — stone, cold, without thought or purpose.

They fought. Suzanne tried her best to focus, to will Tirzah's arms to loosen, to get an advantage, but the pain drove all concentration away, and so she struck out with mindless furor. There were stunning blows, blood, and agony. They panted, pounded, and swore, and the crows in the braches flew away in fluttery horror. Locked in each other's death grips, Suzanne and Tirzah went down onto the stony ground, smashing, biting one another. Tirzah screamed and laughed, Suzanne just screamed. She could not let Tirzah win, she could not let this insanity have its way.

Damn you, Tirzah!

Tirzah shouted, freed herself from Suzanne's grasp, then jumped up and stomped Suzanne in the chest with her heel, driving her breath from her lungs. Suzanne gaped, gobbled, trying to draw air. She rolled onto her side, holding her chest. Polly began to cry and Tirzah said, "You cry and you're next!" Polly went silent.

Tirzah howled triumphantly, and then turned to grin at the other girls. "Do you see? Do you see my power? Do not dare to challenge me as Suzanne has, or her fate will be yours!" In that barest moment, as Tirzah was speaking, Suzanne gritted her teeth, focused her mind, and willed the thorned branch up and off the ground. It shook, rolled, and flipped upward with a whistle against the air, slamming its vicious spikes into Tirzah's cheek. She wailed and pulled at it; it came away, taking bits of skin and leaving brutal puncture wounds. Suzanne struggled to her feet, grabbed the stone with which Tirzah had struck Rosemary, and with every bit of her strength hurled it at Tirzah. Tirzah roared, raised her hands before her, caught and heaved the stone back around. It struck Suzanne's forehead.

The world shattered.

A thousand fragments of reality flew away.

And then there were the images, floating up into her mind from some foul abyss. Not dreams but memories, one slamming into the other into the other, Faith Gansy, limp in the barn, the little rabbit Benjamin sleeping in the grass, her mother's hand striking out again and again and again while singing about Jesus, Madame Harlow's incessant appeals to God for some favor or other, the Morgans on the grassy lawn, practicing magic and watching over their shoulders so they would not be detected, Tirzah's increasing anger and mania, Reverend Leeman crying, "Woe! Woe!" to the faithful as they writhed beneath the tent in the clearing, Rosemary lying beside the stream, motionless, one hand trailing in the water, fingers fluttering like dying butterflies.

And then…silence.

Everything gone.

Each memory, each spark of awareness sucked away, leaving a lightless, hollow void.

A dark moment that held perfectly still and did not bleed into another.

An abyss, empty of everything.

Nothingness.

Nothingness.

Nothingness.

Then a spot of light overhead.

A tiny spot, painfully bright.

It widened, growing less intense now, a bluish light patterned with the shape of leaves, branches.

Suzanne coughed, groaned, struggled back to awareness. She pulled herself upward, fell back, and then sat up again. She heaved into the leaves, a nasty, wretched clot of sour rocketing out from her gut. Her mind spun like a child's top.

At last she was able to stand. And she was alone.

It was then she realized she did not know her name. She had no idea why she was in a forest in the fading sunlight. She did not know why her body was so bruised, with some of her skin and hair ripped away, her knee wobbling and some of her teeth loose in her head.

And so she ran. Ran from the terror and uncertainty. Ran from the pain. Ran until she was saved or died, and she didn't care which came, as long as it came.

FIVE

1903

1

At some point a group of young men found Suzanne — young, cautious men with brown skin, hesitant faces, and simple uniforms who were traveling in a wagon filled with musical instruments. They bundled her up and carried her away to their little school down near the river. The students and staff at the Colored Waifs' Asylum were kind and gentle, and tended her wounds. For weeks she lay in the little bed they gave her in the attic, weeping uncontrollably for reasons she could not express, sleeping off and on, awakening from nightmares she did not want to share. They called her Rachel for lack of a better name, for Rachel was a woman of the Bible whose life had been filled with difficult challenges and hard travels.

Time's healing blanket served its purpose, and several weeks after her arrival Suzanne arose from her bed, ready to do something other than toss and turn. She was still sore, and her head ached if she turned it too quickly. And she had no idea where to go, for her past and her life were mysteries. But she told the headmaster, a gentle, hunchbacked white man named George Sandston, "I don't want to wear out my welcome," and made to go, hoping beyond hope that he would ask her to stay. And he did. He offered her a job as assistant cook if she cared to stay, and she accepted with great relief. She savored the peace and simplicity of her chores — chopping vegetables, baking breads, frying fish, sweeping and hauling scraps, washing dishes, and keeping the stove fire going. She came to love the sounds of the asylum band as they practiced each morning in the auditorium, offering lively marches, peaceful lullabies, and elegant waltzes that drifted through the little school and lit up every room. All of the instruments were old, donated, many dented and lacking luster, but in the hands of the boys they produced musical magic.

Cittie Parker, the thirteen-year-old who insisted the band rescue Suzanne from the road, befriended her most closely. He sat with her in the little attic room as she recovered, helping her with her meals when she was too weak to eat then sneaking treats of cookies to her when her appetite recovered. Even later, when he sensed she'd had a particularly rough day, he would go to her room and sit with her until she fell asleep. He took great care, as such a close friendship would be a breach of the school's code of conduct. During these late and sleepless hours, they talked. Sometimes about the day's events. Sometimes about upcoming band trips or which boy was having trouble with his classes. Then they would talk about what they wanted to do some day, when they were full adults and off on their own. Cittie wanted to be a professional drummer, perhaps play in a band in Chicago. Suzanne wanted to get a job as a typewriter or maid, and a nice cozy apartment, though she was in no hurry. "I'll leave when you do," she told Cittie. "I don't want to go out alone."

It was in April, nearly two full two years into her stay at the asylum, when Suzanne had a new vision. She was in the kitchen in her apron, preparing to wash dinner dishes in the large tin basin on the sink, when Cittie came in and handed her the tray of plates he had collected from the dining tables. Her thumb brushed his and in that instant she felt a tickling, then burning sensation at the back of her neck. She pulled back and gasped. The tray dropped to the floor, sending the dishes and flatware in a clattery, fragmented spray across the floor. The current immediately spread upward into her head, leaving her gaping, afraid to move. And then, in an image overlaying the kitchen and the dishes and the soapy water in the basin, she saw Cittie.

She knew it was him from the look of the eyes, the nose, the shape of the jaw. Yet it was a younger Cittie, no more than nine or ten. He was quite thin and hunched over, trudging along a star-lit road in the snow, a burlap seed sack over his shoulder. He was weeping and staggering through the cold. Then as quickly as it had come, the vision was gone.

She stared at Cittie, and then at her thumb, and then at the mess on the floor.

Miss Missy, the leathery white-haired cook, shook Suzanne's arm. "What's this, Rachel? We can't afford to break plates! How careless is that?"

But Cittie knew something had happened; he watched her, his eyes narrowed, waiting for her to tell him what it was. Suzanne glanced at Miss Missy then back at Cittie. "I'm sorry," she said, her hand to her heart. "Oh, dear! So careless of me. If there was something I have that I could sell to reimburse you for this damage, I would gladly give it to you. But I have nothing, so how can I make it better?"

Miss Missy blew air through her lips, shook her head. "Oh, dear, we got to put in a request for funds to buy…three, four, six, no, ten new plates."

Suzanne nodded glumly. "I'll write the request."

"Oh, no, no," said Miss Missy. Her round, wrinkled face softened. "I'll take care of it. I suppose we are all clumsy at times. I've broken my share of plates in my day. Now, sweep up this mess and we'll get to washing."

That night, well after midnight, Cittie came up to the attic and tapped on the door. "Rachel, we got to talk."

And so they did. Hesitantly at first, but then speaking more rapidly, like water rushing through a hole in a crumbling dam, Suzanne told him of her vision. Cittie sat silently, his face stony, his shoulders squared. Then he nodded. Yes, he said, he had indeed run away from home at age nine, leaving the relative warmth of the two-room shack for the snowy road, all his earthly goods, which consisted of two pairs of trousers, some gloves, a mouse-chewed leather belt, socks, a white cotton shirt, a tin mug, and his father's pocket watch (the only thing he'd ever stolen in his life) stuffed into an empty seed sack, seeking a place where he would not be beaten nor forced to work in a textile factory from dawn until nine at night. His father had hated him, being the seventh of seven children his family could barely afford, and so Cittie had decided best to be thought of as an orphan than be thought of as the curse of his family. He headed west from Massachusetts into New York state, his shoes rotting from the damp and his body nearly frostbitten in the cold, sleeping beneath trees and in outbuildings, carefully, silently so as not to be found and beaten yet again. He secured work sweeping floors at a Kingston carpentry shop until he learned of the Colored Waifs' Asylum and their well-respected band, and he traveled north, found the place, and declared himself in need. They took him in, taught him to read and write, and taught him to play the drums.

Suzanne listened without interrupting, her fingers working against each other in her lap, her jaw tight, her breaths shallow. When Cittie was done speaking, he stood and looked out the tiny attic window for many minutes. "How did you see me?" he asked at last. "How did you know what happened to me?"

"I...I touched you. I felt something, a shock, a charge. And then in my mind I saw what I saw."

"I felt it, too, Rachel," said Cittie. "A shock. Didn't hurt but it scared me. Like you had found something secret and had drawn it right out of me."

Suzanne nodded.

"Are you..." he began.

"Am I what?"

"A witch? Or a demon?"

"What? No. Of course not." Something turned in her mind. *Witch? Demon? Someone has called me that before. Who was it? When was it?*

"I don't know what I am, or who," said Suzanne. She rolled over on her side on and gazed at the crusted mud dauber flutes embedded in the cracks of the damp wall. "I wish to God I did. I don't know why I saw what I did, but I am so sorry I frightened you. I'm so sorry, Cittie. It frightened me, too."

"We shouldn't tell nobody."

"No, we shouldn't."

Cittie walked to the bed, reached down, and patted Suzanne's shoulder. She immediately pulled away. "Don't. I don't want to see any more. I think touching isn't such a good thing anymore."

"Oh. All right."

"Okay?"

"Okay. But if something like that happens again, you can tell me. I can keep your secret, you know."

"I know."

And so they didn't touch again. As the days and weeks passed, she began to have visions regularly, several times a week when touching a wall or spoon or bucket. She learned who was stealing cake from the kitchen at night and who cheated on an arithmetic exam. She found out that the headmaster was himself an orphan who, like Cittie, had labored in the textile mills until he injured his hand. She discovered that Miss Missy had a husband who had abandoned her after her first and only born child, an infant daughter, was born and promptly died.

She didn't talk to Cittie about them, but he could tell when they'd happened, for she became silent and withdrawn for a while afterwards, unable to come to terms with what it all meant, and why she was so cursed. He would smile sympathetically, and nod, letting her know he knew. And that, if nothing else, was a small bit of comfort.

Yet though Suzanne did not want the visions, with each new one a bit of her memory returned, pushing itself into her conscious mind at night when the orphans and teachers were asleep. In the darkness behind her closed eyelids she caught a glimpse of an elegant house on a rise above the Hudson and a wealthy woman standing on the front porch. Or a vision of a rabbit beneath a bush, its nose twitching and ears flat against its back. Then a shadowy stall with a body partially buried beneath the straw, an ominous brick school surrounded by a wall and secured with an iron gate, a stone chapel with stained glass windows, a group of girls in school skirts and jackets standing in the shade of tall oak trees and talking in urgent, hushed voices. An evangelist crying out from beneath a tent on a mountainside clearing, "Fear ye the Lord in His righteousness, and fear ye the demon in his trickery!"

In the daytime Suzanne focused on her work, chopping, baking, and frying. Miss Missy let her take short breaks to go to the music room and listen to the band practice before she returned to sweep and clean in the kitchen. She concentrated on each task, thinking about what she was doing, trying to drive out thoughts of anything else. She didn't want to go crazy in front of everyone. She didn't want to lose her home at the asylum. But each evening she climbed the attic ladder and went to bed with apprehension. She feared knowing what lay waiting to reveal itself in the darkness. Yet she wanted to know more than anything, for certainly, with time, the pieces would give her the truth about her life.

It was the third night of November. She lay down on her cot and drew the wool blanket over herself, tucking it tightly all around, making a warm cocoon against the chilly air of the attic. The wind outside was fierce, wailing through the trees around the school, causing the shingles on the roof to chatter. She closed her eyes and saw nothing but darkness. A blessing. Tonight, she would have peace and sleep. But as she drifted down into slumber, there was the sudden image of a woman there behind her lids — her mother, she'd come to realize — her face close and looming, with wild and furious eyes. Her hand was raised in a fist, and she screamed, "You are a demon child, Suzanne Heath! God have mercy on you!"

Suzanne tried to open her eyes but it was as if they were nailed shut, insisting she see what was to come. She struggled beneath the blanket.

Her mother leered even closer, and began to sing, "Jesus Loves Me." The song was sweet and comforting at the Waifs' Asylum, but her mother's enraged voice twisted it into the most hideous and terrifying song Suzanne had ever heard.

Demon child?

"Demon child?"

She kicked herself free from the blanket and fell from the bed, sweating profusely, heart thundering. Shoving her hands against the cold floor, she pushed herself to her feet and stumbled to the window. She placed her forehead on the frosty glass and stared out at the sleet that pattered down from the sodden night sky. "Suzanne," she whispered, her teeth chattering. "My name is Suzanne Heath."

Yes. I know that. I remember that now.

"My home is somewhere on the Hudson River. Now I could find my family if I wanted. Surely if I sought hard enough, I could be back where I belong."

She shivered violently, and it had nothing to do with the frosted window or the sleet.

But she said I am diabolic. She hates me. She has no use for me.

"Dear Jesus, she hates me. My mother hates me."

Were my wounds from her? Did she beat me and then banish me from our house?

She put her forehead on the window and breathed fog onto the glass, then drew a cross into the fog. "Jesus loves me," she whispered. "Jesus, do you love me? If you do then why am I here, just now remembering such terrible things? Am I a witch? Am I a demon? Can you love a demon, or is that prohibited? Is this my punishment for something I've done and can't recall?"

Jesus didn't answer, and neither did God. The sleet continued to tick against the window and slide down out of sight.

"I need to know the rest," she said. "I need to remember it all."

There was no answer. A mouse skittered across the floor and darted under Suzanne's bed, and the wind outside shifted, whistling through a crack in the sill. Suzanne left the window and sat on the mattress.

"I won't sleep again until I know," she said, her whole body tense with the declaration. "I won't move. Damn it all! I will sit here until I remember. I must and I can."

And so she sat on the bed, hands clenched, on the verge of tears but fighting them and a great need to sleep away. In the morning when the bell rang, she did not get up nor get dressed. She sat in her nightgown on the edge of her bed, her mind racing and then going numb, back and forth, over and over like someone opening and then slamming shut a door, her bare feet no longer aware of the cold wood beneath them.

There was a knock, and Cittie said, "Rachel? Are you there?"

She couldn't answer.

"Rachel, may I come in?"

She could not speak.

"I'm coming in."

The door opened and Suzanne heard Cittie enter.

"Rachel, what's the matter? Look at me."

She couldn't look at Cittie. Her eyes no longer obeyed her, having found a water stain on the wall as their focus, though the focus, like her mind, pulsed in and out.

"Are you sick?"

Suzanne shook her head imperceptibly.

"You're not sick?"

She licked her lips. "I'm not Rachel," she managed. "I'm Suzanne."

"Oh. Oh? You remembered your name!"

"And more." Her voice was flat in her ears.

"That's wonderful!" Cittie moved into Suzanne's range of vision and cocked his head. "Is that wonderful?"

"No."

"Oh." A pause, then, "It's time to get up. Miss Missy ain't happy, crackin' and cookin' all those eggs herself. She said you best get down there twenty minutes ago."

"No. I won't. I can't."

"Oh." Cittie pulled the stool over and sat before Suzanne. "Want to tell me about why not? I got to tell her why not or she'll take it out on me."

"I need to know it all. I'm staying here until I remember everything."

Cittie brows drew together. He tapped his knees then said, "Can I help?"

"No. You can't."

And so he left the attic, and Suzanne sat on the bed throughout the day into the evening. At one point Miss Missy came in and put her hand on Suzanne's forehead. Suzanne jerked back and away.

"You ain't got no fever," said Miss Missy. "What's ailin' you?"

Suzanne said nothing.

"You melancholy?"

"In a way."

"I got soup for that."

"I'm not hungry."

"You got to eat and you can't just sit here."

"No. Thank you."

George Sandston came in later, dressed in his headmaster's suit and clutching his hat, his hunched back hunched even more from the pain of having to climb the ladder to the attic. "Rachel, it's nine at night. You've sat here all day as if you've lost your mind. Miss Missy said you won't eat. I'm worried for you."

"I'm not hungry."

"We can't have you up here, staring at the wall. Doctor Terry is on his way."

"I don't need a doctor. But thank you."

Later, an hour perhaps, maybe two, the doctor came into the attic. Suzanne had seen him time and again, tending to the boys when they broke arms or came down with the influenza. "Rachel, the staff is very concerned. They think something has gone wrong with your mind, for you to sit here like this."

Suzanne tried to look at the doctor but her gaze would not leave the water spot on the wall.

"If you can't look at me, or if you can't get up now and talk to me in a rational way, I'll have to take action on your behalf."

"I can't. Please. Leave me alone. I'm almost there, I know it."

"Almost where?" His voice was tightening. He did not like being challenged. "You make no sense."

"Not to you, but to me." She swallowed, took her hands and forced her head around to face the doctor, though still she could not look at him.

"I mean it, Rachel. Stand up. Talk to me. Enough of this nonsense."

"I need time alone. Time to think. Leave me be. Please go."

Doctor Terry was angry now, and his face reddening. "I said stand before me, young lady!" He grabbed Suzanne by the shoulders and forced her up, but two things happened in that moment. First, her knees immediately buckled and she fell back to the bed and out of his grasp. Second, a vision surged through her brain, causing her to gasp and put her hands to the sides of her head. She saw the doctor standing inside a narrow, dark, paneled hallway with several other persons in long, dark coats and severe expressions. Between them, wrapped in a canvas jacket with the sleeves tied in a knot at his back, was a wide-eyed, struggling young man.

"He's yours now," Doctor Terry said, his face calm but his voice registering an unseemly glee. "Crazy as a bedbug, he is. Violent when provoked, refused to obey his parents, knocked his brother down a flight of stairs, breaking the boy's arm in the process."

"I see," said one of the other men. "We shall have none of that here."

"Take care with him. Give him an inch and he'll take you for a mile. Restraints are well-suited in his case."

The young man continued to wriggle. "Let me outta this thing! I ain't crazy! I had to fight 'em or they'd kill me, don't you see? They was out for me, out for blood! They was gonna kill me then eat me!

I swear to God they was!"

Doctor Terry shook the men's hands as the young man writhed, then dropped to the floor, trying to worm his way out of the jacket. "Please!" he cried as he flopped back and forth. "Please, untie me! I can't stand this! I promise to be good! Please, I can't stand this!"

"Thank you, Doctor Terry," said one of the men. "We will make sure he never fights anyone again."

Doctor Terry nodded and turned on his heels, heading down the hallway toward an arched door through which dusty, filtered light shown. The vision vanished.

"What was that?" demanded Doctor Terry. He took a step backward from Suzanne's cot. "Tell me, young lady! What in God's name was that?"

He'd felt it, as Cittie had. A charge or a shock, something drawn from him. And he was frightened.

"I don't know," said Suzanne. She could not confess her visions to the doctor. He was already posturing to send her to that hospital with the dark hall and the canvas jackets. This would make it a certainty.

"But you do know," said the doctor. His eyes were narrow, angry, scared. "Tell me what that was!"

"Static, perhaps," she said simply. "Static that makes our hair stand up at times. What else would it be?"

The doctor stomped his foot, then raised his hand as if to slap Suzanne but then thought better of it. "You are to come downstairs now, and resume your normal daily activities. If you choose to sit here, look into nothing and refuse to eat like a mad woman, then I'll be forced to handle you like a mad woman."

Suzanne clenched her jaws.

"Did you hear me?" demanded the doctor.

"Yes!" she shouted. "Yes, I heard you! The mice in the walls heard you! The spiders in the corners heard you! The sleet outside the window and the trees in the forest hear you! Now leave me the Hell alone! Get out of here. Now! Or you shall rue the day!"

The doctor did, indeed, get the Hell out of there, slamming the door and stomping down the ladder, muttering under his breath that he would be back in the morning, oh, yes, back with help to take her away. She remained on her bed, staring at the wall, trying to force her brain to remember the rest of the missing details of her life.

But the vision of Doctor Terry kept creeping back in, pushing away anything else. Her mind replayed, over and over, the young man in the canvas jacket, fighting, crying, hopeless and helpless, and those in charge ignoring his agony. The night crept on. The clock in the second-floor hall chimed eleven o'clock, midnight, one o'clock.

She shook her head, pounded it with the heels of her hands, but nothing more came clear. She was done. Dry.

Quietly and on shaky legs, she pulled on her clothes and shoes, and opened the door, listening first, and then creeping down the ladder to the second floor. The pendulum in the hall clock swung back and forth, *click click click click*. The single gas lamp on the wall hissed with faint, flickering light. A boy in one of the two bedrooms moaned in his sleep.

Downstairs, in the kitchen, was a notebook in which Miss Missy kept her recipes. Suzanne would write a note to Cittie. She wouldn't give her destination — not only would that be careless but she had no idea, herself, where she was going — but would let him know she was all right and to thank him for his friendship. A knot grew in her throat. Her only real friend, left behind.

Padding down to the first floor, through the dining room and into the kitchen, Suzanne lit a candle and fumbled for the notebook in the shadows. There, on the shelf beside the wooden biscuit bowl. A pencil was tied to a string and marked the last recipe Miss Missy had used. In the very back were blank pages. Suzanne creased the last page then tore it out.

She sat in the candle light at the butcher table, and wrote simply, "Dear Cittie, I had to leave. The doctor was going to send me away. Don't worry about me. I'll figure things out. Take care. You are a wonderful drummer. Your friend, Suzanne." She folded it, unfolded it then folded it again. It was done.

It was finished.

2

Cittie woke before the other boys as he always did, brought back around to awareness by the starlings and blue jays outside the window as they gathered in the bare rose of Sharon to argue over perches and look for pods that still contained seeds. He scratched a patch of dry skin on his knee, washed his face in the basin, then dressed for the day in his gray trousers and jacket, white shirt, and blue tie. On his fifteenth birthday, just last month, he was finally able to move from short pants to long, a major step in the life of a boy at the asylum. In two more years, he would graduate and be sent on his way with a certificate, ten dollars, a new suit, and the heartfelt well wishes of the staff.

Breakfast was at seven, and then his history class at eight. After that, arithmetic and then two hours with the band, preparing for a Christmas concert that was held each year to help raise funds for the school. It was in the band that he felt most alive. His drum, a stained snare donated to the asylum by a Lutheran church, felt like part of his own body when the straps held it firmly against his waist and the sticks were in his hands. The rhythms were as much a part of him as his heartbeats, the rolls against the drumhead as alive with energy as the muscles of his arms. God created him to play the drum. What he would do with it someday, he had no clue. But had no doubt it would come to pass.

Stepping over the warped floorboard that creaked, Cittie went to the door and reached for the knob. It was then he spotted the folded note, poking out beneath the door, with his name printed in pencil in bold block letters.

He snatched it up, looked back to make sure the other boys were still sleeping, then stepped into the hall and stood beneath the glowing sconce to read its message. His head bowed. He whispered, "No, Suzanne."

Twenty minutes later, Cittie found himself on the road that led from the Colored Waifs' Asylum, hunched beneath his ratty winter jacket, his burlap seed sack over his shoulder with all his worldly goods within — his clothes, the pocket watch, and the snare drum, the second thing he had ever stolen in his life. The night was nearly done, the overcast sky to the east bleeding from dark pewter to a steel blue. Sleet hung on the bare branches and as-of-yet-to-fall leaves of scarlet and yellow. His leather shoes, which had cracks in the sides, leaked melted sleet, soaking his socks and numbing his feet.

He caught up with her a good two miles up the road. She was standing beside her little steamer trunk, staring into the forest as if she'd never seen trees before. Her wool coat, donated to her by the local Baptist charity and long enough to drag the ground, was sopping from hem to mid-calf. The mangy fur collar of the coat looked as much like a drowned, chewed squirrel as anything decorative. Her felt hat drooped sadly on her head. She wore no gloves, and her hands were up before her, steepled as if in hopeless prayer.

"Suzanne?"

She looked over, her mouth falling open slightly. Her eyelashes were beaded with the wet and her hair, unpinned, lay flat against her cheeks.

"Cittie."

"You left us."

"I had to. Did you find the note?"

"We always talked about leaving together." Cittie rubbed sleet from his eye. "Don't you remember?"

"The doctor was going to send me away. For nothing more than sitting and thinking. Does he never sit and think? I would guess not with his attitude."

"He's a good man. Maybe he was just a bit worried..."

"I think he gets paid per person he sends to that dreadful hospital."

"What hospital?"

"The one..." Suzanne stopped, looked out at the trees again, her face clouding over like the shadows within. She stared, took measured breaths, and then turned back to Cittie. "Doctor Terry touched me and I saw it. A hospital for the most terribly tormented people. There was a man in that dim and narrow hallway, a poor man terrified out of his wits, struggling in a jacket that was tied so his arms were bound and useless. He begged them to hear him out, but they cared little but to haul him away, lock him away. Doctor Terry was happy to pass the man over to them. He grinned like Carroll's Cheshire Cat, a cold, haughty grin that made my blood freeze."

Cittie stepped closer, one hand extended, tentative. "Suzanne, you really think…"

"I don't think, I know. Had I stayed, he would have hauled me off. There was no choice but to go away."

"Without me."

"Cittie…"

"Without me."

"Without you."

Cittie shivered, more with despair than cold. "Do you want me to go back? I can go back, you want me to."

Suzanne put her hand to her eyes, wiped off the sleet, then sighed. "The world is a hard place, Cittie. You are so young…"

"Not so much younger than you."

"I want you warm and safe."

"Safe from what? Maybe Doctor Terry mean like you think he is, and mayhaps he'll throw me away into some institution for the insane, for tryin' to run away and for stealin' my drum."

Suzanne smiled a sour smile. "Not if you don't sit too long to think. Please go back. I don't know what's out here any more than you do, not really. Dreadful things could happen. I don't want that on my conscience.

"But what about good things that could happen? If I stayed at the asylum, I might miss 'em. Mayhaps it's time for me to leave but I just didn't know it."

"Ah, Cittie."

Cittie stretched his shoulders beneath the seed sack. "I never heard you talk like this before. It's troublin'. Sure, you been down and sad before but not like this. Don't be alone like this."

Suzanne pointed out in the woods. "There, up there, Cittie. This is where I was. This is where I ran, through the trees, down to this very road. Here is where you found me and took me in the wagon. I know that now."

Cittie looked up and down the sloggy road. "Yes, yes, you're right. It was here."

"I ran away, down to this road. I was beaten down, cut, bruised, bleeding."

"You were."

"I felt it through my feet, right through my shoes. I stopped here, went over and touched that little oak. I didn't want to but knew I had to. I sensed, no, I knew I would learn something important if I did. Something that sitting in the attic and thinking for days would never have brought to light." She took a shivering breath, though Cittie could tell it came from within, not without.

"What'd you learn?"

"Who I am." She looked at him straight on, her eyes tight, damp. "Where I was. What I did. Dear God, Cittie."

"Oh."

"I don't think you'd want to be friends with me anymore if you knew. Another reason you should go back to the asylum and forget me."

"Tell me."

"Just go."

"No. Tell me."

"I let her die. Cittie, I let her die! I chose to fight Tirzah rather than go for help, to prove myself or punish her, either, but it doesn't matter now, does it? The reason? All the while, she was bleeding. And she died, helpless, up in the woods."

"Who died?"

Suzanne's clenched fist went to her heart and she spoke as if the words were crushed glass. "My sweet Rosemary."

Cittie stepped closer again, wanting to hold her hand, if even for a moment to ease her agony. Instead, he said, "Tell me, Suzanne. It'll be all right."

And so she did. She told him things she now recalled in vivid detail, detail that at once amazed and worried Cittie. A school for wealthy girls, a club called the Morgans, dabbling in the occult with spells and visions and moving things with thoughts alone. She spoke like an anguished woman at confession, pouring out all her sins before God and man, on the verge of weeping but bearing down to keep the tears from flowing. She told of a trek to hear an evangelist in the mountains, a quiet escape to a fern-covered spot among the trees, and then the fight. She was knocked unconscious and when she awoke, she didn't know where she was or who she was, so she ran, and ran.

"And now I'm running again," she said. "I am going to find a place where no one knows me, where I can live and perhaps do something to make up for what I've done. What I haven't done. My great sin of omission."

Cittie put his hands into his pockets, kicked at an icy stone in the road, then said, "We all done things we shouldn'a. We all not done things we should'a."

"Things that ended up in death?" Suzanne shook her head. "No, not many have done that. And what of the other girls, who were there with us? The other Morgans? Did Tirzah kill them, too? I don't know. I should have led them all away from her, back to the safety of the camp meeting! What I know for certain is I am responsible for Rosemary, at the very least, and imagine her soul cursed me as it flew off to heaven!"

Cittie sighed. "So, what you gonna?"

"I think I'll go to New York City. Find a job. I don't care what anymore. The lowest of the low would suit me fine, short of selling my body. I just want to live my life. I want to find a way to make amends in some way. I have no choice."

"Okay."

She looked up the road as an ice-covered branch cracked and crashed to the ground.

"I'll miss you, Cittie. Now please go back. Hurry, before they see you're gone."

"No."

"You don't need the grief, going with me."

"We're friends. I ain't gonna let you go off alone."

"You're a Negro. I'm white. You know how that will look to most people. That will be grief of a mighty kind."

"We can say I's your servant, I work for you to carry your packs."

Suzanne shook her head. "Good heaven, no. You would be tormented. I would, too. Just the two of us, on the road? You know how that would look?"

"Then we go together, but apart," said Cittie. "Traveling in sight of each other, but not together."

"Cittie, please go back. There is so much for you back at the asylum."

"Not no more." He smiled and held up the seed sack. "I brought the drum with me. Nothing there for me anymore but a cot with a dent in it where I used to sleep."

Suzanne made a soft, tsking sound with her lips, then, "It's a long walk."

"Walked longer in my time. I'll take your trunk."

"How? I had a devil of a time getting it this far. It's small but it's not lightweight."

"Oh, just watch me."

In only a matter of minutes, Cittie made a small travois with string from the seed sack and sturdy sticks from the edge of the woods. He lashed the trunk to it and then grinned. Suzanne nodded reluctantly.

And they walked. Southeast along the ice-slicked road, side by side through the countryside but parting when they heard an approaching wagon or rider, with Cittie slipping behind a tree or hedge and holding low. When they reached a larger road, Suzanne moved ahead and Cittie held back a distance so they wouldn't appear to know each other. Every so often Suzanne would stop and stand completely still, and he knew she was reliving her visions, so he would wait patiently. His heart hurt for her, but there was nothing he could do but what he was doing. Moving on. Following her lead. They slept as poor foot travelers do, in soft haylofts or tucked out of sight in sheds or barns. They ate the biscuits and ham Suzanne had taken from Miss Missy's kitchen and tucked into her coat pocket.

White Plains was a large and busy village filled with horse-drawn trollies, automobiles, produce-filled wagons, and well-dressed men and women bustling about on their daily businesses. Cittie and Suzanne arrived there early in the morning as the shops and offices were opening and the sun lay low on the streets. Suzanne was clearly foot-weary and hungry, though she did her best to walk upright with her head held high. If not for her mangy coat collar, worn shoes, and hair that had been combed and pinned up in a hurry beneath the felt hat, she would have blended in well with the citizenry. As it was, a few people gave her sidelong glances but then went about their chores. Cittie, knowing well how to behave in strange and crowded places, matched Suzanne's pace from fifty feet back, head down, the sack over his shoulder and his hands gripping the poles of the travois. He felt the eyes on him, a strange black boy alone in the town, but said nothing and moved along.

It was a wagon full of young pigs that proved their ticket to

New York City. The wagon was drawn up at the edge of an outdoor market and the driver, a bulbous man with a pimply forehead, was busy loading the squealing creatures from a pen into the wagon. Cittie saw Suzanne stop and glance back at him when they both heard the wagon owner say to the pig merchant, "Getting these pigs to Manhattan and I'll be back in four days. You got more, I'll take 'em. Lot of pork eaters, sausage eaters down there."

When the pigs were loaded and the driver was in his seat with the reins gathered, Suzanne looked back at Cittie and nodded. She mouthed something he couldn't decipher. No one on the street was watching and the customers in the market were engaged in conversation and haggling, so as the wagon turned around toward the road, Suzanne threw herself quite nimbly over the wagon's tailgate and crawled in low among the animals. Cittie had but seconds to untie the trunk from the travois. When the wagon passed him, he shoved the trunk up and over among the pigs and climbed in with his seed sack. He and Suzanne crouched among the smelly, sniffling swine, heads raised just enough to see and breathe over the prickly pig backs. As the wagon picked up its pace, Cittie spied one lone little boy standing in the middle of the road, tugging on his mother's hand and pointing at the wagon. "Mama, I seen them get in there!" he shouted. "Look, Mama, look at them people!" Happily, the mother merely jerked the boy and took him on his way.

They rode nearly eight hours, alternating between kneeling and sitting, being thumped and bumped about by their porcine companions, trying not to groan when sharp little hooves came down on their hands or thighs. Cittie clutched his seed sack close to his chest so those same little hooves might not step down and through the treasured snare drum. The pigs grunted, sniffed, snorted, urinated, defecated and farted, at first curious about their human co-travelers, then quite disinterested. Cittie also urinated among the pigs, thankful for the cloak of tightly packed animal bodies. He suspected Suzanne might have done the same but was happy not to really know, ill at ease with even the thought of such an intimate thing.

Cittie suspected the driver might stop to check on the pigs and they would be discovered, and so he spent his time devising various alternate escape scenarios. But the driver was just as happy to steer the horses onward, stop for a meal at a small tavern along the way, then on down into New York in the late afternoon. The scenery changed more quickly than Cittie would have imagined, with houses and shops, factories and office buildings, tenements and water towers becoming more closely packed together with each quarter mile, then each city block. Carriages, wagons, trams, carts, and automobiles jockeyed for position on the ever-widening streets. People were everywhere — businessmen in fancy suits, laborers in grimy coveralls, ladies in large hats topped with feathers and bows, factory girls in sad shoes and braids, maids and butchers and beggars, children of the rich, children of the poor, eyeing one another with curiosity as they passed along the streets in their respective social manners.

The wagon reached the heart of Manhattan. Cittie was shocked to see that some of the more elegant buildings reached a startling, mind-numbing eighteen or more stories high. His stomach twisted as he gazed up at them from among the pigs. What would happen, he wondered, should a strong wind knock those buildings down? God help those within, and God help those without, standing or riding in the pathway.

The driver steered the wagon off a wide boulevard and onto more narrowed lanes, away from the elegant stores and aura of wealth into shabby neighborhoods that reeked of need. Street surfaces were covered with crumbling paving stones and deep potholes. A dead horse lay in the road with its head upon a plank walkway as little boys poked it with a stick. Cittie's heart pounded a fast and furious rhythm, one of hope and fear, uncertainty, determination.

"Suzanne?" he said, the first word spoken since White Plains.

"What?"

"We're here."

"We are indeed."

"Are you scared?"

"I hope I'm not."

Down a long, muddy street littered with trash and children, the driver at last drew the horses up in front of a large, one-story wooden building surrounded by a splintery plank wall and alive with squeals and squawks, grunts and bellows. A sign painted on the plank wall read, "Lawson and Sons, Slaughterhouse." Even above the smells of the pigs in the wagon, Cittie detected the scents of the other animals, of their fear, their death. The driver coughed, spit onto the road then spoke to the slaughterhouse foreman who had come to the gate. "Got some good ones for you. Forty-six young porkers. Receipt's here. Let me in and we'll unload them."

Cittie's body tightened. He had pictured the end of the trip, but had prayed there would be a few moments to climb out and away, undetected.

"Cittie!" whispered Suzanne. "What do we do?" He saw her worried eyes above the mud-caked head of a particularly restless pig.

"Follow me." He squirmed through the pigs to the wagon's rear. Perhaps, as the foreman was looking over the receipt, they could get out and steal away.

But as Cittie hunched himself up and over the tailgate, dragging the trunk and sack with him, he heard the foreman shout, "Who in Christ's name are you?"

"My name is Cittie, sir," began Cittie. He turned back to face the driver as the man threw down the reins and jumped to the ground. Cittie glanced briefly into the wagon where Suzanne still held still and quiet, eyes wide and terrified.

"City?" scowled the driver. "What are you talkin' about? New York City? You a simple-minded colored boy?"

"No, sir, Cittie's my name, sir." He looked at the ground, kicked at the road. "I just hitched a bit of a ride, sir. I'm sorry."

The driver and slaughterhouse foreman stomped to the rear of the wagon. The driver's face looked like a crumpled red rag. He shook a fist at Cittie's nose. "You little black bastard! Hitching in my wagon, scaring my pigs! Probably thought to bash me on the head at some point, yes, and steal me blind!"

"Yeah, boy! Have you 'rested for this, beat, too!" said the foreman. He reached out for Cittie's arm but Cittie skipped back several steps. Then he reached into his pocket and pulled out all he had there, money he'd earned over the past four years by doing extra chores at the asylum. Eleven silver dollars, eight dimes, and twenty-seven pennies. He held them out toward the two men. "Here, sir, I'll pay you for your trouble. I didn't mean no harm, sir, I promise I didn't." Then he pretended to stumble and the coins flew high and wide, landing on the wet ground in a spray. The men shouted angrily but went after the coins, and in that moment Suzanne rolled from the wagon and the two of them ran off up the street, coated in pig filth, Cittie carrying the trunk like a babe, the sack tucked beneath his arm with the bulk of it flapping and bouncing against his back.

Around a corner and into an alley they went, skidding to a stop behind several rain barrels to catch their breaths.

"My God, Cittie! Do you think they'll come after us? Will we go to jail?"

Cittie shook his head. "No, no, don't you worry none. They got money and they got business to tend to. We be all right."

"Sure?"

"Sure." He wasn't, but he hoped he might be right.

Suzanne let out a long, low breath. She wiped her nose. "Do I look as bad as you do?"

"I think you might."

"Oh." Suzanne peered into the rain barrel at her reflection, and her shoulders fell. "Curses, indeed I do. I'm coated, head to foot. I can't find a job this way. No one will hire a ruffian like me! And I can't find a place to stay."

"Don't worry, Suzanne. We'll figure somethin' out."

They moved deeper into the shadows of the alley, stepping carefully over the refuse and human waste and around a tall pile of fly-coated garbage so they could wait and rest. Several cats hissed and ran out of the mess, dragging food scraps and dead mice with them. Cittie took off his coat and put it on the ground for Suzanne to sit. She hesitated, but then gave in, and thanked him.

"I didn't know you had money," Suzanne said as she stared at her knees, "and for you to waste it all on us. Cittie, I should not have climbed into that blasted wagon. We should have stayed on foot."

"You was beyond tired for the walkin'," said Cittie. "And it ain't wasted if it bought us our getaway. Have to do what we have to do."

Suzanne raked her fingers through her hair, pushing it from her face then grimacing at the state of her hands when she took a long look at them. "What shall we do? We don't know a soul in this city to go to for help. I've never known anyone to look so dreadful as we do."

Cittie grinned behind his hand, because he'd never seen anyone look so dreadful before, either, and it was all he could do to swallow the laughter. At last he composed himself. "Now, don't you worry. Ain't nothing what's ever's got dirty that can't be got clean again. Don't the Bible say that?"

"I don't know. Does it?"

"I think so. If it don't, it should."

Within the hour, darkness had blanketed the city, and while the electric streetlights, standing proudly at each intersection, burned steadily and with enthusiasm, the streets themselves seemed illuminated with little more than pale moon glow. The deep corners and alleyways were as black as midnight in the mountains.

"Got an idea," said Cittie, stretching his shoulders against a pinch.

"What is it? I hope something good. I can't sit here any longer."

"Come on."

He led her through the streets, staying to the shadows with his face turned away so no one would yell or hit him for being who he was and where he was. Bars spilled muddied light and drunken patrons out onto the streets. A gang of gnarly boys fought in a loud tangle in the center of the road. Cats prowled, dogs growled. Automobiles rumbled by, bouncing across potholes, the headlights reminding Cittie of dragon eyes, cutting the night in search of prey.

"How much farther, Cittie?" asked Suzanne, stopping to scrape a stone from her shoe.

"Not much, if I remember right. I'll find it."

It wasn't much farther, another few blocks, but he did find it in the center of a widened section of avenue in what appeared to have once been a wealthier neighborhood but had begun to slide into the rot around it. It was a large fountain in the shape of a Roman woman holding a pitcher. The woman had lost her head but the pitcher in her hands remained on her hip. No water was spouting from the pitcher, and probably hadn't in quite a while, but the pool around the fountain was quite full from recent rains and sleets. Wagons rumbled past, and men on foot, a few women with men and a few women alone, but they showed no interest in the two at the fountain.

"Noticed this as we passed by this afternoon," said Cittie. "Free bath!"

"What? No, Cittie, I can't."

"Course you can," said Cittie. "Just make it quick. Do it same time as me, so it's all done fast and we're out."

Cittie put down the trunk and sack and climbed into the pool, lay on his back and splashed the water over his body, dragging his hands across his jacket and trousers, trying to scrape off as much crusted pig residue as possible. "It's not so bad, Suzanne. Cold but good and wet."

"What else would water be but wet?"

Cittie smiled.

Suzanne shook her head, grimaced, but then followed suit, removing her coat and hat and stepping into the water. "Cittie, it's freezing!"

"Water cleans us, cold or warm. Don't matter which it is, just decides for us how long we gonna stay in it."

She hesitated, clenched her fists, then sat on the low edge of the pool and leaned into the chore, rubbing the soiled hem of her skirt, her shoes, and her sleeves. She scrubbed her face and hands. Unpinning her hair, she lowered herself onto her knees, bent over and rinsed it with wide, swirling motions, trying not to make noisy splashes but making them, anyway. "I can barely stand the cold, Cittie," she whispered through chattering teeth.

"Then make it quick."

Cittie climbed from the fountain pool and shook hard to get off the worst of the wet. He stood trembling, his feet stamping, and his arms around himself as Suzanne finished with her hair and stepped out of the pool. A milk wagon drove past, followed by a sputtering black automobile with just one headlight working. Several men spoke in raised voices down the way. An old man, inebriated or demented, stumbled past, waving his hands. "The Rebel's hidin' in them trees! Lay low, lay low!" he shouted, and Cittie and Suzanne stepped back to give him even more room.

"We'll die here in the cold like this," Suzanne said. "What were we thinking? This was insane. Doctor Terry should haul us both to that hospital and throw us in canvas jackets!"

"Put your coat back on. Then we'll go find a place to change into our dry clothes."

"I can barely move. I'm frozen in place!"

"No, you ain't."

She huffed her resentment, but her huff was muffled and close to tears. She slipped into the filthy coat, snatched up the dirty hat, and trailed Cittie up the street and off into an alley that ran behind a row of tall, shabby tenements. Clothes hung on drooping lines between the porches of the various stories and fire escapes clung to the exterior of the buildings like giant, skeletal insects hoping to gain entrance through a window. An outhouse was erected behind each tenement.

Cittie took the seed sack behind the first outhouse where the ground was muddy from rain and other liquids he didn't care much to think about. As carefully as he could, he peeled off his wet clothes, slung them over the wire fence behind him, and stepped into the clean ones from the sack. His muscles immediately relaxed and he let out a breath that he felt he'd been holding since three days back. His wet shoes soaked his dry socks right away, but that was a small price for being close to clean again.

Suzanne took her turn behind the outhouse, carrying with her a few choice items from the trunk. When she came back around, she looked surprisingly calm and composed, in a fresh skirt and blouse, her wet hair combed and pinned once more on top of her head. "I can't wear the coat anymore," she said. "It's done for."

Cittie studied the clothes on the lowest line then grabbed an old, discarded plank from a pile of garbage. *Just the right length*, he thought.

Suzanne frowned. "You aren't going to steal clothes, are you?"

Cittie shook his head. "No, I only stole twice in my life and am done with it. I'm just gonna make a trade is all. Gimme your coat, please."

"No. Why?"

"Maybe you can't clean it in a fountain but mayhaps somebody can clean it in their wash tub. It's a fine coat under all that dung, after all. Please?"

She pursed her lips, unconvinced, but handed the long coat to Cittie. He hooked it onto the end of the plank and then, following a few mis-aims, tossed the coat onto one of the clotheslines. Then he knocked free a well-worn but thick quilt and held it up proudly. "Not a coat and not a cape, but you might could wear it as a shawl. Keep you warm, I think."

A dog in the yard next door began to bark. Another dog down

the road began to bark, too.

"Now we got to get out of here," said Cittie. He handed Suzanne the quilt, which she held for only a few moments before flinging it away with a grunt of horror.

"What? It got lice in it?"

Suzanne stared at the blanket on the ground, her shoulders heaving. "No. No. A baby died in that blanket. I saw the mother weeping, holding him, cooing to him, praying for him, and then his eyes rolled up in his head and he died."

"I'm sorry. I..."

"You didn't know. You couldn't know. It's my curse, Cittie. Always has been and probably always will be. My curse until I have paid for my sins, if that's even possible." She lifted her head and looked at the moon, so far above the city, so far away. "I don't need a coat or shawl. I'm dry. I'm fine."

"Suzanne..."

But she didn't care to talk about it.

It was years before she talked about it again.

Suzanne found work in a Brooklyn mattress and pillow shop, and housing in a shabby apartment with two young women from Scotland. Cittie didn't find work with any of the New York club bands, so he made a few dimes a day drumming on street corners with a cup at his feet. His take was not enough for rent, so he sometimes slept in alleys and other times lodged with various fellows, some of whom were nice enough to give him a blanket and a corner but others who were just looking for someone, he discovered to his dismay, to rob or someone to rape. He found himself beat up more than he would want to admit, though often those who decided to roll him for his meager tips ended up with a split head or broken arm, for Cittie did not take attacks lying down. A few nights he spent in jail for vagrancy. The company there was terrible but the food tolerable. The winter was the worst, with snows that blew around him like razor-teethed demons determined to bite through his coat or claw down into his collar, up his sleeves or into the cracks in his shoes. Through the depths of winter his fingers were often too cold to drum, so in January and February he made a few coins begging or performing odd jobs when odd jobs presented themselves — hauling firewood and coal, delivering messages, shoveling pathways from store fronts to street-side through the dense and heavy snowfalls. Once a week, regardless of weather, he took a note to Suzanne's apartment and slipped it into her mailbox, to let her know he was alive.

But spring came at last, and in May he walked to Coney Island after finding a handbill promoting new shows at the Dreamland amusement park. One was a band of men claimed to be "bloodthirsty Zulu warriors," men who danced around in outfits deemed savage enough by the show's promoter, Dick Bergman, tooting wooden flutes, clacking painted sticks together, banging drums, and shaking rattles adorned with lion's teeth and tiger claws, which in truth were the claws and canines of St. Bernards or Great Danes. Cittie sat outside the Dreamland office on a small bench, waiting politely for Bergman to speak to him. The man came out, in a hurry, and so Cittie followed him on foot across the broad expanse of the park, explaining how he was an excellent drummer and would do the band proud. He even did some rolls on the snare drum as they walked, and at last Bergman, tall, red-haired, and impatient, stopped and gave Cittie a quick, cock-eyed once-over, straightened his bowtie and bowler hat, and said, "Huh. Well, you're dark enough. If you got rhythm and can howl and pretend not to know English and obey orders, we have a spot for you. Our main drummer is a fool, always bucking the system, trying to tell me my job. I don't tolerate that and he's out on his ass as of tomorrow. I'll take you on if you ain't one to get uppity when you don't like what's going on."

"No, sir, ain't uppity. I just like to drum."

"Drum and dance and howl."

"Yes, sir."

"And wear what we tell you to wear."

"Yes, sir."

"Then go see the wardrobe over at the Zulu band pen. He'll suit you up."

The job hours were long — from the time the park opened at 10 in the morning until it closed at 2 a.m. Cittie's costume consisted of a felt loincloth stitched with clay beads, a feathered headdress that looked more American Indian than African, and leather leg and armbands that grew tighter over the course of the day in the heat. He'd had to endure a piercing of his nose, through which a sharpened bone was shoved through for added effect, a bone he had to sleep with for more than a month before the hole healed and he could take it out at night. But the money was the best he'd ever made, and in June he wrote an actual letter and bought a postage stamp, and mailed it to Suzanne, telling her of the various jobs to be found in any of the three Coney Island amusement parks, of the gaiety and sea air, of the fact that they might be able to visit with one another every so often without being noticed or harassed. He wrote, "If there was ever a place somebody could forget the past, it's here at Coney. Always lights and music and laughing. There's work if you want it. Please come."

Suzanne did. She quit her job at the mattress and pillow shop, moved to Coney, got a room over the Moons' store and a position selling tickets at Luna Park. She never told Cittie if she liked it better there or not, she never seemed happy or at peace, but at least now he could watch over her as best he could, even if he knew he was just pretending to be her protector.

SIX

August 1909

1

Sleep came at some point, though it did Suzanne no good. She dreamed of fires and flashes of white, of a dead woman with no head rising up off a hotel bed to pursue her down a narrow hall filled with mirrors to a corner where there was no retreat. She screamed against the wall, screamed as she slid to the floor, then screamed herself awake. Mrs. Moon was pounding on the floor from below, shouting, "Shut up, up there! I've had just about enough of your nightmares! Learn to sleep quiet or find yourself another place to live!"

2

Six days following the murders at the Capital Hotel, more took place inside the Pavilion of Fun at Steeplechase Park. A young mother, Julia Palmer, and her two young daughters, Jane and Susan, were the victims, their heads crushed much like those of the Capital victims and their bodies left in the Mirror Maze beneath a long crumpled coat where they were found by a maintenance man after the park closed for the night. Fingers were immediately pointed at possible suspects, from the woman's drunken husband to a retarded teenaged boy who got away from his father while in the park to the old man who helped escort riders on and off the most popular of the park's attractions, the Steeplechase Ride. Of course, park owner George Tilyou wouldn't stand for any time lost in making money, so he closed only the Mirror Maze to the public and even offered

a special "two patrons for the price of one" admission the day
following the deaths.

Suzanne received the second note from Lieutenant Granger as
she stood sweating and selling tickets to impatient customers at the
entrance to Luna Park. She grimaced as the messenger boy handed
it to her, and felt the curious gaze of Coralie Granger immediately
fall on the folded paper in her hands. Suzanne stepped away from
her booth, waving her customers over to Adelaide's line, and went
out to the street where Coralie could no longer ogle. She unfolded
the paper, took a deep breath, and read the request, written in
harried, hesitant pen.

"Miss Heath. I don't plan on making a habit of asking for your
help. In fact, it could well be you can't or don't care to help. But as
you picked up on something at the Capital Hotel, and this newest,
most heinous crime bears a similar aspect that you may see for
yourself, I wonder if you might come to Steeplechase as soon as
possible. If you would rather not, I understand. I promise my men
will not give you grief should you show up."

God. Damn it.

Suzanne refolded the paper and put it in her pocket. She glanced
over at the ticket takers and then west up Surf Avenue where
Steeplechase Park held a prominent, garish, and powerful presence.
An airship ride spun a good seven stories above the ground, a giant
Ferris wheel turned round and round, and the enormous, enclosed
Pavilion of Fun — a five-acre building of glass and steel — glared
in the sunlight, hinting at the excitement within. On the exterior
wall, hanging high for all to see, was Funny Face, a large, smiling
countenance of a man with way too many teeth in his mouth.
Funny Face always chilled Suzanne. Many thought him amusing
and enticing. She found him cold, calculating.

Asking leave from Mr. O'Rourke and only gaining begrudging
permission because the request had come from the Coney Island
police, Suzanne changed into her street clothes and walked the
bustle of Surf Avenue toward Steeplechase Park. She had only been
inside this place once, at the recommendation of Cittie who said
she might find some light-hearted entertainment within. On the
contrary. She hated the place the moment she entered, for unlike
Luna and Dreamland, which had ordinary, arched entrances that

opened onto broad, sunny plazas filled with food booths and trinket stands, and then broke into various pathways leading to shows and rides, Steeplechase forced everyone who paid for their tickets to first enter the park's Pavilion of Fun by way of the automated Funny Staircase and the Barrel of Love, a slowly revolving, six-foot-wide, twenty-foot-long wooden cylinder intended to throw those who passed through off their balance, off their feet, and into any others who happened to be in the barrel at the same time.

While Steeplechase Park fronted on Surf Avenue, the main entrance was on the side, off the Bowery. Suzanne took Bushman's Walk into the crowded hubbub of independent shows, theaters, rides, shops, game booths, and eateries. Bright posters and billboards promised everything from "best lunches in all the world" to "most fun you'll ever have." Countless American flags flapped overhead as people of all shapes, sizes, and ages squeezed past, laughing, shouting, arguing, carrying parasols, packages, babies, cheap prizes. Past Henderson's Vaudeville Theater, Stauch's Restaurant, clam and crab vendors, pony rides, haunted houses, and the steep and narrow Drip the Dips roller coaster. Stepping over spilled beer and ice cream, downed toddlers and lost handkerchiefs. Then, like a behemoth appearing through the fog, there was the gigantic, garish Funny Face, grinning with huge red wooden lips and vicious white wooden teeth, hanging directly over the entrance to Steeplechase. Suzanne watched as cheerful patrons paid for their tickets for the park and then elbowed their way onto the rising staircase to vanish in the darkness of the barrel at the top. No one seemed concerned that a family had been killed and left like forgotten bits of sandwich inside that very pavilion. Having fun was serious and important business, to take precedence over anything that might dampen it.

Suzanne showed Granger's note to the ticket seller and he waved his hand, giving Suzanne permission to step upon the upward-moving staircase. She got on just behind a mother with several young sons who turned on the rising steps to stare at Suzanne. She avoided their gazes and watched over their heads as the Barrel of Love grew closer, larger, a black shadowy maw into which people at the top of the stairs stumbled, giggling, squealing.

Had this family been here just a day earlier, perhaps they would have wound up the victims in the Mirror Maze. Life smashed into death. Left like trash for the custodian to clear away.

Suzanne took a breath and tightened her shoulders. A job to do. Amends to make, if the bottomless pit of her sin could ever to be filled with acts of contrition. If there was a connection to the murders at the Capital, she hoped she would find it, so they could determine then apprehend the killer. And she would be done with her duty.

Perhaps. Perhaps not.

The stairs dumped the mother and sons out into the Barrel of Love, with Suzanne immediately behind them. The mother did her best to walk ahead with shuffling steps to the left to keep herself upright, but the boys let the barrel have its way with them, and they tried to climb up the revolving sides only to slide back down again, a tumbling tangle. Suzanne held back several feet, trying her best to imitate the mother's careful steps. The wood was slippery, however, from polish and spit and sweat, and her shoes couldn't keep purchase, and down she went on her hands and knees. Behind her, an elderly gentleman entered the barrel and shouted, "Fred, what is this? I'll break my hip!" The bemused reply, "Move on, Papa, the quicker the better!"

Suzanne crawled the rest of the way out, and then drew herself free to the applause of people who had gathered to watch and laugh at the clumsy exits of those who came after them. One of the little girls spun about and tried to crawl back into the barrel but her mother grabbed her hand and said, "Come on, Sadie. This way, dear!"

Come on. This way, dear! That could have easily been what the mother told her two girls when they entered the Mirror Maze. *It's not frightening, it's fun! Hold my hand, you'll be fine.*

Stop it, Suzanne. Find it. Find Granger. Do your job.

She took the flight of steps down to the main floor, glancing up as the wooden Steeplechase horses whooshed past along the exterior of the western glass wall on their steel rails, their riders clinging to the reins and leaning forward as if to urge their colorful wooden steeds onward to victory.

The Mirror Maze was in a far corner, past the Insanitarium stage where a little clown poked men with a cattle prod and gusts of air sent giggling women's skirts up over their heads, the spinning

Human Roulette Wheel, and the giant plaster elephant from which were dispensed cold beers and lemon phosphates from alternate holes at the end of its trunk. The maze was cordoned off, and Officer Osier, thin and blond and bored, stood inside the rope. He just hitched his chin in the direction of the maze entrance, then crossed his arms and looked out across the milling pavilion crowd.

There was little Suzanne hated more than mirrors, and so she focused on the floor rather than the walls as she felt her way in through the tight passages and sharp turns, following a red ribbon someone had put down to lead to the crime scene. She could hear the voices deep within, mumbled, monotone. The corridors grew narrower with each turn, now no more than two feet wide. The light from the entrance was swallowed up, and only tiny bulbs, spaced well apart, offered any illumination. How anyone could think wandering through a confusing labyrinth, coming face to face with oneself at every turn and every dead end was fun was beyond her. If nothing else, it made her feel as if she were walking into Hell. She paused, closed her eyes to still her nerves, and then continued on.

The bodies were in a central area of the maze, a room the size just a bit larger than Suzanne's small bedroom. At their deaths they had been shoved up against the wall and covered in a large black coat. In the darkness beneath the coat they would have not caught many laughing, preoccupied people's attentions. The lights in the room gave a deathly yellow wash to everything they touched. The bodies were still against the wall, but the coat had been removed.

Granger and Whitman stood still as the photographer, a man no taller than a child with broad shoulders and smoldering cigarette clamped in his teeth, positioned his camera near the feet of the victims, angled it down on the tripod, and snapped a shot. The flash and pop were startling. Suzanne flinched. Another position of the camera, another flash. Another position, another flash.

Granger said, "Thank you, Woods. You can go on, now." Woods nodded, flicked cigarette ash onto the floor, and then began packing his equipment into a leather suitcase. Whitman looked down his crooked nose at Suzanne, and then at the bodies, as if daring her to say something.

When Woods was gone, Granger said, "I wasn't sure you'd come this time, Miss Heath, but appreciate you offering your help again."

At the word *help*, Whitman coughed loud and long then shrugged as if he'd really had a rasp to clear away.

"The…faces, heads, crushed like those of the couple in the Capital. I don't know if there is a connection, but there are no witnesses and no clear evidence around or about. I'll only ask you this one more time, and pray God this is the last of this sort. If you can let us know if there is a connection, then at least we'll have that. We'll have something to go on."

Suzanne nodded.

"Seems actions spurred by a fit of anger, the destruction of the bodies. Or perhaps the killer has an issue with faces. Or perhaps wants to leave the most bloody spectacle possible, to show his power."

"Perhaps."

Suzanne looked at the woman and the girls. A sob caught in her throat, and her stomach clamped, threatening to send her breakfast up and out. She angrily swallowed both the sob and the half-digested food and knelt on the floor. It was slick with dried blood.

"I suppose you've considered tracking down the owner of the coat."

"We will. But if one man owns that same coat, then one hundred do. And there are no witnesses we can find who saw anyone go in with a coat and leave out without one."

"I'll do what I can," she said.

"You don't want to be here, do you?"

Suzanne huffed and glanced over her shoulder. "And you would ask me that? I do what I must, just as you do what you must. Please don't say any more about it."

The mother's hand was cold, stiff, the fingernails broken below the quick as if there had been a violent struggle prior to her death. A delicate feature, once warm, once sensitive and likely kind, always available to hold her daughters' hands, stroke their hair, wipe away their tears of fear, of pain. Suzanne would not touch the little girls, for what the mother experienced, they experienced. The pain she felt, they felt. The fear that engulfed her engulfed them. If she were to feel and experience the woman's death, so be it. But she could not bear to feel the death of a child again. Not ever again.

The dead hand lay still in Suzanne's own and Suzanne waited

but sensed nothing. She peered briefly over at the mother's face, a face with one pale green eye open and the other crushed into the back of the skull. The cheekbones were flattened nearly to the floor, and her teeth lay in the glistening mass of blood and pulp that once was her jaw. There was no nose to speak of, and pink brain tissue oozed out through the top of her head into the hat that clung precariously to the tangled, crusted hair like a frightened animal.

"Anything?" asked Granger.

Suzanne shook her head. She hoped there would be nothing. But nothing for Granger would be nothing for the butchered family. Nothing for justice. No movement toward forgiveness. And so she focused. She drew down hard in her mind.

"You saw white at the other scene," Granger prompted. "Something about white."

"Please, shhh," said Suzanne.

Whitman chuckled dismissively.

Suzanne put the mother's hand down, and then gently lifted the woman's arm. She could feel the broken bones shifting within the flesh. She put the arm down, touched the abdomen, and then jerked her hand away.

"The woman is with child."

"Did you sense that?" asked Granger. "Are you seeing something now?"

"No, I felt it, as anyone would have with a bit of pressure."

"Four victims, then," said Whitman. "Quite a day for the killer. I wonder if he knew her condition. Again, I suspect the husband, Michael, a factory foreman with muscles big as a bull's. You talked to him, Lieutenant. Can't you imagine it? He works long hours to feed his family, breaks his back and slaves day after day, and here they are, wasting his money on frivolity."

"The father was devastated, Whitman. He said they'd received free tickets to Steeplechase, and he was happy they were going to have a fun day of it. He'd given them money for the day, with his blessing. And he has a solid alibi. You know that."

"Puh. I heard that. Not sure I believe the man, nor his co-workers. Could be covering for him as a friend."

Suzanne held the mother's hand again. Waited. Bored down.

Then, "I have nothing for you. Nothing other than her family way condition."

"Did you try?"

"Would I waste my time coming here just to have a look at dead bodies? Would I come here just for sport?"

Granger rubbed his mouth, seeming more irritated than disappointed this time. Suzanne suspected he had been ridiculed lightly at her first invitation to help, but now would be blatantly made fun of. Perhaps even reprimanded by a higher-up.

Shit.

She caressed the woman's cold hand.

"Miss Heath?" said Granger.

"Shh!"

"Huh," said Whitman. "Here we go again."

"Shut your mouth, Whitman, or get out of here."

She tucked her head. And there. Faint but certain. The prickling at the corner of her eyes, the tightening, the sense of lightheadedness. She drew air through her teeth.

"Anything, Miss Heath?"

A sudden flash of white. A blast of fierce cold that takes her breath away.

It slammed into her consciousness, as if the spirit of the dead mother was demanding vengeance, demanding to be heard.

Or perhaps the evil deed was an entity unto itself, and wanted to play with Suzanne's soul and heart, to torment and haunt her.

"You're shivering," said Granger. "Are you cold? Is it cold where…where you are now?"

Freezing, milk-white air, swirling around her. Suzanne works to maintain her balance, measure her breathing. The cold sears her lungs.

"Miss Heath, you look ill."

The white whirls round and round, erasing everything beyond it. Suzanne feels herself spinning, too, round and round with it, slow at first then faster faster.

"Miss Heath, are you ill?"

Faster faster faster faster. Dizzying. Horrific.

"Miss Heath!"

Round round round faster faster faster faster. She begins to sweat in the cold white, sweat from nausea and the thick dread that wells in her stomach like rancid bile. Round round round round round round.

Oh, God, stop the spinning! Please God help me!

And then there are sharp-toothed rabbits just beyond the veils of white, visible in rapid winks, a moment there, a moment gone, dreadful, shadowy creatures with glowing pink eyes and twitching, spider-like whiskers.

Blink.

They grin and their teeth are razor-sharp.

Blink.

Closer now, closer through the white. A scent swirls with the white, a cloying, sweet scent that she remembers but can't recall.

Blink.

Grinning rabbit mouths filled with clattering, chattering teeth, close enough to touch.

Blink.

Spinning faster round round round round. She can't catch her breath. Her lungs hitch impotently.

There is a face now behind the sharp-toothed rabbits, indistinguishable except for the wide, gaping, Hell-dark grin.

"Stop!"

A hand came down across her face, a stinging blow that threw her out of the white and into the middle room of the Mirror Maze. "Miss Heath! Enough! What's the matter?"

Suzanne touched her face, the stinging spot where Granger had slapped her. What a blessed bit of pain.

"I'm sorry, Miss Heath. You looked as if you were going to die, yourself. Your face was white and it seemed you were choking. I can't have any more dead people to deal with."

"It's all right."

"Are you sick?"

"No."

"You looked like you'd eaten something, something poisoned. It looked as if you were having a hard time breathing."

"I had a foul slice of cheese few days ago from over at Stauch's," said Whitman. "Bound me bad for days. Couldn't make anything come out no matter. 'Bout to rupture my ass."

"Shut up, Whitman!"

Suzanne stood. Granger offered his hand but she waved him off.

"I saw white," she said. "Again. Cold white, swirling like a tornado. There were rabbits with teeth sharp as sharks, and a smiling face behind it all."

Granger's brow arced. "White? Rabbits?"

"Perhaps the murderer is Alice in Wonderland," said Whitman.

"A grinning face," said Granger. "Maybe it's Steeplechase's Funny Face."

"Oh, certainly, that's a lot of help there," said Whitman. "As if we didn't know where the murder took place."

Suzanne faced Whitman. "Damn it, just get the Hell out of here!"

"And you are?" Whitman squared his shoulders. "Not the officer in charge from where I'm standing. I don't take orders from some woman."

"Get the Hell out of here," said Granger.

"You aren't serious. I'm just expressing my opinions."

"We talked before this. We'll talk later. Get out. Now."

"That's twice you've been excused," called Suzanne as Whitman stalked from the room. "Shame you couldn't behave!"

"Was that necessary?" asked Granger.

"I thought so."

Granger shook his head, his lip curled in frustration. "Tell me what you think. Don't leave me without something to take back, Miss Heath."

"Not until you cover the bodies again."

Granger spread the coat over the three, though the fingers of the youngest girl protruded from beneath the edge, a tiny and silent plea.

"I'm still at a loss," said Suzanne. "What I saw was quite vivid. With that grinning face, it could be the murderer works here in Steeplechase Park, or someone who comes here regularly. It could be he raises rabbits, hates rabbits, is afraid of rabbits. Maybe he's an albino. I'm grasping at straws, here."

"Did you hear a voice? Something you might recognize again?"

"No." She put her hand to her temple where a headache was brewing.

"Damn it all. What am I to do with this? What you saw with

Coralie's situation was so much more clear. We had no trouble identifying the attacker."

"I don't know what to do with it. I want this off my plate as much as you want it off yours. If this is the same killer, and I suspect it is now, then I want him stopped as much as you."

Granger glanced around the tiny room. "I hate mirror mazes."

"I hate mirrors."

Granger nodded.

"At the very least, have the place fingerprinted. They're using them to help determine some criminals, I understand. Faurot would encourage it. You might find a match in the files."

"I know my job, Miss Heath."

"It was just a reminder."

"We've already taken care of it. We are not as backward as you might think."

"All right then."

He held up his hand. He'd had enough. "Good day, Miss Heath. Once again, should anything else come to you, please let me know. With God's good graces and the stealth and care of the men on our force, we won't find another situation like this, and so I won't be calling you out on a case again."

"We'll see."

"Besides, I have no doubt there are things you'd much rather be doing. Taking a holiday of your own. Shopping with girlfriends. Stepping out with your young man, perhaps."

Suzanne watched him as he spoke. It was obvious he was probing, picking, trying to figure her out, and with little more finesse than his daughter.

"Lieutenant Granger, I do what I must do."

They left the Mirror Maze, following the ribbon out to the open, sunlit arena that was the Pavilion of Fun. Suzanne blinked in the brightness. Osier said, "Have a good day, Miss Heath" and Suzanne only nodded at him. She could feel his smirks at her back as she walked away toward the exit.

3

Coralie caught Suzanne as she exited Steeplechase Park down the winding Silly Slide, yet another one of the park's offerings to those looking for a good time. Most of the patrons slid down with huge smiles on their faces — children, women, men, youths, and even the elderly in their black jackets or bonnets, shocked into cheerfulness as hems fluttered and top hats popped off. Not Suzanne Heath. Even as she careened downward in happy, slippery spirals, her face was solemn. Infuriatingly detached.

"Hello!" Coralie said as Suzanne's feet hit the ground and she gathered herself. "Suzanne! Hey there!"

Suzanne's brows drew together. "What are you doing here? It's not quitting time."

"No, it certainly isn't. I told O'Rourke he could take a long walk off a short pier. I'm done with that place."

"You resigned?"

"That's nice way to put it. I told him I'd had enough of sticky coins and grumbling old women and prissy young misses and this god-forsaken scratchy costume. I said, 'Find yourself another ticket seller, Mr. O'Rourke, I'm done in and gone!'"

Suzanne cocked her head, shrugged, and said, "So be it, then. I hope you can afford the new hat and shoes you are so fond of."

"Oh, no worries," said Coralie. "I've got my plan. There's a couple jobs opening up over at the Hell Gate ride in Dreamland. I know I can get the job. It's inside, out of the heat and dust. I wouldn't have to smile and pretend to like the customers who come through. All I'd have to do is wear a little devil costume and poke at folks at they ride by in their boats. Much more entertaining than a coin from you and ticket from me, a coin from you a ticket from me."

"I hope you get the job." Suzanne hiked off, up the narrow street, squeezing between patrons, holding her skirt.

"Wait!" Coralie called. She trotted after Suzanne, bumping into people, shouldering through. "Suzanne, slow down."

Suzanne looked back. "What do you want?"

"You went into the Mirror Maze."

"Yes. You know I did."

"So, tell me. Please tell me." She lowered her voice against the crowd. "Did you learn anything about the murders?"

Suzanne rubbed her forehead. "Coralie, enough. Just let this all be. I'm trying to help your father; I'm not trying to gather unseemly gossip for you to share about Coney Island."

"Oh, quit being so much gloom and doom. I just want to know what you saw, and if you learned anything. Come, Suzanne. Tell me."

"Gloom and doom? The deaths of a family is a bit more than gloom and doom."

"Oh, I know, and I'm sorry for them. But I'm just curious is all. My father tells me so little and my life is so boring! I swear I won't tell another soul. Come on, now. Should you help solve these cases, you'll be famous. You'll probably be given reward money, and that would be thanks to me for telling my father about you, for suggesting you get called in." She cocked her head and smiled as sweetly as she could manage. It almost always worked with the young fellows. Perhaps it would soften Suzanne a bit.

Suzanne stopped at a lemonade booth and slid a nickel over to the vendor. He poured some of the yellow liquid into a small glass, and Suzanne took it and drank it.

"Buy me one?" said Coralie lightly.

"Are you thirsty?"

"I could be, for a free drink."

Suzanne handed the glass back to the vendor and wiped her hand along her lip. "Coralie, go apply for your new job. Lost time is lost money, lost opportunity. I'm not going to tell you anything about the cases. I owe that much to the dead, that they retain the respect they deserve. I owe that much to your father, and his responsibility in finding the killer without loose talk spreading around."

"You are such a spoil sport!" Coralie pushed Suzanne slightly, causing the other woman to stumble into a little girl reaching for her own glass of lemonade. "Oh, sorry!" she said to the child. "Let me buy you another one."

"You certainly should," said the father, standing behind the little girl, arms crossed. "Clumsy and careless."

Coralie bought the child a drink, then followed Suzanne on though the Bowery's tight walkways. The day was growing almost unbearably hot, with the briny air from the ocean blowing down through the corridors and small spaces between the buildings.

"Did you feel anything when I touched you?" she called from behind. "When I pushed you?"

Suzanne ignored her.

"Suzanne, damn it!"

Suzanne picked up her pace. A tall and bulky young man in fine clothing stepped out of a trinket shop in front of Suzanne, doffed his cap, and said with a grin, "Well, a good morning to you, my dear and lovely lady. May I treat you to an ice cream or pastry?"

Suzanne said, "No, thank you," and kept on walking.

Coralie, however, stopped beside the man and said, "Just ignore her. She's quite the cold thing, no interest in men whatsoever."

"Indeed?"

"Indeed. I, however, would adore an ice cream. And I know every ice cream seller in Coney Island."

"Yes? And you are a foreign girl?"

"Foreign?" She glanced down at her outfit and laughed aloud. "Oh, no! I just quit my job working over at Luna Park. But I think it's quite dandy, don't you? I could be a senorita from Spain, couldn't I? I only need some castanets to make music."

"You like music?"

"I like everything here. I'm from here, you know. I love ice cream, music, moving pictures, roller coasters, handsome men."

The man put his cap back on his head and crooked his arm for Coralie to take. "Then I think you and I shall have a most lovely day. Perhaps even a lovely evening."

"Perhaps you're right."

She slipped her arm in his, felt the power of freedom once more, and decided that applying for the Hell Gate job could wait until tomorrow.

4

Both the Symposium of Secrets and the 3000 A.D. theater were closed for the day, for the proprietor had big plans. Plans that sat like a sweet treat on the tongue—delicious, beautifully addicting and perfectly satisfying.

The proprietor sat on the back bench in the 3000 A.D. theater, silently, thinking, as Rex swept the floor clean of the bits of candy trash left behind by the audiences the night before. Rex hated being watched so closely, which made it all the more enjoyable to do so.

He swept and sweated, glancing at the proprietor every so often to see if he was doing a good job. The proprietor never let on one way or other. Always best to keep Rex on edge. It was also best to constantly remind him who was boss and who was the peon. It was all part of his management. It worked like a charm.

After a long moment, the proprietor said, "Rex."

Rex stopped and looked up, anxiety in his large eyes, the broom shaking in his hands. He knew the tone of the voice.

"Rex, I'm not pleased."

He paused, then, "You ain't? How come?"

"I don't have to explain myself to you, now do I?"

"I ain't done what you asked? I tried. I tried hard."

"Yes, you have. But that doesn't mean I'm not pleased."

Rex waited. The growing fear on his face was just what the proprietor wanted to see, and it was mildly entertaining.

"What you want me to do, then? I'll get you something to eat, maybe? Hot dog? Fish sandwich? Maybe a cup of chili?"

"No, no," said the proprietor. "I'm not hungry."

"Oh."

"Bring out the drones."

Rex dropped the broom and hurried behind the stage. With some muffled grunts and shouts, he drove the mindless minions around to the stage where they stood, staring at nothing, some licking their lips, others drooling.

"You want me to make 'em dance for you? I got it so they can take a few steps at the same time, together. Maybe we could add a little music to the show, like they's a chorus line. Maybe?"

"Dancing would make this a comedy show," said the proprietor. "You think this is a comedy show, Rex?"

"Some people laugh sometimes..."

"And most are horrified as they should be."

"Yeah."

The proprietor looked at the drones on the stage, then back at Rex. "I'm not pleased because I'm bored. Bored. You know what bored is, don't you?"

"Uh-huh."

"Do you ever get bored, Rex?"

"I don't know..."

"You don't. Simple-minded people don't get bored with their circumstance. In a way, I suppose that's a blessing."

"I guess so."

"You know I get bored easily."

"I guess so."

"Cheer me up, Rex."

"What?" He swallowed hard. His hands were already glistening with nervous sweat. "How you want me to do that?"

"I'd like to hear a song. Something different from those blasted bands that blare up and down the Bowery walkways and never shut up. Sit."

Rex sat, but even then was a head taller than the proprietor. He looked at his fists, balled in his lap, and waited.

"Sing a song for me, Rex."

Rex looked up. "Huh?"

"You heard me. Sing."

"Sing what?"

"Something I will enjoy."

"I don't know what you like. Never heard you say nothing 'bout what you like."

The proprietor leaned in close and hissed. "Sing! And I best like what you sing! Do you understand me?"

Rex opened his rotted mouth and through his rotted teeth sang a tangled rendition of "In the Shade of the Old Apple Tree." The proprietor listened, hands in pockets, foot tapping to the rhythm, the only thing Rex had right.

When Rex was done, he looked at the proprietor with great hope in his baggy eyes. The proprietor said, "I don't care for that song. It's pathetic. You best try again and do better this time."

"I don't know what to sing," whimpered Rex.

"Something that will please me. Don't you know yet what pleases me? You've worked for me since May and you still don't know?"

"No. I mean…" Rex licked his lips. Then began on a hopeful high note, "Take me out to the ball game, take me out with the crowd. Buy me some peanuts and Cracker Jack, I don't care if I never get back. Let me root, root, root for the home team, if they don't win, it's a shame. For it's one, two, three strikes, you're out, at the old ball game."

"Damn, but I hate baseball," said the proprietor. "What a waste of energy, money, time it is."

"Oh."

"Enough of this. Stick out your tongue, Rex."

"What? Why? I'll sing something else. Something you'll like, I promise."

"Since when do you question me?"

"Oh, God, please don't do nothing to me."

"Now, Rex."

"Please. No."

"Now!"

Rex stuck out his tongue. He babbled around it, "I din know you din like bathesball! Pleathe don' do nothin'!"

The proprietor stared at Rex, head cocked, eyes narrowing to slits. "You know my power. You know I can move things, destroy things, can even stop or start things sometimes if I focus long enough."

"Yeth. I do. Pleathe don'..."

"Hush! Now. You've seen what I can do. I think I need to remind you, however."

"Buth why...?"

"Because I'm not pleased. Because I'm feeling bored. Because I just feel like practicing a little. And a little practice never hurts."

Rex's eyes grew even wider.

"Well, it won't hurt me, that is," chuckled the proprietor. "Now don't say another word or it shall be all the worse for you."

Rex began to whimper.

The proprietor gazed at Rex's tongue, fat, stinky, flopped out of his mouth like an old cod. "Hold still now." The proprietor stared at the tongue, concentrated, focused. Rex began to shriek and blood welled in his mouth. He struggled to his feet but the proprietor said, "You sit down!" He fell back onto the bench, eyes fish-belly white and his shoulders jumping.

"Now, where was I. Oh, yes, the tongue. Stick it back out."

Rex stuck it back out.

"This evening I am attending a private meeting in Manhattan, a dinner party," said the proprietor as Rex's tongue, with a wet crackling, ripping sound, was slowly and steadily torn from its root. Rex sobbed, dug his fists into his chest as the blood poured bright and red down his chin to his shirt. "It's a gathering of those who follow the teachings of Aleister Crowley. They study his books, think they might claim some power by learning of the man, obeying his law. Fools. The man's a sloppy charlatan, spouting worthless magical nonsense."

The proprietor considered the tongue, now dangling from a small strip of flesh, and Rex's puffed, agonized face. "Ah, to Hell with it, let's finish this quickly." And with a single force of thought, the tongue ripped itself the rest of the way out and flipped onto the floor like the stub of a cold cigar. Rex squealed and folded over against the pain.

"As I was saying, I shall visit the group, share with them a sampling of what I can do, what I've learned and perfected over the years, and see if they are smart enough to turn their attentions from following the ridiculous Frater Perdurabo to following me. I don't doubt they'll see the wisdom in a switch."

Rex fell to his knees and clawed at his mouth. He wailed and choked up thick gouts of blood, then turned his eyes pleadingly up to the proprietor. The proprietor patted his hair.

"Yes, yes, hold on. I don't care for you to bleed to death. You have helped me in many ways, so I at least owe you that." The proprietor found a polishing rag balled up on a windowsill and shoved it into Rex's gaping mouth. "Press down onto the wound until you stop bleeding."

Rex coughed, gagged.

"Do you understand?"

Rex nodded, weeping, and grunted around the rag. His eyes pleaded, *Why?*

"Why did I do this? I told you. I was bored. And because I can. Get up now, and quit complaining. I've actually done you a favor. For how often did you really need to talk? Your job is to listen, to watch, and to do as I say. You might find it refreshing to not have to worry about replying anymore. One less thing to think about."

Rex rubbed his scarlet lips, pushed at the rag, wept.

"Enough of that. I said get up! One of our idiots up on the stage has shit down his leg. Seems you forgot his diaper or you haven't changed it recently. Get to work."

Rex gulped, gagged, rubbed his snotty nose. He nodded meekly.

"See?" said the proprietor. "You don't need to say a thing to do what you must do."

Rex stumbled to the stage and herded the minions behind the curtain. The proprietor looked at the blood on the floor. "And when you're done back there, come mop up this mess!"

5

It was the sweet smell that disturbed her almost as much as the sight of the dead mother and dead daughters in the Mirror Maze. She knew the scent, but couldn't recall from where. It was a key, one of the keys, yet it hung in the back of her mind in the darkest corner where the fingers of concentration could not reach.

Suzanne sat on the sand in the dark, waiting for Cittie, her knees drawn up beneath her skirt, her fingers linked together around them. No one was out in the waves tonight; there had been shark sightings earlier in the day and word had gotten around. There were a few couples down the beach in either direction, cuddling on blankets, giggling in the moonlight, drinking, smoking. Suzanne's headache was only now beginning to recede.

Was the scent from a flower she should recognize? A cologne? A fruit, perhaps? She bore down, trying to touch the scent and bring it out but it eluded her. It was there but beyond reach and beginning to fade. In another few hours, it would be gone.

A man in shirtsleeves and rolled trouser legs trotted up the sand with his dog. The dog, a large yellow creature with friendly eyes, slowed and walked up to Suzanne, sniffed her hand ever so gently, then padded back to his master. In that brief touch, Suzanne caught a warm, soft vision. A little apartment, a soft pillow on the floor, a fire on the hearth, a gentle hand on the head, soothing words. A man's voice saying, "Good boy, Fletcher. Good boy."

"Good boy, Fletcher," said Suzanne softly. The dog stopped, looked back at Suzanne, and then went on with his master.

There was warmth in the world. There was caring, compassion, even love. Out in the world. In other people's homes, in other people's lives. Back at the Waif Asylum.

She looked down the beach at the couple. They were now deep

into petting, his hand under her blouse and she was trying to muffle her squeals of delight with her face into his shoulder. Perhaps this was love, or the beginnings of it. Even in the dim light, he looked happy. Even with the sound of the waves against the shore and her face against him, her soft giggles were happy. A cop might come along and whack the young fellow with his stick and chastise the young woman for loose morals. He might even arrest the two for their behavior. But at the moment, the couple seemed content and convinced that the dark of night kept them safe.

Suzanne picked up a handful of sand and threw it. The biggest chunk of the wet clot flew far enough to land in the water. Maybe she should try out to be a ball player, be a Bloomer Girl, travel around the country, see things she'd never seen before. It might be nice to take a trip across the ocean, to see England or Scotland. As a student she'd read the books by the Bronte sisters. *Wuthering Heights. Jane Eyre. The Tenant of Wildfell Hall.* She had been fascinated with the heroines' universal struggles against temptation, deception, and their strivings for love and redemption. She was swept away with the descriptions of the wild and rugged moors, of the winds over the vast wilderness. One could roam for hours, perhaps even days and not see another soul. One could be alone with the grasses and rain, the sunlight and moonlight. There would be time to listen to the call of birds or humming of insects. Time to lie back upon a day-warmed field and consider the clouds. One might even find God there.

Someday, I'll go there. When all this is over, I will go and find peace. I will find joy.

She thought of Cittie, and smiled. In England, she'd heard, society didn't scoff at a white woman with a black man, nor arrest them. If Cittie went with her, they could be together. Maybe she would even trust him enough at that time to touch him, let him touch her, hold her, explore her body, and her his, tenderly, freely, urgently…

We will find joy.

Then her imaginings fell apart, as they always did. The moment of hope was crushed and thrown away like a handful of sand and deep sadness rose up to fill its place. "What is joy, anyway?" she muttered. "Mirror Mazes are supposed to be joyful."

Several other couples came along the beach, closer into focus, then moving on, the night softening them into gray, featureless beings. The yellow dog ran back up the beach, chased by his master, who was laughing and calling.

Perhaps the killer was on the beach at this very moment, in the darkness beneath the Steeplechase Pier or Dreamland's Steel Pier, watching, waiting. Selecting the next victim, cudgel or hammer in hand, ready to smash another head. Or heads. Suzanne placed her palms on the sand and pressed, wondering if she might detect something there in the ground, a faint current that would let her know if danger stood poised on the shore. But there was only the sense of cool, the sense of grit.

"Maybe we should both start carrying a weapon."

Startled, Suzanne looked up to see Cittie beside her, arms crossed.

"What?"

"A weapon. I heard about the murders at Steeplechase. Mother and children? God have mercy. Crazy man on the loose, smashin' people to bits. I don't want nothin' to happen to you, or to me." Cittie sat, looked at Suzanne. "You hear what I'm sayin'?"

"I hear you."

"Just keep a little knife with you, in your pocket. Something to poke his eyes out, should he come after you. Okay?"

"Maybe I will."

"No maybes, Suzanne. You hear me?"

"I hear you."

"You ain't lookin' too good, if you don't mind me sayin'. You look twisted up, worn out."

Suzanne considered Cittie's face in the pale moonlight. His once-round face now more squared, young yet strong. His eyes showed a thoughtfulness that had always been there but had been honed more keenly over time. There was even a remaining trace of innocence in spite of what he'd seen and experienced in his life. It made her want to cry for him and for her, but she only took a long breath and said, "Thanks. That's quite the compliment."

"Anything you wanna tell me? About, well, you know."

"I didn't determine the killer, obviously, or I'd be looking at bit better than I obviously do. I wanted to know who it was, and I didn't want to. It's almost a certainty that the same person who killed the family in the Mirror Maze killed the couple at the Capital Hotel. But I have nothing at all concrete, just some bizarre images that don't mean anything."

"Want to tell me what you saw?"

"I just have to think about it, not talk about it. Sorry, Cittie."

"S'okay. You'll figure it out, if you want to."

"Perhaps."

Cittie sighed. "I feel so sorry for you, though. Back at the asylum you used to smile and even laugh. Back when you was Rachel. Now, though, I think I only seen you smile once, maybe twice. And laugh? When was the last time you laughed? You know what I'd pay to hear you laugh? Well, maybe not a whole day's pay, but a half, I'd guess."

Suzanne chuckled. "Thanks, Cittie."

"There you go! Want half today's pay?"

"You keep it."

They sat as they always sat, listening to the waves, watching the white lip of foam on the black water as it rose and fell, always reaching out for them but never quite touching them.

Then Cittie said, "I wanna try something."

"What?"

"Trust me?"

"Sort of. Yes."

"Hold my hand. You ain't got those gloves on now. I want you to hold my hand."

"No, I don't think so."

"So you don't trust me?"

"Cittie, it's not that."

"Here." He held out his hand.

"Cittie, don't."

"What you think you'll see if my skin meet yours? Somethin' dark and terrible? You know more 'bout me than anybody else in this world. Ain't nothin' I got to hide. But I remember hearin' in a church meetin' once that we were given hands to work and to hold one another. Think that's true?"

Suzanne looked at the hand, dark skin against the dark sand.

"You're scared."

"Yes," she said.

"My hand ain't nothin' but an offerin'. I want you to know there's people you can really trust."

"I trust you."

"Not so much as you think."

"I trust you as much as I can."

Cittie looked at her, then at his hand, then withdrew it. He pulled a half-eaten Hershey chocolate bar from his pocket and offered a bite to Suzanne. She declined.

"One day, girl, I'm going to cheer you up." Cittie smelled the chocolate then took a bite. "I kid you not. I gonna have you laughin' so hard you'll pop your seams. Things gonna turn 'round for you. One day, we gonna be sittin' here on the beach and you gonna look up at the moon and say, 'This is good now.'"

"Is that so?" Suzanne smiled slightly.

"Oh, you bet it's so." Cittie nodded enthusiastically. "You just wait. I promise you someday you'll say, 'This is good. This is right.'"

"Okay. I'll hold you to that."

"Good then." He took a bite of chocolate and then put it back in his pocket. "And get you a weapon, Suzanne. Get you a knife. I got me a wrench, right here in my pocket. Gonna keep it with me at all times. Nobody gonna get the best of Cittie Parker."

6

"I think we should go on to dinner," said Coralie as the young man slammed his shoulder against the guest room door, shoving it open to reveal the other young men in the room. The beers he'd consumed over the last three hours had made him a little less than steady on his feet, though he still had a great deal of energy.

The young man's name was Robert, and he was a rich dandy at that, fun-loving, rich, surprisingly affectionate, and someone who loved riding Coney's coasters, slides, and revolving swings as much as Coralie did. He enjoyed ice cream and drink, dancing and holding hands. Then, after an hour or so at Henderson's Music Hall, he said he wanted to treat her to a sumptuous meal as a thank you for spending the day with him. He'd walked Coralie back to the Grand Harmon Hotel, in which the well-known and popular Harmon's Restaurant was located.

But first, he said as they entered the hotel lobby, he needed to get some more cash out of his room. They took the stairs to the second floor, down the hall to the room. He opened the door and led her in by the hand.

Immediately, Coralie's stomach turned uneasily.

Two other young men were there, sitting on the beds, drinking dark liquid from fine glasses. A bottle of Bayer Heroin sat on the dresser beside a near-empty bottle of Scotch and full bottle of brandy. Clothes were scattered all over the floor. The window was open, letting in moths that danced and swooped around the gaslights on the wall.

"The restaurant in this hotel has the best sea bass and duck to be found," said Robert as the other men grinned at Coralie. She forced herself to grin back. "Let me find my money, it is here somewhere." He picked up a dark coat and dug through the pockets.

"Well, well, hello, my lovely young thing," said one of the young men, a thin chap with red hair and a curly beard. It seemed an effort for him to speak, though he was quite cheerful with the effort. "Did Robert bring you back for us? Thank you, Robert, that is so thoughtful of you."

"Watch what you say, Paul," said Robert. He pulled a money pouch from the jacket pocket and shook it in Paul's direction. "This is one fine lady. I'll not have you speak disrespectfully to her."

"A fine señorita," said Paul, his mouth lopsided and his eyes rheumy. "*Habla inglés*, señorita? Are you Robert's new friend? We're his new friends, thanks to his father's money! Robert's quite daft, you know, but we like him for his generosity. Don't we, Robert?"

The two men burst into gales of laughter that in a moment caused one to cough and spit into his hand.

"I'm not Spanish," said Coralie. "Robert, let's go on. It's late, and I'm hungry."

The second young man on the bed eased over onto his side and patted the mattress. "Come here, young woman. Did you tell us your name? What's her name, Robert? She looks pretty but I can't see all that well at the moment. Come here, my lady. I want a better look." He smirked, and Paul laughed.

Robert strode to the bed and backhanded the man across the face.

"Damn you, Robert!" said the man, struggling to his feet. "You want a round of fisticuffs with me?"

"Sit down, Barnaby!" said Robert. "You shan't challenge me, for who is it that is financing your time here?"

"Oh, go to Hell, Robert." The man sat back down, hard, on the bed.

Coralie lifted her head with as much feigned confidence as she could grasp. "I've had a grand day, Robert, and I thank you. But I didn't realize how late it was. I need to get home. My father will be waiting and I need to change out of this costume."

"I'll help you change out of the costume," said Paul. "Come here, darling."

Coralie spun about, pushed past Robert and into the hallway. She collected her skirt and hurried down the carpeted corridor until a hand grabbed her upper arm and whipped her back around. Robert's face was tomato red, and close, and furious.

"What was that?"

"I have to go home, Robert."

"Don't you ever walk away from me, Coralie!"

Coralie snarled. "I will if I want to!"

The blow stung her face, snapping her head back and driving her next retort down her throat. He grabbed the lacy collar of her Mexican blouse and hauled her nose up to his. His breath was thick and his eyes wide, strange. "No, you will not! You are my lady, Coralie. I know you are. I could tell the way you stayed with me today, took my arm, accepted my kisses. You are mine now. I will tell you what to do and what not to do."

"Ho, no, just wait a moment, Robert," said Coralie, steeling herself as best she could against the ever-increasing fear of her pounding heart. "We had a fine time, that's for certain. And I'm very thankful for your attentions and your treats, but…"

He slapped her again, and she lost her balance, falling back against the wall, knocking a framed print off and down to the floor. "What are you doing?" she cried. "Don't you dare strike me!"

Robert yanked her up and held her tightly. She struggled and kicked until he slapped her three more times, four. Her face burned and sparks flew before her eyes. Then, panting, she held up a resigned hand, forced a trembling smile, and said, "I'm sorry,

Robert. I think it was the beer making me act so." She softened her body, let her shoulders slump. "Do you forgive me?"

Robert's eyes stayed cold and wide, then slowly his lids lowered. "Oh, dear Coralie! Of course I do. I love you, you know. And I know you love me."

"Yes, Robert."

"Shall we have dinner?"

"Yes, Robert.

They walked down to the restaurant and he bought her a most expensive meal of roast mallard duck, boiled English potatoes, sweet breads with truffles, braised olives, and frozen puddings. He laughed and complimented as Coralie ate and tried to devise her escape.

It was nearly eleven as they left the hotel. Coralie thanked him again, profusely, and then reminded him that he offered to pay for her trolley ride home.

"Oh, you shan't ride home alone, my lady," said Robert. "I shall take you there myself, to make sure you are unharmed."

"Oh, no, no, I will be fine. No need to worry. I'm a Coney girl, remember. I take caution as I must. And my father will be waiting for me at the end of the line."

"You told me he works late this evening at the station, nearly 'til midnight, didn't you?"

"I...I don't recall."

"Well, I do," said Robert in a disturbingly cheerful voice. "Come now, darling, and we shall hop on the trolley!"

They did, and they rode north to Coralie's apartment with Robert holding Coralie hand and caressing her hair. At the stop he tried to insist he come in with her to "make sure no miscreants are hiding to hurt you." But Coralie convinced him that sometimes her father did come home earlier than planned and he would be furious to find her with a young man he didn't know. Robert acquiesced, saying should he and Coralie have a daughter someday, he would likely feel the same way. He kissed her soundly and said, "I have decided I won't be returning to Philadelphia, as my heart is here now. I will see you tomorrow, my sweet."

In the apartment, alone at last, Coralie dropped to the divan and buried her face in her hands.

7

She is at home in Tarrytown, in her childhood bedroom. It is early morning, and the sunshine has just begun its lazy crawl across the small Oriental rug on the floor, the one her father brought home from his most recent, extended trip. China dolls are lined up along the delicate white doilies on the bureau. Framed prints showing laughing children and their dogs playing in the grass hang on the walls. A rocking chair holds its spot near the bed. The bed is made up with a white satin spread and lace-trimmed pillows.

Suzanne sits on the floor near the spot of sunlight, petting a small gray cat. It purrs, looks up at her with squinty, contented cat eyes, and nuzzles her arm. Suzanne can hear activity round and about in the house. Someone is hammering downstairs, perhaps hanging up a painting. Someone is singing a song with a sweet tune that she almost recalls. Someone is walking up the steps, and they creak. She looks over at her door, waiting to see who it is.

The cat squirms in her lap and she looks down to find it is no longer a cat but a rabbit. The rabbit lays its head down on Suzanne's arm and says, "I'm Benjamin Simmons." It is cute, the way it said that in its tiny little rabbit voice, and Suzanne put out her fingers to pet the bunny on the head. But then its head cranes about and it opens its mouth, and Suzanne can see it is filled with razor-sharp teeth. She screams but can make no sound. She tries to stand but cannot move. The rabbit's ghastly teeth clamp down on her hand, drawing blood. Suzanne she flicks her hand and sends the bunny flying. It strikes the windowsill with a splat, leers back at her, winks, and then hops out the window.

The door swings opens. Suzanne's mother is in the doorway, holding some azaleas she'd cut from the side yard. Her head is enormous and her mouth is huge, smiling ear-to-ear like Steeplechase's Funny Face, like a giant clown's balloon, showing countless teeth that remind Suzanne of overly-polished piano keys. She holds out the azaleas; they melt like ice, dripping down her arms in dark pink rivulets. "Jesus loves me, this I know," she sings off-key and most gleefully. "But not you, child, to the devil you go. You, foul girl, will burn with fire, as angels play a cheerful lyre."

Suzanne is on her feet now, holding a little knife. She waves it at the hideous balloon-headed mother and backs into the bed. She tries to scream for Della but cannot. The knife goes limp in her hand; now it is a daffodil. She lets it fall.

The balloon-headed mother laughs, shrill and long.

The sunlight on the floor turns scarlet, bleeds outward across the floor in all directions and then up the walls. The entire room is engulfed in red. Suzanne watches, then turns back to her mother, but her mother is gone and Rosemary Reynolds is in her place. Rosemary, dead but on her feet, her mouth eaten away by time and decay, her eyes washed a sour-milk white, glazed. They don't blink but face Suzanne in a steady, lifeless yet accusatory gaze. Her hair, what is left of it, is covered in pine needles and a shiny, gelatinous mass. She sighs heavily, the air whooshing out through the rotting flesh of her chest, causing the ragged scraps of her school blouse to flutter. She steps forward, one foot dragging behind, for there is little left of it now. Animals have gotten to it. Animals up in the mountains.

Suzanne waves her arms. "Rosemary, no, no. Please, go back!"

Rosemary doesn't go back, but thumps slowly across the floor, across the spot of sun on the rug, trailing coagulated blood and something tiny and yellow that squirms within it. She opens her destroyed mouth and Suzanne can see that her tongue, too, is gone. Rosemary's upper lip, of which there is still a bit of skin, curls in a sneer.

Suzanne screams, climbs up onto the bed, slams her back against the headboard and can move no more. She shoves with her heels, hoping to drive herself through the headboard and wall behind it, to get away, get away! It does not work. Rosemary reaches the bed, her knees striking the side, and then fumbles and scrabbles up onto the mattress, drooling bloody saliva. Her teeth clack together, and they are sharp teeth now, like the rabbit's teeth, pointed like tiny spikes, glistening, chattering.

Oh my God, get away!

Suzanne throws her back against the headboard again. It rattles but does not give.

Rosemary crawls forward, teeth tapping, white eyes staring, one rotting hand groping forward for Suzanne's face.

"You loved me," Rosemary says, though she has no tongue, and it is the gurgling voice of a drowning woman, "but you let me die."

Get away! Suzanne puts her hands over her eyes but she can see through the fingers as if they were glass, see Rosemary's dreadful face coming closer, closer.

No!

Rosemary's mangled hand caresses Suzanne's check. She leans in for a kiss.

"God, no, get away!"

Suzanne jerked hard, opened her eyes. Her mattress was soaked and her heart thundered. Her breath came in frantic gulps, dry, sand-blasted. She rolled off the divan and stumbled to the window, shoved it open farther, and leaned out. A faint breeze stirred beneath the south Brooklyn moon. She looked up at that moon, at the faint, gray face there, who in that moment appeared, rather, like her dear friend from Madame Harlow's school so many years ago.

I can't undo what I did, Rosemary. I can't make it right. I can only try to make other things right.

She splashed her face with water from the basin, dusted her arms and chest with talcum powder, dressed, and quietly left her flat. It was not quite four in the morning, and most of the world was still, but there was the faint sound of voices in the apartments she passed by, horses nickering in their stalls, an occasional cock crowing in a backyard coop, confused by the time.

The fourteen-block walk to the Coney seemed longer in the dead of night. In the morning, when everything and everyone was alive and moving, the stroll was, if not pleasant, at least filled with distractions. Now, though, the walk seemed an eternity, with the streets stretching far beyond what they should stretch, with the breeze whispering conspiratorially from around the corners and unseen packs of dogs snuffling and growling at one another.

Some electric lights continued to shine in Coney Island, atop light poles along Surf Avenue and on the front porches of the more elegant hotels. Strings of lights outlined Steeplechase Park, Luna Park, and Dreamland. More lights came from several of the Bowery dance halls and bars, which would remain open as long as there were patrons willing to shell out coins for drink and music. But most of the places were shut and locked down, and the darkness between the pools of light was deep. Suzanne walked hard along the street, angry, wanting to drive out the bad with each footfall, wanting to stomp away the sin of this place by pounding it into the dust. East along Surf Avenue, past the Capital Hotel, which looked at her with callous rectangle eyes, content that it knew a secret that she did not. Past the chillingly still Steeplechase Park and down to Kensington Walk, where she entered the Bowery. The empty shops and stores and diners and rides, standing so close to one another, seemed to lean in over her and whisper in ominous voices. Suzanne wrapped her arms around herself tightly; it was a hot night, but an icy chill coursed through her body just beneath the skin.

Dim lights and an occasional bright one, piano and trumpet music through open doorways, stumbling drunks both men and women, and then long patches of shadows in which rats' eyes winked like fireflies. The Bowery did not feel dangerous during the day, with its bright awnings and flags and people dressed in their best holiday outfits, more often than not polite with one another even in the oppressive crowding. But at night, when the more genteel thrill seekers had gone home for supper, prayers, and bed, and the parks and most of the independent attractions were silent, there seemed to ooze from the pores of the Coney Island darkness a sticky seediness that clung to one's flesh like an oily sweat.

Suzanne walked up and down the Bowery alleys — Kensington Walk, Schwieckert's Walk, Stratton's Walk, Thompson's and Henderson Walk — her jaw set, fists clenched, feeling like someone ready for a boxing match with no ready opponent at hand. She sensed she was pacing the world, like she had to pace the world, pace it all, that nothing short of that much effort would make any difference. Out to Surf Avenue, then angling back into the Bowery by way of Henderson's Music Hall, past more late-night bars and eateries, more sots and a few pickpockets watching for easy targets, a couple cops on corners, silent coasters and silent cars of the Witching Waves ride, more skittering rats, more stray cats. She walked down to the entrance to Steeplechase Park, and stared at the Funny Staircase, now motionless, and the black spot at the top that was the Barrel of Love. Then her gaze shifted up to the giant, toothy Funny Face looking down from on high. She stared and it stared back.

"You're hideous," she said.

And you're grabbing at straws, it replied.

She removed one cotton glove and touched the locked metal gate in front of the staircase. The metal was surprisingly cold in the summer's night's heat. Perhaps there was something there, if she focused. If she thought about the mother and daughters and concentrated harder than she ever had before.

There was nothing.

The large billboard beside the staircase read, "Steeplechase Park, 25 Attractions With Admission of 25 Cents! George C. Tilyou welcomes you, yes, YOU, to the most wonderful place in the world!"

I wonder how many attractions the mother and her daughters saw before they decided to go into the Mirror Maze? Did they get their quarters' worth before they got their heads smashed?

What are those damnable rabbits? The fire? The white?

Cursing George Tilyou for not having better security in his park, Suzanne left Steeplechase, back down the central Bowery alley, her stride faster now than before, as if she was running toward something or away from something, she wasn't sure. It was as if the whole of Coney Island knew who she was, what she had done, what she wanted to do, and was daring her to give it her best.

Though she feared her best would never be enough.

She stepped into an unseen puddle of vomit, and then quickly stepped out. Her shoe stank and the sole was instantly sticky. It was all she could do to keep from vomiting, herself.

Oh, shit. Okay, not shit, vomit. She chuckled once, humorlessly. *I've got to get down to the shore and wash this off.*

She turned south onto Stratton's Walk and hurried beach-ward, wishing there was a handy rain barrel along the way. Several men came toward her in the middle of the walk, their arms linked, trying their best to hold each other up and get each other home. They glanced at Suzanne with rheumy eyes and continued on their way.

She walked as fast as she could without attracting attention. Passing on either side, in rapid succession were Becky's Beef House with its garish statue of a red-lipped woman riding a cow, The Green Peacock Bar, Coney Souvenirs, a small fenced area for "A Penny, A Pony" with a miniature riding ring and little stalls visible over the fencing. Tiny equine faces peeked out, muzzles munching on the evening's meal of old hay. Then came Wilton and Company's Fine Photography, then 3000 AD, Anderson's Eatery...

She stumbled, stopped, and whipped around. She stared at the closed and bolted door of the 3000 A.D. theater.

It had been so powerful it had shot up through her feet. A charge that had raced up her legs as if she had stepped on a frayed electrical cord, causing her knees to buckle.

Something, someone incredibly powerful had passed there or had stood there. Someone with enough concentrated psychic energy that Suzanne did not need to invoke it or take it through the naked flesh of fingertips or palm, but strong enough to drive into her from the ground.

Suzanne stared at the theater's wooden door, which was secured with a lock and chain.

He was here. He walked here.

"He visited this place," she whispered, her mouth dry as old bread. "Maybe now I can know."

Maybe now I can see...

She took a breath. Moved to the door. Reached out with her bare hand.

"What'cha doin' there?"

A young girl came out of the night into the faint light that shown from the bulb over the theater's door. She could not have been more than seven, with a little blue dress, button leather shoes, and a drooping bow in her black hair.

Suzanne frowned. "What are you doing here, child? It's very late. You should be in bed! Where is your mother?"

"I don't know. Somewhere."

"Go on, now, find her. Or your father. It's much too late for a little girl like you to be out."

"But what'cha doin'? You look like you's lost or somethin'." The girl smiled, blinked her huge, lash-fringed eyes.

"Go on!"

Suzanne glared at the little girl. Then she drew a sharp breath. Stepped back. The girl's face shifted in the shadow, morphing slowly into...

Faith Gansy....

Rosemary Reynolds…

Olga Heath.

Staring at her, accusing her…

"Leave me alone!" Suzanne cried.

I must still be asleep! This is just my dream, carrying on to further torment me! I have not walked to Coney, I have not wandered to Steeplechase Park nor stepped in some tippler's foul spewings!

Then the little girl stuck out her lips, her plain little face her own and not some sleep-fashioned one from the past. Pouting, she turned and wandered away. In the distance up the alley, a woman shouted shrilly, "Lillian, get yourself back up here this minute or I'll tan your hide!"

Some mothers don't give a whit for the suffering of their own. Curses on them.

Suzanne shook her head.

No, curse you, Suzanne, don't think about that now.

Back to the door of the 3000 A.D. theater. The broadside, nailed on the wall to the right of the door, boasted many outlandish claims: "A Warning to All Humanity to Be Ware and Be Aware! Watch! Be Vigilant Against Them! Or Our Race Shall Perish and Our Very Souls Shall Be Consumed!" Some kind of ridiculous playact, intended for the incredibly gullible as well as those who wanted to watch something peculiar for a lark, a good laugh.

And maybe a murderer wanting to slip away into the darkness for a bit, to hide out, to think back and savor the details and let the dust of his crime settle.

She knew she would see something when she touched the door.

She touched the door. Tucked her head, focused.

Nothing, then the tingling, the stirring, the dull headache waiting for its turn.

It struck.

She is in a small, windowless room, looking at a chair in the center of that room. It is an odd chair, with leather straps that would buckle around the person who might sit there. There is laughter behind her—heavy, low, a raspy, guttural chuckle. She wants to turn, to see the face, but can't force her body to do so.

Blink.

She is in the chair now, with the straps around her. They cross her chest, abdomen. There are two on each arm. A man's voice says, "You gonna try it, see if it works?"

Blink.

She is spinning now, spinning in the chair. She does not feel sick, however. Whoever's mind she is in now seems to actually enjoy the sensation. The man's voice, somewhere beyond the spinning, says, "Go faster?"

The head, her head, nods.

Blink.

Another room now, another place. The smells are more earthy and the air is more stifling. There is a stage, and upon it are people who have been shaved clean and are dressed in cotton shifts that don't even reach their knees. They stare out from the stage, eyes unblinking, like the eyes of the dead. A stick pokes out from between the rear stage curtains and whacks them on the legs. This causes them to move. They shuffle back and forth, bumping into each other on occasion, and then lifting their bare arms to make mild slashing motions through the air as if trying to be threatening. Suzanne is standing in the back of the audience, can feel the rough surface of the wall as she leans into it. Whoever it is she is at that moment smells sweet, that scent again…

Who am I? When am I?

She wants to put her hand to her face, to feel it, sense it, braille it. Her arms are crossed over her chest, and all she can feel are crumpled sleeves.

Blink.

She is in another room, a very nice one with electric lights glowing in a crystal ceiling chandelier. There are elegant tapestries over the windows, drawn against the night, a grand piano topped with silver candlesticks, potted ferns, several mahogany bookshelves stuffed with volumes, red velvet drapes separating this room from another. She walks toward the piano, strums fingers across the keys, bringing out a sweet but discordant tone. Tightening her thoughts, she attempts to look down at her hands, but can't.

Who am I?

There are voices in the room through the red drapes. Clinking glasses, knives against plates. Dinner conversation. These people sound cultured in tone, dignified in volume. But she cannot understand what they are saying.

She touches the piano keys again then pounds them with her fist. The voices in the other room go quiet. Silence. Then chairs scrape. They are coming from their dining, they will come into this room in only a moment.

Suzanne feels herself turn from the piano and walk to the far wall, where several oil paintings hang, and beside them, a large mirror in an ornate frame.

Yes! I want to see. Let me look in the mirror. Then I will know!

Her heart clenches.

Closer to the mirror now, moving over to stand in front of it.

Blink.

Gone from the elegant parlor, back in the chair and spinning again, laughter in her ears, from deep in her own chest, the chest of the one in the chair as round and round and round it goes. The lights wink off. Darkness now. And hideous rabbit images appear on the wall.

The sweet smell rises up again. She can almost name it now, she knows she knows it! She has smelled this very same scent before sometime in the past, somewhere far away from Coney. But when? Where?

Something cracked against her ear, and Suzanne was knocked out of her vision back into the Bowery, crashing into the door of the 3000 A.D. theater with vomit on her shoe and pain in her jaw. Before her stood Officer Whitman, his nightstick raised. He looked quite pleased with himself.

"Well, how about this, now. Here you are," he said. "Snooping around, sneaking around! Didn't know I had occasional night patrol here, did you? Thought you could get away with whatever it is you're doing here, didn't you?"

"Damn you, you nearly broke my skull!"

"Listen to your words, unladylike, like an old dock worker or fish wife. I should take you in for cursing."

Suzanne bared her teeth, glared. The pain in her head ricocheted back and forth like a ball kicked between children on a graveled road.

"Then take in just about everyone who walks the Bowery at night, Whitman. I've heard the worst there is. Why aren't they handcuffed behind you?"

"Cursing is the luxury of men, not women."

"Tell that to the women who wander the Bowery at night."

Whitman scowled. "What are you doing here at this hour?"

"Leave me be, Mr. Whitman, or so help me God you'll wish you had. Lieutenant Granger..."

"No, no, Miss Heath. Granger is pretty much shut of you. He said you had nothing worthwhile on the Mirror Maze case, and so has decided not to call on you again. I told him you were merely crazy, and that we needed to find you a nice, cozy madhouse for you to live out your final years. A shame Blackwell Island has closed, but there'd be room in the loony ward at Bellevue, I'm sure."

"Step back, sir. Now. I have no desire for you to be harmed."

"Harm me?" Whitman's laugh was sinister, deep. "Harm me? So now you are threatening me? That is an offense on the books, enough to take you in. You know, from the first time we met I suspected there was something unseemly about you."

"I did not say I would harm you. I said I did not want you to be harmed."

"It's the same thing."

"No, it is not. I'm saying that should you grab me, I will no doubt find out something about you, something beyond the dalliances you have had without your wife's knowledge. Something I could share with Granger, something that could ruin your career."

Whitman flinched. "You shouldn't tell a soul or I should beat you unconscious with my stick!"

"And even through the pain, as you have held that stick so often and so tightly, it will reveal to me your darkest secrets."

"You know I don't believe that is possible."

"I know you suspect that it is possible. And I know well that it is possible."

Several middle-aged men wandered near, and paused to listen to the altercation. These men looked to be business fellows of means, a bit unsteady but still wearing their vests buttoned and their boaters at intentionally jaunty angles.

Suzanne lowered her voice, narrowing her eyes. "I have a question for you, Whitman. Are you the killer? A nightstick could kill quite effectively, could crush a skull right well with enough force behind it."

Whitman took a threatening step forward, his billy club raised again, his teeth set against each other. "You dare suggest that such a thing!"

Suzanne did not move. "Should you beat me for no reason? With witnesses who look the type to appreciate and understand the law? Perhaps even a lawyer in the bunch?"

Whitman stopped, peered over at the men in their boaters, and then back at Suzanne. His voice grew quiet and cold. "All I will say to you is this. I don't trust you. Stay out of my way. Stay out of my sight. I think you're a charlatan, perhaps even dangerous, a woman who never learned her place, a disgrace to the name 'feminine.' I think you need to go to work and go home. That should be your life. Should I see you wandering again, I shall haul you away."

"For what? There is no law against loitering in the Bowery."

"Oh, I'll think of something." Then, his voice raised, he said, "Move on, now, ma'am." He turned to the gentlemen, touched the brim of his hat. "Good evening sirs."

Suzanne went on, doing her best to brush off the encounter with Whitman and focusing again on the visions. She had had visions as long as she could recall, had felt herself in the various scenes as if she had actually been there. Had sensed and smelled and heard and seen what others had sensed, smelled, heard, and seen. But the vision she'd had in front of the 3000 A.D. Theater was different. This time, as it had blasted itself into her body, she felt it in her soul. Never before had she been so engulfed, so totally part of the experience. The sensations were still heavy in her gut, still squirmed there like a parasite that had found its host.

She needed to visit the theater when it was open. She needed to see the show, touch the seats, discover what waited there to be discovered.

Down at the shoreline, she removed her shoe and washed the vomit away in the low-tide waves. Then she stood and stared out across the water, the waves coming, one on one on one. Hissing, purring, crashing. Whispering to her, *It will only be a matter of time before you know who the killer is.*

Or, she thought, only a matter of time before it crashed down and killed her first.

8

As Suzanne Heath made her way from her flat to the Bowery in the pre-dawn hours, Mattie Snow was amazing and terrorizing the guests at a private dinner party in a spacious apartment overlooking Central Park. They were in awe—mouth-gaping, eye-popping awe— and that is exactly what Mattie had intended and expected.

It had not been difficult to gain entrance to the party. She had donned a pair of light blue satin gloves for which she'd spent way too much money and her most elegant dress, one she had had for years but rarely wore, pinned her hair up beneath a black felt hat, allowing just a few teasing tendrils to curl down along her jaw, and put on a dab of lipstick and rouge, not enough to look like a whore, but enough to give her the look of vitality and energy, as if she spent time out in the sun rather than in the back room of a shabby Coney Island amusement. Then, clutching her embroidered handbag, she had taken a trolley from Coney to Manhattan in the late afternoon, spent some time wandering Central Park, watching the swan boats drifting on the Pond, watching children and parents feeding ducks and pigeons, and sitting on a bench as young men gave her admiring glances on their ways past. Then as the shadows grew longer and the park grew darker, she walked across Fifth Avenue to a great stone building where a doorman in a fine blue coat stood before the elegant glass doors.

He didn't seem suspicious, but rather tipped his hat cheerfully and asked whom she was going to see. She told him she was to dine with the Andersons, but he then frowned apologetically and said, "I'm sorry, Miss. Everyone who has invitations to the Andersons' suite has entered, and there are none left to join them. You must be mistaken."

"Oh, perhaps so," she said. "I might have come on the wrong date. My apologies, sir."

"No trouble at all," said the doorman, all smiles again.

"A good evening to you."

"And to you."

Oh, it will be a perfect evening, sir, she thought. *It will be just as I plan it to be.*

Mattie smiled, nodded, and then stepped away, down the front steps to the edge of the street where she pretended to check the buttons on her gloves. Couples, arm in arm, strolled past on the walk, their wealthy chins tipped up and back ever so slightly. Carriages drawn by the finest of horses and shiny new automobiles rumbled by on the street.

I fit in here. I am at home here. And I shall have this. I shall have it all, all that I ever wanted, here and anywhere else I desire.

She looked up from her gloves and gazed intently at the doorman, who was now watching a buggy jostle past, his hands in his coat pocket. She stared at his shirt collar and then focused, imagining it tightening around his neck.

He first ran his finger around his collar and chuckled nervously. "Seems this must have shrunk a bit," he said to himself as if his sudden fidgeting was unseemly and needed an explanation. But then his eyes grew wide, then wider, as the collar drew in even more, at first creasing the skin of his neck, then cutting into it, causing the neck to quickly swell and his face to go red like a ripe summer tomato. He gasped, stumbled with his hand out, reaching for a wealthy family of four who had just come up the stairs to the door. The mother drew her young children back protectively as her husband caught the doorman and said, "Crandall, what is the matter?"

Of course, Crandall couldn't speak, the collar was already chewing into his trachea, crushing it, leaving the doorman lying on his side, clawing his neck, kicking out against the air, and begging for help with his eyes.

"Jane, go inside, call for Doctor Dunbar!" shouted the father. "Tell him Crandall is having a seizure! Hurry!"

The mother nodded, gathered her tots around her skirts and pushed through the glass door. This was all Mattie needed. She darted across the walk and up the steps, moving in behind the family.

"Dreadful!" Mattie said to the mother in the lobby as the mother pushed the elevator button and looked nervously back out the front door. The children clung to her hands, whimpering. "I hope Doctor Dunbar can help!"

"Mercy, so do I." The mother shuddered. "How horrible!" The

elevator door opened and they all entered. As the door closed, Mattie hid her smile behind her glove.

She was now in the parlor of the Bensons, a wealthy industrialist family living on the top floor, a family that made and maintained their money through investments in railroads, Bell's telephones, and Edison's electric company. The parlor was exquisite, with European tapestries rather than ordinary curtains covering the windows, tapestries that seemed to have been created sometime during the medieval period, stitched through with scenes of forests, peacocks and rivers. The chandelier hung heavy with countless rainbow crystals that appeared ready to drop to earth at the slightest urging. There was a piano bedecked with candles, and fabric-covered chairs angled here and about, making some sort of organizational sense to the person who placed them there. A large mirror hung on the wall directly over the piano, its ornate frame finished in gold leaf. Mattie licked her lips and nodded. This, and more, much more, would be hers.

They had been dining when Mattie arrived. After her initial, inspiring introduction, they invited her to join them for veal, grouse, vegetables, and raspberry cream. Mattie declined, telling her host and hostess that she preferred to wander their home, seeking out spots where the paranormal was more strongly sensed, testing the spectral waters throughout the rooms and hallways. This unnerved the Bensons but they agreed, and returned to their plates and glasses of wine.

Mattie did not believe in paranormal spots, nor ghosts, nor spirits, but these people did and she would have no trouble including that in her presentation. Gullible, hopeful, frightened, and entitled they were, the Bensons and their well-dressed guests, with so much money and time on their hands that they could waste a great deal of it on petty wonderings and exciting uncertainties. Mattie could not hear their conversation in the dining room on the other side of the partially closed drape that separated the parlor from the rest of the house, but could hear the hum of their voices, the clinking of their silverware and wine glasses. No doubt that amid their talk of other things, they whispered about their uninvited but now welcomed guest.

The maid, all dressed in black and white like some kind of

prudish zebra or cow, had opened the apartment door to Mattie's knock. Mattie introduced herself, explained that she had come for the gathering, but the maid shook her head, and said, "No, Miss. They're all here," and began to close the door in Mattie's face. Mattie glared at the door, which pushed itself back against the maid, knocking her to the front hall floor. Mr. Benson — George Benson — had heard the thump and came out to see what the commotion was. The maid, still on the floor, pointed at Mattie and began to explain, when Mattie stepped in over the maid, held out her satin-gloved hand, and said, "Mr. Benson, my name is Mattie Snow. I understand you are having a gathering tonight. A gathering of those who have been studying the teachings of Aleister Crowley. I'm here to discuss that with you. And I believe you will want to hear what I have to say."

Benson was enraged, as Mattie had expected, his secret gathering interrupted. He shook his fist and quite girlishly stomped his foot, then ordered Mattie out. "You have no idea what you're talking about, and I shall call the authorities should you ignore my demand!" As he was ranting, Mrs. Benson — Jewel — and their party guests, another six whose names Mattie couldn't recall at the moment and didn't really care to, appeared behind him, equally angry and a bit frightened by the appearance of an abrasive young woman.

But Mattie only smiled and said, "You need me here. You just don't know it yet."

"I need you gone!" said George Benson. "Jewel, call the police department! Tell them to come at once!"

"Mrs. Benson, stay put," said Mattie, and Mrs. Benson did not move, but only glanced at the black phone on the wall behind her. "Mrs. Benson, you and your wife and friends are deluded by the Great Beast 666. He is no beast, and he certainly is not great, but only fancies himself to be so. How sad that intelligent persons like yourself have fallen for his game of smoke and mirrors."

"Young woman, I shall remove you bodily if you are not gone in the next second," said Mr. Benson. "I've never assaulted a woman before but there can always be a first time!"

"George," said his wife, wringing her hands as the other guests stood bug-eyed and mute. "Don't get into a scuffle, I beg you. Your heart, remember."

"No need," said Mattie. "Mrs. Benson, that is quite the lovely bracelet on your wrist. Is it diamond? I suspect so."

Mrs. Benson looked at her wrist, then back at Mattie. Her mouth gobbled for a moment, and she managed, "Don't talk to me. Just get out of here and leave us be!"

Mattie narrowed her gaze, focused on the bracelet, concentrated. Mrs. Benson gasped as the bracelet slid off her wrist and tossed itself through the air into Mattie's waiting hand. Mattie chuckled.

"Merely a sampling," said Mattie.

"Pah! Only an illusion!" said Mr. Benson.

"Pah, truly? An illusion? I suspect everyone here saw just what happened."

Mrs. Benson was already convinced, and she took her husband's elbow. "George, wait…"

"Get out!"

Mattie sighed, shook her head, and considered the mother-of-pearl buttons of George Benson's expensive waistcoat. She focused hard, her jaw set and her face tight, and the buttons each popped free of their stitching, one at a time and they dropped to the floor where they bounced silently on the carpeting. Then, slowly, they crawled about the floor to form the letter "B."

"B for Benson," said Mattie cheerfully.

The guests gaped.

"Now, certainly, I should get a little smile for that," said Mattie. "Or at least mild applause."

George Benson stared at the little buttons on the floor, winking in the overhead electric light. Then he stared at Mattie.

"Who are you?"

"I told you. My name is Mattie Snow."

George drew himself up, trying to regain his wealthy industrialist demeanor, for not to lose face in front of his friends. "How did you know about my gathering? Why did you come here?"

Mattie looked at the door. "Am I invited, then?"

Mrs. Benson nodded vigorously.

Mr. Benson looked at all the other guests, whose faces were screwed up with worry. "All right. Damn it all."

And so she spoke with them in the foyer, explaining that the spirits had told her of their meeting, and that she needed to be there to offer important corrections to their evolving belief system. Though no spirit had come to her, as no spirits existed, but rather Rex had followed the Bensons back to Manhattan from Coney several weeks earlier, riding near them on the train, pretending to be deep in his own thoughts but listening, learning, ready to report back to Mattie.

Mattie had noted the couple weeks earlier as she'd stood on the Bowery's main corridor eating a cup of chowder. Over the years Mattie had learned to listen to other people, to subtly eavesdrop, to catch little details that might at some point become handy. Nearly everything she heard was worthless, stupid, day-to-day chatter, spewed out in the air like droplets of spittle. Every once in a while, however, a man's or woman's comment would catch Mattie's attention and pique her interest enough to investigate. This couple she felt well worth following. She'd heard the man quietly mention Crowley, and wondered what the Beast would think of the illusions and trickery that made up so much of Coney's entertainment.

Perfect.

And so Mattie ordered Rex to their trail, on the train, then on a trolley to Central Park. He spent the night across from their apartment, and then a morning and into the afternoon. Then he stole the apartment's exterior cast-iron letterbox when he saw Mr. Benson place envelopes inside for the carrier to pick up. It wasn't hard to do. He waited until the doorman was helping a young woman with her baby buggy up the steps and into the lobby, and then shouted to those near him that a girl was being attacked in the park and needed help. As nearby pedestrians raced into the park to the rescue, Rex slipped across the road, dropped behind the juniper bushes against the brick wall, then reached up and pried the letterbox off with the steel rod he kept up his sleeve for protection. He spirited the box away just as the doorman was patting the baby on the head and turning back to his job.

On his return, Mattie first beat him for being gone so long, forcing her to close her amusements, and then rewarded him with chocolate for bringing the letterbox, which was full of invitations to the Bensons' "Beast 666 Private Dinner Party and Evening of Conversation."

Mattie wandered about the parlor as the others finished their meal in the dining room. There was a mother-of-pearl encrusted box on the cherry writing desk; she opened it to find it filled with cigars from Cuba. She took one out and lit it with a hard stare. She had never smoked a cigar, but this felt like the place to do it. She drew on the tip, fought back a cough, and then let the smoke curl out through her lips. Nasty thing, a cigar. So many men on holiday smoked them and tossed the stubs out on the ground where they would occasionally stick to the bottom of her shoe. But the rolled tobacco did feel good between her fingers. This fat, brown finger could be just right for pointing at someone for emphasis, or sticking on someone's skin for punishment. She moved back to the piano, checked her hair and face in the mirror, touched the faded scars from a long-ago fight, and then banged on the piano keys. The dining room went silent. There had been enough waiting. They could damn well eat dessert later. She was in charge, and the sooner they realized that, the better.

When the Bensons and their guest had gathered in the parlor, the women seated primly on the chairs and the men standing beside them, Mattie told them what they needed to know. They listened intently, convinced by her demonstrations, amazed at her knowledge of magic and the paranormal. As George Benson watched begrudgingly but attentively, she explained how since she was a young girl she had sensed in herself something powerful, and came to realize it was something she should embrace. She told them her power had increased greatly over the last few years as she practiced and studied. She did not condemn Crowley outright but dismissed him as worthless. When George scowled and squirmed nervously in frustration, Mattie forced his lips up into a huge, grimacing smile and then asked the others if they needed any more convincing. They all shook their heads. Even George, who shook it on his own, without any nudging from Mattie.

"I am not ready to claim my kingdom yet," Mattie said. She strolled slowly back and forth in front of her new converts. "The foundation is still being laid, things still being perfected. Nothing of value has ever been done in haste, for things brought about quickly crumble quickly. Consideration, care, caution, calculation, the four c's of successful and enduring creation."

The gathering nodded, waiting, rapt, frightened.

She told them that she was in the process of gathering a race of drones who would serve her when the time came, doing the menial tasks that she, and people like the Bensons, would find beneath them. "And should you decide to join me, you shall be my second-in-command. Now, Crowley stated, 'Do what thou wilt shall be the whole of the law.' I amend it to this: 'Do what our leader wills shall be the whole of the law.' But obedience to me, for those such as yourselves, people of breeding and education, shall be profitable and pleasurable, indeed. You think you have all you want now? You can't begin to dream what lies ahead. Money, property, and power beyond your imaginations. No one will be able to counter or cross you. They would not dare. Over time, this city will be in your hands, then the nation. Eventually..."

"The world?" said one of the lady guests.

And quoting Jesus, someone she had been taught about at a girls' school when she was younger and had long since dismissed, she said simply, "Yes, it is as you say."

"Obedience." This was from a young man with dark curly hair and a trim mustache. He was struggling with her demand and his youthful sense of rebellion. He could hardly stand still. "I'm will admit I have been impressed with your displays. And perhaps I'd be willing to help you with your...your kingdom. But I obey no one but my own self."

Mattie paused, considered the young man then went to stand before him. She could hear the quite inhalations of the others, waiting to see what she might do.

"You would have obeyed Crowley had he come to this gathering, yes?"

The young man raised a brow. "Perhaps. I don't know."

"Perhaps?"

"Probably. But he is he and you are you. He is well known among certain circles. He has earned a following. As for you, I've never heard of you before this evening." He glanced at the others, as if hoping they would chime in on his defense. But they said nothing. "None of us have. Yes, you have a certain talent with popping buttons and stealing bracelets without touching them, and even forcing a man to smile against his will. But to come in here and suggest we become your obedient servants, why, that is beyond arrogant."

Mattie laughed low and long. It sounded more like a growl than a sound of amusement. She stared at one of the unlit candles on the mantle. With a little flick, a flame was then dancing on top of the wick. "I don't use that power often," she said. "But it's good to know it's there if I need it. Pipes to light, anyone?"

The guests in the parlor froze.

Mattie turned her attention back to the young man. "What's your name?"

The man hesitated, but he held his head high. "August."

"August. Do they call you Augie?"

"No, they best not."

"All right, then Augie, I suggest if you don't care for what I'm offering, that you leave. Now."

"No. I was invited here. This is not your home. You can't order me out for merely speaking my mind."

"Miss Snow, let's take this a little more slowly," said George Benson. "You're throwing a great deal at us at once. We need time to absorb it, consider it, and then make our decisions. You yourself said certain things take time."

"I have had you, this gathering, under my scrutiny for quite a while, so no, nothing is being rushed here." A lie, but lies were only tools to a goal, nothing more, nothing less. "The groundwork is being laid, you needn't worry about that. All you need to do is give me your allegiance, and when that is done, I'll tell you what I need from you."

"I see a magician here," said August, pleading his case again to the others, who still said nothing. "Little more. I say we bid her good night and go on our way. In the morning we'll be glad we did."

Mattie sighed and shook her head. "Sad, sad. I didn't think I'd need to show you more than I did, though perhaps to you, Augie, it seems a sleight of hand. Let me offer one more demonstration, and then we'll see who would prefer to join me rather than challenge me. For, you see, I shall not be denied."

August scoffed, curled his lip, but his eyes registered naked terror as Mattie took another step toward him and focused her gaze on his forehead. The women looked at their husbands, the husbands looked at their wives. Then all looked at August.

This was always hardest. Mattie could certainly make it happen and had proved that five times already, though it always left her exhausted. She had planned on saving this method of execution for only those who fit her special criteria, but she intensely disliked this August fellow, and so decided to give him her unique treatment. He would be out of her way, and the others would eagerly embrace her as their master once this was done.

"Sorry, Augie," she said, almost gently.

"What are you…" August began and then his face contorted. "Oh, my God!"

Mattie gazed intently at his head, concentrating, making it happen.

August slammed his palms against his temples and then stared at Mattie as if she were the devil, himself. "What are you doing? Stop…" he began, and then the pain cut off the words and all that was left was a pig-like squeal. He dropped to his knees, his arms over his head, wailing. The women jumped to their feet, reaching out, but when Mattie turned her icy gaze from August to them, their husbands grabbed them and held them back. There was nothing they could do for their friend. He was on his own. She smiled, nodded, and then concentrated on August once more.

It didn't take long for his head to be destroyed. The temples caved in from the sides, the forehead folded back into the brain, the back of the skull forced its way forward, all at once, like a box being flattened for scrap. Ten seconds, maybe, fifteen. One of the man's eyes popped before it was half done; the other blew backward into the gray and white matter that once had held his thoughts, his dreams, his hopes. His incisors shot out in a satisfactory little spray, *plink, plink, plink,* hitting a bare spot on the well-polished oak floor in front of his knees. Skull fragments and bits of brain appeared through the man's well-combed hair, and then he was done. He flopped over with an almost surprising slowness, and lay in a fetal position, blood running down through the shattered bone and staining the edge of the Oriental carpet.

The women screamed. In unison, as if they'd rehearsed. Screamed, screamed, until Mattie told them to hush. "You don't want to draw the attention of anyone else in the apartment building, do you?"

They went quiet immediately. Or as quiet as four horrified rich women who had just witnessed their friend's head destroyed could be.

Mattie took all their names and addresses down on a piece of stationery Mr. Benson happily gave to her. She folded it and slipped it into her skirt pocket. Then, with a clap of her hands she said, "Did someone say there was cake for dessert? I would love a slice!"

After dessert, she took Mr. Benson to his bedroom and locked the door. George didn't argue. Mrs. Benson didn't complain. The sex was mediocre, as a horrified man doesn't often make for a virile lover, but she was too tired to hope for much, anyway. And at least he'd been able, with trembling fingers and tongue, to pleasure her to a degree. It was good enough.

Good enough for the time being.

9

Cittie wrote a note to Suzanne during the band's midday meal break, carefully penned and carefully delivered, first through band member Moses to one of the boys who cleaned up tiger shit from the Bostock's Wild Animal Circus in Dreamland, who took it out to a street sweeper on Surf Avenue, who walked over to Luna Park and handed it to Suzanne, saying, "Excuse me, Miss, but I think you dropped this on the road."

This was Cittie's usual way of communicating with Suzanne without coming right up to her in broad daylight like a white friend would have, or having to spend two cents to mail it to her room over the Moons' store.

It read:

S —
I want to treat you to a day off. Tomorrow is Sunday. You don't work Sundays and me either. Meet me at entrance to Dreamland at opening. Fun is on me.
C.

He hoped to hear back from her. He wouldn't see her that evening since he was going to have to work double-shifts with the band. It was always that way on Saturdays. Long day, banging, shaking, marching, scaring park patrons. To make it even more difficult, Dick Bergman decided last week to add more make up to everyone's faces to make them even more ominous, and the makeup — white and red streaks across almost every bare part of their bodies — itched and ran when they sweated. This made Bergman angry, but he didn't give up because he'd spent a crate-load of money on the makeup. In between marches he made them reapply the stripes. Now, sitting with the rest of the fake Zulus in the shade of their dressing and lodging tent in a rear, obscured corner of Dreamland, Cittie did his best to eat his pork sandwich without smearing the makeup any worse than it did on its own. Alfred, Moses, and Cletus sat on the bench and leaned over with their knees spread, letting the oily meat drip onto the sawdust on the ground. Cittie liked grease, figured it was healthy to eat all of what was given him, so he ate by tipping his head back. Lightnin', on the other hand, was being Lightnin', which meant being obstinate and unpleasant for no good reason other than making the other band members uneasy. He ate one bite of his pork sandwich, a meal provided by Bergman as all meals during the workday were, then pretended it was a crow that had come to peck his eyes out. He jabbed the sandwich against his eyes, jumped up and hollered. Weeks earlier, the other Bloodthirsty Zulus would have caught him and sat him down and asked what was wrong and did he need a doctor. Now, they just ignored him. The man was crazy, or wanted everyone to think he was crazy. Of course, this made for good showmanship when the band was out among the vacationing crowds. Nobody could shake a rattle or blow a bone flute in a more threatening manner than Lightnin'. He would make music and dance and holler and go into a frenzied spasm. Then he would jump as closely as was allowed toward ladies in the white summer gowns or young boys with lollipops, lick his lips, bug his eyes, and clack his teeth at them. The women would scream, the little boys would cower, and the gentlemen who had come with them would laugh and give a tip to Bergman, who wielded a rifle and a leather-tip pouch.

Cittie finished his sandwich and drank a cup of water from the pitcher on a wobbly table in the tent. It was a scorcher outside, close to 100 degrees at least. And yet they came, the curious, the bored, the thrill-seekers. One of the wandering acrobats had fainted with the heat and had to be taken to the hospital. One of the lions in Bostock's Wild Animal Circus had even succumbed to the high temperatures while in its cage waiting to perform. Cittie filled another cupful of water, then poured it over his head, savoring the temporary coolness.

"Don' waste water," said Moses.

"Shut up," said Cittie.

Bergman was there then, at the open flap to the tent, wiping moisture from beneath his pith helmet and unenthusiastically waving his rifle. "Come on," he grumbled to the Zulus, who popped the rest of the unfinished sandwiches into their mouths, picked up their instruments, and went out into the harsh sun. "Step lively now. Got to show these folks a real bloodthirsty band so we can make the cut for next season."

The Zulus tooted and banged and shook and hollered. They pranced and danced and made to chase after people before Bergman threatened them with the rifle to keep them in line, to keep them playing. Around the park they went in the brutal heat, sweat pouring down Cittie's face, taking the freshly reapplied streaks of makeup with it. Past the impressively tall and garish Beacon Tower, the man-made, green-tinted lagoon into which Shoot-the-Chute riders careened down a 280-foot ramp in flat-bottom boats to splash and skim across the water. Past the pagoda-inspired Japanese Teahouse where diners sat at tables covered in white linens on bright white decks, enjoying exotic fare and watching the frantic human activity below. Past the theater in which the End of the World show acted out in terrible and glorious details the Biblical accounts of mankind's inevitable damnation or salvation. Past the Trip Over the Alps scenic railroad, a slow-moving coaster that took folks on a ride through mountain scenery created with plaster and decorated with stuffed mountain goats. Past the Vaudeville Stage, Bostock's Circus, and the Dreamland Ballroom. Up toward the park's entrance now and the grand building in which the Creation show was performed, then the Moorish Theater, the Fighting the Flames show, and the ominous, Satan-guarded ride called Hell Gate. Back past the entrance to Freak Street where forty human monstrosities were on display.

Women shrieked and laughed as the band passed them. Men chuckled and scoffed. Children wound themselves up in their mothers' skirts. Teenaged girls watched nervously as teenaged boys taunted the band, threatening to capture them or shoot them. If a threat seemed a bit too real, and Lightnin' looked to be ready to take them on in earnest, Bergman would step in and, in his lowest and most authoritative voice, tell the youth that all was under control and they best move away.

Cittie drummed his drum, sometimes wanting to break into one of the more pleasant rhythms he'd learned at the Waifs' Asylum but reminding himself that he was a savage from Africa and best make his music sound like it.

The night came, and with it the brilliantly bright lights of Dreamland, a full million of them, lit up the world. The band took a brief supper break then began their second shift, playing, dancing, charming the crowds with their fearsome appearances and sounds, earning Bergman a few tips on top of his salary, from which he paid the band members. Thankfully, the heat began to bleed away, and a cooler ocean breeze came in from the south.

As the night crept on and Cittie drummed and drummed and drummed he thought about Miss Missy and George Sandston, about white people and Negros and Du Bois' The Soul of Black Folk, the last book he had read while at the asylum. He thought about the smelly tent that had become his home in Dreamland, a home he shared with the rest of the band except for Lightnin'; nobody knew exactly where Lightnin' lived, and nobody cared to ask. He wondered how long he would work in Dreamland. He daydreamed about trying out for a real band once more, and winning the spot. He thought about Suzanne, and how if she were black he would ask her to marry him in a heartbeat.

Midnight rolled over and passed with the sinking moon, and the band retired to the tent. Moses pressed into Cittie's hand a damp note he'd gotten from the sweeper on their last trip around the park. He sat on his cot, wiped the remnants of makeup from his body with a towel, rubbed his sore feet then opened the note.

C —

You are relentless, you know that? As much as I want to say no I will say yes so you'll stop pestering. I can't imagine what you have in mind, as we could never be seen together.

What a friend I have. How lucky am I? Truly.
S.

Cittie went to sleep with a smile.

10

Suzanne stood on Surf Avenue outside the entrance to Dreamland, a 75-foot-tall, 50-foot-wide, and 150-foot-deep and shaded archway before which stood a giantess, a stone statue of a half-naked, classically Romanesque woman who represented art and beauty and wonder, everything Dreamland hoped its patrons would expect inside. Everything it hoped its patrons would pay to find. Ticket sellers sat to either side of the arch, with a burly man watching from the shadows to make sure no one entered without paying their ten cents. Attractions inside the park, of course, would cost extra. Dreamland had, since its opening in 1904, touted itself as more dignified and cultured than either Luna Park or Steeplechase. This resulted in it making less money in past years than the other two, and which in turn resulted in the owners adding more shows such as the Freaks and the Bloodthirsty Zulus and rides like the Leap Frog Railroad and Shoot-the-Chutes. Had to keep up, somehow.

People pushed around Suzanne, heading into Dreamland, rushing as if they wanted to be the first to see, to do, to eat, to buy. The day threatened to be as hot as the day before, so Suzanne wore her lightest shirtwaist and more airy hat. She had on her cleanest pair of cotton gloves. Who knew what she might touch, and she had decided to a least give Cittie three hours in which she was not trying to learn something or trying to avoid learning something. When they were done in Dreamland, she was going back to the Bowery. She was going to visit 3000 A.D.

A morning of mindless entertainment, if she could handle it, would be the best way to start the day.

"Excuse me, Miss."

Suzanne glanced over to see a tall woman apparently from the Middle East, dressed from head to toe in a long dark blue tunic and dark blue veil. Only her eyes were visible through a small opening in the veil.

"Yes?"

"Are you going into Dreamland?" The voice was peculiar, unnaturally high-pitched and halting.

"I am. Eventually. Why do you ask?"

"Will you accompany me?"

"I..." began Suzanne. Then she laughed and shook her head. "Cittie, you amaze me. Where on Earth did you find that costume?"

"I borrowed it from Sadie at the Arabian show. I promised not to get it dirty or tear it."

"It might be difficult for you to see, don't you think?"

"I can turn my head as well as the next fella. See?" He turned his head side to side. And though Suzanne couldn't see his lips, she knew he was smiling from the crinkles at the corners of his eyes.

"Ready?" he asked.

"Ready."

Dimes paid, the pair entered Dreamland. Few people stared, as Cittie's getup could just as easily be a show promotion as an exotic foreigner. Suzanne did her best to smile when Cittie pointed out displays and free shows along the Promenade — little monkeys doing tricks, clowns blowing bubbles, ponies prancing, and dogs jumping through hoops. She declined the offer to tour the display of Dr. Courtney's incubator babies but accepted a ride down the Shoot-the-Chutes. She and Cittie sipped tea in the Japanese Teahouse, a delicious and relaxing brew as nearby patrons cast curious smiles at the veiled figure.

"Your hands show a bit," whispered Suzanne. "They might suspect."

"Ah, some Arabs are dark like me. Don' worry. Have fun."

"I'm trying."

"I know."

She found it hard to sit still through the Fighting the Flames show. It was too real and too troubling, as on the huge stage the façade of a six-story hotel went up in flames and 120 firefighters rode to the scene in their engines and hose wagons drawn by real horses. People screamed from windows until the firefighters raised the ladders and rescued them all. The audience, seated on bleachers, cheered and applauded madly. Suzanne could only close her eyes and be glad it was done.

"How about Hell Gate as our final amusement?" asked Cittie in his pinched woman-voice, as people closed in tightly around them as they left the Flames show. "I been in it once. Not scary, Suzanne, in fact it'll mostly make you laugh."

"I don't know. I'm not fond of devils."

"C'mon."

Suzanne stopped outside the Flames show, adjusted her hat, and looked across the wide and sunny Promenade to where Hell Gate's brick building stood, a huge, looming Beelzebub slouching over the entrance, the wide staircase leading up to the near-perfect darkness. *Coralie works there now,* she thought, steeling herself. *Has for four days. Maybe I can wave to her, at least.*

"All right?"

"All right."

"Suzanne."

"What?"

Cittie hesitated.

"What, Cittie?"

"I think you should give up tryin' to help the police find the murderer. I think it's not good for you, all that death. All that evil. I worry somethin' bad will happen to you."

"I'm careful, Cittie. I watch where I'm going."

"Not just bad to your body. Bad to your mind."

Suzanne looked at her shrouded friend, at the eyes in the little opening. Then she looked out at the cheerful folks having fun in Dreamland. Innocent people, for the most part. "I have to, Cittie. There's no choice. Can you understand?"

"I don't know if I want to."

"I have to, Cittie."

"Oh. All right, then."

"All right."

"So, are you having fun, maybe just a little?" The eyes within the little opening in the veil appeared hopeful.

"A bit."

"Then that's good."

Just walking up Hell Gate's broad staircase was unsettling. The hot summer air went instantly colder the higher they went, as if they were preparing to enter a mysterious cave, which, as the interior suggested, they were. Cittie handed the tickets to the man, at the top of the stairs. The man was dressed all in black and wore a skull mask.

The large, dark room before them, lit only by several flickering torches secured to the walls, was in fact a pool with water than went round and round in a whirlpool. Small boats were docked in a steel-barred lock, waiting to be pushed out and into the pool. Suzanne stood silently, tensely, as the customers before them, a young married couple, climbed into boats and were then set free by the boat master, another man in black and a skull mask.

"Hold on now, watch, they're goin' round and down," said Cittie, leaning close to Suzanne.

"Oh, dear. I'm not sure I like this."

The boat caught the current at the edge of the room and then drew the boat inward, spiraling around toward the center in constantly narrowing circles as the woman screamed gleefully and her husband held her tightly. In the middle of the room the boat plunged out of view into the unknown below.

"Oh," said Suzanne through her teeth.

"It's fine. You ready?"

"I don't know Cittie…"

"Trust me. And we already spent the nickels and can't get 'em back."

Okay, Cittie, for you. Only for you.

The boat master nodded at Cittie and Suzanne, cocked his skull-masked head, and gestured toward the front boat in the lock. "Watch your step, my dear ladies," he said with a low chuckle. "And watch out for…your souls!"

Suzanne gave the man a hard look, then sat in the boat on the little bench seat, scooting over so there would be enough room between herself and Cittie that they wouldn't have to touch. She reached out and clasped the wooden bar in front of her.

"Fare thee well, if well there may be!" said the boat master, and he opened the gate, setting their boat adrift in the pool. It was immediately swept up in the whirlpool, drifting slowly around the room's blackened walls, and then picking up speed as it circled inward toward the center. Firelight splashed and bobbed atop the water like luminescent fish. Around and around, preparing to throw them down the giant drain. Suzanne tried to focus, to watch the light from the entrance to keep nausea at bay, but her stomach would have none of it. She felt the sausage she'd had for breakfast churning, seeking the fastest route out. Cittie laughed, "This is swell!"

Round, round, round, faster, faster, faster.

Round and round and round like the chair, like the room where the razor-toothed rabbits grin and the white swirls and the fire dances.

"I want out, Cittie!"

"Can't, Suzanne. Just hold on."

Closer to the black hole in the middle.

"I can't do this..."

Suzanne clutched the bar harder, took deep breaths, fighting nausea and dread. She glanced over at the entrance to catch a second's impression of the boat master's grinning skull face.

Then the floor fell out from under them and they plummeted to the depths.

Suzanne closed her eyes as the boat careened down the steep ramp.

Then the boat splashed, bobbed, and Cittie said, "We're down now. S'okay. Open to look. See?"

Suzanne looked.

They were in a narrow man-made river, drifting forward through the darkness, with more flickering torches on the craggy plaster of Paris walls. Up ahead, around a curve, were strange voices and thumping sounds.

"No worse than the Shoot-the-Chutes, now was it?"

"I don't spin well," she managed. "The drop, okay, I'm just glad that's done with."

Cittie sighed. "No fun, then, is it?"

Suzanne wished she could touch his arm, to find reassurance there and to offer it in return. But even with her gloves on, she didn't trust what might transpire. And so she lied as kindly as she could, "Yes, Cittie. I'm having fun. Bless you for being who you are and doing what you've done for me. I can't think of anyone who has ever been as kind."

Cittie hesitated then said, "Thank you. And Suzanne?"

"Yes?"

"I wanna tell you somethin', but I can only tell you here in the dark, 'cause I'm not sure I want you to see my face when I say it."

"Say what?"

"I don' want you feelin' awkward 'round me."

"Say what, Cittie?"

"That you're my best friend. I never felt close to anyone like you, not then, not now. I don't know what I'd do without you to talk to. I hope…I hope you don't mind."

Suzanne smiled, and the smile caught her by surprise. "Thank you, Cittie. And you're my best friend, too."

"You know, I'd hug you if you'd let me."

"Best not."

"Sure."

The boat took the curve then, and they entered Hell.

The walls were wider here, with great juttings of jagged plaster rocks, vicious stalactites, sabre-sharp stalagmites, and riverside pools that bubbled and churned, releasing smoke and a most foul odor of sulfur. More torches were jammed in the walls at peculiar angles, flaring orange and red. And then from behind the rocks and cave formations jumped a shrieking hoard of demons waving bright red pitchforks. They danced around and jabbed their weapons at Cittie and Suzanne.

They were all sizes, these play actors, and Suzanne noted that some of the costumes were a tad too tight while others a tad too loose. They wiggled their horned heads and shook their fork-tailed behinds. Some did handstands and backflips, all the while hissing and wailing. Others just snarled and jabbed. None of them was Coralie.

Cittie whispered, "You think Hell looks like this? I don't think so. This is kinda silly."

"Maybe." *No, it looks nothing like this. It's worse, much worse. I have no doubt about that.*

The boat floated on, away from the demons and into a narrow passage that bore right then left then right again. Out into another larger room next, where even more demons were dancing and pounding pitchforks, more flaring torches and angry plaster rock formations. This time, however, the demons' domain was being watched over by Satan on a throne adorned with skulls and leg bones. The Dark Master, himself, had a huge red head the size of a carriage wheel, glistening white fangs, scaly red skin, and clawed hands and feet. His tail, as thick as an anaconda, coiled up and over the arm of his throne and twitched back and forth ever so slowly.

"He's mechanical," said Cittie.

"He is, indeed," said Suzanne.

"It'd be funny should he break down during the ride."

"It would." *I hate this place. Let it be over soon!*

"I wonder if Satan really looks like that? Or maybe people made up what they think he looks like. The Bible say anything about Satan havin' a tail?"

"I don't know."

"Or horns?"

"I don't know. Do you think it matters?"

"To some folks, it might."

Suzanne scanned the demons, watching for Coralie. Even in the makeup and costumes and flickering, irregular torchlight, she knew Coralie's face well enough to recognize it if it was there.

And there it was. Coralie's face staring out from the headpiece of a tight red demon costume. Little black-pointed horns were tied onto her head. She stood beside a stalagmite and half-heartedly, thrusting with her pitchfork, swaying back and forth in a pretense of dancing. She stared at nothing, not reacting to any of the other demons, not focusing on the riders in the boat.

Suzanne had never seen Coralie looking so distant, so faded.

"Coralie!" she called.

Coralie stared, shook the pitchfork.

"Coralie! Look at me!"

Some of the other demons stopped in their tracks at the shout, losing their demon attitudes, jerked back to the fact that they weren't actual demons but were actors getting minimal pay to pretend. They looked at Cittie and Suzanne, then over at Coralie, who at last had stopped moving. She looked at Suzanne, her face now registering who was calling her name.

The boat continued to float on toward another turn, around another wall, another curve. Suzanne turned in her seat and watched Coralie. The girl, the former Luna Park ticket taker, the cheerful, full-of-life Coney miss, looked like she had had the spirit beat out of her. She looked like she wanted to die.

"Coralie!" Suzanne called, but then the boat took the turn and Coralie and the other demons and old Satan on his throne were gone, and there was the end of the ride up ahead — a man helping the young married couple out of their boat and directing them to the steps that would take them up and out into the daylight of the world once more.

11

Outside Dreamland's grand entrance, Suzanne thanked Cittie for treating her to a morning of entertainment and said she hoped to see him tomorrow night on the beach. Cittie told her she was very welcome. Then he shoved his hands into his trouser pockets beneath the long blue Arabian gown and watched as she headed back up Surf Avenue, head high, hat steady. In just seconds she was swallowed up by the crowd.

She'd smiled at him once or twice, and that was worth all the dimes and nickels he'd spent. He'd never make her wholly happy, that wasn't anything another person could do for a friend. But if he could offer moments of distraction or a touch of fun, then it was enough.

And he'd had enough of the Arabian outfit. He'd been sweating like a bull beneath the cloth, and couldn't wait to get it off and return it to Sadie. He'd kept part of his promise. He hadn't torn it. But it was damp and dirty from sitting in that blasted Hell Gate boat. Maybe he would wash it first. That might be best.

As he turned back toward the park, he noted a police officer leaning against the western base of Dreamland's arch. His lips were pursed and his arms were crossed. The man was looking at Cittie.

Oh, God. Let that just be a passin' glance.

Cittie strode quickly toward the entrance, looking straight ahead, trying to catch up with and blend in as best he could with a large family heading the same way. But then the officer called, "Ma'am, you in the blue robe!"

Cittie pretended not to hear, not to see. He walked faster.

Then the voice was closer, "You in the blue robe! Ma'am, stop right there!"

No, no, no!

"Ma'am! Stop right there!"

Cittie stopped.

The officer came around to face Cittie straight on. He wore a most disturbing smile, one that made Cittie instinctively reach for the wrench in his trouser pocket. He would not use it, but wrapping his fingers around the handle gave his nervous fingers something to do, something to bear down onto against his fear.

The officer had black hair and a nose that looked like it had been knocked askew during a fight. He angled his face, as if trying to see inside the veil through the eye-slit. Then he said, "What's your name?"

Cittie's heart picked up a fast, heavy beat. He did his best not to shake.

"You hear me? What's your name?"

Cittie put his right hand to his mouth, keeping as much of his hand covered by the blue fabric as possible. He tapped his lips and shook his head.

"What? You tryin' to tell you you can't talk?"

Cittie nodded.

"I know you can. I watched you talking to that young lady a moment ago. Suzanne Heath. You know Suzanne Heath, don't you?"

Cittie said nothing. People pushed around him, staring with brief curiosity at the officer interrogating a figure in a long Arabian gown and veil.

"You know her. You came out with her, out from Dreamland, talking like old friends. Now, you want to talk to me here? Or do we need to go to the precinct house?"

Cittie took a breath and in his best woman-voice said, "We just met."

"Don't give me that nonsense. You talked like old friends. I know the difference. Again, who are you? You don't tell me, I'll take that veil right off."

"No, please. It's 'gainst my religion." Cittie's woman-voice cracked. "Men shouldn't see beneath a veil."

"And you should not lie to an officer of the law. And you're no woman." With that, the officer grabbed the top of the veil and yanked it clean off. Cittie drew back, put his hands out before him, preparing to be clouted on the head.

"Oh, so my ears and eyes didn't deceive me," said the officer. "Not only are you a man, but a colored man at that! A colored man spending time with a young white woman. And Suzanne Heath, in particular."

"I am an actor, sir," said Cittie. "I perform in Dreamland."

"You play a woman?"

"No, sir." *Jesus, help me.*

"So you just like to dress like a woman? You one of those men?"

Cittie's throat was dry, but he fought against a cough. He needed to sound certain, strong. But he knew white officers when they confronted black people they considered suspicious. His arms shook mightily beneath the robe. "No, sir."

The officer rubbed his chin threateningly. "If this isn't your costume, then you're in disguise. Why are you in disguise, boy? Could it be you are in love with a white woman, and she is in love with you? Now, wouldn't that just be dandy!"

"No, sir. You got it wrong."

"I don't think I do."

"I got to get to work, sir. I don't wanna be late." He tried a smile and it failed. "So if you please, sir, I'll be on my way." *Oh, please, God, I got to get out of here!*

"I don't think so. Take off that ridiculous outfit."

Slowly, Cittie shrugged out of the gown. It remained, pooled at his feet like shed blue skin.

"Now, what's your name, boy?"

He couldn't say it.

"Tom. Tom Brown."

"Tom Brown? I don't think so."

God...!

"Well, Tom Brown, we got some talking to do. And it's too hot out here in the sun, so we'll just take a little trip back to the precinct house where it's a bit...what's that in your pocket, boy?"

Oh, my dear God!

"Hold now. Is that a wrench? Let me see that, boy, give that..."

Cittie broke and ran. Shoving past the cop, past the people in line for Dreamland tickets, dashing into the arched, shadowy entrance amid shouts of, "Hey, watch it!" "Be careful, there, boy!" and the bellowing commands of "Stop him!" from behind. He reached the end of the arch and raced out into the garish sunlight.

A fast look to the right, left, straight ahead.

Which is best? God, where to go!

He darted to the left and into the early-afternoon shadows that rimmed the Promenade and shaded the brightly-adorned carts and wagons offering foods and souvenir knickknacks. Bending low, he skirted the narrow space behind the vendors, causing some to frown and kick at him but others to just watch with mild interest.

I know this park, I know I can hide!

He did not look back. He did not want to see or know if the officer was close, ready to grab him up and beat him. Instead, he ran.

Behind a towline of ponies with cheerful children astride them, behind the brightly-costumed Amaldi twins performing their sword-swallowing act, alongside the meandering Mini-Train with its patriotic bunting, behind Marcus Ferguson and his Trained Pups. He slipped on a spilled drink, went down on his hands and knees, and then shoved himself upward again.

There! The entrance to Freak Street. Cittie rounded the corner, skidded, nearly knocking over an elderly man and woman who were strolling away, shaking their heads in dismay at the human monsters they had just witnessed. Cittie wormed his way into the crowd, fighting against their current.

Dear Jesus, help me!

He shouldered through the tight clot of holidayers on the straw-covered corridor. Pushing around them, past them, head down. And then, there were the displays. A row on the right, another on the left, iron-barred cages in which the human monstrosities offered their mutilated and malformed bodies up to the horrified admiration of the curious in order to earn their daily bread. The Snake Boy with his scaly skin. Chimp Woman, covered in hair from head to toe. Clyde the Cyclops, a dead and stuffed baby with a single eye and pig-like nose growing from its forehead. Sultry Sally, a belly dancer with three arms. The Human Spider, with limbs so withered and lifeless they appeared to be the chitinous appendages of an arachnid, and with four other false legs protruding from her clothing to complete the disturbing effect. Freak Street was one of the free exhibits in Dreamland, though a greasy, bug-eyed photographer worked there, offering to take pictures of park visitors standing next to their favorite freak. The photographer was currently occupied, positioning at his tripod, preparing to snap a photo of a rashy-faced young man ogling Sultry Sally.

Cittie quietly wormed his way behind and under the Cyclops' cage.

In the smelly shade, lying flat with gnats up his nose and mice sniffing his feet, he looked out at the feet shuffling in the straw — poor men's cracked leather boots, rich men's Creedmores. Ladies' button-up Oxfords and girls' patent leathers. Boys' leather shoes with buckles coming undone. The footwear of countless people seeking the thrill of fun and fear, gasping, laughing, dropping cigarette butts and hacking thick wads of phlegmy spittle onto the ground.

He held still, silent. Praying the officer did not see him come into Freak Street, praying that amid the hubbub nobody noticed the young black man scooting among them to hide in the narrow space beneath a cage in which a dead, stuffed baby stared out with a lifeless, unblinking eye.

12

The 3000 A.D. Theater was not open on Sundays. Peculiar, as almost everything else was. Perhaps the owner was a religious man. Perhaps he gave the day to the Lord, and spent the time attending church and having meals with his family.

Suzanne stood helplessly before the locked theater door in the fierce Sunday afternoon sun, giving the proprietor credit for obeying his religious teachings, but likewise cursing him for delaying her visit. Several other people pooled around her, looked at the closed sign, grumbled, and moved on.

She would move on. But she would be back.

13

Mattie lay on the cot in the back room, watching the swirls behind her eyelids, admiring the patterns there. Her mind, her imagination was a bottomless vessel, always filling with new ideas, new possibilities and new goals. Though new things materialized slowly at times, and sometimes they came with pain and stress, the well was never draining. It was always filling.

She had tracked down six of the extended family members. Painstakingly, carefully, gathering information through impersonations, falsified letters, theft, and outright spying over many months. Hours of headache-inducing concentration focused onto this task. Of course, there were more of them, there would always be more of them, much like rats or cockroaches or flies around piles of dung. But she did what she could and would continue to do so, wiping as many of their pathetic footprints permanently off the face of the earth as was possible.

The real targets, though, they were on hold. Mattie licked her lips and smiled. Let them sense what was happening. Let them come to the realization that something was in store for them, as well. Something even more dreadful than what their relatives had faced.

And now, with the help of the wealthy and well-connected Bensons and their friends, the former Crowley-philes, she should be able to find more of them. Stamp them out. Crush them into oblivion.

The first to go had been Maude and Mary O'Connor, sisters living in north Brooklyn, from the poor-trash side of their particular family, women who eagerly accepted Mattie's offer of two free tickets to a day on Coney Island, which required a return note saying when they would be arriving. The two women, giddy with the excitement of a paid holiday, stopped by the Symposium to pick up their park passes. Mattie let Rex take care of the face-to-face while she watched through the rear curtain. Tracking the ladies after that was relatively easy, though Mary and Maude parted ways and then only one could be followed and dispatched. That Assistant Alderman Harper had been with Maude wasn't so much worrisome as a nuisance. She'd ached for hours afterwards, lying on the cot in the Symposium's back room with a pillow over her head and instructions to Rex to put the "Closed" sign on the door until mid-afternoon.

The mother and her daughters, Julia Palmer and her kids, were a sister and nieces, a respected working-class family, but the three were happy to accept the free ticket to Steeplechase. Mattie had hoped to catch them in a more private place, but the crowds that day were intense, even more so than usual. She and Rex had followed them into the Maze, then Rex gave Mattie his coat and stood at one sharp turn, pretending to be lost, steering the other maze-goers into another direction that confused them and turned them around for a good five minutes. That was all it took, as children's heads were smaller and took less effort.

The reply from the next target had arrived this morning. Anna Dow. Another sister. "I am very happy to accept this free pass, and shall be stopping by in a few days with my husband to pick the ticket up. Thank you for selecting me from your random sampling of citizens. I will be happy to give a review of the park when our visit is done."

Anna would be stopping by the Symposium to collect her ticket. With her husband. A minor problem, however. Rex would be instructed on how to take care of the young man. And when the time came to destroy Anna, Mattie was the master.

All is coming along as planned. All is good.

Mattie had been perfecting her talents for seven years. Seven. A magical number. In those seven years, holed up in small flats and shacks and anywhere she could find a place to be alone, she read and studied and practiced to become stronger, to become the best, to become the most powerful. Her skills at telekinesis and motion-generated hypnosis were the most impressive but they could always be improved upon. At times she could touch an item or a person and gain insight into something about their past. Once, on a fluke, she had been able to stop time for everyone but herself by staring hard at a clock or watch face. It had lasted all of two seconds, and had not proved useful at all, save to see a boy stop in mid-leap and a Ferris wheel pause in mid-turn for two or three moments. That effort left her in bed for more than a day afterwards. Sometime in the future, on her plantation, she would have the time to work on the control of time and then concentrate even more fully on the prediction of future events. There were many delicious, glorious options ahead. For now, however, she had her hands quite full. "Practice makes perfect." She knew that old chestnut well. Practice on the sisters and cousins and daughters and mothers, and then she would be fine-tuned for the final, most delicious targets themselves.

Out in the Symposium's front room, beyond the heavy curtain, she could hear Rex grunting and stomping about, doing the card and handkerchief tricks for a small gathering. No, he didn't need to talk. His voice had been a guttural irritant, anyway. Now he had to be a bit more dramatic with his body and his hands, which made for a better show.

A few minutes later, there was mild applause, some coughing and muttering, and the crowd left. But then Mattie heard a young man's voice say, "Hey, what's back there? What you got hiding behind the curtain? Can I have a look?"

It was time for Mattie to get up, go out and introduce herself. To find out if the young man was alone or if someone was outside waiting for him.

She hoped he was alone. She just loved working the spinning chair, and it would offer one more imbecilic drone for the kingdom.

14

She saw him in the fading sunlight at the bottom of the Hell Gate steps, dressed in his dandy's clothing, complete with black jacket, top hat, and gray pressed trousers. A small white boutonniere was threaded through his top jacket buttonhole. In his hand was a batch of yellow daisies.

No, no, no!

She drew back from the top of the stairs into the deepest shadows and stood beside the boat master who was now out of his skull mask and was mopping sweat from his brow.

"Mighty brutal evening, this," the boat master said to Coralie. "Feels like God put a big old sweater on the earth right now in worst of the summer. You'd think He'd take a bit of pity on us, wouldn't you?"

"I don't know. He can do what he wants," said Coralie softly, not taking her eyes off Robert, who worked his shoulders and ran his finger along inside his collar, excited, clearly, to be seeing his one and only again. He licked his lips, a habit that drove pins into Coralie's nerves.

"Why did you come up through the hatch?" asked the ticket taker, inclining his head toward the hatched escape route. A ladder led from the downstairs "Hell Level" up to the trap door on the pool floor. Nobody used it. There'd never been a fire or other emergency in Hell Gate.

"Felt like it," said Coralie.

"You're a strange one."

"I've been called worse."

The ticket taker pulled off his skull mask. It had left a red impression on his face. "The rest of you demon actors change downstairs and then go out that exit."

I came up through the hatch because I thought I could trick Robert. I thought he'd be waiting for me there, but no, shit, here he is out front.

"Let it be," said Coralie. "It doesn't matter in the greater scheme of things, does it?"

"Fine. I'm not a busybody. Do as you wish."

A young man with long legs and shiny, overly-pomaded hair took the stairs two at a time and snatched the skull mask from the boat master's hand. He grinned at Coralie and put the mask on. It was seven o'clock. Time for the second shift. A moment later, the replacement ticket taker, a squatty boy who never smiled, hauled himself up the stairs, huffing with the effort, and pulled on his skull mask.

"You just going to stand there? Customers are lining up down front," said the masked ticket taker.

Maybe I should go back down the hatch. He hasn't seen me yet, I could scoot around and out the rear entrance before…

"Coralie!" Robert raised his hand and came rushing up the stairs, his face split in a most disturbingly happy smile. "There you are! I waited for a few minutes at the back, but then the other actors said they thought they saw you heading this way. And here you are!"

Damn it to Hell!

"When we're married, you shan't work, my dear. I won't allow it." Robert took her arm and she cringed. "I'll tolerate it for now, since you are still a single woman." He leaned in close and gave her a moist kiss. His breath smelled like tobacco and alcohol, quite a bit for it not even being past dinnertime. He steered her down the stairs with a firm grip on her elbow. Coralie's instinct was to wrench away, to tell him to go to Hell, to scream for help from anyone nearby who might understand what a circumstance she had gotten herself into.

But she only smiled and nodded and let herself be guided down the Promenade toward the Starlit Café, one of Dreamland's many small diners that offered ordinary foods with overblown names such as "Milky Way Sandwich," "Moon Cream," and "Galaxy Stew." She knew what would happen if she did scream or fight. Two nights ago she had done just that when Robert had fondled her under Dreamland Pier. She had been rewarded with bruises the size of dinner plates on her hip and upper arms. As strong as Coralie was, Robert was stronger by far. And crazy as a bedbug. And as dangerous as a tiger. After he beat her, he had kissed her and said, "Now, there's my Coralie. There's my girl. You shall behave now, won't you?"

She had not told her father. Her pride had kept her from it, her need to remain as independent as she had always been had prevented her from confessing her terrible dilemma. But she knew she would have to. As she and Robert walked along Dreamland's lagoon and as riders on the Shoot-the-Chutes careened down the slope to splash in the water, yelling and cheering, she realized that she was no match for everything in Coney. As much as she'd always thought it so, she had come to know that she was no match for an insane man with a lot of money and the delusion that she was his property.

All she had to do was make it through tonight. When she got home, she would tell her father everything. When she got home, she would put the police lieutenant on the case and with luck, Robert would find himself the property of the Coney Island jail.

Robert pulled her close and whispered in her hair, "I love you, my dearest. Over dinner, let us plan our wedding."

Coralie said nothing. Robert jerked her arm, hard, causing her head to snap back. "What do you say?"

"That sounds good," she said around a mouthful of glass.

15

Coralie's replacement as a Luna Park ticket girl was a young thing no more than fifteen, a beautiful child with perfect teeth, ebony hair, and near-black eyes. Her name was Anita, and was the only actual Mexican girl to wear the Mexican outfit. Adelaide and Eliza were particularly intrigued, and immediately tried to mimic Anita's lilting accent, and the little tosses of Anita's head that seemed to have such a fun yet dignified flair. O'Rourke, likewise, seemed especially fascinated by his new employee, and he tried to impress her by being more thoughtful and considerate when around the ticket girls. So, if for no other reason, Suzanne was glad Anita was there.

But she was concerned for Coralie. The girl had never looked so distressed as she had in the bowels of Hell Gate. All the other demons pranced and danced and played their parts, but Coralie looked as if she were terrified. As if she feared the old plaster Satan might pull himself up off his throne and bite her in half. Coralie never let her worries show. She was tough as iron.

But not yesterday.

It clawed at Suzanne's heart.

Something is wrong. Poor Coralie. She's so puffed up, but so vulnerable.

Men and women and boys and girls and children and babies rushed at her from all directions, waving money and flashing grins, full of hopes of a fun day in Luna Park. An occasional disgruntled grouch or pouting child. Suzanne took the money, handed the tickets, took the money, handed the tickets.

I can't do this today.

Took the money, handed the tickets, took the money, handed the tickets. Caught a bit of conversation between Anita and Eliza. Eliza wanted to know how to say something in Spanish and Anita was struggling to help.

Money. Tickets. Money. Tickets.

I can't stay here today.

"You gave me the wrong change!" said one prissy gentleman with an equally prissy woman at his side. "Are you a thief, to pocket the discrepancy and hope I won't notice?"

Suzanne re-counted the change, handed it over.

Money. Tickets. Money. Tickets.

Lunch break was too far away.

A little girl tugged on her father's hand, screaming, "I don't want to go in there! There's a elephant in there! I don't like elephants!" And the father said, "Be quiet, Myrtle, we're going and you're going to like it." Coins were slammed down on Suzanne's cart. "Two, please." She gave him the tickets.

I can't lose my job but I can't stay here today.

"Mi nombre es Eliza," said Eliza.

"Bueno!" said Anita.

"I like handsome men," said Eliza. "How do I say that?"

Anita giggled. "Tengo gusto de hombres hermosos."

Suzanne put her hand to her forehead and bent over her cart. She moaned. Loudly.

Adelaide looked over from her cart. "What's wrong?"

"I don't feel well at all. I've caught something."

"Oh, dear. Is it bad?"

"I'm quite dizzy."

"Oh, dear. Do you think you should go home?"

"I think that's best. Please tell O'Rourke for me."

Adelaide grimace. "Can't you, Suzanne? Please? You know what he's like. He'll bark at me."

"I don't care to lose my breakfast in front of him, or in front of you."

"I don't know, Suzanne, it would just take you a moment..."

"Anita?" The girl looked over from her cart. "I am ill and must leave. Please tell Mr. O'Rourke I am sorry but had to hurry."

Anita shrugged. "Oh, certainly. I will. I hope you feel better."

Suzanne left Luna, knowing O'Rourke would be enraged yet again, but also knowing that all full-time Luna Park employees were allowed two days off a year for sickness, and she'd never taken one. And knowing that Anita's charm might make the news of Suanne cutting and running go down easier for O'Rourke.

She headed east up Surf Avenue, past the dark and grim Great Deep Rift Coal Mine ride and a shop selling photo postcards, over the trolley tracks and across the street to Dreamland. She paid to enter and pushed through the throng to Hell Gate's front steps. She put her hands on her hips and told the ticket seller, "I need to see Coralie Granger. Immediately."

The ticket seller frowned. "Who?"

"Coralie Granger. She works here. Down in that ridiculous—"

"I don't know her and I have work to do."

"Then let me go up and talk to the boat master. He might know her. It's very important."

The skull-masked boat master seated a family of four in a little boat then sent it off into the whirlpool. "What? That's impossible. She's down there. I'm up here. It'll have to wait until she gets off at the end of her shift."

"Her father sent me to get her. Lieutenant Granger of the Coney Island police force. I don't think you'd care to challenge his request."

"Oh." The voice changed. A bit meeker now. "Oh, well, I'll see what I can do." He tugged the sleeve of the masked ticket taker. "I need to get downstairs for a moment. Hold the crowd until I get back. Five minutes at the most."

The ticket taker scowled, or at least Suzanne imagined he did, as the boat master pulled up the hatch in the floor and crawled down the ladder into the man-made bowels of Hell. Five minutes he was back, shaking his head.

"Sorry, she never came to work today."

"Did she send a message? Was she ill?"

"I don't know. Now go on, Miss. We have work to do."

Suzanne took the steps back down to the Promenade. *All right. Maybe Coralie was ill yesterday. Maybe that's why she looked so stressed.*

"I'd rather her be sick than scared. Poor, dear Coralie."

She would check with Coralie's father today. Make sure Coralie was doing all right. Sick at home would at least be safe at home. Coralie was too wild for her own good, and some time being quiet or reading or resting would do her good.

Now the most important chore of the day faced Suzanne. She would face the 3000 A.D. Theater.

The thought of it cramped her stomach, and this time, she actually felt sick.

16

There were many disturbing sights in Coney Island. Funny Face's terrible grin. The desperate yet very realistic screams of the trapped hotel guests in the Fighting the Flames show. The poster advertising the freaks of Freak Street and the sign encouraging folks to pay to stare at premature babies in boxes on display in Dreamland. The dark and gaping maw of the entrance to Hell Gate with its guardian devil looming overhead.

But this was the most disturbing of all.

Suzanne sat on a wooden bench in the back of the 3000 A.D. Theater with an audience of twenty-some others, watching some pathetic, poorly-dressed halfwits shambled about on a low, flat stage, waving their arms mechanically, emitting soft grunts as a cane poked at them from behind the rear stage curtain. A scratchy phonograph recording played eerie trumpet music, attempting, it seemed, to sound otherworldly.

The audience sat whispering, chuckling nervously, eating roasted peanuts from little paper bags. A baby squirmed off his mother's lap and began to crawl about on the floor.

Suzanne had removed her gloves in preparation. She had her palms pressed to the bench beside her, waiting, dreading, hoping something would come to her as it had the other night. If nothing in a few minutes, she would scoot to another spot on another bench. There was no doubt the killer had been in this very theater. At last she had a true sense of direction. It terrified her. It relieved her.

There was nothing where she sat, so she excused herself, went around and encouraged the others to move down a space, then sat at the far end of the bench. She touched the wood. Waited. Braced herself. Nothing. She pressed down. Still nothing. The creatures on the stage continued to move and grunt.

Then the music faded and a voice came out from the recording.

The low, matter-of-fact voice of a woman.

"You may wonder what it is you are witnessing. You may cower at their terrible countenances. You may shiver at what appears human but what appears to be anything but. And you are right in your discomfort."

Suzanne cocked her head to the sound. Froze.

"What you are witnessing is something beyond belief, but it must be believed. While the human race was not paying attention, aliens from Mars came to Earth. They bred with unsuspecting humans, producing this race of half-Earthling half-Martian. Such crossbreeding produces mindless creatures who might seem harmless, but when the Martians decide it is time to call them into action, we will see a power beyond our imaginations."

I've heard that voice…

"These few have been caught and are kept locked for our protection. But more are being born every day."

Dear God, I've heard that voice. Who is it? I can't remember who it is. Damn it!

"So pay attention. Be ready. The day is coming."

The strange music picked up again. The audience looked at one another in bemusement.

Suzanne began to shake uncontrollably, causing the man next to her to give her a disapproving look. She excused herself and stood against the wall, staring at the figures on the stage, bearing hard into her memory.

Whose voice? Where is it from?

It was deep inside, deep like the sweet scent whose name eluded her, at the back of her mind in the darkness. The fingers of her memory struggled to reach, stretching, almost touching but falling short.

Think, Suzanne. Think!

The unnamable sweet smell passed by her nostrils then faded away.

Think!

Then from behind her, cold, invisible arms rushed out, wrapping around her, binding her back against the wall in a frigid embrace. She gasped but no one heard her because one of the alien humans on the stage had tripped and fallen over the cane with a loud thump. She wrenched back and forth, the cold binding her, caressing her, holding her as tightly as a canvas jacket. Then hands she could not see bore into her, diving through her chest, through her ribs, to her heart.

She knew in that moment that she was going to die. Whatever

power it was that had come into this place, whatever force it was that had found her, would at that very moment in that very sorry place crush her heart and leave her on the floor.

But then, *NO!*

She wouldn't allow it.

Damn this to Hell! I'm stronger than this!

She closed her eyes, fought with every cell of her body. In the darkness, razor-toothed rabbits and the swirling white appeared, threatening to catch her up and spin her again. Her eyes snapped open.

No, no, NO!

Her mind scrambled, recalling the past, remembering a power she had dabbled with long ago, and with all her might she pinpointed that tiny spot in her brain, the long-ignored ability to move something, to push something away, with the power of thought.

Now!

She focused into and against the hand at her heart, *Let go, let GO!*

The cold fingers touched her heart; it skipped a painful beat. Her lips curled in terrified defiance.

Let GO! Get BACK!

The fingers touched her heart again. Probing. Taunting.

"I said get BACK!" she screamed.

The hands vanished. The arms evaporated.

The audience spun about on their rears to glare at Suzanne.

"What's wrong?" she managed. She stepped away from the wall. "Never heard a woman yell before?"

Heads shook, eyes rolled. They all turned back toward the stage where the figure on the floor was still struggling to stand back up. His cotton shift caught up on his hip and revealing that yes, he was indeed male. Mothers covered their children's eyes. Young women giggled. One man jumped up onto the stage and pulled the floundering alien human upward, then said, "Enough of this. I want some chowder."

And so the show ended earlier than expected, and the crowd filed out, ushered by a silent, frantic-eyed giant who came out from behind the stage's rear curtain to hold out a tip can. No coins were dropped inside it.

Suzanne was the last to leave, hating the place, dreading another encounter, yet knowing this place held the answer.

The answer to the murders.

And the answer to a question she had not even asked. A question she did not even know existed. One she could not even comprehend enough to put into words.

17

Cittie had slept under the Cyclops cage — an angry, disturbed sleep that came only in brief periods of dozing and left him exhausted, sore, and covered with insect bites. Throughout the day and into the evening, each pair of men's black boots topped by gray trousers had caused his heart to clench, certain that his time was up, the police officer had found him and would drag him out by his ears.

But the officer didn't come into Freak Street, or if he did he didn't pass by the Cyclops cage. Yet Cittie still suspected the man was nearby, in Dreamland, asking questions, sniffing around. And so he stayed put, burying his face into the crook of his arm, cursing himself for being careless, cursing the officer for being so suspicious, planning his next move.

The world awoke just after six in the morning, with golden sunlight and birds that nested in Dreamland singing their territorial claims. An hour later, he could hear the employees arriving, preparing for the day. Carts wheeled into place, booths and stands opened, fish frying, hot dogs boiling, umbrellas opened and actors heading for their buildings to costume up for the first show.

I think I'm safe.

He pulled himself forward so his head was peeking out from under the cage. None of the freaks were in place yet — they had rooms in the back of the Creation building — but would be coming soon. Cittie crawled out and stood on shaky legs. He blew his nose several times, dislodging dead gnats.

He sneaked to the end of Freak Street and peered out. The vendors and magicians and animal trainers were busy preparing for the long day ahead. No one looked over at him.

Quickly, then, but not running so as not to attract attention, Cittie made his way past the shows and rides, beyond Beacon Tower and the bright blue lagoon, around the teahouse and back to the Bloodthirsty Zulu tent. The band members were in various stages of wakefulness. Lightnin' was still snoring on his cot, his mouth wide as a cavern, drooling into his pillow.

"What the Hell happened to you?" asked Moses. "You're all banged up. Bit up. Your eye's swelled, too."

Cittie touched his eye. It was a bit puffy. Bug bite. He looked at Moses. Moses, he could trust. The others, he wasn't so sure. But to take Moses aside to tell him about the cop, about his disguise, his day with Suzanne, and the wrench that was still in his pocket would generate too much suspicion in the others. Best to let it be for now.

Plopping down on one of three stools in front of the small dressing table, Cittie dug his fingers into the red makeup jar and slathered it on in thick globs. Then the black. Then the white.

"Hold on there," said Cletus. "You wastin' that. Leave some for us!"

Cittie ignored him. The more disguise the better. Cletus grabbed the jar away and gave him a look.

Out into Dreamland they marched in their loincloths and bones, skirts and tiger teeth, painted into terrifying figures, banging, tooting, dancing, rattling, their fearless white leader marching beside them with his rifle at the ready. Cittie watched the crowds as he drummed, skimming the faces, breathing hard, praying all was well and that the officer had decided Cittie wasn't worth the effort and was off to chase after real criminals.

They performed, scared folks, made others laugh nervously, hooted, hollered, pretended to be cowed back into line by Dick Bergman. They sweated and the makeup ran, but on they went, around and around Dreamland, hissing at children, shaking rattles at haughty old men. The sun rose high, began to lower to the west, and it was time for the midday meal. Dripping with sweat and white face paint, they returned to the tent.

Cittie stopped just inside the flap.

In the middle of the floor, holding both the blue Arabian costume and the wrench from Cittie's trouser pocket, was the police officer.

"Ah, I knew you would be easy to find," he said with a sniff of his crooked nose.

The band stopped, looked at Cittie, at the officer. Bergman tossed his rifle onto the nearest cot. "What's this about?"

"I suggest you ask your drummer there," said the officer. "What's his name, now?"

"Cittie Parker," said Bergman.

"Not Tom Brown, eh?"

"Tom Brown?" Bergman scowled. "No."

"And here you are, Cittie Parker, trying to hide in plain sight. Sorry, boy. I'm not that green."

Cittie stared. First at the costume, then at the wrench.

Oh, my Jesus, no.

"My name is Officer Mitchell Whitman," the policeman said to Bergman. "I noticed your boy here acting suspiciously yesterday afternoon, going around in this….this outfit…out on Surf Avenue. He'd borrowed it from one Sadie Schroeder, apparently. Wasn't hard to track it down, take it as evidence, find out where the borrower worked, then wander on over here."

"Evidence?" asked Bergman. "Of what?"

"Several things, actually. First, he was with a woman I suspect of no good, a Luna Park girl with shady behavior."

"Oh?"

"A white woman, Mr. Bergman."

"Oh."

"And then I noted this in his pocket." Whitman waved the wrench. "Without going into detail best kept at the precinct for the time being, this speaks volumes about a major investigation, and gives me even more reason to arrest him this very moment. I'm sorry, but you'll have to find yourself another good niggra for your band."

Dear God. I'm dead.

"I always thought somethin' was wrong with you, Cittie," said Lightnin'. He flopped down on his cot and laughed. Moses gave Cittie a look of horror, and then Whitman turned Cittie around and marched him out of Dreamland.

18

Mattie shut down the 3000 A.D. theater and wired George Benson to secure a wagon and haul the drones away under the cloak of night to a warehouse he owned out on Long Island. When he arrived, he was taken aback by what he saw, and insisted that Rex herd them into the truck so he didn't have to touch any of them. He promised to hire a few underlings to feed and care for them until another suitable location could be secured.

After the drones were gone, in the gray light just before sunrise, she set fire to the little building by stuffing straw under the stage and gazing at it with her concentrated stare. It smoldered, caught, and spread quickly, burning bright and wild. She and Rex stood down Stratton's Walk a ways, watching it burn, watching the first frightened man — the fellow who ran the pony rides — pass by then run off to call for the fire department. The little clam shack beside the theater caught fire as a breeze tossed flame onto its roof, and half the shack and the entire theater were gone before the firemen were able to pump enough water onto the conflagration.

A crowd gathered as they always did to admire disasters, shaking their heads and crossing their arms, saying what a shame for the theater and shack, and how lucky it was it didn't spread any farther than it did.

Mattie and Rex returned to the Symposium — Rex to sleep in the corner of the front room with his blanket and pillow, Mattie to the cot. However, she did not sleep. She crossed her arms over her chest and looked at the light bulb overhead, a new replacement since she'd shattered the last one. Her heart raced and her stomach was knotted. She hadn't felt like this in a long time. She hadn't experienced such panic since she was much younger. There was danger nearby. There was someone in Coney Island who had at least as much power as she did. Someone who had come to the 3000 A.D. theater and had sat on a bench, stood against the wall.

Someone who was looking to find Mattie and stop her.

And so she had burned the theater down. It infuriated her to do it; nothing confirmed one's one insecurity like having to destroy something one had built just to thwart an enemy. Better to stand up against them, challenge them face to face.

But Mattie didn't know the face. She didn't know the name or the voice. She only sensed the proximity of the enemy. If Mattie's keen senses were not on full alert during the day, she might even pass that person on Surf Avenue or Stratton's Walk and not even know it.

Not knowing was dangerous.

Oh, she thought, she could order the Bensons to buy her some land and help her move to the South with her entourage. But that wouldn't be dealing with this immediate problem. And this problem had to be eliminated. If not, she sensed it would follow her and continue its attempt to destroy her. Mattie needed to rethink, to lay low and pay attention with every fiber of her being, to scout out the enemy and kill it. Until then, she would not be able to continue with her work. Whoever it was would suffer and then die, and as he died, she would gleefully tell him about her plans, plans he had not been able to stop.

Mattie clenched her fists, gritted her teeth.

The new light bulb shattered, sending shards to the floor.

19

Cittie sat in the corner of the cell on a piss-soaked bench, watching between the huge, scarred, slobbering man seated on the floor beside the door, a thin man asleep on a second bench, and a preacher of some sort on his knees, facing the wall, speaking in words Cittie could not understand. There were no windows in the cell. The floor was concrete with a drain in the middle. There was no bedpan; when Cittie had called through the iron-barred door to tell the guard he needed to relieve himself, the guard said, "That's what the hole there's for. We don't give pans to black criminals no more. Had pans full of shit and piss thrown at us more times than we can count. Animals, the lot of you!"

Humiliated more than he could ever remember, Cittie squatted over the drain hole and voided his bowels. Had he his street clothes, he could have covered himself with his jacket or trousers, but Officer Whitman had dragged him out of Dreamland in his Zulu costume, which, at the precinct house, had made him look all the more crazy and dangerous.

He finished, found nothing with which to wipe, and so resigned himself to sitting back on the bench as he was, realizing now that the dark marks on the bench weren't just piss stains.

The room was cold, and there were no blankets. The guard had told him as he'd pushed him through the door that this was just a holding room until the judge could hear the charges and Cittie would be arraigned.

Whitman had been quite proud of himself, presenting Cittie to the officer at the desk, demanding to see Lieutenant Granger because certainly the skull-crushing murderer had been apprehended. Whitman had chained Cittie to a chair beside his desk in the large, open communal office — most likely, Cittie thought, to let the other officers see his catch — as he wrote up his report. The office had been stuffy, but the cell was sweltering.

The slobbering man had studied Cittie carefully on his arrival; he'd looked like he was imagining Cittie as a big slab of beef on a platter. The sleeping man had been sleeping, and continued to. Had he not shuddered on occasion, Cittie would have sworn he was dead. The preacher had asked, "Who are you, my son?"

Cittie hadn't answered. He felt the less his cellmates knew about him, the less he was noticeable, the safer he would remain.

But once he was taken out for arraignment, he would face Hell. The Coney Island police were champing at the bit to solve the Capital Hotel and Mirror Maze murders. Whitman had seen Cittie's wrench.

Whitman had seen Cittie with a white woman — Suzanne Heath, to be exact.

Cittie had been in a disguise.

Cittie had run from Whitman, which would certainly increase the suspicion of his guilt.

All the way to the precinct house, Whitman had laughed about the electric chair up in Sing Sing. "Used to be in Albany, but they moved it. Quite a fancy piece of hardware, I understand. Strap you in with leather straps, crank you up good and tight against them, put on a metal cap, attach a leg wire, say a little prayer, then let the current rip! I understand some men die right away but most sit and sizzle and jump for oh, a good minute or so. Smells something fierce. So bad sometimes the inmates near the death room complain.

Sometimes they have to flip the switch again to kill 'em. Wonder what it feels like, getting fried like a live perch in a pan? I think you'll be able to find out. Too bad you won't be able to tell me what you felt, though."

It was all Cittie could do to keep from throwing up. He clenched his jaws, tried to pace his breathing, and gave his fate to God for the Coney Island police would never accept his plea of innocence.

Cittie knew he was a dead man.

The preacher, on his knees before the wall, began to wail and rock, then scream like a tortured man. Cittie put his hands over his ears but the sound poured in like water.

20

"Cittie."

Cittie looked up from the bench. Suzanne stood outside the door, her hands on the rusting bars, staring into the shadow cell.

"Cittie, it's Suzanne."

Cittie scratched his arm and sat up on the bench. His torso was rolled in a small, ratty blanket. His feet and legs were bare. Several other men shared the cell with him — a jabbering man squatting in a corner, a large man pressed against the walls, and a slight man, little more than a boy, sitting alone on a second bench picking at the skin on his chin. The room reeked, but Suzanne did her best not to show her disgust.

"How'd you know I was here?" Cittie's voice was ragged, low.

"Lieutenant Granger sent word to me that there would be no more need for me to help them with their investigations. He said they'd caught their man, someone who had been spotted with me in a disguise, and carrying a wrench in his pocket."

Cittie nodded, tried to smile but there was a huge welt on the side of his face that made it nearly impossible. Suzanne's heart clenched.

"God. Did they beat you?"

"Couple hours ago. Took me out back, stripped me clean, gave me what they called 'a taste of my own medicine.' Said they'd leave me alive so's I could fry in the chair for what I done."

Damn them! "They have no proof of anything. You haven't done anything."

"I'm their murderer and I won't confess."

Suzanne looked left, up the narrow aisle off which were six cells for colored inmates. The door leading from the colored cell block was open. Beyond that were the cells for the white men. There had been lots of white men in those cells. Here, in the colored section, were only these three men, all crammed into the one cell. "They said I could visit only a minute. They said usually they don't let white folks visit the Negro cells. Especially not white ladies."

"Glad you came. Thanks."

"You're welcome."

Cittie scratched his arm, hard. "Got flea bites. Fleas pretty fierce in here. Hot, too."

"Then why are you wrapped up in that blanket?"

He looked at her, and his expression told her why. When they'd stripped him, they hadn't given him anything to put on but had tossed him back into the cell naked.

"You hungry?"

He nodded. "Ain't fed us for nearly twenty-four hours."

"Bastards. I'll tell them to get some food in here."

"Thanks." She could tell he knew her request would be worthless.

"Why'd they let you come in to see me? It don't make sense."

"I'm not sure. Whitman isn't here, he's out on rounds. Maybe they're eavesdropping in hopes you'll tell me something you wouldn't tell them. You notice no one is here with me. But I would bet they are listening."

"Could be."

"I will get you out, Cittie. Now more than ever, I will find the murderer and have you set free. I swear this to you."

"At the asylum they always said swearin' ain't good. Don't swear, Suzanne."

"I'll vow, then. I vow to exonerate you. If it's the last thing I do, I promise."

Cittie looked at her sadly, his face contorted with the swelling, his brows pinched.

"Stay strong," she said.

"I'll do the best I can."

"It won't be long before I hear you say, 'This is good. This is right.'"

He smiled a little. Then, "Don't get hurt, Suzanne. You be careful."

"I will be. You, too."

He nodded.

She left.

It wasn't until she was walking hard south toward Surf Avenue that she was aware of the tears on her cheeks. They burned like acid.

21

"I haven't seen her in three days now," said Lieutenant Granger. He stood at the top of the rickety steps outside Suzanne's room above the Moons' shop, trying to stand tall and confident, but trembling beneath his uniform. It was early morning, with a mild breeze blowing and starlings and pigeons fluttering closely overhead in search of food. Greasy smoke hung in the air; someone was cooking fatty meat nearby. Down on the road, a milkman rattled by with his horse and cart. The Moons could be heard arguing in their shop. "There have been times that she's gone off for a day or two, and that makes me mad with worry, but she has always come home. Always. I sent men out last evening to find her, as I began to suspect something foul has gone down. But they didn't find her. I thought maybe you might have talked to her, you might know something..." he trailed.

"She works at Hell Gate now, in Dreamland." Suzanne's words sounded odd, as if from outside herself. There was a soft ringing in her ears and her stomach was tight as a stretched canvas jacket. Cittie was in jail. Cittie could die.

"Yes, I know," said Granger. "They saw her leave Sunday night. But she didn't come home Monday night, nor last night. I hoped that, as her friend, you might have talked to her. She might have told you where she was going."

Suzanne shook her head, pulled the door closed behind her and locked it. "I'm sorry, Lieutenant. I don't know anything. I wish I could help." *I was right*, she looked terrified down in Hell Gate. *It wasn't illness, it was fear. Perhaps she's the murderer's next victim. Perhaps it's my fault that the killer is still out there. Oh, God. God damn me.*

"Maybe she told you to keep a secret? Girls do that, you know. A secret she was afraid to tell me?"

Suzanne started down the steps. Granger followed. "No secrets."

"Think harder. Please?"

Suzanne reached the walk, steeled her legs beneath her, and turned to Granger. "I saw her in the Hell Gate ride Sunday morning and she didn't look at all happy. I guessed perhaps she was sick. But maybe not."

"I'll walk you to work," said Granger.

"There's no reason." *Just go on, leave me alone.*

"Maybe not. Indulge me." There was naked fear in his eyes.

"All right."

"You don't look well, Miss Heath."

"My friend is accused of murder, there is a murderer loose in Coney, and now your daughter is missing. I would say I'm due to look less than perfect."

Granger humphed.

They walked in silence all the way to Surf Avenue, moving with the growing crowds of trolleys and wagons, pedestrians and happy stray dogs out for a trot. Clearly Granger was hoping to give Suzanne time to reconsider what she'd said, to either come clean with what she knew or to recall something she had forgotten.

As they turned onto Surf Avenue beside the Capital Hotel, Suzanne stopped and held up her hand, hoping he didn't see it shaking. "Lieutenant, I have nothing to tell you. She might just show up this evening. She might not. What more can I tell you?"

Granger tightened his jaw, looked up and down the street at the bustling holiday crowds and the rattling trolley as it passed, then looked back at Suzanne. "Maybe if I gave you something of hers? Some clothing, perhaps, that you could hold? You might see something?"

Suzanne caught the inside of her lower lip with her teeth, and then let it go. "I don't know. You know it's not something I can always control."

"But maybe?"

"Lieutenant…"

"Maybe?"

"Maybe."

"Good, yes, thank you. I tell you what, you go on to work and I'll find something she wore most recently and send it over, or I might bring it over myself if I can and…."

"Wait. You want something from me. I want something from you."

"How much?" Granger fumbled for his front jacket pocket, unbuttoned it. "I don't have a lot of extra money but I can offer what I have."

"No, no money. I want you to let Cittie Parker go."

"Who?"

"Cittie Parker. The man you are holding for the Capital Hotel and Mirror Maze murders."

"Surely you're joking, Miss Heath."

"Do I look like I'm joking? No, I look sick to you. And I am. Sick at heart over cruelty, violence, and injustice."

Granger wiped his mouth, frustrated, desperate.

"He is innocent. I know it. I've known him for years."

"You think you know him, Miss Heath. Obviously you don't."

"Some things we may think we know. Sometimes we might not be sure that we know. In the case of Cittie, I know without a doubt that he is not guilty."

"So have you touched him, then? Have you seen his comings and goings? Have you determined his innocence as you determined the guilt of the man who attacked Coralie and sent her to the hospital? Have you seen his inner thoughts by catching his elbow or putting your hand on his shoulder?"

"I…" *No, I've never touched him.* "I can swear on my life that Cittie had nothing to do with the murders."

"I can't release him, Miss Heath. He'll have his trial."

"After one of your officers has beat him half to death again?"

"He tried to escape."

"No, he didn't. They stripped him and beat him for the fun of it. If they told you he tried to escape, they lied."

"My officers don't lie," he said, but the tone of his voice said he knew they were capable of lies.

"So you can't help my friend? Yet you want my help."

"There is no way I can just let him go. He's in the system, there is evidence against him…"

"No evidence at all. Circumstantial at best."

"Damn it, Miss Heath! He was in disguise. He ran from Whitman. He had a wrench in his pocket, a wrench that could easily smash a skull!"

"Any blood on the wrench? Brain matter?"

"How easy to wash a wrench. The boy's very likely guilty. Whitman is certain of it."

"Not to mention Whitman saw Cittie and me together, and Whitman likes me about as much as he would like a sandwich filled with shit."

"The court will decide his guilt. I tell you most truthfully. But I can offer to you his protection from further harm."

"How?"

"I can give him a cell alone, and give instructions to all on the force to let him be."

A little boy ran up to Suzanne and sprayed her with water from his little tin gun. It struck her skirt and he chortled loudly. His mother snatched him up, gave Suzanne a cursory "I'm sorry, ma'am," and hurried off into the throng of bodies and vehicles.

"He'll be safe, I can promise you that much."

It's not enough. It's not enough!

"And warm clothing."

Nothing is enough that is short of his freedom!

"Please, Miss Heath."

"You could sneak him out, sneak him free, and he could go off where he couldn't be found again."

Granger cringed. "There is no way to do that, no back door from the Negro cells. And I can't risk my career on that."

"Not on your daughter?"

"Damn it, Miss Heath! Listen to me! If I could, I would. Let me tell you that. But there is no way to get him past twenty or more officers on duty at any one time. The chief has a special guard on him, as the murder suspect. It would not work. I would be arrested, charged, convicted. Then Coralie, if she is indeed safe and just being careless and shows up at home, she won't find me. She'll be alone for the first time in her life. And as confident as she pretends to be, or even imagines herself to be, she is vulnerable like any woman. She couldn't make enough to pay for lodging and food. She has no prospects for a good husband to care for her. It's a risk I don't care to take, and for you to ask that of me is cruel."

Suzanne looked at the sky. Just tilting her head back made her feel for a moment as if she were spinning. She closed her eyes, opened them again, but the sensation of going around was just barely diminished. Herring gulls circle 'round, white clouds drifted past, crisscrossed by the countless electrical wires above the street. Then she managed, "You must see that he eats well. I don't care if you have to smuggle steaks in beneath your jacket or in your hat there. He will be well cared for. And I will be able to visit him when I want to without any interference. During that time, I will continue to seek out the true killer. If I need your help, you'll give it to me."

Granger nodded.

"Bring to me something she wore most recently. And know that I can promise nothing. But I do promise I will do my best to find something that will help you."

"Good, good."

"And I will try my best to find the murderer. No, I will find the murderer. That, I swear to you. And when I do, Cittie will be released and never harassed again."

"I understand. Thank you."

Suzanne left Granger by the Capital Hotel. Up to Luna Park she went, dragging her feet, feeling as if God's hands were on her, pressing her down into the ground, challenging her to stand upright, to keep on moving. Upon her arrival, O'Rourke told her that she was no longer employed there for taking two sick days in a row. He didn't care that she was due the days, and she saw her replacement at her cart already. Another young Spanish girl with bright eyes and flowing black hair.

Suzanne turned away. O'Rourke could choke on his cigar for all she cared, or get caught with one of those young girls by one of their fathers, and pay the price.

She had a terrified friend to save from death. She had a killer to find. She had her life to correct.

Oh, Dark World, are you Hell's hell? Is there light to swallow you up, waiting in the wings for angels of earth to tear open the door? Or do you laugh at those who struggle, and feed off their torment, growing ever stronger, ever more dark?

22

Suzanne started from the beginning, retracing, first revisiting the Capital Hotel. She took the steps with effort and then wandered down the hall to room forty-six. She told the couple staying there that a double homicide had taken place in that very room which caused them to snatch up their cases and clothing and demand another room from the manager. The manager was furious at Suzanne but backed down when she said she was on assignment from Granger and he best not interfere. The hotel had a telephone and she knew the manager might call the police precinct house to check, but so be it. It would still give her some time.

Avoiding the mirror, she focused on the bed frame, the door, the walls, the windowsill, running her bare fingers along them, trying to clear her mind of all thoughts, trying to let what might be there soak in. The mattress, pillows, and rug, had been replaced, of course. A bit hard to get customers to settle in with blood and brain bits scattered all about.

Suzanne closed her eyes, recalled the bashed assistant alderman and the hapless Miss O'Connor. She moved slowly, trailing her fingers waiting, concentrating. She picked up images of a little girl with her face pressed to the wall, playing count-to-ten with her brother. She saw an old woman clutching the foot of the bed frame in a faint as a woman who was likely the old woman's daughter tried to coax her to sit down. There were voices, old and young, discussing rides and shows in the parks and in the Bowery, those enjoyed and those dismissed as a waste of money. She smelled a clean baby, diarrhea, powder, sweat. All the input made her dizzy but she moved on, around the room.

Then up to the bed's headboard. She touched it, held it, waited, prayed for something to help save Cittie. There was nothing.

Nothing.

She pressed down.

Come on.

Nothing.

Please! I can't do this much more! It's too much! Give me something! Something I can use!

She closed her eyes.

Something!

And then the face of Maude O'Conner was up against Suzanne's face, huge and close and hideous and bloody and crushed, the eye sockets scarlet and pooled, the eyes smashed deep and back yet staring out from the depths like puppies hoping to be saved from a sewer drain. God! Suzanne gasped, stumbled, but did not let go of the bed frame.

Let me see more. Let me know more.

A soft rustling sound — the killer? — moved away from the bed toward the door. The door opened, closed, trailing a sweet scent. The sweet scent she knew but didn't know.

Suzanne's hand grew wet with perspiration, her breaths fast, her heart a rock thudding against her ribs.

I need more! Who did this? What is the smell? By all the angels and demons, I have to know!

But her mind could not find it amid all her vast and tangled memories. Again, it eluded her.

To Steeplechase Park, then, with a quarter for admission in her clammy hand. She thought briefly of what it would mean, now that she was without work. No money to buy food, not that she was hungry or could even fathom being hungry again. No money to pay the Moons, not that she would care right now should rain or snow fall on her and kill her. But life was what it was, and she would have to eat, would have to have shelter. Perhaps the Moons would give her a few weeks to find another job. Or perhaps they would turn her out. There were many factories; she would find something. The Triangle Shirtwaist Factory itself employed hundreds of girls. She'd seen advertisements for workers off and on in *The New York Times*.

Up the Funny Staircase between several school girls in their white dresses and several school boys who were determined to get up to where the school girls were, she pushed past Suzanne as if she weren't even there. She caught passing senses of their desire but their equally strong sense of insecurity about their looks. On through the Barrel of Love, sliding, cursing under her breath, toppling, then out again. Down to the first floor, across to the Mirror Maze.

She stood at the entrance, letting others go in front of her, holding herself together against herself, dreading the idea of trying to make it through to the middle without the ribbon to show her the way. The mirrors winked at her, sparked their ominous greeting, tried to get her to look full on. She looked away.

"You buyin' a ticket, Miss?" asked the ticket seller at the podium beside the entrance.

"I don't know."

"Well, step out of the way so others can get through, please."

She stepped out of the way. A steady stream of cheerful folks in summer jackets and billowy summer frocks filed past, buying tickets, moving into the maze and disappearing. From deep within she could hear them laughing, shrieking, moaning happily as their confusion increased.

"Don't worry," the ticket taker called over the Suzanne on the sidelines. "You get lost for more than an hour, I'm supposed to send someone in to find you and bring you out."

"Really? You send someone in?" *How long were the mother and daughters in there? You sent no one in for them. They had to be discovered like discarded garbage once the park closed down.*

"Yep. It's policy."

"Damn poor policy if you don't follow it."

The man frowned, handed a ticket to a middle-aged woman. "Excuse me?"

"Nothing," said Suzanne.

She watched the customers going in, coming out. Like waves on the ocean. In, out, back, forth, a constant stream. The sheen on the mirrors flashed with each movement of the crowd, whispering, *Come in, Suzanne. You'll find what you need to know in here. Come in. Come in.*

She walked away, found a bench, and sat holding her knees, watching the tips of her shoes. The world spun beneath her. Voices of passersby sounded like hissed accusations. She could not hear the words but knew the tone. Condemning. Damning. She clamped her teeth, preventing the bile that rocketed into her mouth from coming through her lips. The taste was foul, bitter.

She couldn't go into the maze, regardless of what it might offer. For if she went in she knew she would never come out. The mirrors would make sure of that. They would bind her and reflect her guilt back to her and never let her go.

I'm losing my mind. That's what this is.

I'm losing my mind in trying to find truth.

She swallowed hard against the bile and forced herself to her feet.

No, she thought. *No! I have to hold on. I can't go crazy, not now, maybe later. Maybe later when the crimes are solved and I'm absolved and there is nothing more I have to do. Then I can go insane and it won't matter anymore.*

I must keep my mind to save Cittie.

The 3000 A.D. theater awaited her. It held the best possibility to find what she was looking for. It was the most psychically charged. It held the most terrifying but important possibilities. She would do that for Cittie. She would do that for whatever future victims there might be.

Thank God, the theater had no mirrors.

23

Anna Dow looked quite a bit like her older sister, Darlene Andrews. Petite, pale, freckled, with curly hair, a weak chin, and ears a bit too big for her head. She was prim and pinned and dressed well, suggesting her husband was well employed. Her dress was pale pink and her hat, as wide as a buggy wheel, was bedecked with fabric fruits of all types. Mattie watched through the back-room curtain as Rex opened the door to the tapping and let Mr. and Mrs. Dow enter. Both wrinkled their noses as they looked about at the magician table, the benches, the bare walls, clearly uneasy with the tawdriness of the place but willing to bear it for the few minutes it took to claim their free ticket. *Funny*, Mattie thought, *rich folks seem to love free things more than poor folks. Grab something, and another something, and another something. Hold it, don't let it go. It's why they remain rich.* The thought made Mattie grin.

Mattie came through the curtain, startling the husband and wife. "Hello, my name is Mattie Snow." She held out her hand and offered her most disarming smile. Anna took the hand, squeezed it slightly, let it go. "You are the winner of the free ticket. Nice to meet you. Mrs. Dow? Mr. Dow?"

The couple nodded. Mr. Dow said, "Your sign says you're closed.

Thank you for letting us in."

"You're welcome."

"We're here for the free ticket to Luna Park. A pittance of a prize if you ask me, but Anna was happy to have won."

"That's nice. I'm happy she is happy."

Anna cocked her head and said, "You are a lovely young woman, I was expecting, I don't know…"

"A grizzled carnival barker with bad breath and a wooden leg, perhaps?" Mattie laughed lightly. "I hear that frequently. How could someone like you be involved in the tawdry business of running an amusement? I realize it's not the ordinary path for a woman of my background, groomed to be a steward of home, family, church, and society. And yet I selected this as part of my long-term goal."

Mr. Dow frowned. "Long-term goal? Have you no husband?"

"Oh, no. And no prospects at the moment, either. No matter, however. What I've studied shall make me more than capable of taking care of myself."

Anna touched her chin delicately. "You said education. Where did you go to school, may I ask? Something you said caught my attention."

"That I'm not grizzled and I don't have a wooden leg?"

"Ah, no, not that."

"That I know my path is not ordinary?"

"No. What you said about being a steward of home, family, church, and society. That's the motto of the school my sister, Darlene, attended."

"Is it indeed?"

"Yes. Madame Harlow's school. A reputable place, and I was planning on attending, as well, but then there was the incident during a tent revival meeting, which shook their confidence in the ability to manage the students. My parents decided to send me elsewhere."

"Madame Harlow's school. Yes, I know of it. Did Darlene like her time there?"

"I suppose so."

"And our free tickets?" Mr. Dow was growing impatient.

"Ticket, sir, one ticket, for your wife. It looks as if you could afford to buy your own."

Mr. Dow snapped his fingers, and Mattie handed over the Luna Park ticket. She had made sure the paper was stained a bit, and had a chew mark on the side. Mr. Dow looked disgusted but put the ticket in his pocket.

"On second thought," said Mattie, "you are such a nice couple. I would be very happy to give you not only a free ticket to Luna Park, but one to Steeplechase, Dreamland, and the Iron Tower as well, Mr. Dow. Just step back through the curtain with me into the rear room. I have the tickets in a box there."

Mr. Dow shook his head. "No, no thank you. I don't like it here and I'm not convinced you aren't some kind of sneaky miscreant or pickpocket. Luring folks with free tickets to take their wallets."

"Patrick, that's uncalled for," said Anna.

"No, it isn't. I wondered about the free ticket to Luna, but decided to let you have your fun…"

"I'd never won anything in my life before," Anna said to Mattie as if hoping for a bit of help.

"…and I've not been to Coney Island since we came with Uncle Samuel and Aunt Lattrice two years ago. But something is odd here, something I don't like."

"Mr. Dow…Patrick," said Mattie, "I'm sorry you are distrustful. But come with me into the back room. I will let you select the tickets you want for yourself and your wife. There are several for an evening at Henderson's Music Hall. It includes free beer."

"Patrick," urged Anna.

"No."

"Patrick? Let's select a few other tickets. She's trying to show you she is not a pickpocket. I appreciate that."

"She'll get me into the back room and roll me, I suspect."

"Patrick! I'm ashamed that you would be so distrustful! Miss Snow, my apologies."

"That's all right," said Mattie. "Caution can be a good thing. I understand and I'm not offended. You two have a wonderful day in Luna with my blessing."

"Patrick? At least the Henderson's tickets?"

Patrick Dow blew an exasperated breath, tapped his teeth, and then nodded. He and Anna followed Mattie through the curtain into the back room, where Rex grabbed the man and forced him into the spinning chair and into the straps while Mattie held Anna and made her watch. The chair spun 'round and 'round and the lights went off and the horrible rabbits appeared and Patrick went limp with insanity.

Then Mattie made Anna sit on the floor, and proceeded to crush her skull with her mind.

24

The 3000 A.D. theater had burned. Nothing was left but charred planks and puddles, the stench of ash and a couple half-benches still lying on their side in the middle of the mess.

He knew.

Suzanne stared at the remains, one hand over her mouth. People moved behind her, in front of her, glancing at the burned boards, shaking their heads and shrugging, and moving on.

He knew. This was no accident. The murderer knew I was looking for him and so burned this place to the ground.

Suzanne stood motionless, with only her chest heaving in and out in dismay.

"He knew."

"What's that?" said a man passing before Suzanne. "Did you say something, Miss?"

"No," said Suzanne. The man went on.

But how could he know? Suzanne, you're losing your mind for certain. While seeking visions of truth, you are letting in ridiculous imaginings. There is no way the killer could have known you were there.

She moved slowly to stand toe to toe with a fallen beam. The acrid scent stung her nose. She pulled off her gloves, reached out, touched it. Her body tensed with what was to come.

But there was nothing.

She focused her mind, her heart, her soul. *Come on, damn it! I'm better at this in spite of myself and I won't have suffered it all for naught! Show me what I might see. Show me who came here! Show me, show me the killer's face so I can save Cittie!*

Nothing.

Something!

She pushed her hand harder against the wood.

Damn it, give me something!

Nothing.

She knelt on the ground beside the blackened beam, her knees instantly wet through her skirt, her hand still flush against the wood. She would not move until she felt something. It was still there, beneath the damage. It had to be. Just as there was still wood here, deep within the carbonized outer fiber of the plank, there must still be a bit of information, too. Deep, but there, still. Her teeth bore down against each other, her molars snagging a bit of cheek and drawing blood. Her breaths grew uncomfortably fast and sweat beaded and rolled down her face, her arms, her chest.

Something! Give it to me!

A flash of memory — sitting on her cot in the attic at the Waifs' Asylum, refusing to move until she found the answers she needed. Doctor Terry declaring her crazy for doing so, threatening to send her off to where the canvas jackets awaited her.

Men and woman moved behind her and she felt their disapproving looks, could hear their critical comments to one another. As long as Whitman didn't come along and drag her off, she would stay. As long as he didn't arrest her and throw her into the looney bin.

Come on, demons, gods, angels, whoever is holding back!

Tears welled and fell, mingling with her sweat, sliding down her cheeks, trailing her throat toward her heart.

Show me! I shall not be denied! I have the power to know!

Who is the killer?

"Tell me!" she cried.

"Ma'am, let me help you."

An arm reached out to her and she violently leaned away and said, "Don't touch me!"

The arm drew back, went on.

The smell.

It was there, rising in her mind, just beneath the foul smell of fire-ravaged wood. Sweet, flowery. Familiar.

She bore down, harder, concentrating. She felt her jaw pop with the effort.

What is it the smell? How do I know it?

Flowery. A scent of spring.

Perfume. No, no. Toilet water. Rose.
Dear God, yes...!
Buerger's Floral Rose Toilet Water.
Suzanne gasped, pulled her hand back from the wood.
No. That's impossible.

Rosemary Reynolds wore Buerger's Floral Rose Toilet Water. Suzanne had known no one else to wear it, for the year after Buerger's put it on the market it was recalled and replaced with Floral Lilac. Rosemary didn't care for the lilac, and used the rose scent sparingly so it would last.

Rosemary would have nothing to do with this. Surely this was only Suzanne's frantic mind scrabbling and grabbing straws.

But the scent was persistent.

It meant to be detected.

Rosemary....

It was unmistakable.

Suzanne stood and stared at the wood. Had Rosemary been in the 3000 A.D. theater recently? *Oh, dear God, is she in Coney Island? Is she involved?*

And that thought was more insane than any Suzanne had ever entertained.

25

Rex shaved Patrick Dow, dressed him in a shift, and strapped him back into the chair. Wouldn't do to have him wandering. As to Anna Dow, Mattie bagged her pulped head in the pillowcase from her cot, and then stood to consider the handiwork.

"I'll call Benson. Tell him we have another one and to come today to take him out to the warehouse. As to the dear Mrs. Dow here, I need to decide where to put her to be found. Tonight, after the parks close, you and I will spirit her over to Barney's Saltwater Bath House, prop her up behind one of their hedges and wait for her to be discovered. I'm sure her sister Darlene will take notice. Perhaps compare the family lines of the O'Conners and the Palmers. Find the connection, maybe? If not, then perhaps the next one to die will give her a better breadcrumb trail to follow."

Rex nodded, made to say something then remembered he didn't

have a tongue, so he only nodded again.

"Stay here." Mattie put on her little straw hat. "I'll be back soon."

Rex nodded, choked, rubbed his drooly lips, and sighed.

The nearest public telephone was in Feltman's Restaurant. She entered the foyer, a cool and shady area that smelled of pine oil and cigar smoke. To the left was the bar, a long room with numerous electric chandeliers, blue carpeting, and cozy little tables around which couples drank beer and held hands, and men gambled at cards. Every table was filled; each stool at the bar was taken. Glasses clinked, bartenders and waitresses moved silently and easily about like fish in an aquarium. Mattie held her head high and haughtily to blend with the customers, and walked through to the cherry-wood booth at the far side of the room. A man was on the telephone, his hand cupped around the mouthpiece. He was yelling into it, his words shaped by a bit too much beer or whiskey. "No, no, lishen to me. Lishen rye now!" The man bleary red eyes turned in Mattie's direction; he tried to wink one but couldn't quite manage it. Then he pointed to Mattie, shook his head, and said, "My brother's shnot lishnin' to me. Heesh blabbin' on and on!"

"I need the telephone, sir. Can you hurry?"

"Jush a minute, jush hol' on." The man shook his head.

Mattie smiled sweetly, focused her gaze on the receiver to yank it away from him and into her hands. But she didn't need to, for in that moment he grabbed his mouth, dropped the receiver, and stumbled away to throw up in the direction of the brass spittoon on the floor at the end of the bar. Well-bred patrons cringed and moved away. A drunk man on a stool laughed and the bartender shouted, "Benny, get over here. We got another pile of mouth shit to clean up."

Mattie gave the operator the number. George Benson wasn't home but his wife was, and Mattie could hear her terror over the line. "Tell your husband that I have another delivery that must be made to his warehouse. It needs to be done today. There will be consequences if not."

"I'll tell him, and..."

Mattie hung up. She didn't need to hear anything else Mrs. Benson had to say. Chatty old biddy.

She squeezed her way back through the bar, ignoring the leers of some of the sops, smiling at the polite acknowledgments of the gentlemen, considering the number of people who had gathered in this one spot to drink and visit with each other. Sixty, seventy perhaps? A sizeable group. Yet a fraction of everyone in Coney Island at that moment. Everyone in Coney Island at that moment was but a fraction of everyone in New York, and all those in New York a fraction of those in the States, and that a fraction of the world.

All waiting for her to take charge.

The headiness of it was more gloriously intoxicating than any liquid spirit on the face of the Earth.

She pushed out through the front door onto the street, and then stopped.

Gasped.

The enemy was nearby. Had passed by that very spot recently, leaving a pool of charged air in his wake. Mattie spun about, spine rigid, blood cold. *Where are you? Who are you?*

She looked right, left, and back at Feltman's door. The charged air was fading. She hurried west, lost the trail. Then quickly east, losing the trail. She crossed Surf Avenue to sense nothing. Went back to Feltman's, took the door, grabbed the door knob...

She is standing at the bars of a jail cell, holding the cold, crusty bars, looking at a young black man seated on a cot within. The man looks as if he's been hit by a train, his face puffed up and his eyes squeezed nearly shut. He is wrapped in a blanket. He says, "Took me out back, stripped me clean, gave me what they called 'a taste of my own medicine.' Said they'd leave me alive so's I could fry in the chair for what I done."

The body which Mattie now experiences looks right, left, then back into the cell.

She wants the body to speak, she wants to hear the voice. She wants to look down at what she is wearing, for that could help her find the enemy more quickly.

Who is the black man? Why am I seeing this? Is he the enemy? No, he's incarcerated, so he can't have left the psychic residue I felt a moment ago.

Or has my training at last allowed me to see something of the future? What? What is it? I must know!

A man elbowed Mattie aside from the door, giving her a barely tolerant look, and escorted a woman old enough to be his mother into the restaurant. Mattie's vision broke apart and vanished.

The enemy had come in. Into Feltman's. Mattie followed the man and old woman inside. She scanned the crowd, walked among them, focused, tuned in as hard as she could to sense the enemy's presence.

Another pocket of charged air there, beside one of the tables where three men sat sipping beers and chewing tobacco. She stopped, looked at them, uncertain of how to proceed. Then she touched one on the arm. "Sir, don't I know you?"

The man grinned, "I don't think so, Miss. But I wouldn't mind getting to know you better."

Mattie pulled away. It wasn't him. She touched the other two in turn, getting a shy smile from the second and a bemused rolling of the eyes from the third. In none did she sense a charge.

I should have focused as much on detection as my other talents over these last years, she thought as she continued through the room, watching faces. *How pathetic and shortsighted have I been? There is someone seeking to destroy me, and all I have are tiny scraps that don't even come together to make a corner of this puzzle! Was he here just now or last week? Or will he be here tomorrow? Am I seeing the present? The future? The past? All I know is he is after me and I'm not prepared for this!*

It was all she could do to keep from kicking chairs and screaming. At herself, at her enemy. It took every bit of her emotional reserve to keep from crushing a few nearby skulls just reveal her power. Instead, she excused herself with an overly-wide smile and left the restaurant, barely noting the young, brown-haired woman at the far side of the bar, speaking into the mouthpiece of the telephone.

26

The toll operator didn't understand the request at first. She couldn't get the last name right. "Remmolds? Rendols?"

Patience, Suzanne. Maybe her ears are clogged up. She grit her teeth. *Sure, but if her ears are clogged up then what is she doing at work? Doesn't an operator need a clear head?*

"Reynolds. I shall spell it for you. R.E.Y.N.O.L.D.S. The Rufus Reynolds family of New Milford, Connecticut. I'm sure you can find them."

"Hold on a moment. Reynolds, right?" The operator sneezed, cleared her throat.

God. "Yes. Rufus Reynolds."

"Yes, I see now. Stand by, dear. I'll ring you once your party is on the line."

"Thank you."

Suzanne put the receiver back on the hook, and then crossed her arms. Rosemary wore Floral Rose Toilet Water. Perhaps Rosemary survived the attack. Perhaps she was here, in Coney Island. Perhaps the injury to her brain had caused her to lose her personality and take up another one. A hateful one. A vicious one.

No, that was impossible. Not Rosemary. Nothing could have altered her and made her a killer.

Then why the Rose Toilet Water? It meant something. It wasn't just a memory from the past.

The phone rang. Suzanne picked up the receiver and put her lips to the mouth piece. *Oh, God, I'm afraid what they might tell me.*

"Miss Heath? I have your party on the other end. Good day to you."

"Good day. Thank you."

The voice on the line was heavy, male, tired. "Yes, hello?"

"Is this Mr. Reynolds?"

"Yes, it is. Who is calling?"

"My name is Suzanne Heath."

"All right, Miss Heath. What do you want?"

"I…I attended Madame Harlow's School seven years ago. I knew your daughter Rosemary, very well. We were good friends."

There was a long pause, then, "Yes?"

"Rosemary is your daughter, then? I have the right Reynolds family?"

Another pause. "What do you want, Miss Heath?"

Tread softly. Speak carefully. I hope he can't hear my heart pounding.

"Mr. Reynolds, is Rosemary living in Coney Island now? I wonder, as I think I might have…might have seen her at a distance. There was something that reminded me of her, and I thought maybe you might let me know."

"Miss Heath?"

"Sir?"

"You know what happened. Every girl at that school knows what happened."

"Sir?"

"Rosemary died. She was killed. She wandered away into the woods and was killed. No one paid attention. No one knew she'd left. Now don't you play ignorant with me, Miss Heath."

Oh, God.

"Killed by a bear or wolf. Left in the woods for animals to find and drag away."

"Oh, my God," Suzanne whispered.

"What was that, Miss Heath?"

"Sir. Do you…do you know who killed Rosemary?"

"One of the girls she spent time with. I don't know. No one knew, no one confessed, no one was punished."

"And Rosemary…"

"Never found." It sounded as if the man choked back a sob. Then, "If you went to Madame Harlow's School then you know all this. Do you call me to torment me with my loss? The wound will never heal and here you are, calling to pick at it to make it worse?"

"I'm sorry, Mr. Reynolds. That's not why I called. I truly thought…" *I thought I smelled her cologne, I thought she might be involved with some brutal killings.* "I don't know what I thought. I'm so sorry. I loved her. She was my best friend."

"Is that all, Miss Heath?"

"That's all."

He hung up without saying goodbye.

Rosemary was dead.

Though perhaps not. Her body had not been found.

She might be here on Coney Island. Or she might be bones scattered up in the woods.

She might be a murderer. Or she might have been murdered.

More information.

And no closer to the truth.

27

Granger was furious in his fear, and he shoved a blouse toward Suzanne as she approached the police desk in the hall of the precinct house.

"There you are!" he said. "I went home after we parted this morning, found this, and returned to Luna as quickly as I could. They told me you'd been relieved of your duties. That you'd been let go this very morning. So what was I to do? I sent a few fellows out to find you, and the scoured the area to no avail. Where were you? You knew I needed your help, yet you, what, went out and about on a jolly jaunt?"

Suzanne frowned, stepped back, refusing to take the blouse. "I had important business, Lieutenant Granger. Don't you dare point a finger at me, accusing me of wasting time. I'm still on your murder case, if you didn't know. I'm run ragged with it all, sleeping very little, eating even less. So watch how you speak to me!"

Granger blinked, grumbled, glanced around to see how many officers had heard this woman correct him for his behavior. The men in the hallway pretended that they had not.

"Come with me, then," said Granger, his voice lowered.

"No, I'm here to visit Cittie. To see how he is faring."

"Not until you take this blouse and see what you might see. Time is wasting, Miss Heath. Coralie cannot have us wait for you to spend time chatting with your friend."

"Checking on his health is not mere chatting."

"All right, fine. You're not here to chat. But for God's sake, take this. See what you can see. Please."

Suzanne nodded. She followed Granger into a small interrogation room. The single window was open but the summer air was dead. The room was stifling and smelled like years of guilt and regret. There was a chair, one desk. A bookshelf with only three volumes, slid over on their sides. Granger shut the door.

"Have a seat, Miss Heath."

She sat.

Granger's brows furrowed. His jaw trembled. He held the blouse out again. "I really do hesitate to give this to you. I'm afraid of what you mind find out. I'm afraid to know, but I'm more afraid not to. Will you help me, please?"

Suzanne took off her hat, placed it on the table. Her whole head was wet and her hair matted down like a wet sponge, wrung out. "Lieutenant, I'll do what I can. But I have to tell you, recently I've had so much input, so many visions, one on top of the other, that I'm not sure anything I'm finding out will ever come together. And it's taking its toll."

"I'm sorry. But please help me. Help Coralie."

To Hell with it, to Hell with me, let's try again. If I die with this all, then my debt is paid. The slate is clean. She took the blouse.

"Focus hard, please. It's what she was wearing Saturday night. The last night I saw her."

Suzanne cut Granger a silencing stare, then folded the blouse to her chest and closed her eyes. "I may discover nothing, you know that."

"I know that. Now concentrate."

"I know what to do."

She heard him draw air through his teeth, but he said no more.

Focus. Open to it. Let it in. Let me see. Let me know.

The blouse smelled sweet, not of roses but of sandalwood, Coralie's preferred scent. Suzanne buried her nose in the soft cotton fabric. Pressed it to her cheeks, rubbed it gently on her chin. *Coralie, are you there? Is there something I might find? I'm willing.*

The heat of the room made her woozy. The silence in the room was claustrophobic.

"Miss Heath?"

"Shh!"

Coralie? Can I help you?

It came to her not violently but slowly, a fog opening to reveal a room in which the bed was not made and the blankets dangling to the floor. It was evening. The curtain was open and hazy stars could be seen floating in the black. Suzanne was in a body. It smelled like a woman's body. It smelled like sandalwood.

Am I Coralie?

"Miss Heath?"

"Shhh!"

The man's voice says, "Don't you dare turn away from me, my love. I've told you before. You will do as I say, and in that you shall be happy. Here I sent my friends away to another room so we could have our own without their tawdry interferences. And yet you look away from me when I speak to you."

Suzanne turns with the woman's body, and looks at the man

who spoke — a dandy in an expensively-tailored suit, polished black shoes. He looks familiar. Suzanne has seen him somewhere. Tall, broad smile, broad shoulders, bulky. Yes, the Bowery. He had approached Suzanne and she snubbed him. She had then heard him turn his attentions to Coralie.

"Do you understand me, Coralie? You shall never look away from me again."

Yes, Suzanne thinks. *I'm Coralie. All right now, let me know where she is. Let me know what happened.* She braces herself against a rising fear as keen as a butcher's knife.

"Robert," says Coralie. "I'm tired. I want to go home now. Let me go home now. I need some sleep." It is Coralie's voice, but Suzanne has never heard her so submissive, so conciliatory. So anxious.

"No, no, I know what you need. You need dinner. We'll have a fine Sunday night dinner first. We'll order a meal to be brought up here, won't that be fine? We shall eat, then you shall return home with me by your side. We shall wait for your father to arrive from his work, and we shall tell him together of our impending marriage."

"Robert, please, listen to me. I'm not quite ready to marry you. I've not known you but a week, perhaps? Let's take time to…"

Robert takes a broad step forward and slams his fist against Coralie's jaw. Suzanne feels the explosion of agony as she crashes to the floor. Robert stands over her now, his smiling face twisted now into a mask of insane rage. Spittle hangs from his lower lip. "What did you say?"

Suzanne feels Coralie's anguish, terror, and rage building inside, a growing knot, hot, relentless, ready to explode.

"I asked you a question!" Robert kicks Coralie solidly in the ribs. Suzanne feels one of them crack. Coralie squeals.

"Answer me!" shouts Robert.

Coralie can't, for her jaw is broken.

Robert's eyes shift from brown to a hideous, glowing black. He raises one hand as if to strike her again, then he laughs and turns away. "I'll be back with our dinner, dear. I'd rather go select it myself than have them bring it up, unchecked. The cook is not always as good as he imagines himself to be, and I want fresh fish, not day-old." He leaves the room, closing the door gently as if he doesn't want to disturb Coralie with a bang.

Coralie sputters, spits out a raw-rooted tooth…

Blink.

Coralie is still on the floor. There is no sense of how long she has been there. The door opens and there is heavy footfall. Her vision is fogged with pain, but she sees the shoes, the bottoms of the legs. They are not Robert's shoes. These are smaller, brown shoes. It is another man in the room. There is a grunt, a soft rushing of air, and something sharp buries itself into Coralie's brain.

And she is gone.

"She's gone." Suzanne shudders back to the present. She slumped against the chair, panting. Her body stung with the effort and the realization of what has happened. It was no longer hot in the room, but uncomfortably chilly.

Granger looks horrified. "What did you say?"

"I said she's gone."

"No, she's not. She's not gone."

Suzanne nodded. Her head pounded with the effort. "I'm so sorry. She's dead. She's been killed."

"No, no, don't tell me that! Please God, don't tell me that!"

"I'm sorry. I'm so sorry." Suzanne rose just as Granger's foot lashed out and kicked the chair across the room. She gasped, screamed, "What? You would do that to me for what I've done for you?"

Granger threw his hands over his face, bent over, and howled like a wounded animal.

Suzanne's heart tightened. She stepped forward, wanting to comfort him, knowing his anguish and hating that she couldn't touch him even with the simplest gesture of compassion. "I'm so sorry. Truly."

When Granger at last looked up, there was fire in his red-rimmed, puffed eyes. "Who did it? Did you see? When did it happen? By God, whoever it is will wish he had never been born!"

"Sunday evening. They discussed dinner."

"Who? Where were they?"

"Coralie. Coralie and a man named Robert. I don't know his last name."

"Where were they?"

"A hotel, I think. It looked like a hotel room. And he said he would go down to get dinner from the hotel restaurant."

"The Capital Hotel?"

"I don't think so. They don't have a restaurant, do they?"

"No, no, of course they don't." Granger's nostrils flared and his lip twitched. "Tell me now. What happened? I want to get this Robert and tear his arms off."

"It wasn't Robert. Robert hit her, and hard. Knocked her down."

"Bastard!"

"But then he left. Left Coralie on the floor. Another man came in. He had brown shoes."

"Brown shoes?"

"It was all I could see. He was a smaller man. Smaller feet, thin legs, not as muscular as Robert."

"Is that all you saw? Good God, woman, you have to tell me more!"

"He was smaller, but strong. He...he struck Coralie with something hard. That killed her."

"He smashed her skull?"

"I fear so, yes."

"Sunday night?"

"Yes."

Granger paced to the window, to the door, and back to the window, his face set, his eyes unblinking. He stopped. "Your friend wasn't caught until Monday morning, Miss Heath."

"Wait a minute. What are you saying?"

"Oh, you were so sure Cittie Parker could not be a killer. Him and his disguises and furtive behavior and pocketed weapon, just right for bashing in the heads of women and men and little girls!"

"No, that's impossible."

"That colored boy has brown shoes. Whitman collected his clothes and brought them here from Dreamland. Brown shoes, yes! And he's a small man. Add that to what we've already suspected..."

"No, Lieutenant Granger, you're desperate! You're frantic! Brown shoes? You're going on that alone?"

"Clues add up, Miss Heath!"

"Go find the hotel, find your daughter! Take fingerprints, talk to witnesses what they might have seen. Don't make me tell you how to do your job!"

"How dare you speak to me in that manner?"

"Don't throw this on Cittie's shoulders. I know he is innocent."

"I have my doubts, oh, yes, big doubts. Oh, what I would do to him should I have him alone for a minute."

"You promised to be good to him while he was locked up. You promised that should I help you find Coralie, you would make sure he isn't harmed."

"A promise is based in trust and in truth."

"Nothing has changed that. Go, find Coralie before you assume anything."

"Oh, I will." Granger yanked open the door and stalked out with Suzanne behind him, calling several officers to follow him out. Suzanne stopped in the middle of the hall.

Oh, God. Cittie.

The mustachioed officer at the front desk gave Suzanne a scowl, a sniff.

"I need to see my friend," Suzanne said, turning to him. "Lieutenant Granger has given me permission."

"Now, I don't remember hearing anything about that, Miss."

"Oh, but he did. I need to go back to the colored cells."

"Not on my life. Now go on, Miss. We have work to do."

"I must see Cittie!"

"You must go on your own or have one of our officers escort you to the street."

"Cittie!" screamed Suzanne.

"Callahan," shouted the desk officer, "take this woman out of here!"

28

Lying on the bench in his cell, wrapped in his filthy blanket, Cittie was awakened by a cry.

"Cittie!"

It had sounded like Suzanne. Maybe she was there. Maybe he had dreamed she was there.

He rolled himself up more tightly in the blanket and drew his knees up. Across the cell, on the floor, sat a shivering old man, wiry white hair, misshapen fingers, dirty shirt and torn trousers.

The old man said, "You hear something?"

"I thought I did."

"Your name Cittie?"

"Yes."

"A woman come to see you?"

"I hoped she would."

"She didn't sound happy."

"No, she didn't."

"What you in here for?"

"They think murder."

"You do it?"

"I didn't do nothin' but wear a disguise, carry some protection, and run away. What'd you do?"

"Stole some money. Man dropped his wallet. Money was right in it. I didn't take all of it, just ten dollars. That was about half. I never would steal all a man's money from him."

"That's thoughtful."

"I know it is."

The men went silent. Cittie listened to see if he might hear Suzanne call again, or if she might be coming down the aisle to see him. But he didn't. And she didn't.

29

Newsboys barked the headlines up and down Surf Avenue, waving meaty copies of *The New York Times,* happy to have a grisly story to whet the appetite of potential sales customers.

"Coney Island's own police lieutenant's daughter found murdered in the Grand Harmon Hotel! Read all about it! Get your copy of the *Times* here!"

Suzanne stood on the side of the road, shading her face from the mid-morning sun, watching as customers swarmed the newsboys to buy their copies. She didn't want to read the story. She'd heard enough conversation on the street.

"Killed by a blow to the head! Such a pretty girl. Such a shame."

Were she not pretty, would it have been a shame? Suzanne thought, knowing that her own appearance was as far from pretty now as it ever had been. If it ever was. Very little sleep for two days. Hair not brushed, clothes beginning to stink. She'd lost her favorite straw hat at some point and couldn't recall where. She was able to keep down water, but that was all. There was no drive in her but to save Cittie. For now there was talk of moving his trial up, make it speedy, within the next two weeks if possible. Folks of Coney Island were salivating over the idea of an execution. It was almost like a new amusement ready to be erected and enjoyed.

As a clot of people gathered around the newsboys and other pedestrians strolled the street with candies and ice creams and trolley cars clanged by and automobiles rumbled in and around them all and roller coasters that bordered Surf Avenue rattled over their steel tracks with passengers shouting in joy and terror and a brass band marched westward, watching for piles of manure so as not to stomp down into them and white-coated barkers called to passersby to fork over a nickel for a straw-stuffed dolly, Suzanne just stood and stared at it all.

She had come here looking for her new life. She and Cittie, cautiously hopeful, leaving the asylum for...this.

This.

A tortured life for me and certain death for Cittie. I can't save him. And I can't redeem myself.

Clues. Oh, yes, I've got clues. Sharp-toothed rabbits and Rosemary's Floral Rose Toilet Water. Spinning in the dark and white tornadoes rising and fire and crushed skulls and death!

Granger said clues came together to solve a crime. None of the clues she'd found came together. As much as she knew Cittie was innocent, she knew Rosemary had never come to Coney Island on a murder spree. Even if Rosemary were indeed alive and here, she would be married and a mother, a loving mother.

Wouldn't she?

"Curses on it all. Damn it all to Hell."

An elegant old matron in black, passing Suzanne on the street side, said, "My dear! Such words for a young woman!"

Oh, but I could say much worse, you old biddy!

There was nothing to do but make the rounds again, and again, gloves off, touching, exploring, gathering whatever might be there, discarding the senseless and trying to force-fit pieces that might be of importance. Wander 'round and 'round. Sisyphus relieved of his rock-pushing to tread the same ground over and over. A Flying Dutchman doomed to travel Coney Island in search of a port that would never be reached.

Suzanne rubbed her heat-scorched lips and braced herself for yet another day of torment.

Then a man on the street called ahead to his buddy, "Just heard there was another murder. Woman found with her brain beat in, found down at the Saltwater Bathhouse. Damn, what a place this is. Don't think we want to go there now. Let's peruse Luna Park, instead."

Another murder. Another woman.

Cittie is in jail. He could not have done this. They can't accuse him of this. Here is his freedom!

For the first time in days, Suzanne felt a spark of hope.

The woman had been wedged behind one of the many holly bushes along the front of the bathhouse, seated on the sandy soil, crumpled over with her head dangling against her chest, discovered by a child who had been chasing a mouse. The body had been dragged out and stretched flat with a towel over the head.

Horrified, fascinated bystanders stood back, whispering, gaping. Police officers prowled about — Osier, Whitman, Granger, and others — going over every inch of the area, looking for something that might help. Osier was cursing under his breath. Whitman looked unaffected, knocking aside bushes with his boot. Granger was talking to the mother of the child who had found the body. The child was nowhere to be seen. Probably off to Bellvue for evaluation. What child, seeing such a sight, could keep his wits?

Suzanne moved slowly into the scene, gloves off, her hand trailing the tops of the holly bushes.

Granger looked over. "What are you doing here?"

Suzanne continued to feather the prickly holly leaves with her fingers. "You know why I'm here. You've asked for my help before. I am still determined to find the murderer of all these people and stop the killing. And I will save Cittie."

"Miss Heath, go on. We don't need you. We found Coralie in the hotel, killed much like the others. Because of the timing and the method, your friend is still our main suspect."

"Her head not destroyed, I heard. Clocked but not crushed.

Coralie's death is not connected to these others." It sounded matter-of-fact and cruelly harsh, but so was the image of Cittie in an electric chair.

"Oh, but it is connected."

"Yet here is a sixth victim by the bathhouse, killed like Julia Palmer and her children and Maude O'Conner and your alderman friend."

"Oh, this? I believe someone has decided to copy Cittie Parker's crimes, to gain some sort of notoriety as well. Villains will do all sorts of things. Clearly you know very little about the mind of a criminal."

Suzanne grappled for a response, shocked into silence. Then, "And you call yourself an investigator, that you would make up facts to suit your anger?"

"Get out of here, Miss Heath." This was Whitman. "Or I'll arrest you for interfering with our investigation."

"I've done nothing to interfere."

"Just being here is interference enough. And my God, woman, you stink! Perhaps you should go into the bathhouse and take a bath. Or better yet, go out in the ocean and let the waves clean you off."

Suzanne backed away into the crowd of the curious, avoiding touching them, still staring at Granger, at Whitman, and at the body on the ground.

I have to touch her. If I touch her, I think I'll know.

A horse-drawn ambulance pulled up to the bathhouse, and men in white gathered the body onto a wooden-handled canvas stretcher. Suzanne tried to move over to reach the stretcher but the men were fast and the body was gone in a moment and the ambulance slammed shut.

The morgue was in the precinct house. Getting to the body now would be almost impossible.

A man in a dapper, green-and-white-striped bathing costume reached down into the grass and picked up a small envelope. He called to Osier, "This fell from the dead lady's blouse."

Suzanne snatched it away. She held it close, felt it. She sensed nothing. Then she looked at the address. "Anna Mannetti Dow."

Osier growled and snatched the envelope away. "Give me that!

Now move on, Miss Heath!" He glared at the crowd. "All of you! Leave now, go on about your amusements or down to the beach or we'll whack some ears and haul you in!"

Anna Mannetti Dow.

Susanne knew the maiden name well. While there were certainly plenty of Mannetti families, she knew of only one.

Darlene Mannetti. One of the Morgans from Madame Harlow's School.

Darlene had a sister, several of them. They wrote back and forth to each other while Darlene was at Madame Harlow's. Suzanne was certain one of her younger sisters was Anna. Darlene joked about her sister, calling her Anna Banana.

Darlene's sister.

Rosemary's cologne.

A connection at last.

Then who were the other victims?

Suzanne locked eyes with Granger before she turned away.

30

The reporter at the *Times* office in the twenty-five-story-high Times Square Tower was willing to help a lovely young woman named Sally Jones who was interested in becoming an investigative reporter. She told him she admired the earlier work of Nellie Bly, and saw great value in learning to follow leads subtly and keenly.

Suzanne had bathed body and hair, perfumed herself with a twenty-five-cent bottle of lemon essence, practiced tipping her head coquettishly and speaking softly and alluringly. He found her charming, and she found herself in a sunny corner of the third floor of the office building, looking through his notes about the Coney Island murders with him standing proudly by.

Maude O'Conner was survived by her father, Arthur O'Connor, and her mother, Beatrice Broome O'Connor, sister Mary O'Connor, her Aunt Dotty, and cousins Mary Alice and Peter. Julia Palmer was Julia Rittenhouse Palmer, survived by her husband, Michael, a brother Charles, and a sister Caroline, and a list of cousins, nieces, and nephews.

Each one was related to the Morgans.

Suzanne looked up from the notes, stared at the wall. Her spine flushed cold. It was hard to focus, to stand straight.

"Miss Jones? Are you all right?"

Suzanne swallowed. "Yes."

"Did you find what you were looking for?"

Yes.

"No." It took great effort to look at the man, to hold an expression of mild disappointment. "I'd wondered if the victims had all come from Brooklyn. Only one did, Miss O'Connor. I thought perhaps the killer was scouting out people from a particular neighborhood. I understand the insane and criminal mind will sometimes do something like that. Believe there is a coven of evil in a certain place, or that the devil has taken over folks who live near to one another."

"Hmm," said the reporter. "I've never heard that. Interesting theory."

"I think so. Well, thank you so much for your time, sir."

"Oh, wait, that's all? You're leaving? I thought perhaps I could show you around the office a bit more. So much to see here. And lunch is in less than an hour." He smiled. It was a kind smile. A trusting and trustworthy smile. Suzanne made herself smile back. He at least deserved that.

"No, I must get back home. But thank you again."

The trip on the open-air trolley from lower Manhattan to Coney Island seemed endless, and the noise near deafening. Clattering, clanking, squealing brakes. Babes in arms crying, mothers shushing children, old men arguing, young couples laughing.

But it was merely a garbled backdrop to Suzanne's thoughts. Dark, terrible thoughts. Stomach-churning imaginings.

The murders were all linked to the Morgans. Not Morgans themselves, but their relatives. A definite decision on the part of the killer. A warning of some sort to the Morgans, wherever in this sprawling country they now lived. Or perhaps the beginning of a clean sweep of Morgan families? Who would hate them so, to do this? Who was that dangerous and violent?

Ah, but I hate you all even more!

Oh, God.

Oh, you'll be sorry you ever knew me!

Tirzah.

She had been crazy with wanting power, demanding control.

And then when the other Morgans challenged her or rejected her, she'd flown into a rage. Slamming Rosemary with a rock. Leaving her in the woods. Knocking Suzanne unconscious. Leaving her in the woods, too.

How might time and rage and a desire for power twist and squeeze the human mind to an even more distorted and dangerous creature?

No, it's not Rosemary in Coney Island, killing for sport. It has to be Tirzah.

Suzanne rubbed her forehead, trying to piece it together. *But what are the razor-toothed rabbits? What is the swirling white, the relentless spinning round and round?*

Those should help me find her. If I can find them.

"If I can find them," she said to the tall tenements and warehouses passing by in the heat of the midday sun.

A fat woman decided to switch seats, moving over and squeezing down next to Suzanne. There was no way to get away from the big woman's hip. For the rest of the ride Suzanne struggled with images of crushed skulls and carnivorous rabbits intermingled with visions of the fat woman's husband humping her on their squeaky, smelly bed, grunting and farting and smelling like motor oil.

31

The lot on which the 3000 A.D. theater stood had been cleared out and razed, ready for a new tenant to build another amusement. There was nothing to touch, to draw from, not even a forgotten piece of timber, to find Tirzah Simmons.

And so she asked the vendor across the corridor — a man who ran a shop that sold candy shaped like butcher's meats — who might own the empty lot. He said, "One moment," as he hung a red, rubbery confectionery steak on one of the little meat hooks that rimmed the open front window of his shop. From those hooks also hung pink, sugary sausages, pork and lamb chops, and even candies that looked like various fish caught fresh from the sea. Except the colors were wrong. "All right," he said, wiping his hands on his apron. His dentures clicked as he spoke. "That would be Mr. Paulson McKenzie. Owns mine, that burned one over there, and quite a few others scattered around the Bowery. Why, you thinking of renting the lot?"

"Perhaps. Could you give me Mr. McKenzie's address so I might pay him a visit?"

"He'll be 'round on the by and by. Always checking to see how his properties are doing. Shame he wasn't in time to stop that fire, but like I said, he's busy. He owns lots of lots. Ha! Lots of lots, that sounds funny, don't you think? Lots of lots?"

"Sure."

"He'll be by in an hour or so, should you want to wait."

"I'll wait."

"My chocolate chicken kidneys are just a penny a piece."

"No, thanks."

Suzanne waited. Stood beside the vacant lot, watching people go by. No face the same. Different people, different families, even different nationalities. People with normal lives, normal relationships, normal families.

What a strange thing, normality.

The sunlight began to dim. Establishments along Stratton's Walk turned on the electric lights that rimmed their doors and signs. People, like moths, were drawn to them. Moths, like people on holiday, were likewise drawn to them, and batted themselves to death against the glow. Suzanne waited, her back aching, her shoulders tired, her eyes stinging from airborne grit.

"There he is," said the candy-meat man from his booth. "That's Mr. McKenzie."

McKenzie looked like what Suzanne imagined him to look like. A nose like a hawk, eyes small and critical, tweed, vested suit, boater on his head. And a silver-tipped walking stick, as if he would just as happily whack someone out of his way as look at him.

"Mr. McKenzie!"

McKenzie looked around, frowning, his gaze settling on Suzanne. "Excuse me, did you speak to me?"

Suzanne nodded primly. "Yes. Let me introduce myself. My name is…Katherine Reynolds. I am interested in the empty lot you have there. I might want to rent it to set up a little clothing shop."

"You? You come here on your own to rent a lot from me? That's business best done by your husband."

"I'm Miss Reynolds, sir. And I have the funds and the intellect to make a good business on this lot. If you prefer not to have my money, then I'll go elsewhere."

McKenzie clearly didn't like the idea of losing income. "What do you plan for the lot?"

"A small clothing shop. Finest clothing, of course, which will appeal to the ladies who come to Coney Island. What lady of means could resist a new pair of shoes from Paris or a silk blouse from the Orient?"

"That's not the usual Coney Island fare."

"Indeed, which is why I think it would do well."

"An interesting idea. Much more tasteful than the business that occupied the spot prior to the fire."

"It was a theater, was it not?"

"Yes, a sad little show with shambling idiots. The place smells foul more often than not. I'm not all that disappointed it burned down."

"Who ran that theater, might I ask?"

"Why do you want to know?"

"I like to know who it is I am following. To make sure I do better with my business."

"Oh, you shall do better."

"Who ran the theater?"

"A strange woman named Mattie Snow. One reason I hesitate to rent to a woman again."

Mattie Snow? Who is Mattie Snow?

"Thank you, Mr. McKenzie. Now do you have an office where we can talk business?"

"Yes. On West Eighth Street near Culver Terminal. It's getting late. Why don't you come there tomorrow, and we shall draw up the contract?"

"Certainly."

"Don't you care what the rent is? You are willing to do business without knowing the cost?"

I'm doing business right now without knowing the cost. Though I fear it will be very high for one or both parties.

"I would guess you're a fair man."

"That I am," said McKenzie, and with a tip of his hat was on his way, tapping with his silver-tipped walking stick through the falling evening shadows.

The candy-meat man turned on his electric lights — a sad string of seven bulbs over his door that hung low like one loop of bunting, an attempt at a festive look. Suzanne went up to the open window again. "Do you know Mattie Snow?'

"You're a poet!" said the man cheerfully. Suzanne felt a rush of compassion for the little candy-man and his unabashed cheerfulness. "And did I tell you the chocolate chicken kidneys are a penny a piece?"

"You told me, thank you, but no. Perhaps later? Do you know Miss Snow?"

"Not really. Know who she is. Saw her in and about the theater. She never bought any of my candy, though. Who doesn't like candy?"

"Everyone likes candy.

"I would think so! And I have the best prices."

"What does she look like, this Miss Snow?"

"About your age, pretty, dresses nicely. I don't know. I never watched her very closely. I tend to watch the man who is her assistant, or brother, or husband, perhaps? I tall man, a bit fierce-looking." The candy man leaned close, sticking his head out through the window. "I always thought that man had something wrong with him, too. A bit of a cretin."

"Do you know where she lives?"

"Oh, no, of course not. Like I said, I don't pay that much attention. But she does own that other amusement."

Oh, God, yes. Oh, God, help me.

"What amusement is that?"

"A scrappy little place called Snow's Symposium of Secrets."

"Where is it?"

"Down Stratton's Walk, just before you get to Wade's Boardwalk and the beach. It's down a little dead end off the walk."

"You've been there?"

"Oh, heaven's no."

"How do you know where it is?"

"My wife's been there, once. She loves to spend her Saturday afternoons here. She works up in Brooklyn at a hardware store. Anyway, she said the show at the symposium wasn't worth her coin. Some parlor tricks by that big man is pretty much all."

Oh, my dear God. I think Tirzah is there.

"Thank you, sir." Suzanne started down the walk, but then called back, "I'll buy some of your candy tomorrow."

If I'm alive tomorrow.

"Thank you! What should I put aside for you?"

"A trout and some chicken kidneys."

"That I will!"

32

The old thief had been taken from the cell and had not returned. He'd been replaced by a boy of about thirteen who was as thin as a fence post and scared as a mouse. The boy was dressed in short pants, a shirt that had once been white, and some tattered suspenders. He stood flush against the corner, even though Cittie had offered to share his bench with him.

The boy's eyes were wide and white, and he didn't speak for the first few hours he was there. At last, he said, "How long you been here?"

"Days, maybe a week? I've lost track of time. No windows in here, no sense of day or night."

"Where your clothes at?"

Cittie said, "They won't give me none. Took mine away, gave me this blanket is all."

"They gonna kill us? They gonna take us out and shoot us?

"I don't think so. What's your name?"

"Matthew."

"I'm Cittie, Matthew."

Matthew looked out the barred door, then back at Cittie. "They gonna kill us, you think?"

"Why they arrest you, Matthew?"

"I was with some other boys, just talking. Some lady said we was bothering her. Those boys ran. I didn't. I wanted to tell the cop that we wasn't talking to that lady at all but was just standing around making jokes. Not about her. Just stupid stuff. Not about her, I promise."

Cittie nodded.

"But she said what she said and the cop smacked me and grabbed me and here I am. I think they want to kill me!"

"No, no, I don' think so."

"Then I'll go to prison and never see my Mam again!" He started to cry, great shuddering sobs that folded him over and seemed enough to tear his small body apart. Cittie got up in his blanket and led the boy to the bench. He sat him down and put his arm around his shoulder.

"You ain't gonna die. Don't worry, you ain't gonna die."

I hope you don't die.

The boy leaned into Cittie.

I hope I don't die.

Suzanne, where are you?

33

The symposium was indeed a tawdry little shack holed up at the end of a narrow alley off Stratton's Walk. The garish red sign, "Snow's Symposium of Secrets and Surprises!" seemed to offer something truly curious on the inside for only a nickel. Yet in smaller letters at the bottom of the sign indicated the show closed at 6 p.m. It was nearly 8 p.m. The two small windows to either side of the door revealed no light within.

Suzanne stared at the door. It was likely locked. She took off her right glove. Her hand shook madly.

Mattie Snow. Snow is white. Mattie is a clue to finding Tirzah. Mattie has something to do with Tirzah. There is a connection between the two. There has to be. The swirling white. It was a blizzard. It was snow.

Do it, Suzanne. Move into this. Here is the next step toward your penance. Here is the next step to Cittie's life.

She reached for the tarnished brass door handle, touched it.

It was warm, rough. Vague sensations of the hundreds, thousands, of patrons who had touched it and come through for a magic show. Nothing useful. Suzanne grit her teeth, closed her eyes, but still nothing but the faint chatter of people coming and going.

And, as she expected, the door was locked. So she knocked.

She put her ear to the wood and listened. There was no sound.
She knocked harder.

No one answered.

"Mattie Snow! Are you in there? I need to talk to you!"

No one answered.

The vision struck:

She is in a tiny dark closet, looking out through a small window
in a door. She can see into the next room, a well-lit space where
a tall brute stands rubbing his lips. In the center of the room is a
chair with straps. A man is in the chair, a pudgy man with bulging,
terrified eyes. The brute steps from the chair and Suzanne feels her
foot go up and down on a pump. The chair begins to whirl around
and around and around. The man in the chair gobbles, stammers
as the chair goes faster and faster. The lights shut off. Sharp-toothed
rabbits and horned devils appeared on the wall, glowing as if from
Hell.

I am Mattie Snow. I own this place. I am in charge, I know that.

She hears herself laugh.

The sound is strangely and disturbingly familiar.

Suzanne's heart leaps. *How do I know that laugh?*

Through the tiny window she can see the shadowy chair
spinning round and round as the rabbits and devils taunt from the
wall.

You're the child of the devil, Suzanne!

No, Mother, be quiet, let me know what this is, who this is!

*You're doomed to Hell for your dabblings in devilish spells and demonic
acts!*

Get behind me, Mother!

Blink.

She is out of the closet and in the room now, and the chair has
stopped spinning. The man looks as if someone has performed a
lobotomy on him, with vacant eyes and drooling mouth. The brute
unstraps him, unfolds a cot from the rear wall, and places the man
on the cot.

And then she hears the voice speak. The voice emanating from
the body in which she now resides. It says, "Very well, then. Ugly,
ugly chap, this, but another mindless one, another obedient soul for
my army."

Suzanne's breath snags. Her chest locks. *Oh, my God. Yes, I do know that voice!*

"Yeah," says the brute. He nods and grins, revealing the few teeth that are determined enough to remain in his rotted mouth.

"Get him dressed. Take him over to the theater and lock him up with the others."

I know that voice. From long ago. It is someone I used to know!

"And wipe that damned blood off your lips," she hears herself say. "You look like a mongrel that just ate a rabbit."

Suzanne dropped to the ground on her knees. The vision flew away. A moth spun around her face, bumped her cheek and moved on.

Out on Stratton Walk, the night partiers paraded back and forth, laughing, singing, talking. They couldn't see her there, in the darkness, kneeling before the Symposium of Secrets and Surprises. And if they did, they probably didn't much care.

I used to know that voice.

I think it belonged to a Morgan.

I think it belongs to Tirzah.

Dear God. I fear Mattie Snow is Tirzah.

34

Mattie stood just outside the rear door of the Symposium of Secrets, listening. Rex was beside her, staring alternately at the door and at Mattie, his face rippling with concern.

Mattie had been sitting on her cot in the back room, brushing and pinning her hair, putting a touch of blush onto her cheeks while peering into her little pocket mirror, preparing to go out in style to search for the enemy. But the enemy had found her first.

There had been a knock on the front door, and she knew. She felt a powerful vibration in her bones, and quickly pulled the string on the overhead light bulb. Then she and Rex had stood in the darkness as the voice had called, "Mattie Snow? Are you in there? I need to talk to you!"

The voice was muffled but clear and it was familiar. It was a young woman.

The enemy was a young woman.

The enemy is a Morgan.

Mattie shoved her hairpins and the mirror into her skirt pocket, and quietly opened the rear door and she and Rex had gone out. "Don't say a word," she warned Rex, then grinned at having forgotten he could no longer say a word. "And don't make a noise." She reached for a pin in her pocket, clipped up a loose strand of hair. She didn't have her hat. So be it. Once she was done with the enemy, she would return for it. She would look good for her triumphant night on the town.

More knocking and then silence. Mattie waited, listening, tuning her mind, concentrating, to determine who it was on the other side of the building. No doubt a Morgan. Perhaps Mary Alice, having found a connection between the deaths, though Mary Alice was not one of the brightest of the seven. Perhaps Darlene. Whichever it was, Mattie sensed a power that had been practiced and fine-tuned over time.

Though in no way as fine-tuned as mine. This shall be a lark! This shall be a fine exercise!

"Rex, go away. Go far away. I will find you later."

Rex frowned, but nodded his head and slipped away and out to Henderson's Walk. What he might do, Mattie didn't know and didn't care.

Still no sound. No more calling or knocking. Perhaps the enemy had gone? Had given up and left?

That wasn't likely. If she had found Mattie then she wasn't going to leave. There would be a confrontation.

But Mattie would control that. No matter how powerful the enemy might be, Mattie was more powerful, still. She would play with the enemy a bit, drain her and wear her out first and then bring her down.

What a fine bit of fun, so much more fun than a ride on a coaster or slide down the Shoot-the-Chutes!

35

She sensed Tirzah, nearby, moving among the nighttime Bowery visitors. Suzanne stood in the middle of Stratton Walk, opening her mind and senses to it all, detecting Tirzah's presence but not seeing her face among the many in the passing crowds.

She's here. I know it. I feel her. I must find her!

The hairs on Suzanne's arms raised up, charged as if with the static of an approaching storm. Tirzah was close. Perhaps she detected Suzanne as well. More people passing by, too many faces passing by. The charge grew stronger, stronger, and then began to fade.

Tirzah had indeed passed by, but Suzanne had missed her chance.

Damn!

Did she see me? Did she not? Does she know I'm here? Does she not?

Tirzah was heading north toward Surf Avenue. Suzanne followed. She would catch up to Tirzah, confront her. With whatever dormant power she'd developed years ago at Madame Harlow's school she would fight Tirzah if need be. She would kill Tirzah if need be.

She ran, following Tirzah's highly charged trail. To Surf Avenue and east, along the light-and-shadow-striped street, worming her way past slow pedestrians and darting out of the way of honking automobiles, nearly stumbling over the trolley tracks as a young man, clearly intoxicated, slammed into her and sent her reeling. Toward the blazing glow of Dreamland and its countless electric towers.

She reached Dreamland's entrance. Happy people were paying to go in for the last few hours of operation. On toward the far end of the amusement district she hurried, through the long shadows and blacked silhouette of the Iron Tower and recently abandoned Galveston Flood show, which sat dark and ominous like a crouching animal waiting for its prey.

But then trail faded.

No, no, no!

Suzanne turned around, around, looking for Tirzah in the night-shaded faces. Overhead, a silent slice of moon watched, intrigued. She looked west up Surf Avenue, retraced her steps…

And there! She stumbled into the static trail once more, sending her nerves to jangling and her flesh to buzzing. Up past Dreamland she raced again, past Luna Park, then back into the Bowery on Thompson's Walk, heart thundering.

She knows I'm after her. This is a cat-and-mouse game. She is ready for me. I must be ready for her!

Past dancing girls' tents, shooting galleries, and men on stilts, dancing for tips. Past the Music Hall, past restaurants and bars and trinket shops. They all seemed to stretch, contort, and writhe in her peripheral vision. Lights blurred together into one long luminous sheet, waving and undulating. The world seemed to shift beneath her feet. She fought to stay upright.

The static pathway suddenly flared more intense, hotter, sending painful sparks into her mind and down her spine. She was closing in on Tirzah. And as the distance between them shortened, vivid visions of herself as Tirzah washed over her, visions of the recent and atrocious crimes. Maude O'Connor, lying on the bed in room forty-six, her head crushed not by a cudgel but crushed by the sheer focus of Tirzah's thoughts. Julia Palmer and her daughters, laughing in the middle of the Mirror Maze then turning with wide eyes to face who would become their destroyer; Julia's head caving in first with a cracking, wet sound that caused her little girls to scream and cower until it was their turn. Anna Dow in the room with the revolving chair, against a wall, screaming and squealing as her skull broke and the shards of bone cut into and through her brain.

And then her own visions, her own memories — her mother standing and staring at Suzanne with hate in her eyes. Her first day at Madame Harlow's, standing in the headmistress's office as her mother tried her best to present Suzanne as a good candidate for the institution instead of the demon child she believed she really was. The day on the mountain, in the fern-strewn forest as Tirzah made her declarations to the members of the Order of Morgans. Tirzah striking Rosemary with the rock and killing her. Yes, Rosemary was truly dead. And then looking into Tirzah's face as the two struggled, and Suzanne saw a glimpse of fear in Tirzah's eyes. In one moment, Tirzah was afraid of Suzanne.

The trail turned sharply into a short alley running between two shops. Suzanne skidded to a stop and a strolling couple behind her nearly ran into her. "Watch where you're going, Miss," said the man. "And for heaven's sake, no need to run. We're in Coney Island. Take your time. Enjoy the evening."

The couple went around Suzanne. Suzanne stared down into

the night-black alley. A figure was there, stopped where the alley was clogged with a tall wall of barrels and wooden staves.

It's Tirzah. Here we go.

She could feel Tirzah's mind reaching into her own, cold psychic fingers probing and attempting to get Suzanne to halt. It was a most sickening feeling, but Suzanne pushed through. She walked slowly into the alley. The shadowy figure shifted a bit, but did not make to run or to clamber over the rubbish.

"Tirzah, I know that is you."

The voice, the familiar voice came back, "Tirzah? Ha!"

"Mattie Snow, then. You changed your name to hide."

"I'm not Tirzah, you fool."

The psychic fingers left Suzanne's mind and caught her legs, wrapping them like red-hot wires. Suzanne wailed through her teeth, but continued to walk.

Closer. She couldn't see the woman's face, still. Much too dark.

"I tell you, I'm not Tirzah. You aren't as talented as you thought you were, are you?"

Suzanne took several more steps. So close now. Another foot and she would be able to reach out and touch Tirzah.

"I have something of Tirzah's though, if you want it. I stole it from her before graduation. She didn't know, or if she did, she didn't complain. She'd learned her place by then. Here, it's cheap, anyway."

Something was tossed into the air and Suzanne caught it. It was a small hand mirror.

Tirzah's mirror?

She held it and a vision shot through her like a bullet:

Suzanne as Tirzah, inside Tirzah's body, looking through Tirzah's eyes, striking Suzanne down to the ground.

Blink.

Tirzah, Suzanne, and the other Morgans, back in the clearing where Reverend Leeman was continuing his sermon. Rosemary is not with them. She is somewhere in the woods near a creek, dead.

Blink.

Back at the school in late afternoon. Madame Harlow and Miss Williamson have just noticed that Rosemary is missing. Tirzah doesn't know what to say. Suzanne stares at her as if she will tell of Rosemary's murder. But instead, Suzanne says, "Rosemary wandered off. We don't know where she is."

Blink.

Tirzah pregnant, in a field beneath a tent on a chilly autumn afternoon. On the makeshift stage, Snavely Leeman marches back and forth, waving his Bible. Tirzah's husband, one of Leeman's helpers, sits beside Tirzah and holds her hand. Tirzah has repented of the powers of her flesh and has embraced the powers of the Spirit. The baby moves inside her and there is a warm of pure joy.

Blink.

Tirzah, her husband, and their baby are on a boat on the Hudson River with friends. The boat turns over and Tirzah goes under. Down. Down.

"Tirzah had the good sense to die before I got to her. I would have saved her for last, after the families and then the Morgans themselves. But she's gone and that's all well and good. So, no, I'm not Tirzah."

Suzanne dropped the little mirror.

"But who are you? It's dark but your voice is so familiar. I'd like to know which Morgan I'm going to kill before I do."

Suzanne drew up, steeling herself against what Mattie Snow or Tirzah or whoever this person was and what she had planned. A head crushing, most likely. *I have no power against that. I've not developed anything but my clairvoyance since Harlow's school. All I have are my wits. Stay calm, Suzanne. Calm.*

"I'm Suzanne Heath," she said. "Yes, I was a Morgan. I knew Tirzah. You knew Tirzah. But I don't know who you are. To be fair, tell me or show me who you are."

"Oh, such a silly thing you are!" the other barked. "Suzanne Heath! Are you truly thinking I'll believe that? You're no more Suzanne Heath than I'm Tirzah Simmons!"

Stay calm.

"But I am. And who are you?"

The other just shook her head in the darkness and laughed. Suzanne reached out, grabbed the woman and yanked her into the single spot of moonlight in the alley. She stared into the other's face.

It was her own face.

It was the face of Suzanne Heath, a bit older now, looking back at her with a dreadful and cruel smile. Suzanne wailed, pushed the other away, but the momentary connection sent visions pouring down on her in a torrent, one after the other after the other:

Suzanne, her head still pounding from being knocked unconscious in the woods, stands in the school chapel in the filtered light of a stained glass window, lying to Madame Harlow and Miss Williamson about the disappearance of Rosemary. Her grief over the death of her friend is dissipating and rage at Tirzah is growing. With the rage she feels her power increasing. She will put Tirzah in her place. She will rule over her. Never again will she be controlled by another.

Blink.

Suzanne a year later, out of school, standing on her parents' front porch as her mother says, "Get away from us! We paid for your education, now put it to use somewhere. Don't ever come back here again!" Suzanne reaches out with her mind and grabs her mother's hair and tosses the woman down the steps. Suzanne watches, pleased with what she can do. And oh, there will be so much more!

Blink.

Suzanne bound in a canvas jacket on a hospital bed. An ugly, steel-eyed doctor stands over her. Next to him is a nurse with a hypodermic needle. Suzanne's mind is fuzzy but she can see. She can hear. "You are a troubled young woman, to have hurt your mother. You are lucky she didn't call for your arrest but she had you committed instead. We'll take good care of you." He leans in with the needle. "Good care for the rest of your life."

Blink.

Suzanne stands in small shower, naked, with jets of cold water shooting out on her from all directions. She screams but it is a weak scream because of the drugs.

Blink.

Suzanne in the canvas jacket, drugged, dazed, the doctor saying, "We've done a little operation on you, Miss Heath, at your mother's request. You won't be able to have children now, but that's a good thing. Insanity can pass from generation to generation, and you wouldn't want that."

Blink.

Suzanne hiding in the woods outside the hospital. She has escaped during one of the cold shower treatments, when the orderly was jacking off in the corner, thinking she was too gone to take advantage. She struck him, stole his trousers and jacket. The effects of the drugs are still rolling in her system but she's becoming more clear-headed by the minute.

Blink.

Suzanne alone in an abandoned cabin. She sits at a table with a wobbly leg, watching things move about in the air at her silent command. She laughs, thinking of how someday she will use her power to take what she wants, become who she wants. Damn her mother and her pathetic fears. Damn anyone who curses her. She has her power for a reason. No one will stop her. It will take time but the rewards will be precious.

Blink.

Suzanne, calling herself Mattie Snow, stands inside a brand-new shack she has built with money she stole from her parents' house before murdering them with and moving south to Coney Island to escape into the world of illusion and amusement. She salivates, tasting the adventures that lie ahead.

"I'll ask you again. Who are you?"

Suzanne looks away from herself and picks up the mirror. She hates mirrors. She dreads looking into this tiny sliver of reflective glass.

"I'm Suzanne," said says. "I have to be. I was rescued by the boys at the Colored Waifs' Asylum. I befriended Cittie. I worked in a factory, I worked selling Luna Park tickets. Lieutenant Granger called for me to help solve murders."

"Try again. Who are you?" asked the other Suzanne.

Suzanne looked into the mirror. At first she saw her own face, a face she'd avoided for years. There was the small, straight nose, the gray eyes, the dark, thick brows, and high cheekbones. There, framing her face in the moonlight, was the wavy auburn hair.

But no.

Oh, God wait.

It's not me.

It's Rosemary!

It was Rosemary's face. She was in Rosemary's body, the body that was killed in the summer of 1902. Everything she had done in this life was done in Rosemary's body.

"How? Why?"

"You're Rosemary Reynolds. Obviously you didn't die. You came here to find me. So here I am and here you are."

"No, I am Suzanne Heath! I know it! This is insane!"

"Aren't we both a bit insane?" the other Suzanne laughed. "And I've had enough of you." She raised her hands, tipped her head, bared her teeth, and Suzanne flew backward against the wall. Her head struck, hard, sending flashes through her brain. She staggered up.

"I'm Suzanne," she managed. "I know it!"

"Shut up, you piece of garbage. Now it's time you moved on to join Tirzah in Hell. I am the gate, and you're going through!"

The other Suzanne laughed and then angled her head down, glaring at Suzanne. Suzanne felt her blouse collar begin to constrict. Her hands flew to her throat. The other Suzanne walked over to Suzanne, laughing. Suzanne loosened one hand long enough to grasp the other woman's wrist and squeeze.

And another vision leapt up into her consciousness:

She is in the other Suzanne's body. Time has passed. She stands in the center of Surf Avenue with her hands tied behind her back, staring at the flaming inferno that is Dreamland. Several police officers flank her. Frantic firemen with their wild-eyed horses and steam-billowing engines try to pump enough water from the roadside hydrants to put out the flames. The water arches high and far. But it is clearly not going to be enough.

"Too much of the water's been redirected to the park's lagoon and other attractions!" cries one of firemen. "We don't have enough to put it out!"

And he is right. It isn't long before the arched entrance collapses in on itself, and behind that, Beacon tower and the Shoot-the-Chutes cave in with a deafening roar.

"You can't prove anything!" laughs Suzanne.

"Oh, but I can." This is Lieutenant Granger, though his uniform is a bit different now. He appears to be a captain. "A witness saw you sneaking about, setting little fires here and there. At first he thought you were an act until the flames started in earnest."

"Perhaps I did. But they were not set as you would imagine! I did it with my mind, and I'll do the same to you! And to anyone else who crosses me! You can't hold me. I'm just playing along with you for the fun of it." She wills the rope to untie; it falls to the street. "Do you see? Now say your prayers." She stares at Granger, glares at Granger, who begins to shake in his boots. Smoke coiled around his shoulders and then burst into a column of flame. Screams all around from horrified onlookers, terrified firemen. Suzanne howls with glee, until a billy club comes down on her skull from behind and knocks her out.

Blink.

Again, she is filled with drugs. They are heavy, and subdue her enough to keep her from focusing on her power and causing damage. She is groggy and nauseous, seated in the defendant's seat in the courtroom. The judge talks on and on about evil and justice, how 672 people died in the Dreamland blaze including his friend Granger and sixteen infants in their little incubators, the worst disaster he's ever encountered in all his years. Suzanne wants to make him shut up but can't clear her head enough. He reads the sentence: "On this date, September 6th, nineteen-ten you, Mattie Snow are sentenced to death, having been found guilty of multiple murders." He doesn't ask if she has any final words. The gavel bangs.

Blink.

She sits, doped, strapped securely into the electric chair, a metal cap screwed to her head, an electrode attached to her right leg. For the first time in many years, she is terrified. Fear bubbles up over the effects of the liquid they'd injected into her arm prior to the reading of the death sentence one more time. Some of the guards around her smirk; others appear grim. She struggles, though the struggling is only in her mind. Her body is listless and cannot be ordered.

This shall be the conclusion of her power. This is the result of her life.

Something in her mind stirs weakly. A memory of Faith Gansy and her open innocence. A memory of Rosemary. Her kindness, her example. Suzanne had loved her.

Had wanted to be like her.

Had dreams of a life together. Had dreams of tenderness.

And now...

Now she is bound for Hell. She has opened the gate for herself and will slide right down like those little boats in the whirlwind in Dreamland's ride.

"Goodbye, witch," snarls the head of the guard. He nods to a man beyond Suzanne's line of vision. She tries to brace herself but can't. There is no way to prepare for this. The switch is thrown. Current cuts her mind. She sees flames leaping and razor-fanged rabbits gnashing their teeth and smiling at her.

And in that moment between life and death, she sees herself as two people, the one who chose evil and the one who would have chosen kindness if she had not let circumstances, anger, and selfishness drive her into the abyss. In the crackling, fire-blazing second of her execution, her mind cries out for a choice, and it is granted. She will go back in time to pay a heavy penance for the death and destruction she's caused. She will go back without memory of what she has done, and will be forced through circumstance and conscience to seek out and fight her evil self. She will have no understanding of the whole truth. She will stumble into and will be forced to embrace her lot, and she will suffer greatly in the process.

'I will do it,' she thinks. 'I don't know if I'll gain peace but at least I'll prevent some of the evil I have created. I will do it for the memory of Rosemary.'

Blink.

A new memory of May, 1902. Suzanne, sent back from 1910, awakens in the body of the dead Rosemary Reynolds, lying in the forest. She is rescued by a passing wagon full of boys from the Colored Waifs' Asylum. She proceeds, unknowingly, into the life that will link her years later with her evil self, into the place that will force her to confront what she has done in her first life so she can fight herself, stop herself, and in doing so, seek redemption.

The other Suzanne jerked her wrist away and then howled like a she-wolf at the moon. "You're weak! You've no power but that of detection! You've let yourself go over these last seven years! I can do with you as I will. My first thought is to crush your skull like the others, but you, Rosemary, deserve something more special. You're my first Morgan to die at my hands."

Suzanne shook her head. "No. Oh, no, you won't kill me. I'm not weak at all. I am Suzanne, and everything you have learned over those many years I now remember. I am as skilled as you. It's all a part of me as it is a part of you!"

"Impossible!" The other Suzanne flung her arm out, furiously, causing a mighty and invisible blow to strike Suzanne's face. Suzanne stumbled but she immediately regained her footing.

"I can crush you as much as you can crush me, for I *am* you!" Suzanne clenched her fists and steeled her eyes and felt all the power swirling, collecting, gathering, focusing, and then it flew out of her like a beam of brutal light and wrapped itself around the other Suzanne's head. She screamed.

Then Suzanne's own skull began to tighten with the other woman's enraged retaliation. She shook her head, trying to free herself from the deadly psychic grasp. She sensed the bone about her brain about to crack.

NO! I won't let this happen! I can't let her win!

She screamed, struggled, wrenched her head around, and pushed back so hard she heard some of her teeth break for the effort. The psychic hold fell away.

"Let me go and I shall let you go!" managed the other Suzanne, still twisting under the vice-grip of Suzanne's mind. "Our powers together will be unstoppable! Our dual abilities will startle and subdue the world!"

"I'd rather we die together!"

But then other Suzanne screamed, bucked, and skipped to the right, freed. The other Suzanne laughed and pointed at Suzanne with a trembling, gleeful, damning finger. "No, you'll die alone!" A large brick flew up from the ground and hurtled toward Suzanne's face, but Suzanne growled at it and it was knocked back down. The other Suzanne waved her arm and a large beam of wood shot up from the trash pile and slammed Suzanne in the chest. Pain exploded. She coughed, spit, but managed to stay upright. "You can't overpower me!"

"I can do whatever I want, Rosemary. I was glad to think you dead, and will now be glad to know you're truly dead!" She rushed forward, eyes wild and mad, mouth drawn open in a most hideous, Funny Face grin.

All the rage and frustration, fear and hatred gathered in Suzanne, forming a white-hot orb so intense she was certain that she would be engulfed by its heat. It rushed down her arms and into her hands, causing them to sizzle, and blew outward at that moment.

"She who lives by the flame shall die by the flame!"

The fire roared across the short space and into the other Suzanne. It wrapped itself around her like a golden, blazing serpent, catching her clothes, her arms, her neck, face and hair, creating a human torch that stood strangely tall and stoic for a few second, but then fell to the ground, face down. It was only then that she cried out into the dirt, struggling, trying to kick the fire away.

Her struggles slowed, and she died, curled in a charred ball at Suzanne's feet.

The police showed up not long afterward, alerted by passersby who had seen the fire, to find Suzanne standing over what looked to be a piece of twisted and charred wood from the former 3000 A.D. theater. They determined it to be a human being, and had quite a few questions for Suzanne, who was unable to come up with an answer that satisfied any of them. She was taken in and booked for the fight, the fire, and the death of the other woman, much to the delight of Officer Whitman, who was sitting at the precinct house's front desk that evening.

36

No one believed Suzanne that the other woman, the burned one who had called herself "Mattie Snow," had been the murderer at the Capital Hotel and in Steeplechase's Mirror Maze. No one believed her, for they had evidence this time. And Cittie, for lack of evidence and the discovery of Robert and his willing-to-do-anything-including-attack-a-woman-for-money friends, was set free.

The evidence was conclusive. Fingerprints taken at the hotel and Mirror Maze crime scenes matched perfectly the fingerprints on file of a "Suzanne Heath" who had been incarcerated in a mental hospital for assaulting her mother. Suzanne said yes, she was a Suzanne Heath but not exactly the same one they wanted to prosecute. They laughed sourly at this weak attempt at an innocent plea, and Suzanne could not prove the prints at the murder scenes were not hers, as her own had been burned off when she'd gathered the fire in her soul and hurled it out through her hands at the other Suzanne.

At Mattie Snow.

The idea of electrocuting a woman up at Sing Sing was distasteful, so the court called for a portable electric chair to be brought down to Coney Island and hooked up in the back of the precinct house. There were no witnesses allowed, only the man who knew how to run the chair, Lieutenant Granger, Whitman, and the morgue doctor. In her cell, Suzanne could hear Cittie in the front hall, asking to see her one more time and being turned away. She could hear him sob on his way out. Her heart was broken clean in two for her friend.

She knew what to expect as they sat her in the chair and buckled the straps. She'd been there before. And she was at peace. It was justice, after all. Justice that had been put on hold demanded its final say in the matter.

One quick flip of the switch, and the current was bright and dreadful. She saw flames rising and white swirling and demons with horns and a sharp-toothed rabbit screaming, "I'm Benjamin! Remember me?" She rose with it up and up and up, and then the white was gone and there was nothing but nothing.

37

Suzanne's body was checked for a heartbeat by the old precinct morgue doctor who was more interested in getting home to his wife, his Scotch, and his bed than dealing with a yet another dead body. After a few seconds he stepped back, pocketed his stethoscope, and waved his hand. "Yes, she's gone." Granger nodded. The precinct morgue attendant, a nervous, middle-aged bald fellow named Bernard, was assigned the duty of taking the body out to potter's field on Long Island.

The horse-drawn ambulance didn't get far from the precinct house, however. Bernard heard a noise in the back of the wagon and reined it over along West 21st Street to have a look.

Suzanne was not dead. Distorted, burned, she was still breathing. Shallowly. Raggedly. But she was alive.

It didn't take him long to decide what to do. The wrapped bundle tossed into a grave at potter's field could be anything. The caretaker at the graveyard for the unclaimed and unwanted wouldn't bother to look. Bernard had a treasure here. He turned the wagon around and drove down to Dreamland, where his friend ran an attraction called Freak Street.

38

Snow's Symposium of Secrets and Surprises sat empty into September, when Mr. Paulson McKenzie had it torn down to let another tenant rent the spot. Luna Park, Steeplechase Park, and Dreamland offered their outrageous charms to visitors with as much vigor as they had during the summer, decorated, choreographed, and lit like heaven itself, drawing them in by the thousands, sending them away weary and lighter for their coins spent. Every so often, a hint of impending fall blew through on a chilly ocean breeze, but for the most part it felt as if summer was there to stay.

A new exhibit had joined those along Dreamland's Freak Street. The curious would wander about, giggling uncomfortably at the Chimp Woman and Snake Boy, winking at Sultry Sally, cringing at Clyde, the Cyclops Baby, and then coming face to face with a badly burned woman who barely moved and was unable to speak. The sign propped up beside her cage read, "Hell and Back! This woman died! Went to Hell! Saw Satan face-to-face and was burned beyond hope! Returned to Earth!" Youths, with chattering girls on their arms, sometimes poked at her to see if she could indeed move. Some cultured women fainted and their gentlemen turned up their noses. Some of the visitors jokingly called the burned woman, "Helen Back."

Late each night, after the parks closed down and most of the lights had been extinguished, Cittie Parker covered the burned woman with a soft blanket and took her down to the beach in a wheelchair. The woman could not speak to him, but she was at peace. Cittie fed her small bits of chocolate, and sometimes she would raise her finger, pointed to the old gray moon, and mouth, "This is good. This is right." Sometimes, carefully, Cittie would hold her hand, and she did not need to pull away.

The days ran one into another. She was not affected by the jeers of the crowds. She lived for the nights of salty ocean air on her face, a gentle friendly voice by her side, and an existence free of visions.

It was good. It was right.

And the world of Coney Island continued on, blazing its lights, screaming its music, entrancing and terrifying the millions with its illusions and façades. A world oblivious and unto itself. Forever and ever.

Amen.

About the Author

Elizabeth Massie is a Bram Stoker Award-winning and Scribe Award-winning author of novels and short fiction for adults, teens, and middle grade readers. Massie's favorite genres are horror and historical fiction, and her novels and novelizations include Sineater, Wire Mesh Mothers, Desper Hollow, Dark Shadows: Dreams of the Dark (co-authored with Stephen Mark Rainey), Buffy the Vampire Slayer: Power of Persuasion, Versailles, The Tudors: King Takes Queen, The Tudors: Thy Will Be Done, the Young Founders series, the Daughters of Liberty series, and many more. She also writes nonfiction and fiction for nationwide educational programs. A former 7th grade science teacher with 19 years in the classroom, she now spends her time writing, presenting creative writing workshops, knitting, geocaching, and drawing ghosts, monsters, and other creatures — all part of her Skeeryvilletown cast of cartoon characters. She lives in the Shenandoah Valley of Virginia with her creative and wonderfully wacky counterpart and husband, illustrator Cortney Skinner.

Curious about other Crossroad Press books?
Stop by our site:
http://store.crossroadpress.com
We offer quality writing
in digital, audio, and print formats.

Enter the code FIRSTBOOK
to get 20% off your first order from our store!
Stop by today!

74764399R00143

Made in the USA
Columbia, SC
14 September 2019